DREAMS OF JOY

DREAMS OF JOY

LISA SEE

LARGE PRINT
Oxford

First published in Great Britain 2011
by
Bloomsbury Publishing Plc

Published in Large Print 2012 by ISIS Publishing Ltd.,
7 Centremead, Osney Mead, Oxford OX2 0ES
by arrangement with
Bloomsbury Publishing Plc

British Library Cataloguing in Publication Data
See, Lisa.
    Dreams of Joy.
    1. Chinese Americans - - Fiction.
    2. Birthparents - - Identification - - Fiction.
    3. China - - History - - 1949–1976 - - Fiction.
    4. Shanghai (China) - - Fiction.
    5. Large type books.
    I. Title
    813.6–dc23

ISBN 978–0–7531–8942–9 (hb)
ISBN 978–0–7531–8943–6 (pb)

Printed and bound in Great Britain by
T. J. International Ltd., Padstow, Cornwall

For my father,
Richard See

Author's Note

In 1958, a People's Republic of China government committee developed the Pinyin style of transliteration for Chinese words, but it took some years before it was widely used on the mainland and it wasn't adopted by the International Organization of Standardization until 1982. For these reasons, I have used the Wades-Giles system of transliteration for Chinese words in keeping with the times and with Pearl's background and education. Those who read *Shanghai Girls* will remember that Pearl also uses a combination of Cantonese and Mandarin when speaking.

The Great Leap Forward began in 1958 and ended in 1962. Although the number of people who died in the resulting famine will never be fully known, archival material recently released by the Chinese government along with research done by scholars and journalists suggest 45 million fatalities.

The wail of a police siren in the distance tears through my body. Crickets whir in a never-ending chorus of blame. My aunt whimpers in her twin bed at the other end of the screened porch we share — a reminder of the misery and embarrassment from the secrets she and my mother threw at each other during their argument tonight. I try to listen for my mother in her room, but she's too far away. That silence is painful. My hands grab the bedsheets, and I struggle to focus on an old crack in the ceiling. I'm desperately attempting to hang on, but I've been on a precipice since my father's death, and now I feel as though I've been pushed over the edge and am falling.

Everything I thought I knew about my birth, my parents, my grandparents, and who I am has been a lie. A big fat lie. The woman I thought was my mother is my aunt. My aunt is actually my mother. The man I loved as my father was not related to me at all. My real father is an artist in Shanghai whom both my mother and aunt have loved since before I was born. And that's only the tip of the iceberg — as Auntie May might say. But I was born in the Year of the Tiger, so before the gnawing blackness of guilt about my dad's death and the anguish I feel about these revelations overpower me, I grip the sheets tighter, set my jaw, and try to force my emotions to cower and shrink before my Tiger ferocity. It doesn't work.

I wish I could talk to my friend Hazel, but it's the middle of the night. I wish even more that I could be back at the University of Chicago, because my boyfriend, Joe, would understand what I'm going through. I know he would.

It's two in the morning by the time my aunt drifts off to sleep and the house seems quiet. I get up and go to the hall, where my clothes are kept in a linen closet. Now I can hear my mother weeping, and it's heartbreaking. She can't imagine what I'm about to do, but even if she did, would she stop me? I'm not her daughter. Why should she stop me? I quickly pack a bag. I'll need money for where I'm going, and the only place I know to get it will bring me more disgrace and shame. I hurry to the kitchen, look under the sink, and pull out the coffee can that holds my mother's savings to put me through college. This money represents all her hopes and dreams for me, but I'm not that person anymore. She's always been cautious, and for once I'm grateful. Her fear of banks and Americans will fund my escape.

I look for paper and a pencil, sit down at the kitchen table, and scrawl a note.

Mom, I don't know who I am anymore. I don't understand this country anymore. I hate that it killed Dad. I know you'll think I'm confused and foolish. Maybe I am, but I have to find answers. Maybe China is my real home . . .

I go on to write that I mean to find my real father and that she shouldn't worry about me. I fold the paper and take it to the porch. Auntie May doesn't stir when I put the note on my pillow. At the front door, I hesitate. My invalid uncle is in his bedroom at the back of the house. He's never done anything to me. I should tell him good-bye, but I know what he'll say. "Communists are no good. They'll kill you." I don't need to hear that, and I don't want him to alert my mother and aunt that I'm leaving.

I pick up my suitcase and step into the night. At the corner, I turn down Alpine Street, and head for Union Station. It's August 23, 1957, and I want to memorize everything because I doubt I'll ever see Los Angeles Chinatown again. I used to love to stroll these streets, and I know them better than anyplace else in the world. Here, I know everyone and everyone knows me. The houses — almost all of them clapboard bungalows — have been what I call Chinafied, with bamboo planted in the gardens, pots with miniature kumquat trees sitting on porches, and wooden planks laid on the ground on which to spread leftover rice for birds. I look at it all differently now. Nine months at college — and the events of tonight — will do that. I learned and did so much at the University of Chicago during my freshman year. I met Joe and joined the Chinese Students Democratic Christian Association. I learned all about the People's Republic of China and what

Chairman Mao is doing for the country, all of which contradicts everything my family believes. So when I came home in June, what did I do? I criticized my father for seeming as if he were fresh off the boat, for the greasy food he cooked in his café, and for the dumb TV shows he liked to watch.

These memories trigger a dialogue in my head that I've been having since his death. Why didn't I see what my parents were going through? I didn't know that my father was a paper son and that he'd come to this country illegally. If I'd known, I never would have begged my dad to confess to the FBI — as if he didn't have anything to hide. My mother holds Auntie May responsible for what happened, but she's wrong. Even Auntie May thinks it was her fault. "When the FBI agent came to Chinatown," she confessed to me on the porch only a few hours ago, "I talked to him about Sam." But Agent Sanders never really cared about my dad's legal status, because the first thing he asked about was me.

And then the loop of guilt and sorrow tightens even more. How could I have known that the FBI considered the group I joined a front for Communist activities? We picketed stores that wouldn't allow Negroes to work or sit at the lunch counter. We talked about how the United States had interned American citizens of Japanese descent during the war. How could those things make me a Communist? But they did in the eyes of the FBI, which is why that awful agent told my dad he'd be cleared if he ratted out anyone he thought was a Communist or a Communist sympathizer. If I hadn't joined the Chinese Students Democratic

Christian Association, the FBI couldn't have used that to push my father to name others — specifically me. My dad never would have turned me in, leaving him only one choice. As long as I live I will never forget the sight of my mother holding my father's legs in a hopeless attempt to take his weight off the rope around his neck, and I will never ever forgive myself for my role in his suicide.

Part One

THE TIGER
LEAPS

Joy

Life Savers

I turn down Broadway and then onto Sunset, which allows me to continue passing places I want to remember. The Mexican tourist attraction of Olvera Street is closed, but strings of gaily colored carnival lights cast a golden glow over the closed souvenir stands. To my right is the Plaza, the birthplace of the city, with its wrought-iron bandstand. Just beyond that, I see the entrance to Sanchez Alley. When I was little, my family lived on the second floor of the Garnier Building on Sanchez Alley, and now my heart fills with memories of my grandmother playing with me in the Plaza, my aunt treating me to Mexican lollipops on Olvera Street, and my mother taking me through here every day to and from school in Chinatown. Those were happy years, and yet they were also filled with so many secrets that I wonder what in my life was real at all.

Before me, palm trees throw perfect shadows on Union Station's stucco walls. The clock tower reads 2.47 a.m. I was barely a year old when the train station opened, so this place too has been a constant in my life. There are no cars or streetcars at this hour, so I don't bother waiting for the light to change and dash across Alameda. A lone taxi sits at the curb outside the terminal. Inside, the cavernous waiting room is deserted, and my footsteps echo on the marble and tile floors. I slip into a telephone booth and shut the door. An overhead light comes on, and I see myself in the glass's reflection.

My mother always discouraged me from acting like a peacock. "You don't want to be like your auntie," she always chastised me if she caught me looking in a mirror. Now I realize she never wanted me to look too closely. Because now that I look, now that I *really* look, I see just how much I resemble Auntie May. My eyebrows are shaped like willow leaves, my skin is pale, my lips are full, and my hair is onyx black. My family always insisted that I keep it long and I used to be able to sit on it, but earlier this year I went to a salon in Chicago and asked to have it cut short like Audrey Hepburn's. The beautician called it a pixie cut. Now my hair is boy-short and shines even here in the dim light of the phone booth.

I dump the contents of my coin purse on the ledge, then dial Joe's number and wait for the operator to tell me how much the first three minutes will cost. I put the coins in the slot, and Joe's line rings. It's close to 5a.m. in Chicago, so I'm waking him up.

"Hello?" comes his groggy voice.

"It's me," I say, trying to sound enthusiastic. "I've run away. I'm ready to do what we talked about."

10

"What time is it?"

"You need to get up. Pack. Get on a plane to San Francisco. We're going to China. You said we should be a part of what's happening there. Well, let's do it."

Across the telephone line, I hear him roll over and sit up.

"Joy?"

"Yes, yes, it's me. We're going to China!"

"China? You mean the People's Republic of China? Jesus, Joy, it's the middle of the night. Are you okay? Did something happen?"

"You took me to get my passport so we could go together."

"Are you crazy?"

"You said that if we went to China we'd work in the fields and sing songs," I continue. "We'd do exercises in the park. We'd help clean the neighborhood and share meals. We wouldn't be poor and we wouldn't be rich. We'd all be equal."

"Joy —"

"Being Chinese and carrying that on our shoulders and in our hearts can be a burden, but it's also a source of pride and joy. You said that too."

"It's one thing to talk about all that's happening in China, but I have a future here — dental school, joining my dad's practice. . . . I never planned on actually going there."

When I hear the ridicule in his voice, I wonder what all those meetings and all his chatter were about. Was talking about equal rights, sharing the wealth, and the value of socialism over capitalism just a way to get in my pants? (Not that I let him.)

"I'd be killed and so would you," he concludes, echoing the same propaganda that Uncle Vern has recited to me all summer.

"But it was your idea!"

"Look, it's the middle of the night. Call me tomorrow. No, don't do that. It costs too much. You'll be back here in a couple of weeks. We can talk about it then."

"But —"

The line goes dead.

I refuse to allow my fury with and disappointment in Joe to shake me from my plan. My mom has always tried to nurture my best characteristics. Those born in the Year of the Tiger are romantic and artistic, but she has always cautioned me that it's also in a Tiger's nature to be rash and impulsive, to leap away when circumstances are rough. These things my mom has tried to cage in me, but my desire to leap is overwhelming and I won't let this setback stop me. I'm determined to find my father, even if he lives in a country of over 600 million people.

I go back outside. The taxi is still here. The driver sleeps in the front seat. I tap on the window, and he wakes with a jerk.

"Take me to the airport," I say.

Once there, I head straight for the Western Airlines counter, because I've always liked their television commercials. To go to Shanghai, I'll have to fly to Hong Kong first. To go to Hong Kong, I'll have to depart from San Francisco. I buy a ticket for the first leg of my journey and board the day's first flight to San Francisco. It's still early morning when I land. I go to the Pan Am counter to ask about Flight 001, which goes all the way around the world with stops in Honolulu, Tokyo, and Hong Kong. The woman in her perky uniform looks at me strangely when I pay cash for a one-way ticket to Hong Kong, but when I hand her my passport, she gives me the ticket anyway.

I have a couple of hours to wait for my plane. I find a phone booth and call Hazel's house. I don't plan on telling her where I'm going. Joe already let me down, and I suspect Hazel's reaction would be even worse. She'd warn me that Red China is a bad place and stuff like that — all the usual negativity we're both accustomed to hearing from our families.

The youngest Yee sister answers the phone, and she hands me over to Hazel.

"I want to say goodbye," I say. "I'm leaving the country."

"What are you talking about?" Hazel asks.

"I have to get away."

"You're *leaving* the country?"

I can tell Hazel doesn't believe me — because neither of us has been anywhere other than Big Bear and San Diego for weekend excursions with the Methodist church, and college — but she will later. By then, I'll be somewhere over the Pacific. There'll be no turning back.

"You've always been a good friend," I tell her. Tears cloud my eyes. "You've been my best friend. Don't forget me."

"I won't forget you." Then after a pause, she asks, "So do you want to go to Bullock's this afternoon? I wouldn't mind buying some things to take back to Berkeley."

"You're the best, Haz. Bye."

The click of the receiver going back into the cradle sounds final.

When my flight is called, I board and take my seat. My fingers seek out the pouch I wear around my neck. Auntie May gave it to me last summer before I left for Chicago. It contains three sesame seeds, three beans, and three coppers from China. "Our mother gave these pouches to Pearl and me to protect us when we fled Shanghai," she told me last night. "I gave mine to you on the day you were born. Your mother didn't want you to wear it when you were a baby, but she let me give it to you when you went away to college. I'm glad you've worn it this past year." My aunt . . . My mom . . . My eyes begin to well, but I fight back the tears, knowing that, if I start to cry, I may never stop.

But how could May have given me up? How could my real father have let me go? And what about my father Sam? Did he know I wasn't his? May said no one else knew. If he *had* known, he wouldn't have killed himself. He would still be alive to throw me out on the street as the disrespectful, shameful, deceitful, troublemaking bastard that I am. Well, I'm out now. My mom and aunt are probably up, and still not speaking to each other but beginning to wonder where I am. I'm glad I'm not there to choose which mother to love and be loyal to, even with all their poisonous secrets, because that's an impossible choice. Worst, there's going to be a moment when things calm down and my mom and aunt make peace — and they go over everything again with a fine-tooth comb, as they always do — that they put two and two together and realize that *I'm* the real source of what happened to my father Sam, not Auntie May. How will they react when it finally sinks in that *I'm* the one the FBI was interested in, that *I'm* the one who led Agent Sanders right to our home, causing such devastation? When that happens, they'll be glad I'm gone. Maybe.

I let go of my pouch and wipe my sweaty hands on my skirt. I'm anxious — who wouldn't be? — but I can't let myself worry about how what I'm doing might affect my mom and aunt. I love them both, but I'm mad at them and afraid of what they'll think of me too — and just like that, I know I'll always call May my auntie and Pearl my mom. Otherwise I'll be more confused than I already am. If Hazel were sitting next to me, she'd say, "Oh, Joy, you're a mess." Fortunately, she's not here.

About a billion hours later, we land in Hong Kong. Some men roll a set of stairs to the plane, and I get off with the rest of the passengers. Waves of heat shimmy off the tarmac, and the air is stiflingly hot, with humidity that's even worse than when I left Chicago in June. I follow the other passengers into the terminal, down a dingy hall, to a big room with lots of lines for passport control. When my turn comes, the man asks in a crisp British accent, "What is your final destination?"

"Shanghai in the People's Republic of China," I answer.

"Stand to the side!" He gets on the phone, and in a couple of minutes two guards come to get me. They take me to the baggage area to retrieve my suitcase, and then I'm led down more shadowy hallways. I don't see any other passengers, only people in uniforms who stare at me suspiciously.

"Where are we going?"

One of the guards answers my question by roughly jerking my arm. Finally we reach a set of double doors. We push through them and back into the horrible heat. I'm put in the back of a windowless van and told to keep quiet. The guards get in up front, and we start to drive. I can't see anything. I don't understand what's going on and I'm scared — petrified, if I'm honest. All I can do is hang on as the van makes sharp turns and goes over bumpy roads. It pulls to a stop after a half hour. The guards come around to the back of the van. They talk for a few minutes, leaving me inside to worry and sweat. When the doors are opened, I see that we're on a wharf where a big boat is taking on cargo. The boat flies the flag of the People's Republic of China — five gold stars on a red background. That same mean guard yanks me out of the van and drags me to the gangplank.

"We don't want you spreading communism here," he practically yells at me as he hands me my suitcase. "Get on the boat and don't get off until you reach China."

The two guards stand at the bottom of the gangplank to make sure I board. All this is a surprise — an intimidating and unsettling surprise. At the top of the gangplank, I see a sailor. No, that's not what he'd be called. He's a crewman, I think. He speaks rapidly to me in Mandarin, the official language of China and a language I don't feel confident about in its pure form. I've heard my mother and aunt converse in the Wu dialect — Shanghainese — my whole life. I believe I know it well but not nearly as well as I do Cantonese, which was the common language in Chinatown. When talking to my family, I've always used a little Cantonese, a little Shanghainese, and a little English. I guess I'll be giving up English entirely from here on out.

"Can you say that again, and maybe a little slower?" I ask.

"Are you returning to the motherland?"

I nod, pretty sure I'm understanding him.

"Good, welcome! I'll show you where to bunk. Then I'll take you to the captain. You'll pay him for your ticket."

I look back down to the two guards still watching me on the wharf. I wave, like an idiot. And then I follow the crewman. When I was younger, I worked as an extra with my aunt in lots of movies. I was once in a film about Chinese orphans being evacuated by boat from China during the war, and this is nothing like that set. There's rust everywhere. The stairs are narrow and steep. The corridors are dimly lit. We're still docked, but I can feel the sway of the water beneath my feet, which suggests that this might not be the most seaworthy vessel. I'm told I'll have a cabin to myself, but when I see it, it's hard to imagine sharing the claustrophobically small space with anyone else. It's hot outside and it may be even hotter in here.

Later I'm introduced to the captain. His teeth are tobacco stained and his uniform is grimy with food and oil. He watches closely when I open my wallet and pay for my ticket. The whole thing is kind of creepy.

On my way back to my cabin, I remind myself this is what I wanted. Run away. Adventure. Find my father. A joyful reunion. Although I only just found out that Z.G. Li is my father, I'd heard about him before. He used to paint my mom and aunt when they were models back in Shanghai. I've never seen any of those posters, but I did see some of the illustrations he did for *China Reconstructs*, a propaganda magazine my grandfather used to buy from under the table at the tobacconist. It was strange seeing my mother's and aunt's faces on the cover of a magazine from *Red* China. Z.G. Li had painted them from memory, and he did so many more times. By then he'd changed his name to Li Zhi-ge, probably in keeping with the political changes in China, according to my mom. My aunt liked to pin the magazine covers with his illustrations to the wall above her bed, so I feel like I already know a bit about him as an artist. I'm sure that Z.G. — or whatever he wants me to call him — will be very surprised and happy to see me. These thoughts temporarily alleviate my concerns about the soundness of the boat and its strange captain.

As soon as we leave Hong Kong harbor, I go to the galley for dinner. It turns out the boat is primarily for returning Overseas Chinese. A different boat leaves Hong Kong every day, I'm told, taking others like me to China. Twenty passengers — all Chinese men — from Singapore, Australia, France, and the United States, have also been brought directly to this boat from other flights and other ships. (What does Hong Kong think will happen if one of us stays overnight or for a week?) Halfway through dinner, I start to feel queasy.

Before dessert is served, I have to leave the table because I feel so nauseated. I barely make it back to my room. The smells of oil and the latrine, the heat, and the emotional and physical exhaustion of the last few days hit me hard. I spend the next three days trying to keep down broth and tea, sleeping, sitting on the deck hoping to find cool air, and chatting with the other passengers, who give me all kinds of useless advice about seasickness.

On the fourth night, I'm in my bunk when the rolling of the ship finally eases. We must be passing into the Yangtze River estuary. I've been told it will take a few more hours before we veer onto the Whangpoo River to reach Shanghai. I get up just before dawn and put on my favorite dress — a shift of pale blue dotted swiss over white lining. I visit the captain, hand him an envelope to mail when he returns to Hong Kong, and ask if he can change some of my dollars into Chinese money. I give him five twenty-dollar bills. He pockets forty dollars and then gives me sixty dollars' worth of Chinese *yuan*. I'm too shocked to argue, but his actions make me realize I don't know what will happen when I land. Am I going to be treated like I was in Hong Kong? Will the people I encounter be like the captain and take my money? Or will something entirely different happen?

My mother always said China was corrupt. I thought that sort of thing went out with the Communist takeover, but apparently it hasn't disappeared completely. What would my mom do if she were here? She'd hide her cash, as she did at home. When I get back to my cabin, I take out all the money I stole from her can under the sink and divide it into two piles, wrapping the larger amount in a handkerchief and pinning it to my underwear. I take the rest — $250 — and put it in my wallet with my new Chinese money. Then I pick up my suitcase, leave the cabin, and disembark.

It's 8a.m., and the air is as thick, heavy, and hot white as potato soup. I'm herded with the other passengers into a stifling room filled with cigarette smoke and pungent with the odors of food that's spent too long without refrigeration in this weather. The walls are painted a sickly pea green. The humidity is so bad that the windows sweat. In America, everything would be orderly, with people standing in lines. Here, my fellow passengers crush forward in a throbbing mass to the single processing kiosk. I linger on the edges because I'm nervous after my experience with passport control in Hong Kong. The line moves very slowly, with numerous delays for reasons I can't see or intuit. It takes three hours for me to reach the window.

An inspector dressed in an ill-fitting drab green uniform asks, "What is the reason for your visit?"

He speaks Shanghainese, which is a relief, but I don't think I should tell him the truth — that I've come to find my father but I have no clue where he is precisely or how to locate him.

"I'm here to help build the People's Republic of China," I answer.

He asks for my papers, and his eyes widen when he sees my U.S. passport. He looks at me and then back at the photo. "It's good you came this year instead of last year. Chairman Mao says that Overseas Chinese no longer have to apply for entry permits. All I need is something that shows your identity, and you've given me that. Would you consider yourself stateless?"

"Stateless?"

"It's illegal to travel in China as a U.S. citizen," he says. "So are you stateless?"

I'm nineteen. I don't want to seem like an uninformed and ignorant runaway. I don't want to confess that I don't exactly know what *stateless* means.

"I've come to China in response to the call for patriotic Chinese from the United States to serve the people," I say, reciting things I learned in my club in Chicago. "I want to contribute to humanity and help with national reconstruction!"

"All right then," the inspector says.

He drops my passport in a drawer and locks it. That alarms me.

"When will I get my passport back?"

"You won't."

It never occurred to me that I could be giving up my rights should I ever want to leave China and return to the United States. I feel a door swing shut and lock behind me. What will I do later if I want to leave and I don't have the key? Then my mother's and aunt's faces flash before me and all the tumultuous and sad emotions of our last days together bubble up again. I'll never go back. Never.

"All personal luggage for Overseas Chinese must be searched," the inspector states, pointing to a sign

21

that reads, CUSTOMS PROCEDURE GOVERNING PREFERENTIAL TREATMENT OF PERSONAL LUGGAGE ACCOMPANYING OVERSEAS CHINESE. "We're seeking contraband items and clandestine remittances of foreign currency."

I open my bag, and he paws through the contents. He confiscates my bras, which might be amusing if I weren't so surprised and scared. My passport and bras?

He gives me a stern look. "If the matron were here, she'd take the one you're wearing. Reactionary clothing has no place in the New China. Please throw out the offending item as soon as possible." He closes my suitcase and shoves it aside. "Now, how much money have you brought with you? You'll be assigned to a work unit, but for now we can't let you enter the country unless you have a way to support yourself."

I hand him my wallet. He takes half of my dollars and pockets them. I'm glad I have most of my money in my underwear. Then the inspector scrutinizes me, taking in my dotted swiss shift, which I now realize may have been a mistake. He tells me to stay where I am. When he leaves, I worry that this will be a repeat of what happened in Hong Kong, except where would they send me now? Maybe Joe and my uncle were right. Maybe something really bad is about to happen to me. Sweat begins to trickle down the small of my back.

The inspector returns with several more men dressed in the same drab green uniforms. They wear enthusiastic smiles. They call me *tong chih*. It means *comrade* but with the connotation that you are a person of the same spirit, goals, and ambitions. Hearing the

22

word makes me feel much better. *See*, I tell myself, *you had nothing to worry about.* They huddle together with me in the middle so our picture can be taken, which explains the delays earlier. Next they show me a wall with framed photos of what they tell me are some of the people who've entered China through this office. I see mostly men, a couple of women, and a few families. And they aren't all Chinese. Some are Caucasians. Where they're from, I can't tell, although from their dress they don't appear to be Americans. Maybe they're from Poland, East Germany, or some other country in the Eastern Bloc. Soon my photo will be on the wall too.

Then the inspectors ask where I'll be staying. That stumps me. They see my uncertainty and exchange worried — suspicious — looks.

"You need to tell us where you'll be staying before we can let you leave here," the chief inspector says.

I tilt my head down and peer up at them, suggesting I'm innocent and helpless. I learned this expression from my aunt on a movie set years ago.

"I'm looking for my father," I confide, hoping they'll feel sorry for me. "My mother took me away from China before I was born. Now I've come home to my right place." I haven't lied up to this point, but I need their assistance. "I want to live with my father and help him build the country, but my mother refused to tell me where to find him. She's become too American." I crinkle my face at that last word as though it's the most detestable thing to be on earth.

"What kind of worker is he?" the chief inspector asks.

23

"He's an artist."

"Ah, good," he says. "A cultural worker." The men rapidly discuss the possibilities. Then the chief inspector says, "Go to the All-China Art Workers' Association. I think they just call it the Artists' Association now, Shanghai branch. They supervise all cultural workers. They'll know exactly where to find him."

He writes down directions, draws a simple map, and tells me that the Artists' Association is within walking distance. The men wish me luck, and then I leave the processing shed and step onto the Bund and into a sea of people who look just like me. Los Angeles Chinatown was a small enclave, and there weren't that many Chinese at the University of Chicago. This is more Chinese than I've seen altogether in my life. A wave of pleasure ripples through me.

I stand on a pedestrian walkway that seems almost like a park edging the river. Before me is a street filled with masses of people on bicycles. It's just noon, so maybe everyone is on lunch break, but I can't be sure. Across the street, huge buildings — heavier, grander, and broader than what I'm used to in Los Angeles — sweep along the Bund, following the curve of the Whangpoo. Turning back to the river, I see Chinese naval ships and cargo ships of every shape and size. Dozens upon dozens of sampans bob on the river like so many water bugs. Junks float past with their sails aloft. What seems like thousands of men — stripped to their waists, with light cotton trousers rolled up to the knees — carry bundles of cotton, baskets filled with

24

produce, and huge crates on and off boats. Everyone and everything seems to be either coming or going.

I glance at the map to get my bearings, adjust my suitcase in my hand, make my way through the crowds to the curb, and wait for the bicycles to stop to let me cross. They don't stop. And there's no streetlight. All the while I'm being bumped and pushed by the ceaseless flow of pedestrians. I watch others step into the herds of bicycles and daringly cross the street. The next time someone steps off the curb, I follow close behind, hoping I'll be safe in his wake.

As I head up Nanking Road, I can't help making comparisons between Shanghai and Chinatown, where most of the people were from Canton, in Kwangtung province in the south of China. My family's originally from Kwangtung too, but my mother and aunt grew up in Shanghai. They always said the food was sweeter and the clothes were more fashionable in Shanghai. The city was more enchanting — with clubs and dancing, late night strolls along the Bund, and one more thing: laughter. I rarely heard my mother laugh when I was little, but she used to tell stories of giggling with Auntie May in their bedroom, exchanging jokes with handsome young men, and laughing at the sheer joy of being in the exact right place — the Paris of Asia — at the exact right moment — before the Japanese invaded and my grandmother, mother, and aunt had to flee for their lives.

What I'm seeing now certainly isn't the Shanghai my mother and aunt told me about. I don't see glamorous women walking along the streets, perusing department store windows for the latest fashions sent from Paris or

Rome. I don't see foreigners who act like they own the place, but Chinese are everywhere. They're all in a hurry, and there's nothing stylish about them. The women wear cotton trousers and short-sleeved cotton blouses or plain blue suits. Now that I'm away from the river, the men are better dressed than the dockworkers. They wear gray suits — what my dad derisively called Mao suits. No one looks too thin or too fat. No one looks too rich, and I don't see any of the beggars or rickshaw pullers that my mother and aunt always complained about.

There's only one problem. I can't find the Artists' Association. Shanghai is a latticework of streets, and soon I'm completely twisted around. I turn down byways and into alleys. I end up in courtyards and dead ends. I ask for directions, but people shove past me or ogle me for the stranger I am. They're afraid, I think, to talk to someone who looks so out of place. I enter a couple of shops to get help, but everyone says they've never heard of the Artists' Association. When I show them my map, they look at it, shake their heads, and then ungraciously push me out their doors.

After what seems like hours of being rejected, pointedly ignored, or jostled by crowds, I realize I'm totally lost. I'm also starved and woozy from the heat, and I'm starting to get scared. I mean really, really scared, because I'm in an unfamiliar city halfway around the world from anyone who knows me and people are staring at me because I look so alien in my stupid dotted swiss shift and white sandals. What am I doing here?

I've got to hold myself together. I really do. *Think!* I'm going to need a hotel. I'm going to need to return to the Bund for a fresh start. First, though, I need something to eat and drink.

I find my way back to Nanking Road and after a short walk come to a huge park, where I see a couple of vendor carts. I buy a salty cake stuffed with minced pork and chopped greens wrapped in a piece of wax paper. At another cart, I buy tea served in a thick ceramic cup, and then sit on a nearby bench. The cake is delicious. The hot tea makes me sweat even more than I already am, but my mom always claimed that a cup of tea on a hot day has a cooling effect. It's late afternoon and the temperature hasn't dropped at all. It's still so humid — and without a hint of a breeze — that I really can't tell if the tea has a cooling effect or not. Still, the food and the liquid revive me.

This isn't like any park I've been in before. It's flat and appears to go on for blocks. A lot of it is paved so that it seems like it's more for mass meetings than for play or recreation. Even so, there are plenty of grandmothers minding small children. The babies are tied in slings to their grandmothers' backs. The toddlers paddle about in pants split at the crotch. I see one little girl squat and pee right on the ground! Some of the older kids — not one of them over four or five — play with sticks. One grandmother sits on a bench across from me. Her granddaughter looks to be about three and is really cute, with her hair tied up in ribbons so that it sprouts from her head like little mushrooms. The child keeps peeking at me. I must look like a clown to

27

her. I wave. She hides her eyes in her grandmother's lap. She peers at me again, I wave, and she buries her face back in her grandmother's lap. We go through this a few times before the little girl wiggles her fingers in my direction.

I take my ceramic cup back to the tea vendor, and when I return to the bench to get my suitcase, the little girl leaves the safety of her grandmother and approaches me.

"Ni hao ma?" I ask. "How are you?"

The little girl giggles and runs back to her grandmother. I really should be going, but the child is so charming. More than that, playing with her gives me a sense that I belong and that everything will work out. She points at me and whispers to her grandmother. The old woman opens a bag, fishes around, and then places something in her granddaughter's tiny hand. The next thing I know, the little girl is back in front of me, her arm fully outstretched, offering me a shrimp cracker.

"Shie-shie."

The girl smiles at my thank you. Then she climbs up next to me and starts swinging her legs and jabbering about this and that. I thought I was pretty good at the Shanghai dialect, but I don't understand her nearly as well as I'd hoped. Finally, her grandmother comes over to where we're sitting.

"You've met our disappointment," she says. "Next time my husband and I hope for a grandson."

I've heard things like this my entire life. I pat the little girl's knee, a gesture of solidarity.

"You don't look like you're from Shanghai," the old woman goes on. "Are you from Peking?"

"I'm from far away," I respond, not wanting to tell my whole story. "I'm here to visit my father, but I'm lost."

"Where do you need to go?"

I show her my map.

"I know where this is," she says. "We could take you there, if you'd like. It's on our way home."

"I'd be very grateful."

She picks up her granddaughter, and I pick up my suitcase.

A few minutes later, we reach the Artists' Association. I thank the old woman. I look through my purse, find the last of a roll of Life Savers, and give it to the little girl. She doesn't know what to make of it.

"It's candy," I explain. "A sweet for a sweet." A memory of my aunt saying that to me gives me a sharp pang of anguish. I've come this far and still my mother and aunt are with me.

After a few more thank yous, I turn away and enter the building. I was hoping for air-conditioning, but the lobby is just as oppressively hot as the street. A middle-aged woman sits behind a desk in the center of the room. She smiles and motions me to step forward.

"I'm looking for an artist named Li Zhi-ge," I say.

The woman's smile fades and blooms into a scowl. "You're too late. The meeting is almost over."

I stand there, bewildered.

"I'm not going to let you in there," she snaps harshly, gesturing in annoyance to a set of double doors.

"You mean he's in there? Right now?"

"Of course, he's in there!"

My mother would say it's fate that I should find my father so easily. But maybe it's serendipity. Whatever it is, I'm lucky, even if it's only dumb luck. But I still don't understand why the receptionist won't let me in.

"I need to see him," I plead.

Just then, the doors open and a group of people stream out.

"There he is now," the receptionist says with a sneer.

She points to a tall man wearing wire-rimmed glasses. His hair is rather long and falls in a loose mop across his forehead. He's definitely the right age — somewhere around forty-five — and strikingly handsome. He's dressed in a Mao suit, but this one is different from the ones I saw on the street. It's crisp and well cut, and the fabric looks richer. My father must be very famous and powerful, because the others follow closely behind him, practically pushing him to the street.

As they leave the building, I hurry after them. Once on the sidewalk, the others fall away, melting into the throng of pedestrians. Z.G. stands still for a moment, looking up through the buildings to a patch of white sky. Then he sighs, shakes his hands as though relieving stress, and begins to walk. I follow him, still lugging my suitcase. What will happen if I walk up and announce I'm his daughter? I don't know him, but I sense this isn't a good moment. Even if I thought it was, I'm filled with apprehension. At one point he stops at an intersection, and I pause at his side. Surely he has to notice me since I look so different — after all, everyone else has noticed me — but he seems completely preoccupied. I should say something. *Hello, you're my father.* I can't do it. He glances at me, still registering nothing, and then crosses the street.

He turns onto a quieter lane. Official-looking buildings give way to apartments and little neighborhood shops. He walks for a few blocks, then swings onto a pedestrian walkway lined on both sides with pretty Western-style, two- and three-story homes. I stay at the corner to watch where he goes. He passes the first three houses, and then he opens a low picket fence, enters a yard, climbs the stairs to the porch, and disappears through the front door. I take a few steps onto the walkway. I see patches of lawn, cymbidiums in bloom, and climbing vines. Bicycles lean against porches and laundry hangs on poles that jut from windows. The houses themselves are lovely — with tile roofs, nicely painted façades, and iron grillwork in art deco patterns covering windows, as peek-throughs for doors, and as decoration along the eaves and around mail slots.

This isn't how Joe and my professors described Red China. I expected utilitarian Communist quarters or even an artist's single room. Instead, my father lives in an elegant art deco house with a lovely garden. What does this say about him exactly?

I take a deep breath, and then I climb the steps and ring the bell.

Joy

Two Shadows Lengthening

A young woman answers the door. She wears loose black trousers and a light blue tunic with woven frogs that button at her neck, across her breast, and under her armpit.

"May I help you?" she asks.

Is she Z.G.'s daughter? My half sister?

"I'm here to see Li Zhi-ge."

"What is this about?" Her melodious voice tightens into something like irritation or maybe fear.

"I've come a long way." I give a little lift to my suitcase. Quite apart from that, she must be able to tell I'm not from around here. "It's a private matter, and it's very important that I speak with him."

The girl steps aside, and I walk into the house. The foyer is large. Polished mahogany floors stretch down a long hallway. To my right is a living room filled with Ming dynasty furniture. To my left, the dining room is decorated similarly. Having grown up in Chinatown, I know the real from the fake, and this is real and of fine quality. But what's on the walls shakes me. I see my mother and aunt in poster after poster. They are young and radiant, clad in pretty outfits, and doing all kinds of activities — getting ready to dive into a pool, stepping off airplanes and waving, and drinking champagne at a tea dance. My mother and aunt often reminisced about being "beautiful girls." Now, here they are, framed and displayed as if in a private museum. I'm conflicted because I'm still upset with them, but seeing their faces gives me courage.

"Please sit," the young woman says. I obey, and she pads quietly out of the room. A few moments later, another young woman, dressed in identical trousers and tunic, enters. Without a word, she pours me a cup of tea and then backs out of the room.

My father has servants! This isn't at all how I envisioned his life.

"What do you want?" a man asks.

It's him. Suddenly I'm shaking so hard, I'm afraid to stand up. I've come so far and ruptured so many ties . . .

"May I speak to you?" I ask, aware of the tremulous quality to my voice. "Are you busy?"

"As a matter of fact, I am," he answers curtly. "I'm getting ready to go to the countryside. You must know that. So please leave me to my packing. I have many things to do —"

"Are you Li Zhi-ge?"

"Of course, I am!"

"A long time ago, you used to go by a different name. People called you Z.G. Li —"

"Many people had different names in those days. Back then, I followed the wind by adopting Western customs. I understood my mistake. I changed with the times and I continue to change."

"Are you the same artist who used to paint beautiful girls?"

He stares down at me impatiently. He gestures to the walls. "You can see that I am. I regret those days too . . ."

"Did you ever paint Pearl and May Chin?"

He doesn't respond — again, the answer is on the walls — but his face goes gray and his posture deflates. "If you're here to punish me further, don't bother," he says stiffly.

What's he talking about?

"My aunt is Pearl Chin," I continue. "My mother is May Chin. I'm nineteen years old." As I speak, I watch him closely. His gray diffidence fades into ghostly white. "I'm your daughter."

He sinks into the chair opposite me, staring at my face. He glances at the posters on the wall behind me, and then comes back to me.

"Anyone could make that claim."

"But why would they?" comes my sharp retort. Then, "They named me Joy." I say "they" and hope he doesn't ask why. I'm not prepared to tell him everything right now.

"I heard Pearl and May died —"

"They didn't."

I fumble in my purse, pull out my wallet, and show him a photo taken earlier this summer, when we went to Disneyland for the first time. My mother and aunt thought we needed to be properly attired. Auntie May wore a cotton dress with a cinched waist, full skirt, and petticoat. Mom wore a pleated skirt and a tailored blouse. They'd both gone to the beauty salon to have their hair done, and they'd tied silk scarves over their heads to protect their bouffants. To complete their looks, they wore high heels. Naturally, we'd fought like mad over what I should wear. We'd finally agreed on a pencil skirt, a sleeveless white blouse, and ballet flats. My dad took the photo of the three of us outside the Peter Pan ride.

My eyes begin to mist, and I blink back tears. Z.G. studies the photograph with an expression I don't comprehend. Loss? Love? Regret? Maybe it's the realization that what I've told him is true.

"May." He draws out the syllable. Then, aware I'm watching him, he straightens his shoulders. "Well, then, where are they? Why haven't they come with you? Why would they send you here alone?"

He's saying "they" too, and I'm not about to correct him.

"They're in Los Angeles." Then, to make it sound better, I add, "*Haolaiwu* — Hollywood."

He doesn't seem to notice I haven't answered his other questions, because he says, "May always wanted to go to *Haolaiwu*."

"Have you seen her in the movies? She's in lots of movies. Me too! We used to work together. First we were extras, and then . . . Have you seen us?"

35

He looks at me like I'm a creature from another planet.

"Joy, it's Joy, right? *This*" — he motions around him — "is China. We don't see Hollywood movies here." Then, "Where are you from? How did you get here?"

"Sorry, I thought I told you. I'm from Los Angeles. I've come to meet you and to join the revolutionary struggle!"

His head rolls back on his neck as if to contemplate the ceiling. When his eyes return to mine, he asks, "What have you done? Are you stupid?"

"What do you mean? I needed to meet you," I say. "Don't you want me?"

"I didn't know you existed until a few minutes ago."

He looks over my shoulder to the foyer. He frowns when he sees my suitcase. "What are you going to do? Your Wu dialect is not quite right. It's passable, but most people will know you aren't from here. Even if your Shanghainese were perfect, you don't look like you belong here with your hair and clothes."

Why does he need to make it so grim?

"Your mother and aunt can't possibly have approved of your being here," he adds. I can tell he's trying to get more information from me, but that's still not going to happen.

"Your government has asked people like me to come here," I say, trying to voice the enthusiasm I've felt for months now. "I want to help build the New Society." But it's like a lid being lifted off a rice pot. All my steam has escaped too quickly. Why isn't he happier to see me? Why hasn't he hugged or kissed me? "I'm not the only one, you know."

"You're the only one who is . . . who is . . ." He swallows. I wait for him to say the words I need to hear. "Who is my daughter." He falls silent and squeezes his chin with his fingers. Every once in a while, he looks at me, weighing, considering. It seems like he's trying to figure out the solution to a difficult problem, but what's the problem? He's already acknowledged I'm his daughter. Finally, he asks, "Are you an artist?"

Strange question. I don't think anyone would call me an artist, so I lie. "Yes! People have always said so."

"Then tell me about the four kinds of art."

So I'm to be tested? I bite my lip to keep my disappointment from showing and try to remember things I've seen in Chinatown. Everyone had calendars for Chinese New Year. Even Pearl's Coffee Shop made a calendar that we gave to our most loyal customers.

"There are New Year's calendars," I say tentatively.

"That's right. They are one of the four accepted art forms. They are for peasants — like folk art — and therefore good for the masses. Political portraits and propaganda posters would fall into this category as well."

I remember something I learned at the University of Chicago, and I begin to recite. "Mao said art is to serve workers, peasants, and soldiers. It should be closely associated with revolutionary practice —"

"You haven't finished with the four kinds of art. What about Socialist Realism?"

37

This I absolutely remember from college. "It gives an almost scientific likeness — like a mirror — of the real world: the masses building a dam, young women making cloth in a factory, tractors and tanks rolling down a country road side by side uniting workers and soldiers. Like what you did for *China Reconstructs*. My mother and aunt" — again I don't specify who was who — "used to save the issues with your artwork."

"May saw those?"

May, again. He seems to have more curiosity about her than he does about me.

"Yes, she pinned them to the wall above her bed."

A slight smile comes to his lips. I can see he's flattered.

"What else?" he asks.

About May? About art? I stick with art.

"There are cartoons. Good for politics . . ."

He nods, but I can see his mind is still enjoying that someone far away in another country still aches for him.

"And the fourth?" he asks.

Blood flushes my cheeks. It's as though everything I've ever learned or seen has abruptly left my brain. In my mind, I'm looking at the walls in our house in Chinatown, in the cafés and curio shops I've been in all my life, in the garages and stores . . .

"Landscapes! Flowers and butterflies! Pretty ladies gazing into a pond or lingering in a pavilion! Calligraphy!" One of those has to be right.

"Traditional Chinese painting," he says approvingly. "It is at the opposite spectrum from New Year's

38

calendars. It is far removed from the lives of soldiers, workers, and peasants. Some consider it too elitist, but it is an accepted art form nevertheless. So which is your specialty?"

"People in Chinatown always said my calligraphy was uncorrupted . . ."

"Show me."

Now I'm to do calligraphy for this man — my father? Why do my artistic skills matter? Is this an investigation to see if I'm really his daughter? What if I fail?

Z.G. gets up and motions me to follow him to the desk. He pulls out the Four Gentlemen of the scholar: paper, an inkstone, an ink stick, and a brush. He calls for one of his servants to bring water. Then he watches me grind the ink on the stone and mix in water until I have the desired opaqueness, and then the way I hold the brush and sweep it across the paper as I write a couplet. I don't want to write a common saying, such as "May you be blessed with peace and safety in the coming year." A good couplet requires symmetry — sentence for sentence, noun for noun, and verb for verb. I remember one I did for our neighbors a couple of years ago. For the first part of the couplet, I write the characters *winter gone, mountains clear, water sparkles*. As soon as I'm done, I begin the second part, which would hang on the other side of the door: *spring comes, flowers fragrant, bird sings*.

"Your *ch'i yun* — breath resonance — is good," Z.G. says, "but as the great leader himself has observed, this kind of art can no longer be pursued as an ideal in and of itself. So, are you using tradition to serve the

39

present? No question. Your need is great in this moment and I can see that. I look at your work and I'm not sure if I see feudal dregs or fragrant flowers, but you could learn from me."

I don't understand half of what he's said. How does he see feudal dregs or fragrant flowers in my couplet? But it doesn't really matter for now, because I've passed his test.

"It's a good thing you came today, because I'm going to the countryside to teach peasants art," he announces. "You're coming with me as my helper. I was given enough rice coupons for my . . . trip that I can share them with you. People in the countryside won't know how ignorant you are."

The countryside? Every decision I take sends me farther from everything and everyone I know. I'm fearful but also excited . . . and honored.

An hour later, Z.G. hands his two pieces of Long March luggage to his chauffeur, who packs these bags along with my suitcase and several other boxes and satchels filled with art supplies into the trunk of a Red Flag limousine. Then the chauffeur drives us to the dock, where we board a ferry bound for Hangchow. Once we've dropped our bags in our cabins, we go to the restaurant. Z.G. orders for us, and the food is pretty good. While we eat, he tries to explain a bit of what we'll be doing and I try to prove myself to him.

"We're at the end of a campaign called Let a Hundred Flowers Bloom —"

"And Let a Hundred Schools of 'Thought Contend,'" I finish for him. "I know all about it. Mao encouraged artists, writers, and, well, everyone to make criticisms against the government in an effort to keep the revolution fresh and growing."

He gives me another one of those looks I can't interpret.

"As part of the campaign, artists like me have been asked to leave our studios, meet the masses, and experience real life," he continues. "We're going to Green Dragon Village in Anhwei province. It's one of the new collectives. They are —"

"I know about those too!" I exclaim. "I read about them in *China Reconstructs*. First there was land reform, when landowners gave their land to the people —"

"Confiscated and reallocated is more like it."

"That's not what I read," I counter. "You should be proud of this accomplishment. After more than two thousand years, the feudal system of ownership was destroyed —"

"And the landlord class eliminated —"

I speak over his sour comment. "Then the masses were asked to form mutual aid teams of five to fifteen households to share their work. Two years ago, the collectives started. Now one to three hundred households have been brought together to share the labor and the profits."

"That's a pretty simplistic way of looking at it." Again, I can't help noticing his dry tone. "But you're more or less correct. Anyway, I'm going to Green Dragon Village. After that, we'll just have to test the climate when the time comes."

He turns and stares out the window. I try to remember if I know anything about Anhwei province. Isn't that where the movie *The Good Earth* took place? I practically grew up playing in the set of Wang's Farmhouse, which had been part of China City, the tourist attraction where my parents worked. A peasant farmhouse will be familiar to me: chickens pecking outside the front door, wooden farm tools, a simple table, a couple of chairs.

In Hangchow, we stay at a guesthouse — clean enough but with a squat toilet down the hall for everyone to share. Z.G. takes me to a restaurant on the lake. We chat about the meal: fish soup with rice noodles, pea greens, and rice. He calls me Joy and I call him Z.G. For dessert, we have fritters made with corn fresh off the cob and sprinkled with powdered sugar. After dinner, we stroll along the lakeshore. My stomach and heart are full as I walk next to my birth father. Here I am, in China, by a lake shimmering pink as the summer sun sets. Weeping willows drape their tendrils into the water. I can't decide where to look or what makes me happier — seeing our two shadows lengthening before us or his face in the soothing light.

Joy

A Sprig of Bamboo

The next morning, my first Sunday in China, I'm unsure what will happen. All my life I've gone either to the Methodist mission or church for Sunday school and services. Even when I was in Chicago, I went to services. But today? Z.G. emerges from his room looking very different. He no longer wears his elegantly tailored suit. Instead, he wears loose trousers, a short-sleeved white shirt, and sandals. He sees me in a pair of pink capris with a sleeveless white blouse that Auntie May bought for me at the Bullock's sale last year. She said the outfit looked "crisp, fresh, and young," but Z.G. doesn't appear to care for it.

After a breakfast of rice porridge, rice cakes stuffed with spicy greens, fresh loquats, and strong tea, we take another boat up a small river to Tun-hsi, where we hire a pedicab to the bus station. Tun-hsi is tiny compared with Shanghai and rather featureless compared with the beauty of Hangchow. The town's buildings are modest in size, and there doesn't seem to be any real industry here. It looks to be the place where people in this area bring produce and other homemade commodities to sell and trade. We arrive at the bus station, and it's positively alive with travelers and goods. I see people in ethnic dress — wearing blue tunics, colorful woven headdresses, and hand-wrought silver jewelry. I hear dialects I can't understand, which is strange because we're still so close to Shanghai. People stare at me, but instead of turning away, as so many did in Shanghai, they greet me with broad — often toothless — grins.

We board a rickety bus. The passengers — smelling of garlic and increasingly sweaty — carry crying babies, live chickens and ducks, bags of produce, and jars of pickles and salted things that reek, ooze, and stink up the bus as the day wears on. I look out the window across fields sweltering under the hot sun. Soon the road narrows, then turns to dirt. We're climbing into low-lying hills. I ask Z.G. how much farther to Green Dragon Village.

"I'm not sure. I've never been there. I've been told it was once a prosperous village. We'll be staying in a villa." He juts his chin. My father Sam used to do that instead of shrugging. "I'm unclear what that means."

Z.G. says Green Dragon is 400 kilometers from Shanghai. That's something like 250 miles, but the road — if you can call it that — is so bad that we're just creeping and bumping along. After a couple of hours, the bus pulls to a stop. The driver calls the names of several villages, including Green Dragon. We're the only two people to get out. I have my suitcase. Z.G. has his bags and boxes. We're on a dusty track in the middle of nowhere. Finally, a boy riding a donkey-pulled cart comes along. Z.G. talks to the boy. I don't understand this dialect either, but I catch a word here and there. Z.G. helps me into the back of the cart. Then he throws in our bags and climbs up next to the boy, who, in turn, whips the donkey. On the right, I see men and women working in rice paddies. In the distance, a water buffalo pulls a plow through a water-soaked field. This is such a different world, and for a fleeting moment I wonder if I'll be able to do this — live in the countryside, learn to work in the fields, even help Z.G.

It's about five when the boy reins in the donkey and lets us off the cart. Z.G. straps a couple of satchels to my back and then he does the same to himself. Then we pick up our bags and begin a long, slow hike up a path, over a small hill, and down into a narrow valley, where elm trees provide shade. We pass a hand-painted sign that reads:

CLEAN UP AFTER YOUR ANIMALS.
BE HARMONIOUS.
RESPECT THE PEOPLE AND THE LAND.

We enter the Green Dragon Village Collective. Willow trees blow softly in the wind. A public square — an open area with a single large tree planted in the middle — lies ahead. A young man sits on a rock at the edge of the square, keeping lookout, his elbows on his knees. His feet are bare. His hair is so black that it glints blue in the sun. When he sees us, he jumps up and runs over.

"Are you Comrade Li?" he asks.

Z.G. nods. "And this is my daughter."

The young man's face is open. His teeth are white and straight. His shoulders are broad and strong under his cotton shirt. "I am Feng Tao," he says. "And I'm ready to learn."

"It is I who am hoping to learn from you," Z.G. responds formally.

Z.G. speaks the same rough country dialect that he used with the boy in the cart, but as I listen to this simple exchange, I begin to pick up the nuances in the tones and pronunciation that make this speech pattern different from the Wu dialect of Shanghai or the more standard Mandarin of the region.

Tao takes the satchels off my back and guides us into the center of the square to the shade tree, which has fragrant white flowers that look like sweet-pea blossoms. I don't see a single electric or telephone pole. There are no cars or motor scooters, yet a slight odor of gasoline cuts into the crisp, green-smelling air. Chickens peck at the ground, just as I expected. Tall, thin trees edge a stream to my right. The leaves shimmy in the light breeze. Across the stream, a path leads up a hill dotted by small — tiny — buildings. Those would have to be the real versions of Wang's Farmhouse. To my left is a high gray wall.

Tao ushers us along a path paralleling the wall until we come to an elaborate gate with a mirror hanging above a carved frieze. We step through the gate and into a courtyard. Dried pig legs and a string of dried fish hang on the wall — and this is still an exterior wall.

Tao calls out, "Kumei, come quickly! They're here."

A young woman pushes through a door. She's about my age and carries a boy of four or so on her hip. Two braids tied with scarlet wool swing on either side of her head. Her cheeks are ruddy. She's shorter than I am, but her body is far more solid and strong. She's a pretty girl, except for the raised scars that run down her neck and onto her left shoulder and arm.

"*Huanying! Huanying!* Welcome! Welcome!" she chimes. "I'm Feng Kumei. You're going to live here with me. Have you eaten?"

Yes, I'd like a meal, some tea, and a shower, but I don't have that opportunity, because Tao says, "But everyone's waiting."

"Then please take us directly to where we are to work," Z.G. responds.

We leave our bags with our clothes in the courtyard. Kumei puts the little boy down and tells him to go back inside. After he runs off, the four of us troop outside, walk along the wall to the square, and enter an adjacent building with a tiled roof and upturned eaves.

"This used to be the ancestral temple for the landowner's family and the rest of the village, because everyone here shares the family name of Feng," Tao explains. "Since Liberation, we've used the temple for meetings. Come. Come."

He motions to me. Something about the way his fingers beckon makes me follow him closely. Although from the outside there seemed to be a massive roof, the interior of the temple is more of an open-air courtyard, which allows the last of the day's summer light to

47

stream in. Huge wooden pillars painted blood red support those parts of the roof that rim the courtyard. The middle of the floor is sunken and filled with water. Carp swim desultorily. Green moss covers the stones. The pond gives a feeling of coolness, although the air temperature is no brisker or less humid than anywhere else I've been. Even with the open roof, the smell of gasoline lingers, but again, I haven't seen any cars, motors, or engines since I've arrived.

People — young, old, men, women, and children — sit on the stone floor along the hall's edges. The women are dressed almost identically, in loose blue pants and short-sleeved blouses with a tiny floral print. A few wear kerchiefs over their hair. Most have braids. The men also wear loose blue pants, only with sleeveless undershirts — the kind my father and uncles wore when they sat around the dinner table on hot summer nights but what my girlfriends in Chicago always said was a marker for bad boys, like Marlon Brando in *A Streetcar Named Desire.*

A well-fed man steps forward with his hand extended. He looks to be about thirty-five, and he has puffy half moons of fat under his eyes. "I am Party Secretary Feng Jin, the highest-ranked cadre in the village," he says. After shaking hands, he points to his wife, a plump woman perched on a stone bench, her heavy legs spread wide like a man's. "That's my wife, Sung-ling. She's the second-ranked cadre. We're in charge of all activities in the collective."

Z.G. tips his head in greeting. "My daughter and I are honored to be here —"

48

"No one said anything about a daughter," Party Secretary Feng says bluntly.

"She received permission to come with me," Z.G. assures him. Until now, I hadn't realized that maybe I shouldn't have come with Z.G. or that I might be a problem for him, and I try to keep my face as impassive as his. "She also wants to learn and observe from real life."

The Party secretary eyes me suspiciously — I really need to get some different clothes — but after a long moment, he shifts subject and tone. As he speaks, it's as though his words are meant less for us than for the villagers. "After Liberation, our great Chairman ordered all temples, shrines, and monasteries closed. Diviners and fortune-tellers were banished or arrested. Folk songs, operas, and love songs were banned. Feasts and festivals were discouraged. It's my duty to make sure these rules are followed, but I change with the government. If I'm told to reopen the temple for village meetings, then I obey. If planting songs are once again allowed, then so be it. I've now been told we'll have art lessons." He motions to the peasants sitting and waiting. "We've done our work in the fields and are ready to learn."

He leads us farther into the temple along a wall covered with posters that seem to form a time line of life in Green Dragon Village from before Liberation to now. The first shows Red Army soldiers, smiling and helping peasants repair a break in a dyke. In the next poster, people hold slips of paper. This must be when land was redistributed. Another poster illustrates daily

49

life: a man with a bag of wheat slung over his shoulder, another man screwing in a lightbulb, yet another talking on a telephone, while fat children play at their feet. The slogan at the bottom is straightforward: COLLECTIVIZATION MAKES EVERYONE PROSPEROUS AND CONTENT.

"I'm honored to see that some of my work has come to your collective, Party Secretary Feng," Z.G. says. "I hope it has been an inspiration."

"You did these?"

"Not all of them," Z.G. replies modestly.

The people seated nearby take in deep breaths of admiration. A few cheer and clap. Word ripples quickly around the room. This isn't just any artist. This artist helped shape their lives.

Z.G. isn't shy or uncertain as my father was. He bounds up a couple of stone steps, takes a position in the middle of the temple, and addresses the villagers. But before he gets very far, an old woman in the front row calls out, "But what do I do? I know how to grow rice in summer and cabbages in fall. I know how to weave a basket and wipe a baby's bottom, but I'm not an artist."

"I can teach you how to hold a brush and paint a turnip, but you have something within you that is even more important to create a great painting," Z.G. responds. "You are red through and through. I'm here to teach you, true, but I want you to teach me too. Together we will find redness in our work."

Tao and Kumei help me hand out paper, brushes, and premixed ink poured into saucers. Then Z.G. tells us to sit down and get ready to work ourselves. Yes, he said I would be his helper and that I might know more than the peasants, but I'm happy to learn with the others. This is the kind of equality and sharing I've heard about and was hoping for. Z.G. instructs us to paint a sprig of bamboo. I'm pleased with this assignment, because I did it many times in Chinese school in Chinatown. I dip the tip of my brush into the ink and let the bristles glide across the paper, remembering to be light with my strokes without losing control. Next to me, Tao copies the way I hold my brush and with a look of determination bends over his own sheet of paper.

Painting a sprig of bamboo appears to be a simple assignment, and people work quickly. Z.G. circulates through the hall, making comments such as "Too much ink" or "Each leaf should look exactly the same." Then he comes to Tao and me. He examines my work first. "You cannot be blamed for not understanding the deeper essence of bamboo, but you need to be wary of too much self-expression and too much ink play. With just a few simple brushstrokes you can call to mind the spiritual state of the subject. You want to evoke nature, not copy it."

I'm disappointed that I haven't impressed him and embarrassed to be criticized in front of the others. My cheeks burn and I keep my eyes down.

Z.G. moves on to Tao. "You're very good at the *hsi-yi* style of freehand brushwork," he says. "Have you trained elsewhere, Comrade Feng?"

"No, Comrade Li. This is my first time with a brush."

"Don't be modest, Tao," that old woman from the front row calls out again. She gestures for Z.G. to come closer. "Even as a little boy, Tao entertained us with his drawings in the dirt."

"When he got older," someone else adds, "we would give him paper and a cup of water to practice painting. He used his finger as a brush. The water would go onto the paper, and for a few seconds we would see mountains, rivers, clouds, dragons, fields —"

"And even the butcher's face!" yet another says enthusiastically. "Then the water would evaporate and Tao would begin again."

Z.G. stands there, staring at Tao's painting, pinching his chin with his thumb and forefinger, seemingly not listening to the villagers' crowing. After a long moment, he looks up. "That is enough for tonight." As the others get up off the floor and file out, Z.G. gives Tao's shoulder a congratulatory shake. I grew up in a household where touching was rare, so Z.G.'s gesture is startling. In reaction to this surprising praise, Tao's mouth spreads into the same wide and gleaming smile he gave us on our arrival.

I collect everyone's paintings. They're terrible, with big splotches of ink and no delicacy. This makes me feel a lot better about my painting, until I remember Z.G.'s harsh evaluation. Why did he have to be so mean, and in front of everyone too?

The sun drops behind the hills, turning everything golden as we walk back to the villa with Tao and

Kumei. At the main gate, Tao says goodnight. Though everyone in this village has the same clan name, I thought Kumei and Tao might be married, and I feel a tingle of relief to learn they aren't. As Z.G. follows Kumei through the gate, I linger for a moment to watch Tao stride along the path, cross a stone bridge, and head up the hillside. Then I turn and enter the villa. My suitcase is still in the front courtyard. I pick it up and follow the others deeper into the compound. For the first time, the word *villa* sinks in. I've never been in a place like this. It must have been beautiful and modern a few hundred years ago, but it seems quite primitive to me — a girl from Los Angeles. Narrow stone pathways and corridors link a series of courtyards lined by two-story wooden buildings. It's all very confusing, and I immediately lose my bearings.

We follow Kumei into the kitchen, but it isn't like any kitchen I've ever seen. It's open air with no roof, which is nice on this sticky night. A large brick stove stands against one wall. Another wall rises to waist height. I peek over it and see an empty trough, some dirty hay, and dried mud.

"We had to give our pigs to the collective," Kumei explains, when she notices my interest.

Pigs in the kitchen? In a villa? My mind scrambles to make sense of what I'm seeing. This isn't at all like China City. Are we going to eat in here? It looks pretty dirty — as in *outdoors* dirty. We're practically outside, and I've never even been camping.

Z.G. and I sit on benches that look like sawhorses lined up against a rough-hewn wooden table. Kumei ladles leftover pork and vegetable soup flavored with chilies into our bowls. It tastes delicious. Then we eat some room-temperature rice scooped from a tin container.

All the while, Kumei chatters. The little boy we saw with her earlier is her son. His name is Ta-ming. An old woman named Yong also lives here. She didn't come to the art lesson, because her feet were bound in feudal times, and she can't walk very far.

After dinner, Kumei guides us back through the maze of outdoor pathways and courtyards. She tells us that the villa has twenty-nine bedrooms.

"Why don't more people live here?" I ask, thinking that, if Green Dragon Village is a collective, shouldn't more people be sharing this big house?

"No matter. No matter," Kumei says, waving her hand dismissively. "I take care of it for the people."

Which doesn't answer my question.

In the third courtyard, Kumei takes us into a building. We enter a kind of sitting room with wood walls the color of maple syrup. At the far end, carved wooden screens cover a pair of window openings. Above these hangs an elaborate wood and gilt carving of squirrels playing in an arbor heavy with clusters of grapes. A table sits in the center of the room. A few chairs rest with their backs against the walls. There are two doors on the right wall and two doors on the left wall.

"This is where you will sleep," Kumei says. "You may choose your room."

Z.G. hurriedly checks each room before opting for the second one on the left. I select the room next to his. It's small, but it feels even smaller because most of the space is taken up by an antique marriage bed with a full frame and a carved canopy. I can't believe I'm going to sleep in something so luxurious. On the other hand, I haven't seen a bathroom or any electric lights, and the kitchen was certainly backward. Is this a villa or the home of a peasant?

I set down my suitcase and turn to Kumei. "Where is the bathroom?"

"Bathroom?"

Kumei looks confused. I say the word for toilet, but even that seems to baffle her.

"She wants to know where to wash her face and do her private business," Z.G. calls from his room.

Kumei giggles. "I'll show you."

"When you're done," Z.G. adds, "could you bring a thermos of boiled water and a bowl to my room?"

I want to remind him that this is the New Society and that Kumei is not his servant, but she doesn't seem to mind.

I grab my toiletry bag and follow Kumei back through the compound, out the front gate, and down a path to a water trough. I look at the trough, then at Kumei. She makes the motions for washing her face. Well, okay, she must know what she's doing, so I dip my toothbrush in the trough and brush my teeth. She joins me when I splash some of the water on my face. I didn't pack a towel when I left Los Angeles, so I follow Kumei's example by wiping off the excess water with my forearms and letting the heat of the night dry the rest.

When we return to the compound, I grab Kumei's elbow. "You were also going to show me the place to do my private business?"

She escorts me back to my room and points to something that looks like the butter churn one of my elementary school teachers once brought to class to teach us about pioneer days. It's wooden, about eighteen inches high, wider at the bottom than at the top, and closed by a lid. *I'm going to have to use that thing? Are you kidding me?*

Seeing the look on my face, Kumei asks, "Don't you have these in Shanghai?" I don't know if they have them in Shanghai or not, but I shake my head. Kumei giggles again. "This is your nightstool. You open the top, sit down, and do your business." She pauses, then adds, "Don't forget to close the top when you're done or you'll have a bad smell and lots of flies!"

This information doesn't exactly thrill me, and it causes me to realize that when I left home I didn't bring toilet paper, let alone supplies for what my mother and aunt have always called the visit from the little red sister. Now what am I going to do?

Kumei says goodnight, and I close the door to my room. I sit on the edge of the bed — hard wood covered with feather padding and a quilt — still trying to absorb everything. I want China to be perfect and my time here to be rewarding, but a lot of what I've seen today is either very primitive or kind of scary. I take a breath to steady myself and then look around.

The single window is just an opening covered by another carved screen. Darkness is falling fast now, and the cicadas are making a real racket. A small oil lamp sits on the table, but I don't have matches to light it. Even if I did, I didn't bring anything to read. The walls feel close. The heat is unbelievable. I stare at the nightstool. In my mind I thought I was ready to rough it, but I'm just not ready to use that contraption. I hear Z.G. moving in the central room and go out to join him.

"So how was your day?" Z.G. asks.

His question puts me on the spot. I want to fit in, but I don't look like I belong and I'm pretty sure I don't act like I do either. I want Z.G to like me, but I realize I'm a surprise and an unexpected burden to him. More than anything, I want to love China, but everything is just so strange.

"It's all I imagined but better," I say, trying to answer in a way he'll like. How can I explain this to him? I'm far removed from the comforts I grew up with, but this is just what Joe and I talked about with the other kids in Chicago. "My mother and aunt always said you can't know luxury until you're deprived of it. They lost a lot when they left China, but I've never understood their feelings. Who needs luxury when you have purpose, goodness, and passion?"

"You aren't actually *living* this life," Z.G. points out, catching me on my false enthusiasm. "You don't know what it's like day after day."

"That's true, but that doesn't mean I'm not happy to be here," I counter, feeling sensitive to my new father.

57

"And I think the people are happy we're here too." I pause and then amend my statement. "That *you're* here. They're going to learn a lot from you."

"I doubt it," he responds, and I wonder again why he's so pessimistic. "We'll do our time here, but those peasants aren't going to learn anything from me. You'll see. And I'd have to agree with Pearl and May. People like us are better suited to Shanghai." After a moment, he adds, "Even the way it is today." He reaches into his pocket and pulls out a wad of what looks like beige crepe paper. "To use with your nightstool."

He retreats into his room, and I return to mine. The walls of the room are made of the same thin dark wood that makes up all the buildings I've seen so far in the villa. I mean really thin, because I can hear Z.G. in the next room pee and fart. I take off my clothes, put on my nightgown, and, for the first time, use the nightstool. If my new father has no embarrassment, then I have to get over mine. Nevertheless, I sit on the edge, lean forward, and try to direct my stream in a way that will make the least amount of sound.

I lie down. It's much too hot to pull the quilt over me, and not a breath of fresh air comes through the opening where a glass window would ordinarily be. I fall asleep to the sound of mice scratching and scuttling in the rafters.

Pearl

A Widow Should . . .

I'm on a plane to Hong Kong, a place I haven't been since my sister and I left China twenty years ago. As I sit in my cramped seat, my past churns through my mind. My sister — a self-centered woman, whom I've tried to protect since she was a baby and who repaid me by betraying me again and again and again — haunts me. My daughter fills my heart with worry. My husband, Sam . . . Oh, Sam . . .

I'm a widow now. My mother used to say that a widow is the unluckiest person on earth, because either she committed an unforgivable crime in a previous life or her lack of devotion to her husband caused him to die. Either way, she's doomed to live out her life unloved by another man, for no good family will accept a widow into their home. And even if a family would take a widow, she would know better than to accept, because the world knows that a decent woman should never go with a second man. A miserable existence should be anticipated and accepted.

A widow should pray, fast, and recite sutras. (I'll omit the sutras and confine myself to prayers.) She should dedicate herself to doing good deeds at her place of worship. (This I might only be able to do in my heart for now, since I have no idea what I'll find for a Methodist like me in the People's Republic of China.) She should spend the rest of her life in chastity. (Something that doesn't break my heart, if I'm honest.) She should give up material possessions and devote herself to others like me: the socially dead. (Instead, I'm flying across the world to find my daughter.) I've often been told that a widow's suffering will overcome vanity and attachment by wearing it out. (I've never been vain — that was something I left to my sister — but I cannot give up attachment if it means giving up on my daughter.) A proper widow should confine herself to dark colors and maybe a few pieces of jade of good quality. But why am I even thinking about these things when I'm on a frantic and unplanned search for Joy?

It's fair to say I don't know what I'm doing. I like to plot my life and proceed carefully, but life doesn't always follow a plan. As a young woman I loved Z.G., but I was forced into an arranged marriage to pay my father's debts. Now, as I think about how I raised May's daughter as my own, never knowing that Z.G. was Joy's father, my chest constricts in sorrow and embarrassment at the idea of May and Z.G. together. She is a Sheep, while he is a Rabbit. This is one of the most ideal matches, and yet I believed that Z.G. and I were the ones meant to be together. The knowledge is devastating and it breaks my heart, but right now I have other things to worry about.

We cross the International Date Line, which means it's now been seventeen days since Sam committed suicide, thirteen days since his funeral, and two days since Joy ran away. There was never any question that I'd be the one to chase after Joy. A kind person would say that May wouldn't want to leave Vern, her invalid husband who was never right in the head to begin with, but I know her. She wouldn't want to leave her business or put herself in danger. What's that phrase she uses? She wouldn't want to break a fingernail. Joy may not be my birth daughter, but she is mine and I'll do anything for her. I keep thinking of my mother, who used to tell me I should beware the trait I carry common to all those born in the Year of the Dragon: a Dragon, believing he is just, will often bound headlong into a disastrous situation. My mother was right about many things.

"You're very brave," the woman sitting next to me says as the plane bumps through the air. She's white with fear and her hands grip the armrests. "You must have done this before."

"This is my first time on a plane," I say after a long moment. I'm so paralyzed by grief for my husband and terror for my daughter that I wasn't afraid when the plane took off and have barely noticed the turbulence that started after we refueled in Tokyo. I turn back to the window and stare into the darkness. Later, I hear the woman throw up into a bag.

Finally, the plane begins its descent into Hong Kong's Kai Tak Airfield. Small islands jut up out of the sea, fishing boats glide on the waves, and palm trees bend in the wind. Then we fly right into the city, between apartment buildings, so close I can see through the windows men wearing undershirts and drinking tea, laundry hanging on the backs of chairs, and women cooking. We land, and a group of bare-chested men roll a set of stairs to the plane. I gather my belongings and follow the other passengers to the exit. The scents of coal smoke, roast duck, and ginger mixed into the heavy, humid air fill my lungs. I'm only in Hong Kong, a British colony, but it smells like China to me.

An immigration official asks for my final destination. As a Dragon, I want to dash straight into China, slash my way across the country, and pry open doors with my long claws to find my daughter, but I have things to do first. To do them, I need to go into the city.

"Hong Kong," I answer.

The airport is on the Kowloon side of Hong Kong. As darkness falls, my taxi weaves through the crowded streets toward the Star Ferry Terminal. Garish neon lights edge upturned eaves, scrawl out the names of restaurants in English and Chinese, and advertise everything from free drinks and dancing girls for American sailors to herbs and tonics to bring robust and healthy baby sons. I'm awash in memories. Twenty years ago, this city was a gateway between May's and my escape out of China and getting on the boat to go to America. Again, it's a British colony, but I'm overwhelmed by how Chinese it is. The border with China is about twenty miles away, with Canton about eighty miles beyond that.

I board the Star Ferry and take it across the bay to the Hong Kong side, where tall white buildings grow on the verdant hills. I make my way to the same cheap hotel where May and I stayed twenty years ago. After checking in, I go to my room and shut the door behind me. It's as if all the grief I should have been feeling as a widow suddenly hits me, while the terror I feel for Joy is overpowering. I've experienced many terrible things in my life, but my daughter's running away is the worst. I'm afraid I won't be the strong mother I need to be. Maybe I never was a strong mother. Maybe I've never been good enough to be Joy's mother. Because, of course, I'm *not* Joy's mother.

My mind goes to one terrible place after another before spinning uncontrollably to an even worse one. The shame I feel for failing my husband and daughter burns my skin. I have no one. Not even my sister. I doubt I'll ever forgive her for reporting Sam to the FBI. She gave me her apologies, and when we stood at the airport, she said, "When our hair is white, we'll still have our sister love." I listened, but I didn't believe her. I didn't say anything because, whether I liked it or not, we had to come together as sisters to find Joy. That said, when I allow myself to think about the things May accused me of that last night, I know she was right in many ways. She pointed out that I'd gone to college in Shanghai, but I'd never done anything with it. I'd never taken advantage of the opportunities that were given to me in Los Angeles either. May said I preferred to be a victim and wallow in my sacrifices. She taunted me for being afraid and for running from the past. But May also used to say, Everything always returns to the beginning. She would laugh to see me now, because I've run so hard and for so long that I've run full circle into the heart of my past.

And look at me! Just as May said, I am afraid. I've always been hopelessly and pathetically afraid, but my sister has never given up. Twenty years ago, as we were escaping Shanghai, she didn't leave me in the shack after I was raped and beaten by Japanese soldiers nearly unto death. Instead, she piled me — unconscious — into a wheelbarrow and pushed me through the countryside to safety. She didn't wither into nothing when she had to give me the daughter she'd carried and loved for nine months. Nor did she ever once falter in acting as Joy's aunt for nineteen years. She kept the secret. She honored her daughter and me by keeping that secret. She would not be in a hotel room, weeping and mourning all night.

Just before dawn, I get up, take a shower, and get dressed. I look in the mirror. I'm forty-one, and, even after everything I've been through, I don't have a single gray hair. I've never been like my sister, whose face is her fortune. Nevertheless, despite the trials of these past weeks, my cheeks are still pink. Only in my eyes do I see the depth of my struggling heart, a maelstrom of sadness and loss.

I go downstairs and order a bowl of rice porridge and a pot of jasmine tea. The meal is as plain as I can make it. I'm a widow, who's lost everything. How could I ever eat a Hong Kong English breakfast of eggs, bacon, stewed tomatoes, and toast?

After breakfast, I stop at the front desk to ask directions to the Soo Yuen Benevolent Association, hoping to get advice about going into China and also how to deal with mail to and from my sister once I get there. The association was founded to help people of the Louie, Fong, and Kwong families. My father-in-law used its services for years. Father Louie remained connected to his home village of Wah Hong after nearly a lifetime spent in America. He sent tea money to his relatives, even if it meant we had to sacrifice. When China closed, he had to use the association to get money across the border to his family. After Father Louie died, Sam kept sending money to Wah Hong, which the FBI and INS agents considered one of his biggest crimes. I can almost hear Sam say to them, "We do what we can for our relatives who are trapped in a bad place." That didn't matter to the agents, obviously. So I know that, if May sends letters and money straight to me in Red China, she'll be attacked for being a Communist sympathizer by the FBI, just as Sam was. At the same time, what waits for me on the other side of the border is a mystery. We've heard mail is often opened, read, and censored, or tossed in the dustbin. I know as well that people in China who dare to send letters abroad or receive them — no matter how innocent the content — can also be accused of being secret capitalists or spies.

So, out into the streets. Hong Kong bustles with life: flower and bird sellers, street markets, British businessmen in three-piece suits, beautifully dressed women holding umbrellas to shield them from the sun. I could say that Hong Kong is just a bigger, gaudier, richer, more cosmopolitan version of Chinatown, but then I'd have to admit that it isn't like my adopted home much at all, except for the food, the streams of white tourists, and the Chinese faces. I could say Hong Kong is closer to how I remember Shanghai, with its lively waterfront, the sex and sin for sale, and the smells of perfume, coal, and delectable treats being cooked right on the street, except that it isn't nearly as grand or wealthy as the city of my girlhood.

An hour later, I reach the Soo Yuen Benevolent Association's office and approach a thin man of about fifty years, wearing a cheap suit, standing behind a counter, drinking tea. I extend my hand. "I'm Pearl Louie and I'm from Los Angeles," I blurt. "My daughter was born in America. She looks Chinese on the outside, but she's an American. My daughter . . ." Tears well in my eyes, and I manage to hold them back. "She's only nineteen and she's run away to China — Shanghai, I'm pretty sure — to find her father. She thinks she's smart and she has a lot of enthusiasm for what's happening there, but she doesn't know anything about it."

How can I say these things to a total stranger? Because I can't expect this man to help me, if I'm not honest with him.

"Are you planning on going to the People's Republic of China?" he asks, unimpressed.

"You say that like it's nothing, but China is a Communist country. It's closed."

"Yeah, yeah, yeah," he says in a bored tone. "The Bamboo Curtain and all that."

I can't believe his attitude. I just poured out my sorrows and worries and he acts like neither thing is important.

I rap my knuckles on the counter to get his attention. "Are you going to help me or not?"

"Look, lady, it's a bamboo curtain, not an iron curtain. People go in and out of China all the time. It's not a big deal."

"What are you talking about?" I ask impatiently. "China is closed —"

"The People's Republic of China is very good at propaganda, but so is your country. You Americans think the People's Republic of China is completely closed. That's part of your government's campaign to isolate China — refusing diplomatic recognition, prohibiting trade, restricting family reunification visits . . ."

I'm fully aware that the United States is punishing China for its role in the Korean War and for supporting the Soviet Union in the Cold War. If that weren't enough, there's the constant irritant of Taiwan, as well as the threat of the spread of communism.

"But the British are still doing business there." He leans forward to stress his point. "All those Eastern European countries are doing things there. Even

Americans — journalists invited by Mao and the government — go in and out of China. But mainly, we Chinese have continued to do business there. Hong Kong and mainland China have had a special business relationship for hundreds of years, long before Hong Kong was a colony. How are we to live without Chinese herbal medicine, for example?"

When I stare at him blankly, he answers his own question. "We can't. We need ingredients for all kinds of afflictions — mumps, fever, problems below the belt . . . And remember, in forty years Hong Kong will go back to the People's Republic of China. Don't think those Communists aren't trying to get their fingers in the pie already. Through Hong Kong, the Peking regime can absorb foreign exchange, buy materials that are hard to get elsewhere, and export certain materials to other countries. Not that getting people and things in or out is completely painless —"

"One of my greatest fears is that my daughter went to China and was immediately taken out and shot. Are you saying that didn't happen?" I ask, because nothing he's telling me matches up with anything I've read or been told about what's happening in the PRC.

"Propaganda," he says, emphasizing each syllable. "Again, you don't understand how many Chinese are going back to China every day. Since Liberation, over sixty thousand Overseas Chinese have gone back to Fukien alone. Another ninety thousand have returned to the motherland from Indonesia. You think the government would kill all those people?" he scoffs. "But if you're so worried, maybe you shouldn't go."

"But I need to find my daughter." (And I don't care what he says. I've read the papers. I've seen the news. It's *Red* China, for heaven's sake.)

He looks me up and down, appraising me for the widow I am. Then he says, "As you say, she's a daughter. Maybe she's not worth it. If she were a son, that would be different." Hong Kong may be a British colony, but Chinese ways and traditions are old and deep. I'm so angry I want to hit him. "Forget this stupid girl," he adds. "You can have other children. You're still young enough."

"Yes, yes," I agree, because what's the point in arguing about a daughter's value or putting this man in his place for offending a widow's vows? "Still, I'm going to China and I need help."

"Ah! Square one! What kind of help do you need?"

"Just two things. I need to receive letters and money from my sister, and I need to be able to write back to her."

"Have you done this before — written to China?"

"My father-in-law used this association to send money back to his home village," I answer.

"Tell me your family name again."

"My maiden name was Chin. My married name is Louie."

The man steps away, looks through some files, and comes back with an index card. "Money was sent from your family in Los Angeles to Wah Hong Village until

69

just this month." His attitude seems to change with this knowledge. "Shall I send money to you in Wah Hong?"

"I'm not going there."

"That's all right. We can still get mail to you as long as you're somewhere in Kwangtung province. Our connections are just over the border, as they've been for over a hundred years."

"But I'm going to Shanghai." Joy said she wanted to meet her father. That's where she has to be.

"Shanghai." He grimaces. "I can't send anything directly to Shanghai. We don't have connections there."

"If you send mail to our relatives in Wah Hong, could they send it on to me?"

He nods, but I need to verify what's possible.

"How does it work?"

"You have someone send us money —"

"My sister will send letters and money, maybe even packages. We'll have to consider the cost —"

"And the time. You can send an airmail letter from the United States to Hong Kong quickly and easily, but the cost to send a package by air is prohibitive."

"I realize that. I'll tell my sister to send packages by boat."

"In any case, I'll put whatever she sends in a new envelope — or package — and address it to your cousin" — he glances at the card in his hand — "Louie Yun. I'll give it to one of my men, who'll then take it with him on the train to Canton. From there, he'll go to Wah Hong and deliver the letter to Louie Yun, who'll put the letter in a whole new envelope and mail it on to you in Shanghai.

Obviously, you'll need to contact this cousin to tell him what he'll need to do —"

I want to go straight to Shanghai, but I say, "I'll take care of it." After a pause, I ask, "Does it have to be so complicated?"

"If you want to receive just mail, then it's pretty easy, although it might be read, censored, and maybe even confiscated entirely. If you want to receive money —"

"I don't want anyone in the village to get in trouble," I interrupt. "A while ago, we received a letter from one of the cousins in Wah Hong, saying they didn't need our money any longer. "There are no wants in the new China, he wrote. He was later killed trying to escape —"

The man behind the desk snorts. "China is unpredictable, and the situation there changes from week to week. Right now, the Communists *want* people to send money. They *need* the money. They want foreign investment. Believe me, they'll happily take your money."

"I don't want them to take my money, and I don't want to invest," I say. "I just want to make sure the letters that are sent reach the intended parties — on both ends."

He throws his hands in the air impatiently. "Think, Mrs Louie! If you want them to take some or all of your money, then just have your sister send her envelope directly to you and see what arrives. Or you can have her hide money in a package and use us to get it to you. We — and other family and district associations — have

71

been doing this a long time. We know what we're doing."

"You swear that my relatives will actually receive my sister's letters and that they won't get in trouble."

"If they're caught, yes, they'll get in trouble!" Which is equally true for May sending mail directly to or receiving it from Red China. "So let's make sure no one is caught."

I don't feel confident about any of this, but what can I do? It may not be perfect, but I now have a way to get mail into China: from May to the Soo Yuen Benevolent Association, and then to Father Louie's family in Wah Hong and on to me in Shanghai. The same process will work in reverse for me to send mail to my sister. I wish May and I had a go-between who was blood close, but that's not possible. May and I are related to everyone in our home village of Yin Bo, but I left there when I was three and May was only a baby. My mother is dead. We never learned what happened to my father. I'm sure he's dead — murdered by the Green Gang, massacred in one of the Shanghai bombings, or killed by Japanese soldiers after he deserted us. The people of Yin Bo might not remember me, May, or our parents. And even if they did, could they be trusted?

"May I offer some advice?" the man from the family association asks. "I told you lots of people are returning to China, and it's true. Getting in is easy, but getting out is hard. You shouldn't go there unless you have an exit plan."

72

"I'm willing to remain in China as long as I can find —"

He holds up a hand to keep me from continuing. "Your daughter, I know." He scratches his neck and asks, "So do you have an exit plan?"

"I haven't thought beyond finding my daughter," I admit. "I can't let her be there by herself."

He shakes his head at my doggedness. "If there's a way out of China, it's through Canton. If you and your daughter can get to Canton, then you'll be just two of hundreds who leave every day."

"Hundreds? You said that tens of thousands of people are returning to China."

"That's my point. It's not easy getting out, but people manage to do it. Some days it feels like half of what I do here is send money back to home villages to take care of houses for people who've left. There are whole villages — deserted — just over the border. We call them ghost villages. Some people leave their houses just as they were that morning — furniture, clothes, cupboards full of preserved food — so that everything will be exactly the same when they return —"

"When can I depart?" I ask, cutting him off.

"When will you be ready?"

After finalizing the arrangements — including making a plan for someone to pick me up at the Canton train station and take me to Wah Hong — he offers one last piece of advice. "The People's Republic of China is almost eight years old. It's changing all the time. It's not going to be what you remember or what

73

you think it should be, and it certainly isn't going to be what you've heard in America."

When I get back to my hotel, I ask the woman at the front desk for a form to write a telegram. Then I find a chair in the lobby and write to May: ARRIVED HONG KONG. TOMORROW I GO TO WAH HONG. WILL SEND MAIL DETAILS WHEN I GET TO SHANGHAI.

The next day, I put on the peasant clothes my sister bought for me twenty years ago to wear out of China. I go to the railway station, buy a one-way ticket on the Kowloon-Canton Railway, and board the train. It starts to move, and in minutes we've left the city and are crossing the New Territories, which are still part of the colony.

I wonder how Joy got across. What if she went to China and China didn't want her? They would have known immediately she wasn't from Shanghai. We always thought her Chinese was good compared with that of the other kids in Chinatown, but her accent . . . And I don't know who or what to believe — the man at the family association or everything I've heard about Red China in Los Angeles. Is Joy dead already? What if people decided she was a spy? What if she was killed the moment she set foot in China? This is my greatest fear, the thing that turns my heart black with despair. What point will be served if I follow her? Just another death — my own. Other questions torture me too: If I find Joy, what physical and emotional shape will she be in? Will she even want to see me? Will we be able to repair our relationship, which, after all, was based on a lie?

74

Will she come home with me, assuming we can find a way out of the country?

The twenty miles to the border — a bridge above the Sham Chun River — comes sooner than I expected. The flag of the People's Republic of China flaps in the breeze. Guards come through the train. They check the identity cards of those who are returning home from doing business or visiting relatives in Hong Kong. It's a large number, which confirms what the man at the family association told me. This is, it occurs to me, much like the border between California and Mexico, where many people cross back and forth each day to do business.

When I tell the guard I'm an Overseas Chinese who's returning home, I'm taken off the train, along with a few others. Memories of entering America flood my mind: my sister and I being separated from the other passengers and being sent to the Angel Island Immigration Station, where we were interrogated for months. Is that what's going to happen now?

I'm escorted into a room. The door is shut and locked behind me. I wait until an inspector enters. He's a lot shorter than I am, but he's wiry and tough.

"Are you stateless?" he asks.

Hmmm . . . Good question. I don't have a passport. All I have is my Certificate of Identity issued by the United States. I show it to the inspector, who doesn't know what to make of it.

"Are you an American citizen?" he asks.

If this really is like Angel Island, then I have to follow what May and I did back then — muddle the story to thwart the bureaucracy.

"They wouldn't let me become a citizen," I answer. "I wasn't good enough for them. They treat the Chinese very badly."

"What is the purpose of your return to the People's Republic of China?"

"To help build the nation," I answer dutifully.

"Are you a scientist, a doctor, or an engineer? Can you help us build an atomic bomb, cure a disease, or design a dam? Do you have airplanes, a factory, or property to donate to the government?" When I shake my head, he asks, "Well, then, what are we supposed to do with you? How do you think you will help us?"

I hold up my hands. "I will help with these."

"Are you ready to give up the filthy, stinky American ideals you've cherished in your heart?"

"Yes, absolutely!" I answer.

"Are you a returning student? We have a special reception station in Canton for returning students, who are expected to make a clean breast of their reasons for coming back to China, their ideas about fame and profit, and any anti-Communist thoughts they might harbor."

"Forgive me, but do I look like a student?"

"You look like someone who is hiding something. You don't fool me by wearing the clothes of the people." The scrape of his chair against the concrete floor as he stands feels ominous. "Stay here." He leaves the room, once again locking the door.

I'm confused and scared. The man at the family association said this would be easy, but that's not what I'm feeling. Could Joy have gone through this? Did she declare herself stateless and give up her passport? I hope not.

The door opens, and a woman enters. "Remove your clothes."

This really is too much like Angel Island. I didn't like being examined then and I don't want it to happen now. Ever since the rape, I've been afraid to be touched by anyone, not by those I love and who love me, not even by my own daughter.

"I have other people to search. Hurry up!" she orders.

I strip down to my underwear.

"A brassiere is a sign of Western decadence," she says derisively. "Give it here."

I do as I'm told and then cross my arms over my breasts.

"You may dress."

The inspector returns, and I'm questioned for another hour. My bags are searched and some items, including my other bra, are confiscated. I reboard the train. And then, in moments, we cross the border into mainland China. I don't have a chance to see it, however, because a guard enters the car and orders all shades closed.

"Any time we pass a bridge, an industrial site, or a military installation, you will lower your shades," he announces. "You will not get off the train until you reach the destination on your ticket."

Pearl

Forever Beautiful

I leave the Canton train station expecting to find the car to take me to Wah Hong Village, but it isn't here. I find no private cars, let alone taxis, in the parking lot either. All I see are bicycles and pedestrians dressed in nearly identical clothes. Everyone looks poor. Canton used to be a thriving city, so the changes are a shock. When some of the other passengers — the returning Overseas Chinese students — are hustled past me on their way to their special reception center, I turn and walk quickly in the opposite direction. I'm not a student, but I don't want to be caught up in anything official even by accident. I cross the parking lot to get to the sidewalk. The street is filled with bicycles, but again no taxis. I see very few cars or trucks. A couple of buses rumble past, but I don't know where they go. I ask a passerby how to get to Wah Hong. He's never heard of it. And neither have the next several people I ask. I stand there, gnawing on a cuticle, not knowing what to do. If the man at the family association messed this up, then how can I count on him to handle my mail?

I'm not off to a good start.

I go back to the train station's entrance and sit on my suitcase. I try to remain calm, but I don't feel that way at all. Panicked is more like it. I tell myself to wait a half hour, and if no one comes for me then I'll try to find a hotel. Finally, a beat-up Ford — a remnant of better days — pulls to a stop in front of me. The driver — a kid, really — rolls down the window and asks, "Are you Pearl Louie?"

Soon enough, we've left Canton behind and we're on a raised dirt road taking us through flooded rice fields for what I'm told will be about a forty-five-minute drive to Wah Hong. Canton seemed like it had stepped back in time under communism, but now I feel like I'm jumping back a century or more. We pass small villages made up of a few peasant shacks clustered together. I shiver. I was raped and my mother killed in a shack like these. All these years I've longed for the gay and colorful streets of Shanghai, but I never once missed the Chinese countryside, yet here I am. Bad memories make me put on mental blinders. I'm here, but I'll do my best not to see it.

When we get to Wah Hong, I ask the first person I come across if he knows Louie Yun. This is another of those tiny villages with at most three hundred inhabitants, all of them with the clan name Louie and all of them related to my father-in-law. I'm taken to Louie Yun's home. Are they surprised to see me! Tea is poured. Snacks are brought out. Other relatives crowd in to meet me. But as much as I try not to *see* or *feel* that I'm in a shack, I am, and all kinds of recollections come rushing back.

When I first arrived in Los Angeles at the end of the Depression, my in-laws and all the people I met were poorer than anyone I'd known in Shanghai. We may have been cramped together in Chinatown — the seven of us in a three-bedroom apartment — but that was positively spacious compared with this two-room shack with what seems like ten or more Louie relatives living here. I hear terrible tales of what happened during so-called Liberation to those in the Louie family who benefited from the money we sent. They were called running dogs of imperialism, beaten, or made to kneel in glass in the public square. Some suffered even worse fates. The stories are just what I imagined, and they fill me with dread. But others praise Chairman Mao, thanking him for the gift of food and land.

The accepted practice would be for me to host a banquet, but I don't want to be here that long. I pull Louie Yun aside, give him some cash, and promise more if he'll handle letters for me. I explain the process, ending with "I'm not going to lie. It could be dangerous for you and the rest of the family."

I don't know if it's gratitude for Father Louie's gifts over the years, desire to stave off poverty, or indifference to the political danger, but he asks, "How much will you pay for this service?"

"How much do you want?"

We negotiate until we reach a fair price — balancing the hazards against the value of American dollars —

which May will send to him each month. Then it's back to Canton. I'm driven to the docks, where I find a ship to take me to Shanghai, which will be faster than taking a train and cheaper than flying. I tell myself I've bought Louie Yun's loyalty, but I have no way of knowing.

Four mornings later, I'm on the deck watching Shanghai come into view. A week ago, I stepped off a plane in Hong Kong and was enveloped by odors I hadn't smelled in that particular combination in years. Now, as I wait to disembark, I breathe in the scents of home — the oil- and sewage-infused water, rice being cooked on a passing sampan, rotting fish moldering on the dock, vegetables grown upriver wilting in the heat and humidity. But what I see ahead of me looks like a badly rendered drawing of Shanghai. The buildings along the Bund — the Hong Kong and Shanghai Bank, the Shanghai Club, the Cathay Hotel, and the Custom House — look gray, neglected, and shabby. It doesn't help that nets hang like trampolines from the façades. I don't expect to see coolies. Isn't this supposed to be the New China? But here they are on the wharf: barely dressed, scurrying back and forth, heavy loads on their backs.

This initial impression doesn't dampen my mood. I'm home! I can't wait to get off the boat and onto the streets. For a moment, I wish May were here with me. How many times have we sat together, talking about this or that café or shop, always wanting things to be as they were in our beautiful-girl days?

81

I, along with the other passengers, am herded into a processing shed. I hand my Certificate of Identity to an inspector, who looks it and then me over. I wear a cotton skirt and a pink blouse, because I can't imagine entering Shanghai looking like a country bumpkin. Still, I definitely look different from everyone else. This seems to single me out for extra attention. One inspector searches my luggage, while another questions me about my reasons for returning to China, if I'm committed to giving up my capitalist ways, and if I'm here to serve the people. This is short compared with the border stop. Maybe they hear my Wu dialect and recognize me as the Shanghainese I am. Once their interrogation is finished — and I've lied repeatedly — one of the men pulls out a camera.

"We like to take photos of returning patriots," he says, motioning to the framed pictures on the wall.

I hurry to the wall and search the photos, hoping to find my daughter. There she is! My daughter's alive and she's here! In the photograph, she stands in the middle of a group of men wearing green uniforms and green hats with red stars. A lovely smile lights her face. I ask the men about her. They remember her. How could they not? It's not as though pretty young girls from America pass through their building every day.

"Where did she go?" I ask.

"Her father is a cultural worker," an inspector offers helpfully. "We sent her to the Artists' Association to find him."

I smile for the camera. It isn't hard. I'm happy. Joy found Z.G., which means I ought to be able to find the two of them very quickly. This is going to be much less complicated than I thought.

I pay a nominal fee to leave my bags in the shed and then hurry across the Bund and rush along the boulevards, paying no attention to the sights around me. In the Artists' Association lobby, I approach a woman sitting behind a desk.

"Can you tell me how to find Li Zhi-ge?"

"He's not here!" she snaps.

Bureaucrats are the same all over the world.

"Can you tell me where he lives?" I ask.

She eyes my suspiciously. "What do you want with him? You should not try to see Li Zhi-ge. This man has a black mark against him."

That's alarming. It seems like the inspector would have mentioned this.

"What did he do?"

"Who are you?" Her voice rises. "What do you want with him?"

"It's personal business."

"There's nothing personal in China. Who are you?" she asks again. "Are you a troublemaker too?"

A troublemaker? What has Z.G. done? And please, God, tell me he hasn't dragged my daughter into it.

"Have you seen a girl —"

"If you keep asking questions, I'm going to call the police," she warns.

For a moment, I'd thought this was going to be easy, but nothing in life is easy, not one single thing. And I'm not myself. This is my hometown, but I feel clumsy and inadequate in the new Shanghai. Still, I have to try one more time.

"Have you seen a girl? She's my daughter —"

The woman slaps her palm flat on her desk and glares at me. Then she picks up the phone and dials.

"Never mind," I say, slowly backing away. "I'll come back another time."

I walk out the door, down the steps, and keep going for another two blocks before I stop. I sweat from the heat, humidity, and terror. I lean against a wall, fold my arms over my stomach, and take several deep breaths, trying to bring my fear under control. Despite the effortlessness of my disembarkation, I need to remember the problems I had at the border. I must be careful. I can't end my search before it's even begun.

I have another idea of where to go. I start to walk toward the French Concession. This used to be a lively area — with brothels, nightclubs, and Russian bakeries — but somehow it all looks grim and depressed. Many street names have changed too, but even after all these years I remember the way to Z.G.'s old apartment, where May and I used to model. His landlady is still there, and she's as mean and cantankerous as she always was.

"You!" she exclaims when she sees me. "What do you want this time?"

This, after not having seen me for twenty years.

"I'm looking for Z.G."

"You're *still* looking for him? He doesn't want you. Haven't you figured that out yet? Only your sister, see?"

The words she speaks are like needles jabbing into my eyes. Why would she say this now, when she never said it back then?

"Just tell me where he is."

"Not here. Even if he were, you're too old now. Look in the mirror. You'll see."

All the while she's staring at my clothes, my face, my hands, my haircut. She's probably been taking in my smell too, since years of a Western diet of beef and milk come out in my sweat. She may be a cruel old woman, but she's not stupid. It's not hard for her to deduce I'm a foreigner.

"He returned to Shanghai after Liberation," she recounts. "He paid the rent he owed me and gave me more money for the items I'd stored for him — his paints, brushes, clothes, and the rest of it. He paid my grandson to deliver everything to his new home. Then he paid me even more —"

She's hinting pretty strongly. Maybe some of the old China ways still work.

"How much for his address?"

She probably thinks she's proposing an astronomical sum, but it's little more than one U.S. dollar.

Z.G. lives not far from here on a pretty pedestrian lane lined with graceful Western-style houses built in the twenties. I stop to put on lipstick and run a comb through my hair. Then I smooth my hands over my hips to make sure all my seams are straight and my skirt hangs perfectly. I can't help it. I want to look beautiful.

"He's not here," the pretty servant girl who answers the door tells me.

"May I come in? I'm an old friend."

The servant girl stares at me curiously, but she lets me in, which is surprising until I step inside. My breath catches, and I'm frozen in place by what I see. Old posters of my sister and me are on the walls. They've been hidden from public view and protected from the grimness of the streets. They are for Z.G.'s eyes only. None of this is what I expected — not the posters, wealth, sophistication, or the three servant girls, who line up before me nervously and stare down into their folded hands.

I motion to the posters on the walls. "You can see your" — what would be the right word in the New China? — "employer and I knew each other well many years ago. Please tell me where he is."

The girls shift their feet, refusing either to meet my eyes or to respond to my request. It's been a long time since I've had to deal with servants. I do what I did with Z.G.'s former landlady. I open my purse and bring out my wallet.

"Where is he?" I ask.

"He was sent to the countryside," the girl I assume to be in charge answers. She appears to be the oldest, although I doubt she's more than twenty-five. The other two girls continue to fidget.

I don't remember Z.G. having ties to the countryside. I've also read that being sent to the countryside is a common punishment in the New China.

"Is it because he lives like this? Or . . ." I look again at the young faces before me. Has there been a problem with him living with these three women? All kinds of improprieties used to happen in the past. I'm calculating how to broach that subject when the servant with a short bob volunteers new information.

"Guns always shoot the leading bird," she says in a low voice. "Master Li is in trouble."

"Things always change to the opposite," the third servant pipes in.

"Dog today, cat tomorrow," the girl with the bob adds. "They could have sent him to a labor camp."

"Or killed him," the third servant says, raising anxious eyes to mine.

"Has he been arrested?" I ask. When the girls don't respond, I say, "I want the truth. All of it."

"He's gone of his own choice to the countryside to redeem himself, learn from the peasants to be more humble, and remember the goals of socialist art," the head girl quickly recites before the other servants can start in again with their gibberish.

"When will he come home?" I ask.

"Don't you mean, *will* he come home?" the girl with the bob asks. "A big tree catches the wind, after all."

The one in charge pinches her subordinate to get her to stop talking, apparently not liking the lesser servants stepping out of their places.

"I remain hopeful," the head servant says. "Otherwise, he wouldn't have left money for me to take care of the house."

"And to feed us too," the quiet one mutters.

I glance from girl to girl. They're all about Joy's age. What kind of man is Z.G.? Is he still falling for any pretty face?

"Have you had any visitors?" I ask. "A young woman perhaps."

"We get those all the time," chirps the girl with the bob.

My jaw clenches. For so long, I felt I lived like a servant, but I wasn't a servant. I wasn't impudent . . .

"I'm looking for my daughter," I say sternly. I start to put my wallet away.

"We know the one!"

"Yes! We do!"

"Tell me," I say.

"She came the day Master Li was leaving. We heard her say she was his daughter. She came from a different place . . ."

"Like you."

"Where is she now?" I ask.

"She went with him to the countryside."

It's not the worst thing I could hear, but it's not the best either.

"Do you know where they went? To which village?"

They shake their heads. Even when I offer more money, they can't help me.

After they let me out, I stand in the lane for some time. I've run up against a blank wall, and I'm unsure what to do next. I'm desperate and terrified for my daughter, who is with someone in such trouble that he appears to have chosen banishment over arrest. In my hopelessness, I find myself speaking to May, as though she could hear me so far away in Los Angeles. *I haven't found our girl yet. She's with Z.G., and he could cause problems for her — things we haven't even thought of.*

88

I shake my head as Shanghai begins to push itself into my thoughts. I hear the sound of a trolley and the rumble of a bus or truck in the distance, but otherwise there's very little traffic noise. All the elegant, low-slung foreign cars of the past have been replaced by pedicabs, bicycles, and donkey-drawn carts and wagons. I hear a food vendor calling out a treat. "Crisp and spicy olives! Fresh olives! Buy my olives!" I haven't eaten Shanghai olives in twenty years, and I follow the cries to the corner and down the street to the left. I find a man with a basket hoisted on his shoulder. When I approach, he lowers the basket and lifts a damp towel off the contents. He has three types — fat, thin, and brown. I ask for some of the fat olives. I pop one in my mouth even before I pay the man. My eyes close in appreciation as the alkaline taste blossoms into something light, refreshing, and invigorating. I'm instantly transported back in time, eating olives with May and our friends — Tommy, Betsy, and Z.G.

Somehow this burst of flavor clarifies my mind. I'll have to go back to the Artists' Association to ask more questions, but first I need to figure out the best way either to get information from that woman in the lobby or to get past her. For now, though, I need a place to stay. I'm sure I can find someone to rent me a room, if I pay double or triple the standard rate, but I don't want to do that.

Home. Los Angeles is my home now — and how strange that is after all my years of homesickness for this place — but the word reminds me that I had a home here too. To get there, I'll have to go to the

Hongkew district across Soochow Creek. I don't see any rickshaws, but I doubt I could ride in one now after being married to Sam. If I saw one, my heart might collapse in grief. Still, I can't help wondering where the pullers are. What happened to them?

I hurry back to the Bund. I speak again to the inspector who helped Joy. I even slip him a bribe, but he insists he doesn't know anything more, so this is just money down the drain. Then I have to pay what he calls a handling fee to watch my belongings overnight. I take my one travel bag and ask directions to a bus stop. The streets were crowded when I arrived. Now that work is done, the sidewalks are jammed with people and the roadways are a swelling mass of bicycles. The rings of all those bicycle bells sound almost calming, like cicadas on a hot summer night. I board the bus to take me to Hongkew. For years, May has picked up American phrases and used them until the rest of us were nearly crazy. One of those phrases was about being crowded together like sardines. Now I understand what she meant. People press against me on all sides. I feel the familiar panic rising, force myself to swallow it, and sway with the bony mass of humanity as the bus accelerates or stops.

I get off in my old neighborhood. It all looks familiar yet completely different. Vendors and little shops cram together, selling goods and services: bicycle tire repair, haircuts, and tooth pulling; oranges, eggs, and peanuts; Front Gate men's underwear, Red Flag sanitary napkins, and White Elephant batteries. I turn onto my old street. The houses on my block all still stand. I remember how each spring our neighbors painted them in rich earth tones: dark purple, dark green, or dark red — colors that wouldn't show the dust or the moss that grows so quickly in Shanghai's humid climate. But the houses don't look like they've been painted in years. Most of the paint has peeled away entirely, revealing dirty gray plaster.

The summer evening customs haven't changed much since I was last here, however. Children play in the street. Women sit on steps stringing peas, shucking corn, or sorting rice. Men lounge on chairs or perch on upturned crates, smoking cigarettes and playing chess. Eyes begin to follow me. I'm afraid to look back. Do they recognize me?

My family home comes into view. The magnolia tree is huge now, making the house seem smaller than I remember. When I get closer, I see that the carved wooden screen that prevented evil spirits from entering the house still hangs above the door, but the jasmine and dwarf pines that our gardener once nursed are gone. My mother's rose vines cling to the fence, still alive but dried out and uncared for. Mostly what's "growing" is laundry draped on bushes and strung on lines. A lot of people must live here, but then a lot of people lived here when May and I left too. A man sitting on the front steps rises as I approach. I should have prepared an introduction, but it seems one isn't necessary.

"Pearl? You're Pearl, right? Pearl Chin?" He's tall, thin, about my age, with a distinguished demeanor but wearing shabby clothes.

"That was my maiden name," I answer, uncertain. Who is he?

He reaches out, takes my bag, and opens the front door. "Welcome home," he says. "We've been waiting for you a long time."

My shoes sound loud on the parquet floor. The salon is just as we left it. I can see down the hall and up the stairs, which also look the same. Meanwhile, the man who let me in is calling out names, and people are emerging from rooms, coming down the stairs, wiping their hands as they run from the kitchen. Just as on the bus, I'm surrounded on all sides. They stare at me expectantly. I stare at them, not knowing what to do or say.

"Don't you know who we are?" a middle-aged woman asks.

When I shake my head, they begin to introduce themselves. They're the people my parents let rooms to after my father lost our family's money: the two dancing girls who moved into the attic (only they don't look like dancing girls any longer in their worker outfits of dull blue baggy trousers and white blouses), the cobbler who lived under the stairs (as wiry and wizened as I remember), the woman who took up residence in the back of the house with her policeman husband and two daughters (except she's a widow now and the daughters have married out), and the student who lived in the second-floor pavilion (the courtly man who answered the door is now a professor). I vaguely remember that he used to go by the Western name of Donald. Now he introduces himself as Dun-ao.

"How can you all still be here?" I ask in wonder. "What about the Green Gang? They were going to take the house."

"They did," the professor answers. "But Pockmarked Huang" — even hearing the name all these years later sends a ripple of fear down my spine — "went into exile in Hong Kong. The king of the underworld died there six years ago." The professor snorts derisively. "By then the government had confiscated all his property anyway."

"We're allowed to stay here because we've always been here," the widow says.

My eyes well up. May and I thought we were alone in the world, but here are people who knew us, and they survived. It's a miracle, really.

They suddenly part to let someone through. I have a momentary hope it will be my father. I honestly don't know how I'll feel if it is. Baba's gambling debts ruined our lives, and he was such a coward. But it's not Baba. It's Cook. As hard as I fight them, tears roll down my face. He was an old man when I was a girl. He's probably in his eighties now. He looks frail, and the others treat him with reverence. That's how it should be. The old have always been honored in China.

"May I stay here?" I ask.

"Do you have a residency permit?" The widow turns to Cook and says submissively, "None of us want to get in trouble, Director Cook."

"No one will get in trouble," Cook says. "This was her family home, and we've kept her room." He turns and addresses me directly. "You may stay, but you must follow the rules of the house and the street, or I will report you to the higher-ups."

It's then I realize that the boarders don't respect Cook for his age. They're afraid of him. We kept him on after my father lost everything because he had nowhere else to go. Now, in the New Society, he's respected and feared because he's part of the red class. Director Cook. They don't call him Director Wang, Lu, or Eng, because he never had a name. We called him Cook because that was his title. Now he's running my family home.

The professor gently takes my elbow and leads me up the stairs.

"You must not think that because you've returned home things will be the same," Cook calls after me. "Those days are over, Little Miss."

But maybe not as much as he thinks or else he wouldn't call me by that old endearment and he wouldn't still be answering to Cook. He would have adopted a new name — like Always Red or Red Forever — to go with the New Society.

"You will clean your nightstool and make your own meals," he continues. "You will wash your clothes and do chores. You will . . ."

I've had a lot of surprises today, but none is greater than when Dun-ao opens the door to my room. It's just as May and I left it — two twin beds with white linen canopies embroidered in a wisteria pattern and our favorite beautiful-girl posters on the walls.

"I don't understand," I say. "How can everything be the same?"

"We knew your parents weren't coming back. Director Cook sleeps in their room now. But we all suspected that you and your sister would return one day, and here you are. But no May . . ."

I suppose he expects me to say something about my sister, but I can't. I look away from his kind face and see into the bathroom. The tile, the tub, the mirror . . . all exactly the same.

"Many houses in the city have rooms that look just like this," Dun-ao says. "The Chinese government isn't always good, but Chinese culture is always here, and it respects family. We all wait for those who left to return. Everyone comes back to Shanghai."

I suppose he's right. Z.G.'s landlady kept his things and he returned to claim them. This idea is even what the man at the family association told me was happening in the "ghost" villages just over the border from Hong Kong. But for my house and room to remain untouched all these years? I wish May could see it.

"You look like you need some rest," he says. "I'm sure you have luggage somewhere. When you're ready, I'll go with you to get it. And don't worry too much about Cook. He's a petty tyrant, but we have many of those now. You'll see that in his heart he's still just Cook, the man who loved you as a little girl." He smiles. "I know, because he's told me this many times."

After the professor leaves, I sit on the edge of the bed. Dust billows up around me. I smooth the bedcover and rake up dust with my hand. This room probably hasn't been cleaned since May and I left. I get up and go to the closet. I remember the day my father-in-law ransacked this room, grabbing clothes for May and me to wear to work in China City. He left behind our Western-style dresses, and they're all still here, as are the shoes, furs, and hats.

My eyes fall on an ermine-lined black brocade coat. It's mine. Mama had matching coats made for May and me, but I was the one who really wanted it. I thought mine was elegant, but May said hers was too somber and made her look old. (Which, of course, was a not too veiled criticism of me.) May lost hers the winter before everything changed. I can still hear Baba scolding May for being forgetful and yelling at me for not being a better *jie jie*, who should have reminded her little sister to remember her coat. May was eighteen! Why should I be responsible for telling her to get her coat at a party or from a hatcheck girl at a club? Baba then told me to give May my coat. My sister, even though she didn't like the coat, would have taken it too, except I was taller and she didn't like that it hung down to her ankles.

I shut the closet door and turn away. I go to our dresser. Inside the drawers I find undergarments, cashmere sweaters, silk stockings, and bathing suits. I pull out a nightgown: flesh-colored silk trimmed with handmade lace. It can't possibly still fit, but it does. I stare at myself in the mirror. Reflected around me are images of my sister and me. I've changed so much inside. I'm no longer the girl who was in those posters, but I'm slim as I was back then, and it seems I'll be able to wear my old clothes, although I can't imagine where I'll ever wear them in Communist China.

I'm exhausted, but I sit down and write two letters: one to Louie Yun in Wah Hong, giving him my address, and the other for him to send to May, saying that I've arrived, that I haven't found Joy, and that I'm in our old home. I also explain how she'll send mail to me. Then I stand and go to the bed, where I fold back the coverlet, trying to keep the dust within its folds. I stretch out on the cool sheets and glance at the other bed — May's bed — before turning away. I've come here in search of my daughter, but I've also run away from my sister. And yet May is here, staring at me benignly from the walls. I look into her eyes and say, *I'm home. I'm in our room. Can you believe it? We never thought we'd see this place again. And, May, oh, May, it's just the same.*

I go back to the Artists' Association several times. Even after I give the woman in the lobby a bribe, she insists she doesn't know where Z.G. is. All she can tell me, finally, is that he was struggled against by the membership and that he left town. I'm tempted to ask again about Joy, but I already know she's with Z.G. and I'm afraid of bringing unwanted attention on her. I slip the woman more money, and she arranges for me to meet the Artists' Association's director — a pudgy man with hair graying at his temples. I pay his bribe, and he tells me that Z.G. went to the countryside to "observe and learn from real life" — whatever that means.

"But where in the countryside?"

"I wasn't given those details," he responds.

"Do you know when he'll return?" I ask.

"That's not for me to decide," the director answers. "The case is no longer in my hands. It is being handled by people in Peking."

I leave the Artists' Association feeling both worried and let down. What did Z.G. do to be in such obvious trouble, and why did he have to drag my daughter into it? I've done everything I can think of. Now all I can do is wait, because they'll return one day. They *have* to return. As everyone keeps telling me, everyone returns to Shanghai. I did.

I clean and wash everything in my room. No one helps me. Why would they? Our former boarders are now assigned to live here, paying the equivalent of $1.20 a month for rent, and they don't want to be perceived as helping someone from the bourgeois class. And Cook? I've met Z.G.'s servants and have seen other servants at the market or doing errands for their masters, but Cook has established a place in my family home as a member of the new elite and honored masses — to be respected, not caring for his former Little Miss. Besides, he's too old anyway. He can't beat the dust out of the carpets, polish the floors, clean the windows, or wash and iron my bedding. I do all that myself, and now May's and my room looks almost as it did the day we left. It's eerie and comforting at the same time.

Then one evening, a week after I arrived in Shanghai, someone bangs on my bedroom door. It's a policeman. My insides constrict with fear.

"Are you the returned Overseas Chinese who was born Chin Zhen Long?"

"Yes," I answer tentatively.

"You must accompany me right now."

I'm paraded downstairs and through the hall to the front door past the other boarders, who gawk, point, and whisper among themselves. Did one of them report me? Did Cook turn me in?

I'm taken to a house that's been converted to a police station not far from here. I'm ordered to sit on a wooden bench and wait. Several people pass by on their way to register births, deaths, arrivals, and departures. They stare at me with curiosity and suspicion. Once again, I'm thrust back in time to Angel Island, where May and I had to wait in a fenced area for our interrogations. I'm scared to death. I take a deep breath. I have to appear calm. I remind myself I've done nothing wrong.

Finally, I'm shown into an office. A young uniformed officer sits behind a utilitarian desk. The room has no windows. A fan circulates hot air.

"I am Superintendent Third Class Wu Baoyu," he says. "I'm in charge of your case."

"My case?"

"You've been making a pest of yourself at the Artists' Association. Why are you asking about Li Zhi-ge?"

I don't want to say anything about my daughter, because again I don't know where that will lead or what the implications might be.

"I knew him years ago," I answer. "I wanted to reestablish our acquaintance."

"You should be careful about whom you associate with. This Li Zhi-ge has been struggled against. You are newly arrived, and I will let this go one time, but I must warn you that bribes are no longer permitted."

My insides constrict even more, and my hands start to sweat.

"Now, let us begin," he goes on. "Where were you born?"

For the next hour, he goes through a list of questions on a clipboard. What relatives do I have still living in my home village, what kind of work do they do, who are my friends in China, and how often do I meet them? Suddenly, an announcement blares from a loudspeaker. Superintendent Wu stands, tells me to wait where I am, and leaves the room. A few minutes later, I hear loud chanting. I peek out the door to where a group of uniformed men and women, holding Mao's *Little Red Book*, shout slogans together. I close the door and go back to my seat. A half hour later, Superintendent Wu returns. His questions shift from those about my family and my life to my return.

"Why haven't you reported to the Overseas Chinese Affairs Commission?"

"I hadn't heard of it until now, so I didn't know I needed to report."

"Now you know and now you will go. It is there that you will learn to have a patriotic spirit. It is there that your remittances from abroad will be processed."

"I don't expect to receive remittances," I say, lying. I don't want my money going through a government agency. What if they don't give it all to me like the man in the family association said? "I prefer to work."

"To work, you need a *danwei* — a work unit," he says. "To get a job, you need a *hukou* — a residency permit. To get a residency permit, you need to register with the local government. Why haven't you registered?"

All this frightens me. It's been only a week, and I've been caught and singled out. Now that the authorities know about me, it's going to be much harder to get around. That is, if they don't throw me in a cell right now.

"Can you help me with those things?" I ask, trying to mask my fear.

"You will be given a residency permit to stay in your old home, but I must stress this is not *your* home. It belongs to the people now. Understood?"

"I understand."

"You're also going to need coupons," he continues. "The government has taken over the distribution of all essentials. The government buys directly from farmers and manufacturers, so that city dwellers across the nation must use coupons to buy basic necessities — oil, meat, matches, soap, needles, coal, and cloth — from government-run shops. Rice coupons are, not surprisingly, the most important. As soon as you get a job, come back here and I will help you get your coupons."

"Thank you."

He holds up a hand. "I'm not done. Rice coupons are local. If you travel, you'll have to apply for special national coupons. If you don't have these coupons, you'll have to eat your meal without rice. As a returned

Overseas Chinese you may travel but you may not leave the city without my permission. You have returned to China. You must do what we tell you to do. Understood?" he asks again.

"Yes, I understand." I feel as though walls are being built up around me.

"You are fortunate," the policeman goes on with false amiability. "Peasants are treated harshly upon their return to China. They're sent back to their home villages in their native provinces, where they're assigned to agricultural work in a collective, even if they brought enough money from America to retire comfortably. But it could be worse. Some unlucky returnees are sent to the far west to reclaim and cultivate wasteland."

The room is hot and stuffy, but I'm cold with terror. I can't be sent to a farm somewhere.

"I'm not a peasant," I say. "I don't know how to do that work."

"The others don't either, but they learn." He looks at his checklist. "Are you ready to confess your links to the Nationalists on Taiwan?"

"I don't have any."

"Why were you so friendly with American imperialists?"

"My father sold me into an arranged marriage," I say. It's the truth, but it hardly conveys what really happened.

"Luckily, those feudal days are over. Still, you'll have to go through many struggle sessions in an effort to cast off your bourgeois individualism. Now, let's see." He glances at his list again. "Are you a returning scientist?"

102

He gives me the once-over and decides I'm not. "If you were, I'd have to make you sign a confession admitting that the Chinese moon is larger than the American moon." He sets his clipboard on the table. "The fact is, you're in a different category. You're wealthy."

He thinks I'm rich, and in the New China I suppose I am with my U.S. dollars.

"Upper-class Overseas Chinese are accorded every consideration," he continues. "You are privileged to have the Three Guarantees. You may receive and keep remittances sent to you, as long as you have them processed through the Overseas Chinese Affairs Commission. You may exchange your remittances for special certificates, which will allow you to pay for living expenses, travel, and funerals. You'll also be allowed to buy goods at special shops, where you can use the certificates you get in exchange for your remittances."

"What if I don't want the certificates?" I want to keep control of my money, but I don't say that.

"You won't have to deposit your remittances in a bank unless you want to." Which doesn't answer my question. "And your secrets will be kept." All this sounds like more than three guarantees, but I don't mention that either. "You will come here every month and we will chat. You will also report to the Overseas Chinese Affairs Commission. If you don't go, I will know. I will also visit the place where you live and question the comrades who reside there. Do not think you can hide your bourgeois ways from them or from me."

He thumps his pencil on the desk and gives me a hard stare. "It is one thing to come back to China, but you must follow our rules. I hope you have learned your lesson, and I hope you will behave accordingly." He stands, crosses to a side table, and returns with some pamphlets, which he presses into my hands. "Take these and read them before our next meeting. They contain the fruits of thought reform. I will be asking you to review your past from a revolutionary standpoint. I will not accept an unconvincing confession. You must be honest. You must plunge yourself into the furnace of socialist construction and patriotic re-education."

A few minutes later, I push through the front door. I take a deep breath and let it out slowly. I wasn't expecting to be hauled off and questioned by the police, and it's left me feeling terrorized and panicked.

"Are you all right?" someone asks. I look up, and there's Dun-ao. I'm very relieved to see him, and surprised too that he would go out on a limb for me. "I followed you here. I waited to make sure you would come out."

He's voicing my exact fear — that I'd been arrested. If that happened, no one would ever know what became of me. Worse, I'd never find Joy.

"Let's go home," he says. "We'll have some tea. Maybe I can help you."

When we arrive home, I make tea for the two of us. I tell Dun-ao about Joy's running away, my following her, Z.G.'s problems, my need to wait until they return, and all the rules the policeman told me I must follow. I do it because I've been intimidated and scared and I'm not thinking properly. Dun — as he says he prefers to be called — informs me that I'm actually quite lucky.

"You'll have to attend thought-reform sessions, as we all do," he says, "but as long as you aren't labeled a backward element, you'll have many benefits. You'll have your special certificates. You can get an exit permit promptly and without delays or questions."

"But what about my daughter?" I ask. "I won't leave without her."

"It's better that you're both here," he responds. "It's a well-known fact that the regime treats Overseas Chinese families as hostages to extort remittances from abroad. That's the whole purpose of the Overseas Chinese Affairs Commission. They exploit people here, so their relatives will send more money to use to build the country. For this reason, they're reluctant to allow family members to leave China."

"But you just told me that Overseas Chinese can easily obtain exit permits."

"Ah, good point. Applications for exit permits which are considered prejudicial to the regime's interests are not granted."

"Well, which one is it?"

"Maybe both," he says, unsure.

"In any case," I go on briskly, trying to sound confident, "those requests for remittances are blackmail. Still, if I were in Los Angeles and Joy were here, I would send every dollar I had, hoping to get her out. Now I have to think about how to get the two of us out. I can't be perceived as being rich, but I can't be perceived as being poor either. I need to stay in Shanghai so I can wait for Z.G. and my daughter to return from wherever it is they've gone. I need coupons to live, and I also need to appear invisible while doing those things."

But the police know about me, and in days the Overseas Chinese Affairs Commission will be familiar with me too. Quite apart from that, the last thing I want is to act like a widow by being invisible, a coward, or a victim. It's against a Dragon's nature to wait, but that's all I can do. I need to be a wily, quiet, and cautious Dragon.

"You're going to need a job," Dun recommends.

"I told Superintendent Wu I wanted one. Maybe I could go to work with the dancing girls. They make pens modeled on the Parker 51." I reel off the factory's slogan, which the girls recite whenever they have a chance. "Catch up with Parker!"

"I have a better idea. You should become a paper collector."

"I don't know what that is."

"We have always had a reverence for lettered paper," he explains, sounding professorial. "In the Song dynasty, Lettered Paper Society members collected paper with writing on it, burned it in special ceremonial fires, and then ritually stored the ashes. Every three years, members escorted the ashes to a river or to the ocean, where the ashes would be plunged to be reborn as new words and images. Do you remember the bamboo baskets that used to be on street corners here in Shanghai, where people could properly dispose of their lettered paper?"

I have a vague memory of those baskets, but my sister and I didn't have an iota of reverence for lettered paper, considering that we modeled for advertisements, which were clearly lettered paper of the most commercial sort.

"What was once an honored profession," Dun goes on, "is now little better than being a trash collector. Still, I think it will give you everything you need — anonymity, access to all corners of the city, obedience to the rules you've been told to follow, and a way to get coupons and keep busy until your daughter returns."

Joy

Observing and Learning from Real Life

It's still dark when the roosters begin to crow. I stay in bed for a few minutes, listening to the sounds of songbirds, the creaking of the floorboards in the room next to mine as my father rises, and the people outside the villa calling morning greetings. With the wood slats on the floors, the sliding doors, and the thin walls, no secrets can be kept. I hear every footstep, snore, hack, sigh, and whisper. I get up and dress quickly in loose pants and a cotton shirt with a faded floral print — both soft from use and many washings, all gifts from Kumei. I run a comb through my hair. I wish it were long enough to braid like the other girls do in the village. Instead, I put a kerchief over my head and tie it at the back of my neck. I take a quick look in a small mirror. Others here have told me how much I look like my father and that we share many mannerisms, like the way I sometimes pinch my chin when I'm in thought or the way I raise my eyebrows in question. That might be so, but that doesn't mean we're alike. Anyway, at least I look more like a peasant than I did a month ago when I first got here.

I slide open the door and hurry through the corridors and courtyards to the kitchen. Kumei has already started the fire in the stove and water boils in the teapot. I pour some in a cup, take it outside to the trough, where I went the first night, and use the hot water to brush my teeth and wash my face.

How stupid I was back then! Washing my face and brushing my teeth with trough water seemed fun and adventurous, but I'd gotten sick as a dog and had spent the first few days in Green Dragon with a bad case of diarrhea and vomiting. I'd received little sympathy from Z.G.

"What did you expect?" he'd asked. "This is a village. These people probably only change the water every three or four days. And they probably use it to scrub their feet and armpits too."

That made me sick all over again. My inhibitions about using the nightstool — and within earshot of Z.G. — were completely gone by the time I fully recovered. But I'd learned, just as I'm learning every day. I now know that the carvings with the squirrel-and-grape pattern in the sitting room for the four bedrooms in this part of the compound symbolize the expectation of prosperity for future generations. The wooden screens covering the windows are carved in a lion's pattern to show a person's wealth. The mirror hanging above the main gate wards off evil spirits, while the dried fish tacked to the wall in the front courtyard is there because *yu*, the word for fish, sounds like *abundance*. The dried pig legs that hang in the front courtyard? They're for eating. The odor of gasoline I smelled that first night? That's how people spot-clean their soiled clothes when they don't want to wash an entire garment by hand. The tree with flowers that look like sweet peas in the middle of the square? It's called a scholar's tree. Its blossoms have now turned into fruits that grow in long yellowish pods like strings of pearls. And when I got my period, Kumei showed me what women in the village do: wrap sand in a piece of cloth and wedge it in my underpants. These are just a few things I've learned.

I help Kumei carry the food and eating utensils to the villa's dining room. Z.G. and Yong, the old woman who also lives in the villa, sit at the table with Ta-ming between them. Yong has bound feet, which are truly gruesome. They're tiny, like miniature candy bars sticking out from beneath her pants. One morning when I came into the kitchen, she'd pulled up a pant leg to massage a thin white calf. There, behind her ankle, was this mound of scrunched flesh and bones — the parts of her foot that hadn't been made dainty in her bound-foot shoe. Now I make a point of not looking at Yong's feet. Because of this, I think she doesn't like me. Or maybe she thinks I don't like her. Whatever it is, we've barely spoken.

Today's breakfast is rice porridge, hard-boiled eggs, pickled turnip, and dumplings made with rice flour dyed green with a local water plant and stuffed with

110

spicy vegetables and salted pork. It's all delicious, but I don't eat more than my share. I dip my spoon into my porridge and listen to Kumei and Yong. I've picked up the nuances of the local dialect and have gotten much better at speaking it.

I'm happy that Z.G. and I were sent to live with Kumei. She's become a good friend, even though we're still strangers in many ways. How did she get her scars? Why does she live in the villa? Who was her husband? I've been dying to ask these questions, but I don't want to appear nosy. I've made up a story in my mind though. Kumei probably married a soldier when he passed through this area. He must have died during Liberation. Since her husband was a hero, the villagers allowed her to live in the villa, where she cares for her son and Yong, another widow, because, in the New Society, the villa has been converted to a home for widows. Maybe none of this is true, but I like the story. And I like Kumei. Her name means Bitter Sister, but she doesn't seem bitter to me. She's illiterate, but she hasn't let the burdens of the past hinder her. She goes to classes in the afternoon, along with many other peasants, to be educated.

Kumei leaves her son with Yong, and the two of us set out for the fields. Z.G. stays behind in the villa. I came a long way to meet him and it's already been a month, but he's an enigma. He hasn't asked much about May or even me, and I haven't asked much about him, even though I'd like to know him better. I'm shy around him and unsure what to say. Maybe he's shy too. Or maybe he's unused to having a daughter.

Maybe he can never feel about me the way my father Sam felt.

It's the end of September. The air is still warm, but not as oppressive as it was when I first got here. We walk past paddies, where the rice stalks have browned. Then we begin to climb the short hill across from the villa. I keep my head down, pretending to watch for ruts or rocks in the path, while glancing surreptitiously up the hill to Tao's house. It looks like many of the other houses — small, built from blocks of some sort, and covered with mud — except that it's the only one angled north. The windows are just openings, as in the villa. The tile roof is low and crooked. Some rocks form a little retaining wall, creating a small terrace just outside the front door. An outdoor wood-burning stove is built onto one of the exterior walls, which can't make it easy for Tao's mother to cook when it rains. A wooden ladder with broken rungs lies askew on the ground, but no one has bothered to right it since I arrived. In the villa, the dried fish and pig legs hang protected in the first courtyard; here they're haphazardly tacked on an outside wall just high enough to keep them safe from dogs and rodents. Laundry drips on a line: Tao's undershirts, his father's baggy pants, his mother's dark tunics, his eight little brothers' and sisters' clothes. To me, the house looks very country and very romantic. My mother would be appalled, calling it a pathetic shack.

"Tao was born in the Year of the Dog," Kumei volunteers, noticing the way I'm staring at the house.

112

"Everyone knows the Dog and the Tiger make an ideal love match."

"I'm not looking for a love match —"

"No, of course not. Not you. That's why we have to walk up here every morning at the exact same time. You don't want to *see* anyone in particular."

"I don't."

But I do. If May could give me up so easily and if Z.G. doesn't want to know me, then maybe Tao . . . Maybe I might still be worthy of love . . .

"Everyone likes a Dog," Kumei continues. "A Dog knows how to get along with others and how to lick their hands. He's loyal, even if the master is his wife. He's good at rescuing, as everyone knows. Do you need rescuing?"

If she only knew.

"What about you?" I ask. "You're a Pig, aren't you? Maybe you and Tao should marry." I don't mean a word I say, but perhaps my questions will get her going in another direction.

"Yes," she agrees, considering. "It could work. But I'm a widow and I have a child. No one will marry me now."

"But it's the New China and there's the new Marriage Law. Widows . . ."

As we near Tao's house, he steps out into the sunlight. It's as if he's been waiting in the shadows for us to come near. I'm not the only one to observe this.

Kumei lowers her voice. "Forget about me and let's think about kisses for you. A Tiger needs a practical and good Dog. Such a good match." She sighs theatrically, which only emphasizes that she's teasing me. "Or, since this is the New Society, you could try free love." Then, "Good morning, Tao. Are you going to the fields? Would you like to walk with us? Comrade Joy has been very quiet this morning. She must still be living on city time. Maybe you can wake her up."

I blush. It happens every time I see Tao, but I notice color rising in his cheeks too.

He ruffles his spiky hair and grins. "I might be able to help our city comrade."

Just then Tao's mother joins her son on the hard-packed earth outside the door of the house. The sleeves of her patched shirt are rolled up to the elbow as if she's about to wash more clothes or salt vegetables. She carries a child strapped to her back, and another three children cluster around her legs like little chicks. (Chairman Mao has encouraged the masses to have lots of offspring, so China will have many survivors to replenish the population at great speed in case America drops atomic bombs on the country. Also, as he has said, "With every stomach comes another pair of hands." China needs those hands to build the New Society, and Tao's parents have helped provide them.) Tao's mother gives me a resentful look and says to her son, "Come home as soon as you're done. I'll have a simple meal prepared for you. Simple, because we're simple in our tastes."

Somehow Tao's mother has come to the conclusion that I'm not simple in my tastes. Maybe it's because of the shift I wore my first night here. Or maybe she's afraid I'm going to steal Tao and take him to Shanghai.

We may be living in the New China, but Shanghai has the aura to these people of someplace mysterious, decadent, and sinful.

Tao jumps down from the terrace and strides ahead of us. I've found that men in the village always walk out front with the women behind. I don't mind, because it allows me to watch Tao glide up the hill, the sinews in his arms and legs sliding gracefully over his bones.

It's a good thing Kumei isn't in my head to hear my thoughts.

We reach the crest of the hill. From here we can see five other villages — each comprising its own collective — nestled between or against rolling hills. Neat rows of tea bushes grow in terraces on the slopes. In the valley, rice paddies and fields of corn, millet, sorghum, sweet potatoes, and hay create a checkerboard of food and wealth. We swing down the path and join others in our work team who are also on their way to the fields.

Some days we work on the tea terraces, picking leaves and tending Green Dragon's most precious crop. Or we'll gather sweet potatoes to dry, store, and feed to livestock. We've also labored in water, building irrigation ditches, wells, and ponds. We women are luckier than the men. The government has issued a proclamation that women can't work in water up to their waists. No one, and this is kind of creepy if you think about it, wants any infections to enter a woman through her private parts. Today, though, we'll just be working in a cornfield. Since all tools have been given to the collective, we check out hoes and other implements we'll need from the work team leader.

115

Now that we're with other people, I'm careful how I interact with Tao. When he marches straight into our assigned field, I linger on the edge to put a straw hat over my kerchief to shield me from the sun before stepping out into the ripening rows of corn. Kumei is ahead of me. She chooses a furrow next to Tao, but I go another five furrows over and drive my hoe into the soil to dislodge a weed.

A month ago, I didn't know how to do this work. I did my best, but I was hopeless and exhausted. I kept thinking about one of my professors, who said that the Chinese peasant is "the twin brother to the ox." I wasn't at all like an ox. I'd come back from the fields with an aching back, sore muscles, and blisters on my hands. The hot sun was brutal, and I didn't understand that I needed to keep drinking boiled water and tea. But as they say around here, "Seeing something once is better than hearing about it a hundred times. Doing something once is better than seeing it a hundred times." I've been learning and observing from real life. I'm still a long way from becoming one of Mao's "shock team" women, but I've found what the villagers call an iron spirit.

All around me I hear people working: the *shush shush* as they glide between the cornstalks, the hacking of hoes as they aerate the furrows, and the melodies of a recently authorized harvest song rising into the air from the hayfield adjacent to us. This is everything I imagined the New China would be: rosy-cheeked peasants helping one another and sharing the benefits, the sun warming my back, the sound of cicadas and birds accompanying our songs.

At eleven, some married women arrive from the village with tin canisters tied to the ends of poles and strung over their shoulders. They serve us rice and vegetables — cucumbers, eggplants, tomatoes, and onions, all of which were grown by the collective — and then we go back to work. A little after noon, Z.G. appears. He wears a big-brimmed straw hat and carries a satchel and an easel. He works in the field for an hour or so before going to sit under a tree to draw. No one objects. He's recording our work.

At four, the hottest time of the day, the married women return, bringing tea thermoses and more rice. During our break, people gather around Z.G. to look at his sketches, often exclaiming and laughing as they recognize themselves and others.

"Look, there's Comrade Du's bat-shaped scar!"

"Are my legs as bowed as that?"

"You can see the girls from the irrigation team walking together in this one. You put those girls together and all you get is laughter. They think life is so carefree."

These compliments should be hard for Tao to hear, since he once received them himself, but he knows he's in the presence of a far better artist.

After our break, we return to the furrows. It's almost the end of the day when I hear a woman shriek. The singing stops, but the cicadas continue to whine as we listen through the warm air for the source of the sound. We begin to hear shouts and a woman's pained cries.

117

Kumei and I rush through the cornstalks and into the adjacent hayfield. The harvest has begun in this field, and the far end has already come under a sharp-bladed hay cutter. It's there, in the cleared area, that a group of people cluster together. We run to them and elbow our way through the crowd. A man, splattered with blood, stands over a woman. He looks pale and distraught. The woman's neck has been torn open, and her arm is nearly gone from her body. Blood spurts and pools around her. Three women have stripped off their kerchiefs and are using them to try to stop the bleeding, but it doesn't seem to be helping.

The smell of the blood under the hot sun is thick at the back of my throat. I feel sick and repelled, but flies and other insects have been attracted to the scent and are buzzing about the woman, swooping in to drink her blood. I've seen her before — in the village, at our evening art classes, and on the paths to the fields — but I don't know her name.

"It's not my fault," the blood-splattered man says in a shaky voice. "I was working in my furrow. Comrade Ping-li was next to me. The next thing I knew, she threw herself in the hay cutter's path — low, so I couldn't miss her. She must not have seen me. But how can that be?" He looks at us, searching for an answer, but none of us have one. "She had to see me. We work next to each other every day."

"You're not responsible, Comrade Bing-dao," someone says from the crowd. "These things happen."

Murmurs of assent greet this assessment. But I'm thinking, *These things happen? Who throws herself in*

118

front of a hay cutter? And then more practical thoughts: *Where's the ambulance? Where's the hospital?* But no ambulance or hospital exists within miles of here. And there isn't a tractor, truck, or car to use for transportation even if there were a hospital. All that doesn't matter anyway. The woman is dying. Her skin has gone waxy. The pool of blood has continued to grow, but the spurting has slowed. Her eyes are glassy and she seems unaware of her surroundings. The kneeling women comfort her as best they can.

"The collective will take care of your children," one says. "There are no orphans in the New China."

"We'll make sure your children remember you," promises another.

"Red blood is a sign of socialist purity," the third adds. "And your blood is very red."

Once again, murmurs of approval.

I glance away as the dead woman's eyes are closed and see Z.G. The piece of charcoal in his hand moves quickly over a sheet of paper in his sketchbook.

Later, I'm in the villa's front courtyard gathering art supplies for tonight's lesson when Tao peeks around the front gate. He asks if I'm all right. I answer yes, but I'm still upset — by seeing that woman die. Tao nods sympathetically and then says, "I want to show you something. Will you come with me?"

"I need to get things ready for class."

"For a few minutes only, please?"

119

I look to see if anyone is watching us. I don't see anyone, but that doesn't mean that someone can't hear us the way sound travels in here.

"Comrade Tao," I say formally, just in case, "I will come with you. I want to be useful to everyone in the village."

He grins when I join him outside the front gate. He turns left, and I follow as he walks on the path that runs next to the villa's high wall. He crosses over a small stone footbridge and turns left again onto a path that parallels Green Dragon's stream. If he smells like gasoline, I don't notice, because I now wear that scent myself. I wear it with pride, knowing that I've truly joined village life.

We don't go far before Tao takes my hand and pulls me off the main path. Touching was taboo in Chinatown, but the rules are even more stringent here. I can't believe that Tao's touching me at all or that I'm following him up a very steep set of stone steps built into the hillside. He doesn't let go of my hand. Farther up the hill, nearly hidden in a bamboo grove, is a pavilion about ten feet wide. I'm out of breath by the time we reach it. Round posts with peeling red paint rise up to rafters. Soft green bamboo surrounds three sides of the pavilion. A low stone railing on the fourth side protects us from a long fall into the valley below. Hills, villages, and fields stretch out before us.

"It's lovely," I say. I turn from the view to meet Tao's dark eyes. The air suddenly hangs heavy. I sense what's going to happen next. Maybe I *will* it to happen. When Tao pulls me into his arms, I go easily and submissively.

120

His mouth tastes fresh — like white tea. I feel his heart beat against mine. He holds me and again stares into my eyes. I feel I'm looking into his soul. I see kindness, sympathy, and generosity. I see an artist.

Then he releases me and takes a step back. I don't care what Kumei said. There is no "free" love in China. We don't even have it in America. All love comes at a price, as my aunt May learned. Tao and I were only kissing, true, but what we've done is beyond forbidden in the New China. What am I saying? It was forbidden in the old China too! And let's face it. I'm a good Chinese girl, who was raised in Chinatown. I don't do things like this.

"What is this place?" I ask, desperate to create some distance between what I *want* to do and what we *should* do.

"It's the Charity Pavilion," Tao answers. His voice is strong. Not a single quaver. "It was built by the grandfather of the landowner who once possessed the villa where you're staying. All this was his land. He owned the pavilion, the villa, every building in Green Dragon, and the fields where we work." He gestures to the undulating green hills. "This is how our village got its name. It's like a green dragon running through the countryside."

If he can be so straightforward, then I should be as well. I glance around the pavilion. Couplets are painted on the three rafters: BE KIND AND BENEVOLENT. MAKE A CASUAL STOP ON THE ENDLESS WAY TO THE FUTURE. and PUT ALL TROUBLES FROM YOUR MIND.

121

"'Make a casual stop on the endless way to the future,'" I read aloud. "Is that what we're doing?"

Tao gives me a look I don't understand.

"Is that what we're doing?" I repeat.

"But why do we need to stop?"

I hear this with my American mind. I've been kissed by only three boys. Once by Leon Lee, the son of my parents' friends Violet and Rowland Lee. From the time Leon and I were children, our parents plotted that we would marry one day. That was never going to happen. Leon was too serious for me, and I never wanted to end up striving, striving, striving for the American Dream, buying a house, a dishwasher, and a lawn. Joe Kwok and I kissed a few times in college, and I thought we were serious about each other. I learned he wasn't serious about anything except his own future. And now Tao. I'm a virgin, but I know the dangers, and there's no way I'm going to second base.

"It was fated that you would come to my village," Tao says. "It was fated that your father would be an artist who would teach me. Perhaps it's fated that we should be together."

"I need to get back," I mumble. "I need to help my father."

As I start to leave, he pulls me to him again. There's nothing shy in the way he holds me or the way he runs his hand up inside my blouse to my breast. Now that's something that's never happened to me before, and my mind empties. The pleasure of that. The yearning and desire it awakens startles and unsettles me. He nuzzles my neck, pushing aside the pouch my aunt gave me with his lips. His tongue darts out, tasting my flesh, sending shivers of cold from my neck to my nipples. How does he know what to do?

"You should go back first," he says, his voice surprisingly husky. "I'll come a little late to the meeting, so no one suspects anything."

I nod and pull away.

"We have to be careful," he says. "No one can know . . . for now."

I nod again.

"Go," he says, and I obey.

Attending our political-study class and art lesson in the ancestral hall doesn't calm my restless emotions. I'm walking in the darkness of seeing a woman die and the light of Tao's touch. My feelings are confused, but that doesn't explain the agitation around me. Tonight the men cluster together, keeping their heads down and their voices low, while the women gather on the other side of the hall, with their heads up and their tongues scissor sharp.

"In feudal days, women had to follow their husbands no matter what their lot," a woman states loud enough for the sound to carry to the men. "Husbands said, 'A wife is like a pony bought. I'll ride her and whip her as I like.' Comrade Ping-li's husband forgot that we're now living in the New Society."

"Ping-li was a woman, but she was a person first."

"We're told we're masters of our own fates, but Ping-li was a slave to that husband of hers."

I'm baffled by the anger and the accusations. "Wasn't today an accident?" I ask Z.G., as we sort the brushes and paper that Kumei and I will hand out after the political meeting.

When he gives me an exasperated look, Kumei whispers in a low voice, "Everyone says it was suicide. Comrade Ping-li's husband beat her. He made her work very hard. She asked for a divorce many times, but that only made him beat her more. What other choice did she have?"

Without thinking, I put a hand to my throat as images of my father Sam flood my mind. No one in Green Dragon knows what I left to come here. I make my hand drop as casually as possible and try to wash all feelings from my face. I catch Z.G. staring at me — weighing me, as he always seems to do — and realizing I don't measure up in some way.

"Maybe your New China isn't so perfect after all," he says to me in English, causing Kumei's eyes to widen in surprise.

"You speak Russian!" Kumei beams. Everyone — from Chairman Mao down to this illiterate village girl — wants to emulate the Soviet Union, which they call Lao Da Ge — Old Big Brother. "Today's Soviet Union is like our tomorrow!" She recites the popular saying. Neither of us corrects her. It's better that she thinks I understand Russian than that she suspect I'm from America. Even here, in the middle of nowhere, people hate what they call the American imperialists.

I glance across the hall to Tao. Almost the entire village is present, yet the way he stares at me makes me

124

feel like we're in a room by ourselves. Just the idea of being alone together feels forbidden, and it takes my mind away from the dead woman and the memory of my father hanging in the closet. Tao gives me an encouraging smile. It's as if he wants me to know everything will be fine.

"We came out of our homes during collectivization," one of the women grumbles loudly. "We were told we'd receive equal pay for equal work. We were told we'd have the new Marriage Law to guide us. But where is help when we need it?"

Sung-ling, the portly wife of the Party secretary, marches up to an old altar table and leans her two closed fists on it. "Feudal ways are hard to change," she says in a shrill voice. "When the Eighth Route Army came through our county during the War of Liberation, they taught us to Speak Bitterness. We women were encouraged to complain about the humiliations we endured — rapes, beatings, loveless marriages, and living under the thumbs of heartless mothers-in-law. We directed our sad stories of anguish and suffering into collective anger about the feudal system. If a husband teased us or belittled us, together we beat him in the square until he was motionless like a dead dog, with his mouth, eyes, and nose full of mud, and his clothes reduced to rags."

This speech has the effect of inflaming instead of calming the women, but Sung-ling isn't done.

"But gossiping and complaining like weak women is not the way to make men hear us. Beating a man in the public square won't make him be a better husband,

125

father, or comrade either. Times are different now. You make me look bad with your backward ways. We have to address these matters properly. I will ask the county to send a propaganda team to our village. They will help us put on a play to remind everyone of the rules. I'll need some volunteers."

I have acting experience, so I raise my hand. When they see my hand go up, Tao and Kumei raise theirs as well.

"Good," Sung-ling says. "Now, for the rest of tonight, I don't want to hear another word about Comrade Ping-li. She is dead. That is all we can say." She peers around the hall, practically begging someone to contradict her. She purses her lips and gives a little nod before continuing. "Now, let us begin our political discussion. Please move to your usual spots."

The divided hall grudgingly comes together, and Tao ends up sitting next to me. Despite Sung-ling's pep talk — if that's what it was — the people remain restive. Party Secretary Feng Jin follows his wife's instructions, refusing to mention the dead woman. Instead, he doles out praise to select model workers. Then he recounts some of the Red Army's greatest exploits, which he does every night. I'm getting to like them better than the episodes of *Gunsmoke*, *Sky King*, and *Highway Patrol* my family used to watch.

The first of tonight's stories involves the brave female communication operators during the War of Liberation. "They had to run *under constant fire*," Party Secretary Feng Jin emphasizes, "from one shell hole to another. They sent urgent messages, *life-and-death* messages. If they lost their connection, they turned their own bodies into electric conductors by *gritting wires* between their teeth. Those women were *sisters* in the war of resistance!"

It's not the most subtle morality story, and in many ways it's a strange choice, since I bet few people here have ever seen a telephone, but everyone seems calmer. But I'm not. Tao's leg has fallen against mine. The heat of his flesh burns through two layers of clothing right into my skin. I keep my eyes forward, staring at the backs of the heads in front of me, but my heart thumps in my chest.

"What has Liberation brought us?" Party Secretary Feng Jin asks, and then he goes on to quote Chairman Mao. " 'Everybody works so everybody eats.' What does this mean? Today those same brave women work in power stations. They climb pylons to change porcelain insulators to maintain ultrahigh-tension transmission lines. One day, they will bring telephones and electricity here. Other women work in cotton and flour mills or serve as machine-tool operators, geological prospectors, welders, forgers, pilots, and navigators. Women are educated — whether in a literacy class like the one we have here in our collective or at a university."

A discussion follows, with several men raising their hands to speak. Again we're reminded of the things Chairman Mao has promised in the New Society: Women hold up half the sky. Everyone — men, women, and children — must plunge into political struggle to brave storms and face the world. We all must adhere to the Marriage Law. Party Secretary Feng Jin ends the

127

session with a song. The whole room reverberates with good feeling as the voices of Green Dragon Village Collective join him.

Later, during the art lesson, I'm still aware of Tao — how could I not be with his taste still in my mouth and his touch on my lips, neck, and breast? — sitting next to me. I refuse to look at him outright, but I peer at his hand and try to draw it.

"Something has opened in you, Joy." I look up to see Z.G. Blood rushes up my neck to my face. "Your technique still needs polishing, but I believe your calligraphy lessons have given you a delicate touch." He stands back, with his arms folded, staring at my work with true appreciation. "The hand is the hardest to draw," he adds. "I think you could be good, if you actually wanted to learn."

I smile. What a strange and wonderful day this has turned out to be.

When the lesson ends, Tao leaves with the other villagers. Z.G., Kumei, and I collect the art supplies and return to the villa. Kumei says goodnight, and Z.G. and I walk through the courtyards to our adjoining rooms. Z.G. disappears into his room, while I put the supplies away. He returns a few minutes later with a sketchbook.

"This is for you," he says. "You'll need a lot of practice if you ever want to draw a hand properly. Always try to depict the inner world of the heart and mind. That is the essence of Chinese artistic striving. You could get there, I think."

He says nothing more and returns to his room. I'm left with my first two gifts from my father — his words and the sketchbook.

After that night, I still wake up early and work in the fields as I did before. In the afternoons, Z.G. still works by himself by the side of the fields with his charcoal, pencil, and sketchbook or with brushes, paints, and paper. People still stop to look at his drawings, but he increasingly keeps a lot of his work private, often flipping down another sheet of paper, especially when I approach, so I can't see what he's working on. This hurts my feelings, but what can I do?

At the end of the day, Tao and I lag behind, gathering everyone's tools and securing them for the night. Then Tao and I head back toward Green Dragon Village. We're careful not to hold hands or touch, because we don't want anyone to look out a window or door and see us. We walk to the villa's front gate, pass it, cross the little bridge, and then hurry along the path paralleling the stream until we reach the turnoff to the Charity Pavilion. I've grown stronger. Now I can get to the top of the hill and still have enough breath to kiss Tao right away. Later, we go separately to the political meeting and art lesson in the ancestral hall. We don't sit together any longer, but I sense him nearby, knowing that tomorrow we'll have our secret time in the Charity Pavilion.

I've gone from losing the one man in my life who mattered to me to gaining two new and unique men.

129

They distract me. They thrill me, but in different ways, of course. And for some minutes, and even hours, during the day I'm able to drive my father Sam from my mind. But it's not easy. When I think of my dad, I know he'd be unhappy to see me here. He wouldn't want me working in the fields, washing out my nightstool, letting my skin burn under the hot sun, or — and this he would have objected to most of all — spending time with Tao, alone and for hours on end. My dad never would have said it — he would have left it to my mother — but he would have been very disappointed in me. He would have worried that I had ruined my chances for what he called a real American life.

My remorse over these things is minor. A part of me feels that the harsh sunlight is burning away my past and that the hard work is chopping away my past mistakes. Every night when I crawl into bed — my skin dirty and every muscle exhausted — I feel wiped clean, and I can sleep. In the morning, when the dark mass of guilt inside my chest — which hasn't left me for one minute since I saw my father hanging from a rope in his closet — threatens to well up and overpower me, I throw on my clothes and join the others with a smile on my face. I can't forget the way my mother and aunt lied to me and fought over me, even though I turned out to be so undeserving of their worry or affection. Yes, I've escaped the blaming eyes of my mother and the reproachful eyes of my aunt, but I can't escape myself. The only things I can do to save myself are pull the weeds in the fields, let my emotions for Tao envelop me, and obey what Z.G. tells me to do with a paintbrush, pencil, charcoal, or pastel.

Part Two

THE RABBIT
DODGES

Joy

Standing Against the
Wind and Waves

We've been rehearsing for many days and we're ready to give our show about women, the Marriage Law, and right thinking in the New Society. Drums, cymbals, and horns beckon people from their homes. Firecrackers snap and spark, announcing that a celebration is about to take place. It's late on a Sunday afternoon. Most people have had the day off to rest, mend their clothes, and play with their children. Now everyone in Green Dragon comes to the square just outside the villa to watch our performance. Five little girls — in matching blouses, pink ribbons in their hair, and trailing long paper streamers — run through the clusters of people. Boys dole out paper cones brimming with peanuts or watermelon seeds, which the villagers crack between their teeth.

The makeshift stage is set up in the Chinese way, with no curtain and everything open for all to see. The musicians continue their clamorous tune, while a group of men from the propaganda team's acrobatic troupe tumble and spin across the stage. The program begins with a recounting of some of Mao and the Red Army's triumphs during the War of Liberation. Next, the propaganda team's actors perform a vignette to illustrate the Twelve Point Measure to increase farm production. The content is nothing new. I know the villagers in Green Dragon already do these things, because I've done them or seen them myself. I've carried water buckets hanging from a pole across my shoulders to the fields, spread manure by hand, sprinkled nightsoil on cabbage plants, and every day Tao and I pass a water buffalo that's guided back and forth over rocks to crush them, breaking down the soil so that a new field can be made. In my first days here, I worried about the creature. It wore blinders and had stumbled on the sharp rocks so many times that its legs were bloody and scabbed. My Western sympathies got the better of me, and I asked Tao why someone didn't remove the water buffalo's blinders so he could see where he was going.

"Without blinders, he'd avoid the rocks," Tao answered. "This is his punishment for what he did in a past life."

I still find it hard to believe that Tao can have such backward beliefs, but then this whole evening is about educating peasants.

Another acrobatic exhibition follows the farming lesson, which improves the audience's mood considerably. When the last acrobat somersaults offstage,

Kumei, Sung-ling, and I take one another's hands and step forward. I'll be playing two different roles tonight. I'm the only one of the three of us who's acted professionally, so my parts are the largest. For my first character, I'm dressed as a female soldier in a green jacket, trousers, and cap with a red star. To my left, Kumei appears as a pre-Liberation maiden, with an elaborate headdress with tassels and beading, a brocade jacket, and a long silk skirt with dozens of tiny pleats. To my right, Sung-ling wears the everyday outfit of all the women I've met here in the countryside: a cotton blouse with a floral pattern, loose blue pants, and homemade shoes.

"We three women have found new lives in the New China," I say, addressing the audience. "We've fought against the feudal systems of political authority, clan authority, religious authority, and husband authority. We've fought against class oppression and foreign aggression."

"I'm a girl from feudal times," Kumei announces nervously. When we first started rehearsals, Sung-ling insisted that Kumei play this part. It's pretty hard to imagine Kumei — with her ruddy cheeks and loud voice — playing a demure maiden. I would have been much better at the part, having once played an emperor's daughter as an extra in a movie. Besides, my aunt always said to take the role with the better costume.

"At age five, I was sold by my parents to the landowner," Kumei continues. "In time he dressed me as a present and opened me every night. Oh, how I

137

cried. I had a mouth but no right to speak. I had legs but no freedom to run."

Kumei's arm movements are clumsy, and she has zero stage presence. Still, I'm surprised she's doing as well as she is. She's illiterate, so she couldn't read the script. I worked with her this past week, trying to help her memorize the words, but Sung-ling kept saying that Kumei's version was fine.

"The Kuomintang soldiers did nothing to protect the people against the Japanese soldiers or the elements. Fifteen years ago, drought dried the fields. Eleven years ago, famine took hold of our country. Millions of people went hungry."

Kumei hesitates, stumbling over the words. Then she freezes. People in the audience titter and point. I had thought this would be fun, but I wish she'd never volunteered to help. Sung-ling hisses the next line, and Kumei repeats it.

"My owner hoarded his rice. People left our village to beg. They sold their children. Too many died. When the War Against the Japanese Aggressors ended, we had the War of Liberation."

When the audience erupts in cheers, Kumei takes a few steps across the stage and brings her hands together in a prayerful manner. Her recitation is amateurish, but now she goes on with more strength. "After our great leader liberated the masses, the people accused my owner of terrible crimes. They killed him and ordered me to make self-criticism. I did this before the whole village. And you" — here she spreads her arms to take in the audience — "remembered my red past as the daughter of a peasant family. You let me live!"

The audience is mesmerized, but I could have done a much better job with the monologue. I would have memorized the actual text sent by the government and not spoken so loosely.

Now Sung-ling strides across the stage. She's been typecast as a model village woman. "Our great Chairman sent people to teach us. The first lesson: brush my teeth! I obeyed. Later, he instituted land reform. Everyone got a piece of land. Even women like me had our names on land titles and deeds. At last we were free from feudal landlord oppression."

This isn't exactly a hard part for Sung-ling to play, since she spouts this stuff every day. Now she leans forward to confide knowingly. "But Chairman Mao was not done. He put us on a path from socialism to communism, and we've obeyed. Five years ago, we formed mutual-aid teams. Two years ago, we gave our land, animals, seed grain, and tools to the collective."

I've heard all this before, but for the first time it really sinks in. People had their own land for only three years? But no one here complains. Everyone loves the collective, because . . .

"We no longer suffer from famine," Sung-ling declares. "Freed from the bloodsucking landlord, farm profits have increased and even our children are chubby."

She bows and receives great applause. She raises her head and continues. "Land reform and the Marriage Law came to us at the same time. This is not like learning to brush your teeth or clean your ears. As you will see, we still face much resistance . . ."

In the next skit, Tao and a girl from the propaganda team portray a young couple. They walk across the stage together, not touching. Tao has just eight lines, and not once has he gotten them right in rehearsal.

"I should ask my father to arrange a marriage for us," Tao recites in a dull monotone. I tried to help him with his delivery, but obviously I didn't get through. "Our fathers will negotiate the bride-price and dowry. Then you will come to my home."

The girl primly steps away from him and shakes her finger from side to side. "No, no, they cannot do that. I am not to be bought or sold."

Tao garbles his next line, which is supposed to be "But I've told you I'm happy to make you my second wife."

The girl playing opposite him goes on with the show, as Aunt May would say. "No more multiple wives, child brides, or concubines." Her voice grows sterner as she repeats, "And no more buying of women."

Tao, the unsuitable suitor, persists, awkwardly gesturing at his would-be bride with about as much ardor as cold taffy. "You'll be safe with me. You'll never have to leave the house or the yard. You know the old saying" — and here Tao beams, relieved to be back to something he actually knows — " 'Men go to market to sell their wares, but a woman belongs in her home with her mother-in-law and children.' "

At this, murmurs of approval ripple through the audience, which surprises me given the wholehearted

140

way people accepted the story of land reform. What I understand in this moment is that many families here — like Tao's — still keep their wives, mothers, sisters, and grandmothers inside. I'm so distracted by my thoughts about this that Sung-ling jabs me in the back to push me forward into the scene.

I've been assigned to play Tao's sister, just returned from military service. I raise my arm to the sky in the inspirational style found in government posters I've seen. "Brother, it is time you understand that women can no longer be oppressed or exploited. Look at me. I fought with the army. Today I'm liberated from the four walls of my home."

I have a long monologue, and I've worked hard to memorize it. So far I'm really pleased with how I'm doing.

"Brother," I continue, "ask your bride to go with you of her own choice to the Party leaders of our village to get permission to marry. If she agrees, my sister-in-law will enjoy equal status in your home. If you have a baby girl, you will welcome her. Female infanticide is strictly forbidden! Remember, you are building the New Society. If you persist in following the old ways once you're married, I myself will take my sister-in-law to court to ask for a divorce. You'll be struggled against by the people. They'll weed you out for your counter-revolutionary ways and gladly grant her a divorce if you continue to follow the bourgeois road."

The people from the propaganda team insisted I use that phrase, but I wonder, what do these villagers — as much as I like them — know about the bourgeois road?

141

The propaganda team's director strides to the front of the stage to spell out the lesson. "The groom has realized his mistake and promises to join the right path," he proclaims. "Our young couple will keep their eyes on their own interests and return radiant from their marriage registration."

As dusk turns to night, members of the troupe set small saucers filled with bean oil and lighted with cotton wicks at the foot of the stage. This darker atmosphere seems right for what comes next. Comrade Feng Rui, the dead woman's husband, is brought onstage to make a self-criticism. He keeps his head down, refusing to look at the audience. He wears standard peasant clothes. His hair hangs stringy and lank.

"Remember," Sung-ling warns, "leniency to those who confess and severity to those who refuse."

Comrade Feng Rui quietly begins. "I was a bad husband. I didn't follow the red way."

That's as far as he gets before people start jeering.

"We always thought you were a reactionary," someone yells.

"Your wife called you a wicked element, and she was right," accuses another.

Sung-ling holds up a hand for silence so she can address Comrade Feng Rui directly. "Your wife was a woman, but she was also a person. Still, you treated her like a dog. You beat her and cursed her. You let your mother torment her. What do you have to say? Tell us your bad history so we can know who you are."

Feng Rui mumbles something unintelligible. A part of me feels sorry for him being humiliated in front of the collective. Then an image of his wife's injuries and her waxy flesh in death comes into my mind. He's lucky to be getting off so easily.

"You behaved so badly toward your wife," Sung-ling continues, "that she threw herself into Comrade Bing-dao's hay cutter. And how do you think he feels now? He took a life, but it wasn't his fault."

"It was yours!" people shout from the audience.

I'm at the side of the stage. I've changed into my next costume, and I'm supposed to be preparing for our big finale. Instead, I find myself joining the others in their chanting condemnation of Comrade Ping-li's husband. Adrenaline pumps through my veins as a white ribbon is pinned to Comrade Feng Rui's chest.

"From now on you will wear this ribbon of denunciation," Sung-ling declares. "Everyone will look at you and see you for the rightist element you are!"

With that, Feng Rui is led away, ending the struggle-session portion of our show. I'm excited, ready for my starring role. I give my cheeks quick pinches to bring in color, since none of us wear make-up. We must end the evening on an up note, and our last scene will do that.

I take my place at a table with one of the actors sent by the county. His name is Sheng. I don't have to look all that closely to see that he hasn't followed the lesson about teeth brushing, and it's pretty clear he hasn't washed recently either. We're playing a husband and wife in an unhappy marriage. We're both fishermen. We

143

argue about who does the chores, who minds the children, who sews, and who washes the clothes. Then the accusations shift from domestic to public life.

"So you like to go to sea to show your strength, do you?" Sheng mocks me. "That's like asking a baby chick to swallow a soybean. You'll choke on it eventually."

"But I haven't choked! I'm sailing the seas of revolution like all the people of China. I'm standing against the wind and waves and breaking a new path for women! My female comrades and I have applied Mao Tse-tung Thought to fishing. My boat has caught over seven hundred tons of fish. Everybody works so everybody eats!"

My husband isn't satisfied with my response, and he's even less satisfied with me. I may have beaten my husband at fishing, but now he physically beats me. He won't give me food. He locks me out of the house so that I have to sleep outside. As a girl on movie sets, I was praised for my ability to cry when the director yelled, "Action." I let the tears flow now. I'm so sad, so pathetic, it seems I have no way out. I take a butcher knife and prepare to drive it into my heart. Even men in the audience weep in sympathy for my sorry life.

Just then I look up and see a poster about the Marriage Law. I study the pictures, explaining what I see: "A hurried marriage is not a solid basis for a marriage. Suicide is not a solution to unhappiness. Divorce will be granted when husband and wife desire it."

144

When I turn around, a panel of judges sits at my kitchen table. I tell them my unhappy tale. My husband gives his version. In the end, I'm granted a divorce in accordance with the Marriage Law. My husband and I part as friends. I go back to my fishing vessel and he goes back to his.

"The dark clouds of misery have been dispelled," I tell the audience. "A blue sky has been revealed. Harmony has been restored."

With this conclusion, we take our bows. Our little show wasn't as professional as a movie or a television show, but the audience loved it. I have the same feeling I have after any performance — exhilaration and joy. As the villagers head home, Tao, Kumei, Sung-ling, and I help the county troupe load their costumes and props into wheelbarrows, which will be pushed to the nearest road, a few miles away. As soon as they leave the square, Kumei and her son walk the few steps back to the villa.

"Thank you for helping," Sung-ling praises me.

"Thank you for letting me participate," I respond. "I'm happy I got to —"

"Don't plump your feathers too high," Sung-ling cuts me off. "Individuals should never take credit for a good job. The glory goes to our team and to our collective."

She gives a sharp nod and turns to leave. Tao and I are left nearly alone on the square. I wish we could go somewhere to have a Coke or some ice cream the way I used to do at home, because I'm not ready to go back to the villa. Emboldened by the adrenaline still

145

coursing through my body, I ask if he'd like to take a walk. It's too dark to go up the hill to the Charity Pavilion, so we stay on the footpath that borders the stream. After a while, we stop and sit on rocks at the water's edge. I peel off my shoes and socks and dip my feet in the cool water. Tao slips off his sandals and submerges his feet next to mine. In elementary school, Hazel and I used to tease other girls about their wanting to play footsie with some boy or other. It was the kind of dumb taunting that little girls do when they know absolutely nothing about sex, boys, or romance. But now I let my toes — wet and soft — slip along the arch of Tao's right foot. The sensations I feel from this are not located in my feet however. The performance has given Tao courage too, because he takes my hand and puts it in his lap. I feel his startling hardness and I don't pull away.

Later, when I get back to the villa, everyone is in the front courtyard. Ta-ming sleeps with his head in Kumei's lap. Yong perches on a ceramic jardiniere, her bound feet barely touching the ground. And Z.G. roosts on a step, his elbows on his knees, his head thrust forward. I'm feeling buoyed, but he looks angry, and it really rubs me the wrong way.

"You come from far away, and everyone is trying to be understanding of your different ways." His tone is stern and harsh. "But no one in this house can afford your bourgeois activities."

"What bourgeois —"

146

"Leaving the village with Tao and doing who knows what. This has to stop."

My first response is indignation. *Who do you think you are? My father?* I want to ask him, except he *is* my father. Well, he may be my father, but he doesn't *know* me. He can't tell me what to do. I look for help from Kumei and Yong. We've just seen a series of skits on the liberation of women. Kumei and Yong should be on my side, but their faces are white with what I take to be fear.

"We're in the New China, but one thing hasn't changed," Z.G. continues. "Your actions reflect on all of us."

My actions? I think about the stuff Tao and I just did. Shame, embarrassment, and remembered pleasure burn my face. Still, I respond defiantly. "Nothing happened!"

"If you're caught," Z.G. goes on, "you will not be the only one punished. We *all* will have to attend struggle sessions and make self-criticisms."

"I doubt that," I say petulantly, like I did when I used to get in trouble with my dad. I mean, really. I walked in here feeling really high — from the show, from the way the audience reacted to my performance, and from going to third base with Tao. Why does Z.G. have to ruin it?

"*You* don't know anything about anything. What you're doing is dangerous for our hosts," he says. "In the last two years, over two million people have been moved by force to the far west to cultivate wasteland as punishment for criticizing the government, being social misfits, or acting like counter-revolutionaries. Some of those people were peasants like Kumei, Yong, and Ta-ming, who did something to upset the local Party cadre. How long do you think these three would last out there? They would die very quickly, don't you think?"

"You sound like my uncle," I retort. "Always crying wolf. I haven't seen anything bad."

"What about what just happened to Ping-li's husband?"

"He deserved it!"

Z.G. shakes his head. We haven't known each other very long, but it's clear I'm frustrating to him, and he really bugs me.

"I'm going to say this again," he says, attempting to add gentleness to his voice. "Your actions are dangerous — not only to yourself but to our hosts."

"I refuse to believe that. Why would what I do have any consequences for them or anyone else for that matter?"

"It's also dangerous to me," Z.G. confides. "What do you think Party Secretary Feng Jin will report to the Artists' Association about who I've brought to Green Dragon Village and how you're corrupting the masses?" He switches to English. "You're a foreigner. I still haven't figured out how to keep you safe when we go back to Shanghai."

"Maybe I don't want to go back —"

He brushes aside my comment with an impatient wave of his hand. He takes a deep breath to calm himself before continuing. "I want you to understand that I'm not immune to love. You of all people should know that. I know it's impossible to keep young people apart if they want to be together. It takes only a few minutes, after all."

His crudeness and bluntness shock me. I can't imagine my father Sam ever saying anything like that to me.

"I see only one thing to do," Z.G. says. "Keep the two of you near me. You will walk to and from the fields with Kumei from now on. No more going to the Charity Pavilion with Tao."

"How do you know —"

"This is a small village. There is no privacy here. Everyone sees everything. Haven't you figured that out yet?" He pauses to let that sink in. "In the evening, you will walk with me to the ancestral hall for the political-study session and our art lessons. You will hand out the paper and brushes by yourself. You don't need help."

"Then I'll never get to see him —"

"Next Saturday night," Z.G. goes on, speaking right over me, "we'll have an exhibition of everyone's best work. You and Tao will display your paintings of the Charity Pavilion."

"But I haven't done any paintings there," I admit. "And neither has Tao."

"I'm aware of that," he says drily. "You and Tao are going to need to work on those right away. So, after our lesson in the ancestral hall, the two of you will return to the villa with me."

"I don't want anyone to think I'm special —"

"They won't think you're special when they see how I treat you. I'm going to teach you how to draw and

149

you're going to learn. I'm going to give you homework and you're going to do it. I'm not going to be nice. Everyone accepts that Tao has talent. You? I'm not so sure you have great talent, but you're better than anyone else in this place. Therefore, from now on the three of us will have private lessons in the front courtyard. We will keep the gate open, so everyone can see us. Soon people will understand that your visits to the Charity Pavilion were only about drawing and painting. Nothing else. If you're lucky, they'll forget about you in a day or two. Once that happens, if I have to step away for a few minutes . . ."

Maybe this won't be so bad. Maybe this will even be a good thing. Tao and I can work a full day in the fields and then at night have our special lesson. We'll learn from Z.G., but we'll also be together in a way that won't lead to anything too dangerous. I'm nineteen and I'm not dumb. Things have happened very fast with Tao. And, as Z.G. pointed out, I know perfectly well where making out can lead.

"What happens after Saturday?" I ask.

"Let's see when Saturday comes. Just remember, a person is his — or her — history. If your history isn't good, then you won't be good. A rebel as a five-year-old will be a rebel as a young man and will die a rebel. So what are you, Joy? What is your history and what are you going to be?"

And so my art training begins. As Z.G. promised, he's not easy on me. "Your outlines are good, but your expression still is not deep enough," he pronounces.

"Our great Chairman has said there can be no art for art's sake. You must express the thoughts and feelings of the people. It must be realistic!"

I work harder than I've ever worked in my life. Z.G.'s judgments are tough, but his lessons also allow me to be with Tao, whose presence makes obvious to those who crowd around us at night in the villa's courtyard that the teacher isn't showing favoritism to his daughter.

"Tao has a gift," Z.G. tells the villagers. "My daughter . . . She is learning to paint the same bamboo leaf over and over again. Artists in the Ming dynasty perfected this technique of painting the exact same bamboo leaf again and again and again."

That's right. He still has me painting bamboo sprigs, just as we did on the first night we arrived. I don't understand why, given his criticisms.

"The Ming artists were trying to create the essence of bamboo with their simple strokes," he goes on. "Now consider the way my daughter has painted the bamboo around the Charity Pavilion. It's pretty, but look closer. There's nothing *behind* her strokes. I tell her she must cut to the bone to find her emotional heart."

Pearl

Dust and Memories

My day starts at 6.30a.m. I wake to the sound of rhythmic thumping — the boarders doing physical exercises to a radio program that everyone is encouraged to listen to and follow each day. By the time I've gotten dressed and gone downstairs, the boarders are in the kitchen, bickering and fighting for space, as usual.

"It's my time at the stove," one of the dancing girls snaps at the policeman's widow.

The widow tries reason. "I just want to set my bun near your pot. The warmth from the stove will heat it."

"You know the rules. Go away!"

The widow backs off and bumps into the cobbler. When some of his rice porridge slops onto the floor, he shouts, "Hey! Watch out, you fat water buffalo!"

"Why are you yelling at me?" the widow shoots back. "You caused the problem. You have to make room for everyone in the New Society."

The cobbler grunts, and then puts the bowl back to his lips and slurps noisily. His other hand scratches his rump. No one moves to clean the white mess off the floor, but then it looks like no one has cleaned the floor since Liberation, maybe longer. I rise from my place at the table, pour some hot water from the thermos onto a cloth, and wipe up the porridge. Layers of grime come up, and the tile's cracked-ice pattern that my mother so loved reappears. Thousands of greasy meals cooked by the multiple people living in my family home and maybe not one mopping, but the beautiful tile is still here. I fold the cloth over and scrub my clean spot a little larger. The early morning squabbling ceases and the room falls silent. Six pairs of eyes stare at me: the policeman's widow in contempt, the cobbler with scorn, the two dancing girls in amusement, Cook in concern, and the professor in sympathy. I get up off my knees, rinse the cloth, and return to my cup of tea.

After breakfast, I walk back up the stairs, where, now that I look, the carpet probably hasn't been cleaned since May, my mother, and I left the house. I reach my room and shut the door behind me. I brush my teeth, wrap a scarf around my hair, push my jade bracelet up my arm until it squeezes in place around my flesh, put on a light jacket, and go back downstairs and out the front door on my way to work. No one calls goodbye or wishes me well. It's been this way for six weeks now. Some days I despair that Z.G. and Joy will ever return to Shanghai or that I'll ever hear from May. I've been writing to my sister once a week and haven't yet heard back. Has she received any of my letters? Or was the man at the family association full of baloney when he said my sister and I could send mail to each other through him and Louie Yun in Wah Hong Village? All I can do is wait, and follow one day after the next.

Today the mid-October sky is blue and the air is perfect. The watermelon men of late summer have been replaced by the persimmon sellers of fall. A vendor with a high, thin voice touts his radish and cabbage cakes fried in liver oil. A bean-curd maker pushes a wooden cart and sings the praises of his perfect little white squares. Women — even in this New Society — spend at least three hours a day in food preparation, visiting numerous markets, chopping, cooking, and cleaning. At this hour, they carry thermoses to the hot water store or baskets to government-run shops for fresh soy milk and crullers. I see plenty of servants: peasant girls from the countryside — bumpkins recognizable in their floral-patterned blouses, cotton pants tied up with string, and homemade paper-soled shoes — standing in long lines with their masters' food coupons in hand.

When my bus arrives, I jam myself in with other workers — most of us dressed in monotonous blue and gray, with only the rare splash of red or yellow in the form of a scarf wrapped around a neck or a kerchief covering hair. The bus pulls back into a sea of thousands upon thousands of people on Eternal brand bicycles. We make our way through Hongkew, over the Garden Bridge, and onto the Bund. I get off at my stop and hurry to my place of employment. It's important not to be late for the work of socialist construction.

I sign in with my boss, pick up my basket and other tools, and head back out to the Bund. I now know why the once-grand Western-style buildings are strung with

154

nets. It's to catch people who try to commit suicide. I avert my eyes and gaze out to the Whangpoo. Every morning and every evening I watch the comings and goings of the vessels that ply the river. Twenty years ago, May and I left China by fishing boat, but that would be impossible now. Inspection ships can stop any craft on the river or at sea, and the docked naval ships make me nervous too.

All right then, on to work. I'm one tiny cog in the big machine the Communists call ground cleaning. If everything works perfectly, then soon all that was perceived to be Western, "sinful and corrupt," or individualistic, unique, and beautiful will be eradicated. Today I've been assigned to what was once the French Concession. All the old names — the French Concession, the International Settlement, even the Old Chinese City — have disappeared. It's just Shanghai now. I'll spend the next ten hours patrolling streets and alleyways, collecting scraps of paper that have fallen to the ground, or ripping old posters and advertisements from the walls of houses and shops.

They say that returning to your native land is like coming back to your mother, but I don't see it that way at all. Doing this job has allowed me to see the changes that have happened in my home city — from the most intimate details of daily life to the larger impact of communism on what was once the Paris of Asia. I see sweepers, garbage vans, and people like me — scavengers of every sort — and yet every day there is new paper and other trash to be found. It's as though people are afraid to throw it all out at once. I've stumbled upon old labels and wrapping paper for products and companies that no longer exist in the city — Flaubert's Furs, Lion Brand tooth powder, and British American Tobacco. I've peeled old political announcements and notices off walls and doors. I've found long-discarded love letters, temple offerings, and photographs. I've even picked up wedding couplets that have fallen from overflowing trash bins and onto the street. Many times I've wondered, as I stuff the couplets into my basket, if marriage in the New Society is just something to be thrown away with no regard to custom, tradition, love, or good wishes. Today I find a bill of sale from a scale factory. Farther along, loose sheets of Overseas Banking Company stationery scuff along the street like dust motes.

Around ten, I arrive at an open-air, government-owned market. The morning rush is over, and the area outside the market is heaped with discarded cabbage leaves, bad fruit, and fish scales and guts. A garbage truck stops and picks up everything. By the time it pulls away, the street is once again clean. That, to me, sums up the new Shanghai. The *life* of the city has been cleaned away. The foreigners, who once populated and ran Shanghai, are gone. The only exceptions are Soviet experts, or the few Americans, Frenchmen, or Germans who, guided by what I believe is absolute stupidity, either decided to stay when China closed or abandoned all they had in the West to come here.

The clubs May and I once frequented have disappeared. Where are their taxi dancers, musicians, waiters, and bartenders now? Dead, shipped off to the interior for land reclamation, or working in a factory like the former dancing girls in my family home. The White Russians who lived on the Avenue Joffre are also gone, but so is the Avenue Joffre. It's now called Huaihai Road, which commemorates the second great campaign of 1949, when Mao's soldiers advanced from the Huai River to the sea, putting them in position to take Shanghai. The Race Club off the Avenue Edouard VII in the International Settlement, where my father lost so much money, has been turned into People's Square on what is now called Yen'an Road.

Dead babies no longer lie discarded on sidewalks. They used to be so common that I can remember walking past one or two or three a day without stopping or thinking about it. I haven't seen rickshaw pullers or beggars who've starved or frozen to death overnight either. Still, I've seen plenty of death: a man — probably an unreformed capitalist, who jumped from a building far enough off the Bund that no nets had been strung as a barrier; and another man — a reputed piece of "bourgeois vermin," who was beaten to death by his former employees right on the street.

Once prostitutes were like flowers decorating the city. Now people dress so identically and inconspicuously — in trousers, shirts, and gray caps — that sometimes you can't tell who is a man and who is a woman. Surprisingly enough, Western-style clothes still hang in department store windows — leftovers from better times. In shops, I've found Pond's cold cream and Revlon lipstick. They're outdated and won't be replenished, but I buy them when I see them because I might not have another chance. Once I run out, I'll have to start using Russian-made toiletries, although the scents are sometimes repugnant.

How is it that I can feel nostalgia for prostitutes and beggats? But then I miss everything — the purring foreign cars, the elegant gentlemen in their tailor-made suits and jaunty hats, the laughter, the champagne, the money, the foreigners, the aromatic French and Russian bakeries, and the sheer *fun* of being in one of the great cities on the planet. I wish I'd brought my camera so I could send photographs to May. Nothing I write could be as vivid or believable as seeing it with her own eyes.

What haven't disappeared are rats. They're everywhere. So here's what I don't understand: Old Shanghai, *my* Shanghai, had plenty of sin on the surface but was shored up by the respectability of banking and mercantile wealth underneath. Now I see the so-called respectability of communism on the surface and decay underneath. They can sweep, strip, and cart away all they want, but there's no changing the fact that my home city is decomposing, rotting away, and turning into a skeleton. Eventually, the only things left will be dust and memories.

As usual, I find bits of May and me on my assigned route. I don't know if other paper collectors have ignored these advertisements pasted on walls or if they just haven't gotten to these streets and alleys yet, but it's strange to peel and scrape away our noses, smiling faces, pretty hair-dos, and clothes. I take these pieces — sometimes just an eye or a finger — and slip them into

158

my pocket. One poster I'm able to pull completely from the wall. I roll it up and tuck it inside my jacket. At the end of the day, I'm supposed to turn in everything I've collected, but I'll keep the poster and the other fragments of my sister and me that I have in my pocket to add to what I've already hidden at home.

I turn a corner and enter a small lane. Images flash through my mind: paying social calls on New Year's Day, my mother being helped down from a rickshaw, my father dabbing sweat off his forehead with a linen handkerchief. I know this street. It's where the Hu family lived. Madame Hu was Mama's closest friend. Mama and Madame Hu were always plotting how to arrange a marriage for May and Tommy, the Hus' precious son. Now it's clear that was never going to happen, but back then I thought Tommy and May made a sweet couple. I remember as well the day bombs dropped on Nanking Road and Tommy died. I can look back and recognize many moments that changed my life. The day Tommy died was one of them. Funny we didn't recognize it for the bad omen it was, because that night Pockmarked Huang's Green Gang thugs came to threaten my father.

Why haven't I thought to come here before now? I have to find out if any of the Hus are still alive. The houses on this lane look very different from others I've seen. I've grown accustomed to laundry hanging on poles projected from windows, draped across bushes like blankets of dirty snow, or flopped over fences and walls. There are no secrets in the New China. Everyone

159

knows everyone else just by walking past the laundry — how old the people are who live in the house, their sex, if they're poor or slightly better off. But outside the Hus' house I see no padded pants, patched jackets, baggy underpants, or the limp socks that would indicate that anyone lives here. There's no laundry whatsoever. Instead, the rosebushes still have a few blooms and a mulberry tree offers shade.

I stride up the walkway and ring the bell. An elegant woman with bound feet opens the door. I'd know her anywhere. It's Madame Hu. I've heard about the stay-oners — those who had the money and power to leave when they had the chance but didn't. Madame Hu is one of those. Twenty years have passed, but she recognizes me right away too. Both of us stand there, laughing and crying at the impossibility of it all.

"Come in, come in." She waves me inside and leads me to the salon. It's like I'm stepping back in time. The Hu family's belongings are all still here and beautifully kept. The room is filled with low-slung velvet chairs and couches. The geometric design of the tile floor is clean and polished.

Madame Hu sways to a chair on her bound feet. My breath catches as memories of my mother fill my mind and heart. Madame Hu rings a bell, and a servant appears. "We'll need tea," Madame Hu orders. Then she turns to me. "Do you still like chrysanthemum tea, or would you prefer something different?"

Of course, she'd remember that. When May was still a baby, Mama used to bring me here for tea. I'd listen to the two women gossip, and they'd let me have some

160

of their tea sweetened with two spoonfuls of sugar. I felt very grown-up when I was with them.

"I'd love some chrysanthemum tea," I say.

The servant backs out of the room. For a long moment, Auntie Hu, as May and I called her as a courtesy when we were girls, and I stare at each other. What does she see when she looks at me? Disappointment that I'm dressed in my common worker uniform, or does she see past the clothes to the person I've become? When I look at her — and I'll admit it, I'm staring hard, soaking her in — it's as though I'm seeing my mother, if she'd lived. Auntie Hu is tiny not from age or hardship but because she and Mama were petite. (How I remember their concern when I kept growing, eventually becoming taller than they were, taller than my father. I remember overhearing fretful conversations about whether I would ever find a husband with my unpleasing and unfeminine height.)

Auntie Hu was always fashion and style conscious, again just like Mama, and she's still beautifully dressed. She wears a dark blue silk tunic closed by intricate frog buttons at her neck, across her breast, and down her side. Her jewelry is exquisite — finely carved jade and gold earrings, a brooch, and a simple necklace. I glance at her feet, and they too are just as I remember them — immaculately cared for and dressed in embroidered silk slippers. The odor that emanates from those two precious appendages — a distinct concoction of rotting flesh, alum, and perfume — is something I haven't smelled in twenty years. What strikes me most is that

161

Auntie Hu looks young, or at least younger than I might have imagined. Then I realize that, if Mama had lived, she would have only been fifty-seven years old.

"You shouldn't have come back," Auntie Hu says. "It's dangerous for you."

"I had to," I say, and then I tell her about my daughter and how I've returned to Shanghai to find her.

Auntie Hu shakes her head. "So much sadness and heartache, no? And yet we have to go on living."

"And you, Auntie, why did you stay?"

"This is our home," she answers. "I was born here. My husband was born here. Our parents and grandparents were born here. And of course, Tommy was born here and is buried here. How could I leave him? How could I leave my husband?"

"How is Uncle Hu?"

She doesn't answer directly. "When Mao and his cronies took power, they made it their business to take everyone's property. Not everything was nationalized at once. Instead, they did it by long torture, by taxing people like us out of existence. We had to give up our property piece by piece. Eventually the government took our factory. Uncle was forced to sweep the floors of the factory his own grandfather had built. But those turtle's egg abortions didn't know what they were doing. Production dropped. Workers were injured. They asked my husband to resume his former post as director of the factory but with the same pay he received as a sweeper." She pauses and takes a breath.

"He was dead within two years. Now the factory belongs to the government, but I still have my house."

"I'm sorry, Auntie. I'm sorry about Uncle."

"Fate can't be second-guessed, and we've all lost people."

The servant returns and pours the tea. Without asking, Auntie Hu puts two teaspoons of sugar in my cup before handing it to me. I haven't had sugar in my tea in years. The taste combined with the scent of chrysanthemums and the odor rising from Auntie Hu's bound feet is vaguely nauseating, yet it transports me to the security, luxury, and coziness of my childhood.

"How are you able to still live like this?" I blurt out, forgetting my manners.

"It's not so hard to keep the old life," she admits. "A lot of us do. I have servants, because we were forbidden to let them go after Liberation." She allows herself a delicate cackle. "Chairman Mao didn't want us to aggravate the unemployment situation."

Which may explain Z.G.'s servants, although they would have been little girls eight years ago.

"I still have my dressmaker," she goes on. "I could take you to her if you'd like. Your mother would want me to do that." But she's not answering my question, and she knows it. "I keep my curtains closed, so people won't know how I live. If you look inside any house on this street, you'll find housekeepers, valets, maids, cooks, gardeners, and chauffeurs. Even in the New Society, we have to keep our homes clean and tidy."

Auntie Hu's face wrinkles in wry amusement. "They call it the New Society and the New China, but this is

163

like the olden times my grandmother told me about, when the wealthy kept the exteriors of their compounds gray and simple so that wandering bandits or ill-wishers wouldn't suspect the privilege hidden behind the walls. Our ancestors may have dressed opulently in embroidered brocades and silks inside their compounds, but they donned simple, unadorned clothes when they went into the streets so they wouldn't be kidnapped and held for ransom. That's what we're doing now! Except" — she gives a devilish snort — "we Shanghainese haven't lost our *hai pah*."

It's true, the Shanghainese have always had a unique sense of style.

"I still send my maid to buy peonies when they're in season. I need to put them somewhere. Why can't I use this vase?" Auntie Hu asks, gesturing to an art deco vase with a naked woman etched into the glass. Her eyes come back to mine. "Where are you staying?"

"In my old house, but it doesn't look like this."

"Oh, I know." She shakes her head sympathetically. "After the bombing in 1937 — such a long time ago now — we went to your home when I didn't hear from your mother. We found boarders. Squatters more like it. They told us about the Green Gang. Uncle thought all four of you were dead, but I knew your mother. She wasn't going to let anything happen to you two girls."

"I don't know what became of Baba, but Mama, May, and I left Shanghai together." I reach up under my sleeve and pull my mother's bracelet down to my wrist. Auntie Hu's eyes flash in recognition. I don't have to tell her the terrible details. I keep it simple. "She didn't make it to Hong Kong."

Auntie Hu nods somberly but offers no condolences. As she said earlier, we've all lost people.

"Anyway," she picks up, "I've gone to your house every few years. I've seen how those boarders have treated it. But it could be worse. Your house was divided before Liberation. No new people were assigned to live there. Just don't expect those nails ever to leave."

"Nails?"

"The people who live in your house. Once they're in, you can never pull them out. But it doesn't have to look the way it does," she scolds in a motherly tone. "Visit the pawnshops. I bet you could find and buy back some of your family's belongings."

"I doubt they'd still be there after all this time."

"You'd be surprised. Who was going to buy anything during the war with the Japanese or later during the civil war? All those workers you see on the street? How would they know what to buy, even if they had money? They aren't real Shanghainese. They don't have *hai pah*. You shouldn't be afraid of living as you once lived."

"If what you're saying is true, then where are the nightclubs? Where's the music? Where's the dancing?"

"Dancing in a club all night is completely different from *having* things. Besides, some people — very high up people — play Western instruments, dance to Western music . . . The Communists say they're pure and for the masses, but you go high enough and they're very corrupt. But none of that matters." She leans forward and taps my knee. "You need to fix your house, even with those nails there."

"How can I? Won't I be reported?"

"I haven't been reported."

"You live alone."

She winces, and I immediately regret my remark. But she's a woman of old traditions. She chooses to ignore my rudeness, as though I'm merely an uneducated child.

"Never forget this is Shanghai. Never forget you are Shanghainese. Never forget your *hai pah*. You carry that inside you no matter what new campaign that fat chairman launches."

Later, she walks me to the door. She takes my hand and stares at my mother's bracelet. "Your mama always loved you best." Then she wraps her fingers around the bracelet and slides it up under the sleeve of my jacket. "Please come back and see me."

I spend another hour picking up paper before returning to the office to deliver most of what I've collected. It's dark now, and I have a few last things to do before I go home. First, I survey the ships and security along the Bund. Chairman Mao does not command a great navy: laundry hangs on lines, hats and clothes drape on guns, sailors sit on decks eating bowls of noodles. The soup must be strong and tasty, because the scent of ginger, scallions, and fresh coriander wafts through the air to me. One thing is sure: the sailors aren't paying much attention to anything beyond what they're eating.

I nod to myself, and then, as I do every evening, I go to Z.G.'s house. A week ago, the servants finally became so irritated by my nightly ringing of the doorbell that I don't bother with that anymore. Instead, I linger behind a shrub on the other side of the walk street and wait to see what lights come on in the house. One of these times I'm going to see my daughter but not tonight.

Then it's on to the Methodist mission I attended as a girl. I come here every day. I, like many others, am afraid to enter. I sit on the curb across the street. I'm not alone for long. A few other women approach, and it's as if they are dragging great shadows of memories behind them. They sit on the curb next to me.

Chairman Mao is against all religions, whether Chinese or Western, but that doesn't mean they don't exist. One-Goders like me have been told to "walk the road of socialism", "expose rightist elements hiding behind the veil of Christianity", and "resolutely struggle against anti-Communist, anti-socialist activities conducted by reactionaries, vagabonds, and wicked elements using the fronts of church or free preaching". They can tell me what to do, but they can't keep me from praying.

I tell Him about the loneliness I feel for places and people that are lost to me. I ask about Joy. Does she miss Chinatown as I missed Shanghai as a young woman in a new country? Does she miss her grandparents, her aunt and uncle, her mother and father as I've missed my parents, my sister, and Sam? I let the grief I feel for Sam well up inside me. My head hangs low, my shoulders sink, and my back weakens.

167

Maybe it's better to be in Shanghai. At home, everything would have been a reminder of him: his recliner, his favorite bowl, his clothes, which still hang in the closet where he committed suicide. If I left my house in Chinatown, I'd see the places we went together, the café where we worked, the beach where we picnicked. I wouldn't want to turn on the television either, because I wouldn't want to see any of the shows we watched together. And what if I heard one of our favorite songs on the radio? Any one of these things would have been devastating. But I'm in Shanghai now. I can't turn back the clock, change the present, or influence the future.

I end with a special plea for God to watch over my daughter and Z.G. I haven't once forgotten that his servants said he was in trouble, so wherever they are, I hope he's protecting her. I recite the Lord's Prayer and then I get up. A knife grinder rolls his cart down an alley to my right, shaking metal rattles and calling, "Sharpen your scissors to snip away bad fortune. Make your cleavers sharp enough to cut through all disasters."

The bus is crowded, as usual. I get off at my stop and then hurry to our neighborhood's political meeting. I've been told I've done a good job "participating actively" in what I can only call brainwashing. I listen to the lessons, recite slogans in a loud voice, and join others in criticizing a neighbor for his bourgeois behavior and someone else for her right-leaning tendencies. I keep my actual thoughts to myself. In my own neighborhood, I can't masquerade as an illiterate paper collector. My neighbors know about my decadent past and my long sojourn in the West. I'm considered a person with "a historical problem." I could be attacked at any moment, but, as Dun has advised me, the more I go along with everything that's drilled into me, the better off I'll be. The more I confess — and how easy it is, really — the more I'm trusted.

The streets are mostly empty as I start home. If I had to give a single example that shows how much Shanghai has changed, it's that the city is asleep by nine in the evening. Even cars are not allowed on the streets after nine unless they have a special permit. As soon as I get home, I check the table by the front door to see if I've received any mail. I've been waiting such a long time to hear from May that I've nearly given up hope, but tonight there's a package with handwriting I don't recognize. The postmark shows that it's come from Wah Hong Village. The box has been opened and carelessly resealed. I grab it, run upstairs to my room, and lock the door.

I rip off the paper. The box contains some clothes and other items. An envelope with May's handwriting sits on top. I open the letter and read just the first line — "Good news! A letter has come from Joy" — before quickly searching through the box for another envelope with my daughter's handwriting. I find some sweaters, a packet of sanitary supplies, and the hat with feathers I wore out of China many years ago. I'll be grateful for the sweaters this winter, if I'm still here. The pads are a true blessing compared with what I've found at the local dry-goods store. But I don't find Joy's letter. I pick up the hat. I hid our coaching papers in its lining

169

when we arrived at Angel Island, and later I hid money there. It took me a minute, but only I would understand the significance of this particular hat. I carefully peel back the lining and pull out a twenty-dollar bill and two more envelopes, neither with writing on them.

I open one of the envelopes, and there's my daughter's precise handwriting. The letter begins, "Dear Pearl and May," as though we're friends and not her mother and aunt. Her formality is like a knife in my heart.

I'm writing this on the boat to Shanghai and am giving it to the captain to mail when he returns to Hong Kong. You must be worried about me. Or maybe you're mad at me. Either way, I want you to know I'm fine. I really am. I never felt at home in Chinatown. I'm going to my proper home now. I know you doubt me, and I can practically hear Uncle Vern saying bad things about communism. Please trust that I know what I'm doing. I appreciate what you did for me, but from now on Chairman Mao will be my mother and my father. If I'm wrong in my thinking — but I'm not — I'll live with the consequences. You both taught me how to do that . . . live with the consequences. I was a consequence. I know that now.

I'm sorry I've been a burden to you both. I'm sorry I was a mistake that you had to endure for so many years. Don't worry about any of that now. I'll love you both forever.

Love, Joy

170

I run a finger over Joy's words and try to imagine her as she wrote them. Did she cry as I'm crying now? She's so sure of herself, but anyone can be sure at nineteen. How can she possibly say she never felt at home in Chinatown? We did everything — *everything* — to give her a good home, so my delight at reading my daughter's letter is tempered with disappointment. It's with that feeling that I open the other envelope.

Dear Pearl,

If you're reading this, then you know our mail system works. I put some money in the hat and in the box. If any of it is gone, then someone has pilfered it somewhere along the way. The cousins in Wah Hong? The censors?

I'll keep sending clothes. Search them for hidden messages and money. Have you read Joy's letter yet? Some of the things she wrote break my heart. Maybe you have found her by now. I hope so.

I'm doing my best to manage the café. It will be here when you return. Vern is sad and lonely. The people he loved most in the world — Sam, Joy, and you — have disappeared. His confusion shows me how much he's grieving. I worry about the strain on his health.

Pearl, everyone at your church is praying for you and Joy. I pray for you too and think of you every day. The main thing is we've heard from Joy. I hope you're as relieved as I am.

You have great courage, Pearl. If our Joy is at all like you — and how can she not be? — then she will survive. You have done a lot for me over the years, but I've never been so proud or honored to have you as my sister as I am now.

Stay safe and all my love,
May

I rifle through the things May sent to find her original letter. It's been written in a style to get past the censors. It contains innocuous news about Chinatown, the weather, and a dinner she went to where the hostess served a green Jell-O mold with bananas. Not once did May mention Hollywood, her own business, or anything about herself in either letter. I don't take that to mean she's miraculously changed.

Then I go back to Joy's letter and read it several more times. It doesn't bring me any closer to finding her, but I'm elated to have heard from her, relieved that May and I will be able to communicate, and awfully happy to have seen Auntie Hu too. What a day this has been, after so many weeks of monotony.

I get up off the bed and add the poster I salvaged to a collection of others I've hidden in my closet. I place the fragments of my sister's and my eyes, ears, and mouths in a pear-wood box tucked under my bed. I'm taking a risk keeping these memories of the past, but I can't help myself. If Z.G. can have framed posters on his walls, why can't I keep these things in my room? I know the answers too well: Z.G. may be in trouble, but he's still important, and this isn't even *my* room anymore. So where will I hide Joy's and May's letters? For now I tuck them back in the hat and put it on an upper shelf in my closet.

Today's visit to Auntie Hu and the blast of hope I've received from my daughter have revitalized me. I peel off my work clothes, leave them in a rumpled pile on the floor, and take a bath. Feeling inspired, I go through my closet and drawers again. I put on a custom-made bra and panties in soft pink silk edged with handmade French lace. Over these, I slip a dress of crimson wool that was made for me by Madame Garnett, who once was one of the finest seamstresses in the city. The dress fits perfectly, but what was elegant and beautifully made twenty years ago is now long out of fashion. I put on a pair of alligator pumps that have turned a warm amber hue from age. The silk and wool are soft on my skin after the coarseness of my work clothes. My jade bracelet feels cool and heavy on my wrist.

When I go back downstairs, I try to look at everything from Joy's perspective. Although I still don't know where she is, I have renewed faith that she's coming back here, and soon. When she does, I want the house to look good. Auntie Hu was right; I just hadn't analyzed it properly before. The boarders have lived here twenty years, but they haven't sold or thrown away any of my family's belongings as far as I can tell. That doesn't mean they've taken good care of things either. The wallpaper is stained, dirty, and torn in places. The rugs, draperies, and upholstery are all in terrible shape. But I'm back now, and I'm going to follow Auntie Hu's advice. On my next free day, I'll visit a pawnshop and a flea market. I'm going to buy some things for the house and get myself a camera. I remember how strict the guards were on the train, closing the shades so people couldn't see bridges or military installations. I don't know what would happen if, for example, I tried to take a photo of the navy ships moored at the Bund, but I don't plan on doing that. If I can, I'll find a place to develop my photographs so I can send them to May. In the meantime, looking through a lens again will give me pleasure. I'm also going to complete what I started by accident this morning: clean the house. I'll do it carefully, when the public rooms are empty. Maybe the boarders will notice. Maybe they won't.

The squabbling in the kitchen that started this morning continues for the evening meal. The professor stands at the stove making a pot of noodles.

"You're taking too long," one of the former dancing girls complains.

"And you've made too much food for just one person," her roommate observes. "You shouldn't be so wasteful."

"I'm not being wasteful," he responds, as he ladles the soup into two bowls and puts them on one of my mother's trays along with two pairs of chopsticks and two porcelain soupspoons. He looks at me and asks, "Would you care to join me for noodles in the second-floor pavilion?"

The silence this morning when they saw me cleaning the spot on the floor is nothing like the silence that freezes everyone now. Then they're all squawking at once.

174

"The second-floor pavilion is your bedroom!"

"You never share your noodles with us!"

"You have no socialist spirit!"

Cook stops their twittering with a stern rebuke directed at me. "Little Miss, bad ways will not be tolerated in this house."

I don't say a word as I follow Dun out the door and upstairs to the pavilion. I haven't been in this room since my parents carved up the house to rent to boarders, but here is another oasis in the sea of communist gray that Shanghai has become. My mother must have felt sorry for her poor student renter, because he has some pieces of furniture that I thought had long ago been sold. The bed is neatly made, and the shelves are filled with books. He also has an old typewriter with English letters and a phonograph, which I remember from when May and I were kids.

Dun sets the tray on the table, which also functions as a desk. He gestures for me to sit in the chair, and then he pulls over a stool.

"I hope we don't get in trouble," he says. "I don't want you to be reported to the block committee." What he says next is even more troublesome. "You look beautiful tonight."

I'm a recent widow. I should get right up and go back to my room. Instead, I take a different approach. Dun and I are friends. That's all we can be.

"Thank you," I say, acknowledging his compliment as though it had come from Auntie Hu or even Cook. "And thank you for inviting me to dinner."

"Would you care for a glass of wine?"

He opens the window and brings in a bottle of Lotus wine, which has been chilling on the sill. The flavor is light on my tongue, but it instantly spreads warmth through my chest. We eat in companionable silence for a while. Dun is a kind man — dignified and gentle. He has an elegance about him that surprises me when so much of the city has turned uniformed and dreary. In another lifetime — if things had been different — I might have married someone like him.

When the other residents turn on the radio in the salon for the nightly Russian-language lesson, I push back my chair to leave. I don't have an interest in learning Russian, just as I have no interest in going to see a Russian film in one of the movie palaces where May and I fell in love with *Haolaiwu*. But we're all supposed to want to learn from Old Big Brother — art, science, everything — so in the evenings we learn Russian from the radio. If we have any time left after that, then we can engage in political study, write letters, or mend clothes.

"Before you go," Dun says, "I was wondering if you would consider giving me English lessons."

"English lessons? Wouldn't that be worse than having a woman in your room?"

He ignores my question. "Your mother told me you used to give English lessons. When I was a student, English literature was my subject. Now I teach the literature of socialism and communism — *The Grapes of Wrath* and books like that. Sadly, my English is not as good as it once was."

"Why does it matter?"

"Because it will help me teach, and I like to think I'm a good teacher." He allows himself a small smile. "And one day I hope to go to America."

I give him a skeptical look. How will he ever be able to leave?

"I can dream, can't I?" he says.

"Let's say Tuesday and Thursday evenings," I tell him. "But no wine."

Joy

Loyalty of Redness; Expertise of Brush

"I keep telling you, Deping, to hold your brush this way," Z.G. instructs. "Concentrate! Your turnip doesn't look at all like the one on the table. Look at it! Really look at it! What do you see?"

It's been hard for us not to notice Z.G.'s impatience, but even I feel exasperated and disappointed. A few days ago, Party Secretary Feng Jin informed us that he'd received word from the capital that our time in Green Dragon is done. Z.G. and I are to leave in the morning and make our way south to Canton for a fair of some sort. He's happy to leave. We've been here for two months and the villagers still refuse to hold their brushes the correct way. They ignore what Z.G. says about the amount of ink to soak into their brushes, and the paintings themselves have a crude quality.

"Everyone examine what Tao has painted," Z.G. says. "He uses his brush to put down what he sees. You can see clouds moving across the sky. You can see cornstalks bending in the breeze. You can see a turnip!"

We all know that Tao is in a different category from the rest of us. He isn't confined to black ink. Instead, Z.G. has given Tao (and recently me) a box of watercolors. The result is lusciously vivid images in which the greens, blues, yellows, and reds have great depth and luminosity.

"When you look at his painting," Z.G. goes on, "you feel inspired but also tranquil. Tao believes in what he paints, and he makes us believe in it too."

Tao sits back on his haunches and beams with pleasure. His clothes have been washed so many times they've been bleached nearly white by the sun and many scrubbings. I'd love to be able to create that color — the hidden blues and grays that still linger in the fabrics — in a painting.

"Now let's consider my daughter's work," Z.G. continues, as he makes his way over to me. Here it comes . . . again . . . the usual unfavorable critique. "As you know, she's been working on a portrait of our great Chairman. She's never met him, but she believes in him."

"As we all do," one of the students calls out.

"When we first came to your village," Z.G. says, "my daughter was weak in her technique and she was afraid of color. But what she lacked in skill, she made up for in enthusiasm for the New China. Who can tell me what is best about her portrait?"

"She made his mole not too big and not too small." This comes from Deping, who was so soundly criticized for his turnip.

179

"I like his blue suit. It fits him perfectly," adds Kumei.

"Yes, and she's made him a little thinner than he is in real life," Z.G. adds with a chuckle, and the others laugh along with him.

"Didn't you tell us that the best art glorifies Party leaders, Party history, and Party policies?" Tao asks.

"Absolutely," Z.G. agrees amiably. "These things are the backbone of the New China."

"The next best art recognizes workers, peasants, and soldiers," Tao adds.

"They are the flesh of our country," Z.G. agrees, but he's not done with me. "My daughter has done a good job. I think" — he takes his eyes away from the others to look right at me — "that my daughter is not bad. She's not bad at all."

Which makes me feel like I'm learning . . . finally.

When the class ends, Tao helps Z.G. and me carry the art supplies back to the villa. I know that Tao and I are not allowed to be by ourselves anymore, but I want to have some private time with him before I leave Green Dragon. I'm trying to figure out how to ask Z.G. for permission when he says, "Just be back in an hour."

Tao and I hurry out the gate, turn left, and then follow the stream until we reach the path that leads up to the Charity Pavilion. We're barely inside the pavilion when Tao pulls me into his arms. I'm kissing him, he's kissing me, and it's all very frantic, hurried, and desperate. For too long we've been allowed only to look at each other across a table, separated by my father, during our private lessons. We've had to sit on opposite

180

sides of the ancestral hall while Z.G. conducted his art classes. We've purposely walked to the fields at different times and chosen different jobs to do: picking or shucking corn, harvesting or separating rice, packing or carrying baskets of tomatoes.

Tao's lips are on my neck and he's fumbling with the frogs on my blouse when I pull away. I take a breath and then another. Tao struggles to regain control of himself too. I take another deep breath, let it out slowly, and turn to face the view. When I first came here, the fields spread out before us like green satin. Now it looks like Los Angeles at this time of year, when weeds, grass, and gardens turn biscuit brown. I'm going to miss this place. I'm going to miss the smell of the earth, the sunsets, and the quiet paths that snake through the hillsides and into the valleys. But most of all I'm going to miss Tao. He stands behind me, his hands on my shoulders, his mouth by my ear, his body up against my back.

"May I call you Ai-jen — Beloved?" he asks. His voice holds neither fear nor brashness. He is merely frank and honest. I've heard many of the younger married couples refer to each other by this endearment. Can I really be Tao's beloved?

"Are you sure?" I ask.

"I knew the night you arrived. Chairman Mao says women hold up half the sky. Can't we hold up the sky together? My house is small, and we'd have to live with my family —"

"Wait!" I shake my head, certain that I'm hearing him wrong. "What are you saying?"

"You're the right age. I'm the right age. We aren't blood relatives up to the third degree of relationship. Neither of us has any diseases. Let's go to the Party secretary and his wife to ask permission to marry."

Marry? His proposal, such as it is, causes something wonderful to happen. My mind empties of all worries and memories.

"We barely know each other," I say.

"We know each other a lot more than people did in feudal days. Back then, boys and girls didn't meet until their wedding day."

But marriage isn't something I've been thinking about. Still, to stay here in what seems like a million miles and a million lifetimes from Los Angeles Chinatown, where no one knows me or my past, would be a cure for the guilt and shame I carry with me everywhere I go.

"We both want the same things — to paint, to grow crops, and to help build the New Society," Tao continues.

"I agree, but do you love me?" I have a crush on Tao, no question about it. I can't stop thinking about him. And the fact that he's been forbidden to me these past weeks makes him all the more desirable.

"I wouldn't ask you to marry me if I didn't love you." He grins. "And you love me too. I saw that the first time we met."

I want to say yes. I want to make love to Tao. I want us to be together. But as sure as I am about how I feel for him, I'm not ready. I've just met my birth father and I hardly know him yet. Then there's China. I'm

182

nineteen, and I have an opportunity to do something few other girls get to do. I'd like to see Canton, Peking, Shanghai, and the rest of China while I can.

"Yes, I love you," I say, and I believe I do. I'm *sure* I do. "But do you want people in the collective to think we were sneaking off together? And what about your mother and my father? I don't think your mother is ready to have me in her house." (This is an understatement. His mother clearly doesn't like me.) "And I doubt my father's ready to say goodbye to me just yet."

"We don't need their permission."

"I know, but their blessing would be wonderful."

He puts forth a few more reasons why we should act immediately, but after a while he gives in.

"All right," he says. "I'll wait."

Then he's kissing me again, and I'm happy — truly happy.

"I wish you could come with me," I whisper in his ear. "We could see China together."

"I want to leave this place more than anything," he responds, sounding hopeful and eager. "But I'd need an internal passport and I don't have one of those. Maybe your father can get me one."

Chairman Mao introduced the internal passport just last year. The government wants to keep peasants from flooding the cities, but the new passport has barred peddlers, doctors, and entertainers — apart from those sanctioned by the government — from traveling as well. This keeps villages pure, but it also keeps them

183

isolated. It's one of the things I've liked best about being here.

"Maybe," I say. "Maybe."

Later, when we walk back to the village, Tao says, "I promise I won't forget you, but you must promise to come back to me."

The next morning, Z.G. and I leave Green Dragon, walk to the drop-off point a couple of miles from here, and take the bus to Tun-hsi. From there, we go to Huangshan, where I'm inspired by the soaring peaks and the pines that jut from cliffs at improbable angles. I'm reminded — as so many artists have been before me — of man's insignificance in the face of nature. We return to Hangchow and wander around West Lake as we did on our way to Green Dragon, only this time we stop to paint the Ten Views that Emperor K'ang-hsi enjoyed so long ago. Z.G. tells me Hangchow is China's most romantic city, and I feel that. I long for Tao, and when I paint I feel his breath on my skin. But I also feel something opening in me . . . as an artist. I know I'm getting better every day.

At the beginning of November, we arrive in Canton for the Chinese Export Commodities Fair, which will last a week. The Artists' Association wants Z.G. to represent the work that he so excels at: propaganda that sells China to Chinese and others who are sympathetic to the regime in the outside world. We walk the fair aisles and look at the merchandise: Chinese-made fabric, radios, thermoses, greeting cards, and rice steamers. I walk past 170 different types of tractors.

184

People have literally come from all over the globe to buy steam shovels, auto parts, and fountain pens. Everything is for sale: hairnets, make-up, and mirrors. But isn't it better to tie your hair in practical braids, let the sun rouge your cheeks, and see yourself in the reflection of a pond, stream, or water trough than buy all these things? Do you need plastic buttons or elastic when home-made frogs are so much more lovely and simple string works just as well as elastic to hold up your pants? And honestly, why do you need a tractor when you can work side by side with your comrades to do the same work by hand? I'm told over two thousand foreign businessmen and Overseas Chinese are attending the fair, and they're buying stuff like mad. It's the first time in two months that I see non-Chinese, and it shakes me.

I can't wait to leave the fairgrounds, but I've been in the countryside so long that Canton surprises me with its bustle. Business enterprises — bookstores, barbershops, banks, photo studios, tailors, and department stores — vie for space. I see hospitals, clinics, bathhouses, and theaters. Music, announcements, and news blare from loudspeakers on what seems like every corner. The traffic is a bit like I remember from my brief visit to Shanghai: bicycles, bicycles, bicycles. Entire families — mother, father, and two or three children — balance on handlebars and fenders. Bicycles are also used for hauling gallon drums, boxes and crates, pigs in baskets, and great bales of hay that sometimes rise four feet above the cyclist's head and can be as wide as ten feet in diameter, depending on the number of bamboo

185

poles used for balance. The bicycles I like the most transport a bride's dowry gifts — although in the New China I suppose it would be more accurate to call them wedding presents — down the street for all to admire. A bedroom suite with headboard, side tables, vanity, and dresser is very popular, and to see all that piled on a single bicycle is really something.

On our last night in Canton, Z.G. knocks on my hotel room door. (How strange it's been these past few days to have running water, flush toilets, a bathtub, and even a television.) He enters, pulls the straight-backed chair away from the desk, and sits down.

"I've now been ordered to go to Peking," he says. "I'm to submit my work to a national art competition." He pauses. I can see he's struggling to tell me something. Finally, he says, "We're very close to Hong Kong. This is your chance, with so many other foreigners here, to leave. You could see if you could get an exit permit and then go to Hong Kong by ferry or train with one of the delegations. From there, you could fly home."

It's all I can do to keep from bursting into tears.

"Don't you want me?"

I asked him this when I first arrived at his house. I still don't know the answer. He's my blood father, but we haven't talked about that. I don't call him *baba* or Dad; except for the occasional words of praise for my drawings, he hasn't had any endearments for me either. I'm not his little dumpling, as my father Sam sometimes called me, or even Pan-di — Hope-for-a-Brother — as my grandfather referred to me. But I'm still disappointed that Z.G. would want to send me away.

"It's not a matter of wanting you," he explains. "No one of any importance knows you're here. If you go to Peking and people learn about you, you won't be able to go home."

I think of everything I've seen and experienced — singing in the fields with Kumei, kissing Tao in the Charity Pavilion, helping build the New Society — and then I weigh that against the secret my mother and Aunt May kept hidden from me, how they'll want to fight over me, my uncle Vern languishing in the back bedroom forever an invalid in his body and mind, and my mother's face when she looks at me and thinks about my father's suicide.

"I don't want to go back there," I say. "My place is here."

Z.G. tries hard to talk me out of it, but I refuse to listen. A Tiger can be stubborn, and I've made up my mind. Still, I realize how close I was to being sent away. I need to get to know Z.G. better, and he needs to learn to appreciate that he has a daughter.

The next day when we board the train to Peking, Z.G. sits across from me, his long legs crossed. He's changed out of his country clothes and back into a Mao suit, so he looks quite elegant. I have my sketchbook on my lap and am drawing the fragments of life that flit past the window like picture postcards: a wheelbarrow propped against a wall, a kumquat tree in a pot, a little garden that comes right up to the track, people working in rice fields. I haven't thought much about home since

187

coming to China. In fact, I've worked very hard *not* to think about home. But as the train chugs through the countryside, I'm reminded of Chinatown and all the people who raised me.

I clear my throat, and Z.G. looks up.

"When I was a little girl," I begin, my voicing quavering, "we lived in an apartment." He remains silent, which I take as a sign to continue. "We didn't have a garden and I didn't play with other children. Once I started kindergarten, I began going to other girls' houses. This was Chinatown, so the gardens were small, but they were filled with cymbidiums, bamboo, and maybe a bodhi tree here or there. They were also filled with all kinds of junk: used electrical conduit, dustpans made from old soy sauce cans, and greasy motors. I thought this was how everyone lived."

I think — I *hope* — Z.G. understands why I'm telling him these things. *I want to know you. I want you to know me.*

"Then my mom started taking me to the United Methodist Church for Chinese-language classes," I continue. His eyes widen. Yes, I suppose it's hard for him to believe that Aunt May sent her child to a mission school, but I know just what to say. "My mother and aunt were educated at the Methodist mission in Shanghai, remember? That's why she sent me. Anyway, in order for me to take Chinese classes, I also had to go to Sunday services and Sunday school. One thing led to another, and pretty soon the churchwomen were inviting me and other kids to their houses in Hancock Park, Pasadena, and Beverly

Hills . . ." When he looks at me quizzically, I explain, "Those are good places to live."

"But why did you go to the houses?" he asks.

"To sing at gatherings, to be given presents — as poor children — during the holidays, or to attend piano recitals."

"Rich people." He sniffs. "America."

"I saw gardens with wide lawns and roses. I thought they were peculiar, but then you never can underestimate the strangeness of *lo fan*."

"I remember them from their days in Shanghai," he agrees somberly.

"When I turned fourteen," I go on, "we moved into a house. It had a dried-out garden, but my mom spent a lot of time there, clearing away the grass and replacing it with the kinds of things our neighbors had: cymbidiums, bamboo, vegetables, and a bunch of junk my parents and grandparents picked up by the side of the road."

"When you're poor, you never know when used electrical conduit or an old motor might come in handy," Z.G. says.

I look at him in his dapper suit, his perfectly cleaned glasses, his neat manner. How would he know?

"By the time I went to the University of Chicago —"

"You went to university?" he asks. Pleasure, satisfaction, and maybe even pride fill his voice. How can it be that we've spent two months together and we still know so little about each other?

I nod. "By then I'd been to movie sets, all those houses for church excursions, and even a few homes of *lo fan* kids from high school whose parents were "progressive," meaning they didn't mind having a Chinese girl in their living rooms. That's when I came to the conclusion that it wasn't those places with their manicured lawns that were strange; it was my family's and our neighbors' gardens that were strange."

Z.G. looks out the train window to the little shacks that come right up to the train tracks. He points down at the tiny courtyards and gardens.

"Like these?" he asks. "They have the bamboo, the vegetables, the junk. No old motors or used electrical conduit though. No one here has access to that kind of gear, but people have salvaged other things."

He's right. Plenty of other stuff — broken earthenware jars, a bent bicycle wheel, burlap rice bags — has been collected and saved. I'd always thought people in Chinatown kept all their junk because they'd lived through the Depression; now I see that Hazel's mother and everyone else were trying to re-create South China. Z.G. has helped me understand something about my life in a purely visual way that I never grasped before.

"Exactly like these," I say. "I always thought of the garden as my mother's domain, but she was from Shanghai. Why did she want a South China garden?"

"Maybe the garden was a reflection of the community where she lived, a community filled with South China peasants."

Once again, he's right. My mother and Auntie May were Shanghai girls, but my father, grandparents, uncles, and all our neighbors were South China peasants. Even those who'd been in Los Angeles for two or more generations — some of whom were well educated, spoke good English, and dressed like Americans — were still, at heart, South China peasants. Somehow they'd maintained the visual idea of how things should look — the lushness of South China re-created in the desert of Los Angeles. More important, they still had their South China frugality.

"I'm from Shanghai," Z.G. says, "and May was most definitely a product of Shanghai. You may have these gardens in your blood, but you too are a Shanghai girl."

He says that with such confidence, and in some ways it makes me happy. I'm glad I decided to talk to him, but I can't stop thinking about the woman I always believed was my mother. Judging from her garden, she must have had memories of her home village. Either that or her home village was deep, deep inside her soul, as my love for the countryside is in mine through my father Sam. Through my blood parents, I should be a Shanghai girl through and through, as Z.G. says. Instead, I feel connected to the people outside the window: China's peasants, like the people in Green Dragon Village, like the people in Chinatown, like my father who loved me so much. Now, sitting on the train, I understand in part why I love Tao. He reminds me of my father — not the one sitting across from me in his elegant suit but the one who worried when I was sick, who made special treats for me, who told me bedtime stories.

★　★　★

191

In peking, Z.G. and I go on excursions to the Great Wall, the Summer Palace, and the Forbidden City. All my life I've known about these places from Chinese school and from the photos and pictures my grandfather clipped from magazines to hang on the wall. The sights are beautiful, but I bet they're a lot more enjoyable in the spring, when it isn't bitterly cold. At night, we go to parties, where Z.G. teaches me how to distinguish people of importance. "A regular cadre has one fountain pen in his pocket," he explains at a party in the compound next to the Forbidden City, where the most important members of the Communist Party live and work. "A two-pen cadre is more important. The most powerful carry several pens in their breast pockets. Those are high officials."

Z.G. seems to know everyone. He has good *guan-hsi* — connections — which function like a web that links government relationships, family, influence, and power. People are happy to see him, especially the women, who bring him drinks, cover their mouths to hide their giggles when he speaks, and generally act like they've never seen a man before. We meet plenty of Americans, who make up the largest group of foreigners in Peking after the Soviet experts. We even attend a couple of parties where Chairman Mao and Premier Chou En-lai circulate through the room. I see them nod to Z.G. a couple of times, but they never come our way. These are people I've read about and who have inspired me. They've made history and changed a country. As a little girl, I met lots of movie stars when I worked on film sets. I even sat on Clark Gable's lap once. But none of them have the charisma of China's leaders. When they walk into a room, the air changes, becoming electric in the true sense of that word — sparkly and powerful. I'm utterly in awe.

It's all wonderful, but two things disturb me. First — and I know it's minor — it's freezing around here. Every party we go to has barely any heat. Sometimes a coal brazier or a rickety radiator that looks about a thousand years old pumps out warmth, but that doesn't help much in a big hall or in a drafty house that dates to the Ming dynasty. I take to wearing flannel underwear and undershirts beneath the practical wool dresses Z.G. has bought for me, along with a sweater, scarf, hat, and coat. The other thing that gnaws at me is what I guess I'd have to call hypocrisy. We're supposed to be in a classless society, yet I'm going to parties and banquets with the highest echelon of people in China. It's exciting to be in a room in the capital with Chairman Mao, but this is a long way from the simplicity — and poverty — of Green Dragon Village, and it doesn't make sense to me. That's not to say I'm not having fun. I'm having a great time, but this aspect of China isn't what I expected.

These conundrums aside, I'm swept up in a whirlwind of sightseeing and parties. I eat steamed dumplings, red dates, and candied crab apples on sticks from street vendors during the day and indulge in course after course at extravagant banquets at night, but nothing tastes as sweet to me as the food did in Green Dragon. And certainly no one is as dear to me as Tao.

On the day of the national art competition —
sponsored by the Artists' Association and the China Art
Gallery, both of which are government controlled —
Z.G. and I attend the opening party. Artists from
around China and from all backgrounds have
submitted entries for the best New Year's painting. We
enter the gallery just as the head judge makes his
opening remarks. As I listen, I see that Chairman Mao
is here, as are several other important political figures.
A few smile our way, but as usual the Chairman gives
us only a curt nod.

"Today we're looking for the best painting to
celebrate the coming new year," the judge addresses the
crowd. "If your work is selected, the masses will hang it
on the walls of their homes, factories, and collectives.
You'll be serving the people in the best way by inspiring
them to help build the road from socialism to
communism. To the judges, I remind you that old
habits and feudal taste have no place in the New China.
Fantasy, superstition, and other reactionary elements
won't be tolerated. But remember, the masses don't
want to see history on their walls at the New Year
either!" With that confusing message, he invites
everyone to enjoy the exhibition.

Z.G. stops at every painting. He asks what I think of
it, and then he tells me if I'm right or wrong. He clearly
sees things I don't and understands their deeper
meanings in ways I can't fathom. We pause at a picture
titled *The Great Victory of the People's War of
Liberation*. I tell Z.G. that it should encourage people

194

to reminisce about their joy and celebration at that time.

"Yes," Z.G. agrees, "but is it a proper New Year's picture? The Ministry of Culture tells artists to show politics and history in our work, but as the judge just said, the masses don't want to see those things in their New Year's posters. They long for the old styles, which will call to mind their hopes for good luck, prosperity, and new sons, as well as their moral and religious principles."

"But the judge also said —"

"That we should avoid traditional subjects." He leans in and whispers in my ear. "That instruction must come from Chairman Mao. It's up to us to decipher what he wants while keeping him from losing face. If he loses face, many people suffer."

I draw back, shocked that Z.G. would say such a thing in public. I'm glad that the crowd is noisy and that no one could have heard him.

He drifts away, and I continue through the exhibition. I see how Mao's desires and Z.G.'s suggestion of their meaning have been captured by different artists. Some have chosen to send a political message through images from the past: door gods in military dress or goddesses in peasant clothes. Others have ignored politics and history entirely, focusing instead on good-luck symbols.

I come to Tao's painting, which Z.G. submitted. The style looks childlike next to that of the professional artists. It shows peasants harvesting rice. The colors are bright but flat, with little or no perspective.

Nevertheless, there's something very much alive about the image. I can almost feel myself in Green Dragon's fields, the hot sun above me and the smell of the earth filling my nostrils.

Z.G. has several entries. My favorite shows a young Mao, wearing a long scholar's gown, striding across a field with peasants and soldiers behind him, almost like a god leading his followers. The hills around the Green Dragon Village Collective form the background. I'm sure the Chairman will like it, and I wonder if the judges will too.

I catch up to Z.G., who stands before a painting titled *An Abundant Harvest of Food Crops*. "You've seen most of the entries," he says. "Which one will Chairman Mao want to see win?"

Before I have a chance to answer, a commotion erupts across the gallery, where the judges have clustered around one picture. We hurry over, joining others who want to see what's so disturbing.

"This could have been painted twenty years ago," one of the judges complains. "The pose . . . The colors . . . This is not Socialist Realism."

"The artist has been tainted by foreign elements," another adds roughly. "Our great Chairman has told us that art must be analyzed and divided into fragrant flowers and feudal dregs. This is the dregs."

"The roses are redolent of capitalist ideology," a third judge criticizes. "Do you see the way she has one hand behind her head? We all know what that means. She's selling herself, beckoning us with her bad ways, just like a prostitute."

With disgusted grunts, the judges move on. As the crowd disperses, I edge forward. The painting is of a young peasant woman standing in a field of roses, holding a basket filled with her pickings, and tucking one of the blooms behind her right ear. Who is the central figure? Me! Z.G. has painted me! All those times I saw him with his sketchbook on the edge of the fields at the Green Dragon Village Collective, he was drawing me. Just as with Z.G.'s Mao portrait, this one is a mixture of fact and fantasy. I'm wearing Kumei's clothes — a yellow blouse and light blue trousers — as I often did in Green Dragon, but my hair is longer and braided in the style of so many country girls. I stand in a field of pink roses. I never saw a single rose in Green Dragon.

"You look like your mother," Z.G. says in a soft voice.

I blush. Auntie May has always been considered beautiful. I've never thought of myself that way, but looking at the painting, I can't help wondering.

"I've missed her," Z.G. adds. His eyes meet mine, and for a moment I glimpse the love he still has for her.

And then Chairman Mao is at my side. He's a bit paunchy. His hair recedes from his temples. His face is shiny and full. His smile is warm and embracing. Standing next to him is like standing next to history, and I'm dumb with wonder and astonishment.

"I like this painting very much," he says. "The girl in it is lovely but healthy too. That girl is you, I believe."

"She is my daughter," Z.G. says, with a slight bow.

"Ah, Li Zhi-ge, it's been a long time," Mao says slowly. "Many of us had women in the countryside all those years ago. I didn't know you did as well." His smile widens. "How many more pretty daughters have you left across China?"

I'm not a product of one of those liaisons, but that doesn't seem to matter to Mao, who turns his attention back to me. "Has your father told you much about me? We were in the caves together in Yen'an. Remember the old days, Comrade Li?" Z.G. nods, and the Chairman continues. "Your father was a good fighter — for a Rabbit — but I felt he could do more good and conquer more hearts with his brush than with his bayonet."

Some people say that, once Chairman Mao starts talking, he can't stop. He doesn't want to hear other opinions. He doesn't even want to make conversation the way most people do. You just have to listen and try to understand his meaning.

"As a hero of Liberation, your father has a special place in our society," Mao goes on. "After Liberation, I wanted him to come to Peking. I had use for his special skills. He would have lived with me and others on the Central Committee. He would have been treated as a prince — a *red* prince — but this man missed his home. He wanted to go back to Shanghai. So I made him a member of the Standing Council of the Artists' Association and an adviser to the Shanghai branch. He won prizes at national competitions, but everyone has moments of weakness. Everyone transgresses from time to time."

198

Z.G. clears his throat. "I admit that sometimes I've taken the wrong road, but I'm not a capitalist roader. I've tried to redeem myself by correcting my errors. I went to the countryside —"

"Yes, yes," Mao says, waving his hand dismissively. He glances at me, his face filled with mirth. "Even in Yen'an, we had to deal with your father's Rabbit ways. So cautious, so discreet, but he never fooled us. Under his soft blanket of Rabbit niceness is a strong will and almost individualistic self-assurance." He turns back to Z.G. "Don't worry about those other things any longer. As they say, the Rabbit always hops over obstacles and calamities to land on his feet. So . . . I like your portrait of me. It's a good apology. I think we can do something with it and others like it. Next time, though, make me appear a man of the people — simple trousers, a simple shirt, straw hat, and —"

"A plain background," Z.G. finishes for him. "So the people see only you."

But Mao has lost interest in that conversation. Now he speaks to me directly. "You don't say much."

"I haven't said a thing yet."

The Chairman chuckles. Then his face turns mock serious. "I know the accents from every province, but I'm having trouble placing yours. Tell me where you're from. I ask because in a few days I'm having the Central Committee issue a new and stricter law — Halting Outflow from the Villages — to keep *all* peasants from coming to the cities. We'll be checking the railway lines, highways, river ports, and all points of communication between provinces. So tell me, little

199

one, where did you grow up? Are we going to have to send you back there now?"

To my eyes, he's an old man — certainly older than my mother and father — but is he trying to flirt with me or scare me out of my wits? How can I respond in a way that won't get me sent not back to the countryside but to California?

"Her mother is from Shanghai," Z.G. answers for me, "but my daughter was born in America. She recently came to China."

"Have you brought remittances with you?" the Chairman asks. "Remittances are most welcome from Overseas Chinese. Foreign money helps build our socialist state."

Again, Z.G. steps in for me, and for the first time I hear him brag. "She's done something better. She's returned in person to help the motherland."

"Ah, but is she one of those who will seek an exit permit tomorrow?" Mao asks. "To strengthen our united front among Overseas Chinese, we've had to relax control over these permits. Too many act like caged birds, waiting for the chance to free themselves from captivity. They complain that their rice rations are mixed with coarse cereals. They say we give no consideration to the old, sick, pregnant women, or newborn babies. The West has corrupted them into valuing personal freedom above all else, but now they must obey the Party. Even *I* must obey the Party." He affects the whining voice of an unhappy man who's returned from overseas: "My stomach is accustomed to cow's milk and white bread. It won't accept dried fish and barley." Mao grunts. "What kind of Chinese is this? A Chinese *is* his stomach. These Overseas Chinese can't forget their capitalist roots, and they won't adapt to the socialist way of living."

Z.G. ignores all this. Instead, he says, "My daughter has been helping me in the countryside. We've been learning and observing from real life —"

"Volunteering to go to the countryside was a very clever hop out of trouble for you, Comrade Li."

Z.G. cocks his head in question.

"You did well there," Mao continues, "but then I needed you to go to Canton. You performed well again, so I brought you here. When you first arrived in Peking, I thought you were still about fifty meters from being labeled a rightist. Then I saw the painting done by your student, Feng Tao. It is in line with things I've been thinking about since I returned from Moscow. They think they've advanced very fast, and they have. They launched Sputnik. Now Comrade Khrushchev says the Soviet Union will overtake the United States economically in fifteen years. Why can't we overtake Britain in the same amount of time? Soon the East wind will prevail over the West wind."

A uniformed young woman joins us. "The judges are ready," she says.

The Chairman clasps his hands together and shakes them in front of him decisively. "We'll have to continue our conversation later."

He steps away, and I take a deep breath. I can't believe I've been conversing with Chairman Mao, standing so close to him, hearing him reminisce about the past and talk about his new ideas. A part of me thinks, *I wish Joe could have seen that*. And then Joe's gone from my mind, because Mao has finished consulting with the judges and has moved to the podium.

"I've just had a small struggle meeting with the judges." He grasps the podium, and confides, "They do not want to see anything too popular or that reeks of Western influence. They don't like the beautiful girls of the past. I have a different opinion. Instead of beautiful girls, why can't we have beautiful *working* women — bringing in the harvest, climbing telephone poles, or . . . picking flowers?"

I grab Z.G.'s arm excitedly as murmurs of surprise rattle through the gallery.

Mao smiles. "Comrade Li Zhi-ge, please step forward."

Z.G. makes his way to the podium and stands a slight distance from Chairman Mao. Cameras flash.

"You have come away from your Western ivory tower," Mao says. "At the same time, you have used foreign techniques to serve China. You have shown me the loyalty of your redness over the expertise of your brush. You have won the grand prize."

Christmas comes and goes without a single carol, decoration, or present, but life is still festive and fun. Z.G.'s poster of me is everywhere. Posters can be reproduced in about ten hours from conception to final printing, making them almost instantaneous revelations of the Party's mood, wishes, policies, and positions. As a result of Z.G.'s overnight celebrity, we're invited to interviews and even more banquets. I'm fed all the famous delicacies — monkey brains, lion's head, bird's nest soup, shark's fin, sea cucumber — and all the rice I can eat. Everywhere we go, Z.G. introduces me as his daughter and his muse. I don't object, but I still don't feel like his daughter and I'm not sure I want to be his muse. Since the exhibition I've been wondering if I could be an artist. If so, what would be the right kind of art for me — Mao's idea, Z.G.'s idea, the things I've seen in Western art books? Would it contain beautiful girls like my mother and aunt or have beautiful working women as Mao suggested? And what would be my subject? Art that glorifies the revolution, honors heroes, or promotes Party policies? Nothing *feels* quite right. Emotions are what drive me, and I can think of only one subject: Tao.

I stay out late and sleep long into the day, but I always have time — I *need* the time — to think about Tao. I spend hours drawing him from memory, trying to recall just one finger. I keep reminding myself of the Song dynasty artists who knew how to capture the essence of something with as few strokes as possible. Sketch after sketch, brushstroke after brushstroke, bring me closer to Tao. That's how much I love him. Along the way, I notice that my technique has gotten much more refined.

In January, Chairman Mao goes to the city of Nan-ning to give a speech launching what he calls the Great Leap Forward. Listening to him on the radio, I see this is a continuation of what he was telling Z.G.

and me at the exhibition. "There are two methods of doing things," Mao proclaims, "one producing slower and poorer results and the other faster and better ones." He announces that he's taking control of the economy. He says China can overtake Britain in steel production in fifteen years, just as he said the night in the gallery, but a couple of weeks later he changes his mind and sets a shorter goal. China can do it in seven years. Not long after that, he sets his sights on America, claiming that China can overtake the United States in steel production *and* agricultural output in fifteen years. "We need to push ourselves," he declares. "Hard work for a few years, happiness for a thousand." No one knows what any of it means, but we're all enthusiastic.

In February, after just over three months in Peking, Z.G. and I board a train and head south to Shanghai, because he wants to be home for Chinese New Year. When I left Shanghai, it was unbelievably hot and humid. Now, as we step off the train, it's not as cold as Peking, but it's still plenty cold. Children wear so many layers of padded clothes that their arms stick straight out from their bodies. The adults don't look much better.

When we arrive at Z.G.'s house, I see the posters of my mother and aunt in the salon. I'd forgotten about those. Then the three servant girls, all dressed in heavy padded clothes, welcome us. They show me to my room. Big steel-cased windows look out onto the street. It's winter, so the trees are bare, which allows the sun to warm the room — a good thing since Z.G.'s house has no heat to speak of. I have, for the first time in my life, a vanity, a mirror, and a double bed, plus my very own closet and bathroom. But it's cold! I put on my flannel underwear, heavy socks, and an extra sweater under the coat Z.G. bought me in Peking. I wrap a muffler around my neck and put on my gloves, prepared to wear them in the house to stay warm.

When I go back downstairs, Z.G. takes one look at me, and says, "This is not appropriate. You're in Shanghai now. Please come with me."

I'm not sure what's wrong with what I'm wearing, since he's still in his traveling clothes and is as bundled against the cold of the house as I am, but I follow him back upstairs and then up another flight of stairs to the attic. Some of his paintings lean against the walls. Boxes and chests are stacked haphazardly on the floor, but he knows exactly what he's looking for. He squats, opens a chest, and motions me to come to his side.

"I used to have a studio, where I painted your mother and aunt," he explains. "I went there when I returned to Shanghai after Liberation. My landlady had kept everything. People go away — to war, to sojourn in other countries, to escape gossip — but we Chinese *always* come home . . . if we can. My landlady knew I would return eventually."

He pulls out a fur-lined black brocade coat.

"Here, try this on. It was your mother's. She left it at my studio one day."

I take off the heavy gray-wool blanket thing that kept me warm in Peking and put on Auntie May's coat.

"It's gorgeous," I say, "but isn't it too showy?"

"Don't worry about that," Z.G. assures me. "Women have been wearing fur-lined coats in Shanghai forever."

I eagerly look to see what else might be in the chest. Z.G. hands me a red satin robe embroidered with a pair of phoenixes in flight. "Your mother wore this for a poster I did where she portrayed a goddess. She was lovely in it. And look, there's more."

I don't want to hurt his feelings, but I have to state the obvious. "These are costumes."

"You could wear them for special occasions. You should have seen your mother when she dressed as Mulan, the woman warrior . . ."

I don't understand old people. Does he think if I put on one of these costumes that I'll be like May? Can't he see that I'm not like her at all? I stare at the robe in my lap. The fabric is soft and luxurious in my hands. I look up at Z.G. I still haven't told him the truth about my upbringing, my father Sam, or the anger I carry toward my mother and aunt.

"It's hard for children to imagine their parents when they were young," Z.G. says. "But we had such great fun, your mother and I. Your aunt Pearl was wonderful too, but May was one of those people on whom fortune always seemed to smile. Come, I want to show you something else."

We leave the attic and he takes me to his bedroom. I've never been in a man's bedroom before. My uncle Vern's room was filled with model boats and airplanes. My parents' room was dominated by my mother's things — lamps with frilly shades, a flowered bedspread, and lace curtains. This is something very different: a heavy four-poster bed in dark wood (clearly a leftover from the colonial who lived here before Liberation) dominates the room. Heavy fabric, the deep red color of the Forbidden City's walls, covers the down-filled quilt. Everything is tidy and warm, except for over the fireplace, where Auntie May's portrait hangs. She's draped in some kind of diaphanous fabric, but nothing's hidden. She's absolutely and completely naked. I've known Auntie May my entire life. I slept on the porch with her for six years. I saw her come in late at night from her business dinners — smelling a bit of alcohol and her clothes no longer pin perfect — but I never once saw her like this.

"This is your mother at her most beautiful," Z.G. says.

My mother Pearl flies into my mind: *Compose your face. Don't let him see your shock. Pretend this is just another piece of art.* I nod, trying to be perky, trying to look happy, but I want to throw up. It was one thing to go to the countryside, see the famous sights, and hobnob in Peking, but now I'm in Shanghai, in a house that in many ways is a shrine to my mother and aunt. In just a few minutes here, I've gotten a glimpse of what their lives must have been like, of the way they were. These were not the people I grew up with. And my aunt May certainly did not have a great fortune — living in Chinatown, married to Vern, never admitting I was her daughter.

"It's wonderful," I say. "Everything is wonderful." Another wave of nausea hits me. "I can't wait to hear more about those days, but I haven't seen Shanghai yet.

Do you mind if I take a walk? I'll be back soon. We have so much time, now that I'm here."

"Of course. Would you like me to come with you?"

"No, no. I just want to take a little walk. We were a long time on the train."

I hurry downstairs and step into the night. It's *cold*, but the fresh air is a relief. I put a smile on my face. I came here to be happy, and I'm going to be happy. If I smile, then maybe I can convince my body just how happy I am. I look both ways, and decide to venture to the right. I don't know where I'm going. I just need to walk and keep smiling.

Pearl

Scars on Her Breast

I'm on my way to Z.G.'s house, as I usually am at the end of the day. It's February 15 in the Western calendar and three days before Chinese New Year. I'm a Christian, a one-Goder, but I could only carry the spirit of Christmas in my heart. On Valentine's Day, I could only think of Joy and the cards she used to make for her classmates when she was in elementary school. Now all around me people are busy with their New Year's preparations: buying clothes, sweeping their front steps, shopping for special ingredients. I see Joy everywhere. The first time I stumbled on Z.G.'s New Year's poster with Joy I was overwhelmed. Now it's pasted on walls in cafés, shops, doctors' offices, and schools. I've heard that close to 10 million copies have been sold. Every piece of paper I collect and turn in I hope will be milled and recycled into another poster of my daughter, because her smiling face lets me know that she's all right.

Then I actually *see* her.

Joy!

She's walking purposefully toward me, unafraid of the dark, as though she's stepped down out of a poster, as though she knows the city. She's wearing May's coat, the one my sister supposedly lost. Z.G. must have had it all these years. My stomach roils with that knowledge, but I ignore it because my daughter has returned to Shanghai! She looks right at me, our eyes meet for a fraction of a second, and then she keeps walking. She doesn't recognize me. Have I changed that much? Did she refuse to see what was right in front of her because she couldn't imagine I'd be here? Or maybe she couldn't recognize me dressed in layers of padded clothes with a knit hat pulled down over my hair and ears and a scarf tied around my neck and up to my nose.

I turn and follow a safe distance behind her. A part of me wants to run up to her and take her into my arms. But I don't do that. I just worked all day, and I look like the paper collector I am. I can't let her see me like this. I can't let Z.G. see me like this either. That's right. I've come all this way to find my daughter, and when I see her I'm filled with vanity. How will Z.G. look at me after all this time? For years, I've known he existed somewhere in China. I'd never believed I'd encounter him again, but seeing Joy means that I'm about to see Z.G. again too. I have an urge to hide behind the bush across from his house, watch them through the windows as they move in the rooms, and wait until I can get my thoughts and emotions together before knocking on the door, but I can't do that either.

210

Z.G.'s servants know about me. I don't want Joy to hear about me from them. But it's more than that. I suddenly don't know what to say to her.

We reach Huaihai Road. She turns right, walking toward the Whangpoo River. I know what I *want* to say — you're coming home with me right now — but I also know that would be absolutely wrong. I've been a mother for nineteen years, and I know a few things about motherhood, and my daughter. I'm disappointed in her for being so rash and stupid as to come here, but as she passed me she didn't look sad or disheartened. Far from it. So, what tactic do we, as mothers, use with our children when we know they're going to make, or have already made, a terrible mistake? We accept blame. In my case, I can legitimately accept some blame for having lied to her all those years. I'll tell her about the regret I feel for having failed her. And then, and then . . . *Please come home!* That method isn't going to work either.

I stop walking, watch my daughter disappear into the crowd, and then make my way to a bus stop. When I get home, I bathe, pin my hair into a bun at the nape of my neck, put on some make-up, and go to the closet. I stare at my clothes, all of which are mementos of the past. I see a fox stole. I see my fur-lined black brocade coat, the twin to the one Joy was wearing, the one I wanted so badly, the one Baba tried to make me give May. I pull out a dress Madame Garnett made for me — dark green wool crepe cut on the bias with jet buttons sewn at the hips as decoration. Twenty years ago, Mama said it was too sophisticated for me; now I think it will be just right — modest, a little old-fashioned, and the color will accentuate my black hair. Z.G. might like to see me in the brocade coat, but I can't go that far. I tell myself I don't care how I look after twenty years, but I do, of course. I tell myself that no woman should allow a man to see the scars on her breast or in her heart.

I want to do something to remind Joy of home and that she's been loved and missed. I'll bring a present. (What kind of mother would I be if I forgot her at Christmas?) I take an old perfume bottle off the vanity and wrap it in one of my silk scarves. I bundle back up in my padded jacket and put the gift in my pocket. I pull on my work gloves, but I throw a red scarf made from baby cashmere from my old life around my neck. It's the first time I've worn something this nice on the street, but most of it is hidden under the jacket.

I take a bus back to Z.G.'s neighborhood, walk to his house, and ring the bell. One of the servants answers the door. She nods, as though she's been expecting me, and shows me into the salon. I take off my jacket and gloves. Z.G. enters a few minutes later. I think he's still an extraordinarily handsome man, and I'm hoping he'll have a similar reaction to me, but the first thing he does is look over my shoulder to see if May is with me. In an effort to keep myself composed and not betray a hint of disappointment, I adjust my jade bracelet on my wrist.

"My servants said you were here in the city," he says, and his voice cascades over me like water over rocks. A Rabbit is always gracious and soft-spoken.

"I've come to get my daughter." I blurt it out.

212

"Your daughter?"

His question tells me Joy hasn't been honest with him.

"Joy," I say. "She's mine. I raised her. May gave her to me."

"May wouldn't have done that, and Joy hasn't said anything —"

"You'd be surprised what May would do." My words sound harsher than I want them to be. I twist my mouth into a smile to show I'm not the bad person here. "Joy believed I was her mother and my husband her father her whole life. When she found out the truth, she ran away and came here to look for you and . . . I don't know what."

"Joy has been lying to me — her own father?"

It's disconcerting to hear the disbelief in his voice. He doesn't know Joy at all.

"Sam Louie, my husband, was her father. He's dead now."

Z.G. takes that in, considers, and says, "I'm still her father."

"You lost that honor a long time ago." I hear sarcasm creeping into my voice, but I can't stop myself. Too many years of heartache have passed for him to claim fatherhood. Still, he looks at me without comprehension. "When I came to you that night to say that May and I were going into arranged marriages to men we didn't know, you didn't try to stop me, stop us. Why didn't you do something? Why didn't you *say* something?"

Twenty years of anger and disappointment bubble up in me, but he still doesn't seem to understand. The worst part is I can't stop staring at him. My old passions — despite everything I now know about him and my sister — make my breath shallow and fast. My heart beats so hard it feels like it's going to break right through my chest. And lower down — even though I'm a widow, even though I loved Sam — there's a warm sensation I never felt for my husband. I always thought it was because of the rape, but now I see it's not. I'm ashamed, guilty, and still angry.

"May knew you had feelings for me," he says at last. "She asked me not to tell you about us. She didn't want to hurt you. I didn't want to hurt you either. I just wanted to take care of May."

"She was a Sheep," I say bitterly. "Everyone wanted to take care of her."

During our last fight, May said that she and Z.G. used to laugh at the way I acted around him. Which story do I believe? I've come all this way to find Joy, but what's flickering through my mind is whether or not I might still find love with this man who's been in my heart all these years. It's been only six months since Sam's death, but is it possible I deserve a second chance?

Wait a minute!

"What do you mean you wanted to *take care of May?* You got her pregnant and then you didn't do a thing, not one single thing, to help her. You let her go into an arranged marriage. You left the city. You —"

"She never told me she was pregnant."

214

That gives me pause, because how could it be?

"When you were painting her and she was" — I close my eyes against the memory of it — "naked, couldn't you tell?"

"Did *you* know?"

"I didn't, but I wasn't making love to her. What did you think was going to happen?"

"I wasn't thinking," he admits. "At least, I wasn't thinking properly. In those days, I was caught up in the movement. I was filled with *ai kuo* — love for our country and its people. I thought I could help change China. I didn't think enough about *ai jen* — the love I felt for May. We were all young. None of us thought about the consequences of anything we were doing."

The doorbell rings. We know who it's going to be. I straighten my dress and tuck a few strands of hair into my bun. Z.G. broadens his chest and clasps his hands behind his back. We stand there like two statues as one of the servants hurries to the door.

Joy swishes into the room, all dazzling energy, her cheeks pink from the cold. Even though it's February, I can tell she's spent time in the sun. She pulls off her hat, leaving her black tresses tousled and unkempt. She hasn't cut her hair since leaving Los Angeles.

Joy absorbs Z.G.'s dour look, and her eyes scan the room to see what's wrong. Her delicate eyebrows, pretty nose, and full lips register absolute astonishment at seeing me. Her eyes widen and become even brighter. Then I see not happiness, sadness, or even anger that I'm here. It's worse than any of those. The cool shadows of indifference fall over her features. She stares at me but doesn't say a word.

I smile and say, "Hello, Joy." When she doesn't respond, I hurry on. "I brought you a Christmas present." I go to my coat, fumble in the pocket to get the wrapped perfume bottle, and offer it to her.

"I don't celebrate Christmas anymore."

A long silence follows this declaration. She knows that I'm a one-Goder and that this would hurt me.

"Joy." The appeal in my voice is strong. She'll have to respond.

"I don't want you here. You'll ruin everything."

"Don't speak to her like that," Z.G. says in the calmest voice possible. "She's your auntie."

I drive my nails into my palms to keep the pain of that from overwhelming me.

"And you're my father," my daughter retorts. "That's much more important."

I feel all the things I've wanted to say to her about being ungrateful, cruel, spoiled, and self-centered — *just like your birth mother* — pushing to fly out of my mouth. Z.G. steps forward. I put up a hand to stop him from coming closer or speaking.

"I love you very much, Joy. Please can we talk about why you ran away?" Of course I know the reason — she didn't want to deal with two mothers who had lied to her — but I need to get her to open up. "We never had a chance to talk that night. If you tell me what you felt, then maybe you'll feel better about everything. And maybe I can help."

And like that, my daughter is once again five years old. She pulls her upper lip between her teeth and bites down hard to hold in her emotions.

"Tell me, honey. Tell me so I can understand."

When she shakes her head, I know that I'm approaching this the right way. We are back in a pattern we've lived as mother and daughter so many times.

"I'm sorry I didn't do more for you after your baba died," I say. "I apologize for that. We both loved him." Tears begin to roll down Joy's cheeks. "We should have been holding on to each other."

But what she says takes me by surprise.

"You were right to ignore me after what I did."

"What did you do?" I ask, confused. Again, this is not at all what I expected. My brain hurries to catch up.

"Oh, Mom, it was all my fault. Auntie May and I talked after your fight. She explained everything about Dad being a paper son —"

"May always puts blame on someone else."

"No, Mom, listen to me. The FBI and INS never would have looked at our family if I hadn't been involved with that group in Chicago. Agent Sanders approached Auntie May *because* of me. She was trying to help our family. She was trying to get you and Dad amnesty. She didn't realize I was the real target. If you'd told me the truth about Dad, I would have been more careful, I wouldn't have joined that club, and the government wouldn't have noticed us."

She's right. If Joy hadn't joined that club, it would have made a big difference. Still . . .

"That doesn't change the fact that my sister betrayed us."

"But Auntie May didn't betray you! She was trying to help you in the best way she could. Amnesty, Mom. Do you even know what that means?"

A part of me thinks, *Even here, even after everything that's happened, Joy takes May's side.* But another part of me actually *hears* what my daughter has said. I've blamed May for everything, but what if she wasn't to blame?

"Honey, your dad's suicide wasn't your fault. Don't ever think that. Yes, maybe the FBI used you as a pawn, but they were always going to win the game."

"Nothing you can say or do will change what happened, what I did, or where I've ended up. You can never punish me as much as I'll punish myself."

"Is that why you came here?" I ask. "To punish yourself? But this is too much punishment for anyone."

"Mom, you don't understand a single thing. I want to be part of creating something bigger than my own problems. I want to make up for all I destroyed — Dad's life, our family. It's my way of atoning."

"The best thing you can do is come home. Uncle Vern misses you. And" — this is hard for me to say — "don't you want to get to know May in a new way? And even if you are right — which you aren't — Red China is not the place to atone."

"Pearl is correct," Z.G. says. "You should go home, because you don't understand what you're seeing and experiencing. Lu Shun wrote, 'The first person who tasted a crab must have also tried a spider, but realized

it was not as good to eat.' You've only tasted the crab."
He glances at me and then back at Joy. "The last time I
saw your mother was twenty years ago. I didn't know
about you. I didn't know what happened to your
mother and aunt. Why? Because I went to join Mao. I
fought in battles. I killed men."

He begins chronicling his hardships over the past two
decades, because somehow he thinks this is about *him*.
I guess we're supposed to believe he's really telling us
his life story, but I once knew Z.G. very well and I can
see there's a lot he's not revealing. And why would he?
He's only just met Joy. It's nice to have your daughter
look at you with eyes of love and respect, but I'm tired
of lies.

"You ran off," I say to him. "You became a famous
artist and you destroyed May's and my lives."

"Destroyed? How?" Z.G. asks. "You got out. You got
married. You had a family. You had Joy in your life.
Some might say I've been successful in the regime, but
others might say I've sold my soul. Let me tell you
something, Pearl. You can sell and sell and sell, but
sometimes that's not enough." He turns to Joy. "Do
you want to know the real reason I went to the
countryside?"

"To teach the masses," she answers dutifully.

"I can try to teach all I want, but I cannot teach the
uneducated."

Did I forget to say a Rabbit is also a snob?

"Maybe you're a bad teacher," I say.

Z.G. gives me a look. "I've been teaching my
daughter, and she's learned a lot."

"And you taught Tao too," Joy adds.

I hear a sudden lightness in her voice as she says that name.

"I praised him because I had to praise someone," Z.G. says. "He's not very good. Surely you see that."

"I do not," she says hotly.

Her face radiates indignation. It's a look I recognize from when she was a very little girl and she was told something she didn't want to hear. Her reaction makes me want to know who this Tao person is, but Z.G. asks again, "Do you want to know why I went to the countryside?" This time he doesn't wait for an answer. We're going to hear it whether we want to or not. "Last year, Shanghai was very different than it is now. Jazz clubs reopened for people like me — artists and, well, those who were part of the old elite. We also had dancing, opera, and acrobats. Then Mao launched Let a Hundred Flowers Bloom."

I remember how excited Joy was about this and how she got into fights with her uncle Vern, who believed the campaign would come to "a no-good end."

"We were told we could say what we wanted without fear of recrimination," Z.G. continues. "We criticized the things we thought hadn't worked in the first seven years of the regime. We aired our views without reserve, and the complaints covered everything: that there should be a rotation of power, that cozying up to the Soviet Union was a mistake, and that contact should be renewed with the United States and the West. Artists and writers had their own list of complaints. We wanted to liberate art and literature from the Party. We didn't feel that all art and all writing should serve workers, peasants, and soldiers. By May, Chairman Mao didn't want to hear criticism. By summer, he didn't like it, not one bit. When he made a speech about "enticing snakes out of their lairs," we knew the Campaign Against Rightists had begun. The spear hits the bird that sticks his head out."

I'm not sure why Z.G. has gone off on this tangent, but Joy is mesmerized. She sits down and listens raptly. His story is hitting her in some deep place, that very place that so far I've been unable to reach. Is he sharing his miseries with Joy, who he's just learned has tragedies, sorrows, and guilt of her own — whether justified or not — to give her perspective? I join Joy on the couch and force myself to listen more closely.

"When rectification began, some cadres were sent 'up to the mountains and down to the villages' in remote areas to take up unimportant posts or work in the fields. It was even worse for writers and artists. When someone asked Premier Chou En-lai why this was happening, do you know his response?"

Neither of us answers.

"He said, 'If intellectuals do not join in *manure* labor, they will forget their origin, become conceited, and be unable to wholeheartedly serve the laboring masses.' But shoveling manure isn't enough punishment for those who've been labeled counter-revolutionaries, rightists, spies, Taiwan sympathizers, or traitors —"

"I don't see what any of this has to do with my taking Joy home," I say.

221

"She sees only what she wants to see, and I'm trying to make her understand," Z.G. explains. "When things changed, I was accused of being a poisonous weed and no longer a fragrant flower. The day Joy arrived in Shanghai, I was being struggled against at the Artists' Association, where my friends accused me of being too Western in my outlook, of using Western techniques of shading and perspective in my paintings, and of being too individualistic in my brushstrokes. I didn't go to the countryside to teach art to the masses. I didn't go to observe and learn from real life. I went to avoid being sent to a state camp for reform through labor."

"That can't be right," Joy says, uncertain.

Oh, how sorry I feel for her. To have to see things in a whole new way . . . again. To know that the person she's run to has also been running.

"Think about it, Joy," he says. "They housed us in the landowner's villa because that's where they put the other unsavory and questionable people in the Green Dragon Collective."

"You're wrong," she insists.

"I'm not wrong. Kumei, Yong, and Ta-ming were the landowner's concubine, one of his bound-footed wives, and his only surviving son."

"Kumei couldn't have been a concubine —"

"You thought the villagers were treating us as special guests, but I'm telling you they put us in the villa as punishment."

"But we were serving the people," Joy argues. "We were helping with collectivization."

"In volunteering to go to the village, I was trying to control my punishment," Z.G. says. "I expected to be in Green Dragon for at least six months, but that would have been better than the years I might have spent in a labor camp . . . if I ever even got out. Your arrival on my doorstep complicated things. How could I have a daughter from America — our most ultraimperialist enemy? If anyone asked about your mother, what was I going to say? That she was a beautiful girl? Everyone would have concluded she had Nationalist ties, otherwise she wouldn't have left China. That would have been another black mark against me."

"But Chairman Mao likes you," Joy practically whines. "He told me all those things you did together in the caves in Yen'an."

"We were comrades then," Z.G. acknowledges, circling back to the past. "I met up with him and became a member of the Lu Shun Academy of Art in the winter of 1937. I trained those who joined our cause to do cultural propaganda. Who better to do this than someone who'd been making advertising posters for so many years? It's not hard to switch from painting beautiful girls in imaginary landscapes to painting people like Mao, Chou, and other Party leaders posing in imaginary situations with smiling workers, soldiers, and peasants."

"Those things aren't imaginary —"

"Really? Have you seen the Great Helmsman actually walk through the fields with peasants?" Z.G. asks. He waits for an answer, and when he doesn't get one, he goes on. "As he told you, when we marched

223

into Peking, he offered me an important post, but by then I was disenchanted. In feudal times, people said, 'Serving the emperor is like a wife or concubine serving her husband or master. The greatest virtue is to be loyal and submissive.' This is what Mao wants from us, but I'm afraid I'm good at being loyal and submissive only if the alternatives are labor camp or death. Fortunately, my rehabilitation came after only a couple of months. It began when Mao sent me to Canton."

I hear the word *rehabilitation* and I think of Sam. He too was persecuted by the government, but there was no rehabilitation for him. Joy doesn't seem to pick up on this.

"But Chairman Mao likes you," she repeats weakly.

"He likes *you*," Z.G. responds. "It pleased him to see such a pretty girl leave America to come here. Thank you for helping with my rehabilitation."

"Rehabilitation?" Joy echoes, finally hearing the word.

"Don't you remember his conversation with us at the exhibition?" Z.G. asks.

I don't know what they're talking about, but Joy nods in understanding.

"Why didn't you tell me?" she asks.

"I tried, but you wouldn't listen. When we were in Canton, I wanted you to leave the country."

"That's right," Joy acknowledges. "You did."

"Well, obviously you didn't try hard enough," I cut in. They both turn to me, remembering I'm here.

"The truth is," Z.G. admits, "I didn't want her to leave."

"She's your daughter! You should have been protecting her!"

"She is my daughter," Z.G. says. "I hadn't known she existed. I was selfish. I wanted to know her." He now addresses Joy. "But that doesn't mean you should stay here."

"I don't want to stay here. I want to go back to the Green Dragon Collective."

Concern passes over Z.G.'s face. I don't know what this place is, but I know my daughter doesn't belong in a collective.

"People are shaped by the earth and water around them," he says. "You're an American. You don't know hardship or how to survive. If you go back to Green Dragon, you'll be giving up city life. You won't be able to return to Shanghai. And you certainly won't be able to leave China."

"I don't want to leave China," Joy says stubbornly. "This is my home now."

"How do I explain things to her so she'll understand?" Z.G. asks me. Joy stiffens at that, and I keep my mouth shut. He turns back to Joy. "I begged Mao and Chou for forgiveness with my paintings, but who knows what could happen tomorrow? Mao won't admit when he's wrong. He purges anyone who disagrees with him. Since the recent class struggle, everyone with a brain or a backbone has been sent to labor camp or been killed. Those who remain, like Chou En-lai, are afraid to go against Mao, but it doesn't matter, because he's stopped listening to others anyway. Who will protect China from bad ideas?"

225

Looking at my daughter's lovely face, I can tell she doesn't care about any of what Z.G. is saying. He has tried reason — self-centered though it may be — but my daughter is suffering from something that can't be touched by logic. The dead can claim the living, and guilt and sorrow have claimed my girl.

"Joy," I say softly, "will you come home with me? You've never seen the house where May and I grew up."

"Why would I want to do that?"

"Because I'm your mother and I've come all this way."

"No one asked you to come here."

"Joy!" Z.G.'s voice is startling in its sharpness. She rapidly blinks her eyes, ashamed of herself, fighting back tears. Then to me, he says, "This is all very sudden. We need time to accustom ourselves to things. Let Joy stay here a few days, and then I'll bring her to you."

Pearl

The Sorrow of Life

February 15, 1958

Dear May,

Our girl has finally come back to Shanghai. She's healthy and she's in one piece. These are the most important things to remember. I've been so focused on finding her that I haven't thought enough about how she would feel when she saw me or what should happen next. I don't know how to say this except just to say it. Joy doesn't want to come home. She believes, and this hurts more than I could ever express, that she's to blame for Sam's death. As much as I don't want to accept it, she's at least partially right. If she hadn't joined that club, the FBI never would have investigated us.

As you know, I've blamed you for everything that happened. It's only because Joy ran away and I needed your help that I even stayed in contact with you. You've tried to tell me how you feel — at

227

the airport and in your letters — but I haven't listened or acknowledged you. A part of me is still angry with you, but listening to Joy speak the same words you told me, I heard them in a different way. Amnesty. Do you think they really would have given Sam and me amnesty? I didn't believe your reasons when you told me what you did. I thought you'd say *anything* to protect yourself. But I was wrong. You didn't report us to hurt us. You reported us because you wanted to protect Sam, me, and, I suspect, Joy most of all.

Amnesty. I keep repeating the word, and every time I punish myself a little more. If I was wrong, then Sam must have been wrong too. If we'd confessed, Sam would still be alive and the family would still be together. Oh, May, you should have seen Joy's face when she talked about Sam. It was a knife in my heart. There've been so many mistakes that have resulted in so many tragedies over the years, and now here we are. Sam is dead, and Joy is so torn by guilt that she refuses to come home — either to Los Angeles or even to our old house here in Shanghai. Tell me what to do.

Pearl

I didn't write about Z.G., because I don't want all that old business festering between us. I didn't mention the Green Dragon Collective, Joy's political views, or Tao, who I presume is a young man she met in her travels. When I think about this Tao, my mind fills with the examples of bad judgment my daughter has already

THE SORROW OF LIFE

shown. In this regard, she's too much like her birth mother. But what will be accomplished if I write those things? I fold the letter, put it in an envelope, and write our address in Los Angeles. Then I put that envelope inside a larger envelope addressed to the Louie cousin in Wah Hong Village, along with a note to the man at the family association in Hong Kong to send my letter by airmail.

A letter arrives from May the next day. It was written twelve days ago. I've been receiving regular packages with hidden money from my sister since her first package arrived last October. This is the first time I've received a simple letter. It has been opened, which is dismaying. Fortunately, not a single word has been crossed out.

February 4, 1958

Dear Pearl,

Sadness upon sadness. Vern died last week. He was never the same after Sam's death, and after you and Joy left. I think he gave up, but Dr Nevel says I shouldn't think that way. "Tuberculosis of the bone never has a happy ending." That's what he told me. "And then there were his mental problems." Yes, Vern was always a little boy in his mind, but he never hurt anyone. He was kind. He bore his ailments and his pain quietly. And we both know how generous he could be.

These past few days, I've looked at my life very differently. I was never a good wife to Vern. I was

229

out all the time. I counted on you to take care of him, and you did, as you've taken care of so many things for me. I've never believed in guilt or remorse. I've always resented the way you held on to misfortune. But they've come to me now. When I watched the undertaker and his helpers take Vern out of the house . . .

Now all that's left of my husband are the lingering odors of his sickness and a few of his model airplanes and boats that weren't broken on the terrible night Joy ran away. When I think of how I belittled him for those models . . . When I think of how I always left you and Sam to deal with Vern's diapers, sores, and smells . . . Since you and Joy left, he had only me and the occasional visit from the uncles and their families. Oh, Pearl, now I understand how you felt after Sam died, and he was so much more of a man and husband than my Vern ever was.

I arranged for Vern's funeral to be held at your church. The reverend welcomed me and didn't once reproach me for not coming to services. The women — Violet and the others — treated me as one of their congregation and not as someone who used to laugh at them for their bad clothes and old-fashioned hairstyles. I'm grateful to everyone, because who else would have seen Vern to the afterlife? His funeral banquet was small — only two tables. I came home and lit incense on the altar. Whether he is in Chinese Heaven or your Heaven, I hope he is with Father Louie, Yen-yen, and Sam. Once again, he'll be surrounded by the love he deserved.

I try to imagine you reading this letter. Are you thinking, My sister, what a useless, selfish, and self-centered woman? I've been all those things. Is it too late for me to change?

Pearl, even though you are far away, please know that I think of you every day. Why has it taken me so long to understand the important things in life? I've always relied on others to take care of me. Now I'm alone in this house and in my life. Please come back, Pearl. Please. I need my sister.

Love, May

I weep at the sorrow of life. I pray for Vern and hope that he's finally been released from the pain he suffered all these years. It hurts me to think of him with only May in his last days. It seems like she's finally understood the man she was married to and what a good person he was, but what about Vern? He must have thought of her as an exotic bird that would swish into his room late at night or early in the morning, only to disappear again. His only real companionship had come from Sam and me. I'm so tired of weeping. I'm so tired of heartbreak. I've found Joy, but will I ever have joy in my heart again?

I pull out a pen and paper and begin to write:

We all did the best we could, but sometimes that isn't enough. Vern lived longer than his doctors ever expected. I wish I were there with you, because I understand your pain only too well.

Z.G.'s "a few days" turns into a couple of weeks. I go back to my old routine: taking the bus to work, surveying the harbor, and collecting paper. I stand in line at the various shops to buy oil, meat, and rice with my coupons. I make time for prayer, go in for my monthly interview with Superintendent Wu at the police station, and keep up with my political meetings. And I swing by Z.G.'s house once or twice a day, always changing the time. When I wear my paper-collecting clothes, Joy and Z.G. don't notice me.

I look through the windows, watch the comings and goings of the servants, and learn a lot. Joy sleeps late, has breakfast in bed, takes a long bath, dresses, and then she and her father leave the house around noon. I see them step into a Red Flag limousine with blue curtains drawn shut to keep them protected from prying eyes as they're whisked to parties or wherever it is they go. Sometimes I see Joy in clothes I know. They're costumes May and I once wore for sittings with Z.G.

Z.G. and Joy are conspicuously visible. She seems to relish the attention. In Los Angeles, Sam was forever a former rickshaw puller. In Shanghai, Joy's father is a celebrity. It disturbs me to see the way they live, and I don't understand why Joy doesn't rebel against all the privilege. Worse, they don't care to see much of me. But what hurts the most is that it feels like they're

deliberately leaving me out. I'm completely preoccupied with my daughter. I see her every day, and yet in
many ways she's still very far away.

Then something happens which prompts me to write
to May. I worry that sending so much mail to Wah
Hong will alert the authorities. That said, May needs to
hear this.

March 20, 1958

Dear May,

Today is Joy's twentieth birthday. I invited her
to celebrate at our home. I even asked Cook to
make some of our favorite dishes from the old
days — steamed cel, shrimp with water chestnuts,
and eight-treasures vegetables. But the whole thing
was a disaster. You and I always loved our house,
but it doesn't look like it once did. These past
months, as I've written before, I've bought some of
our old furniture at pawnshops. Every time I find
something, I'm filled with the sense that I'm
righting things. But the way Joy looked at it all? It
made me feel very poor in spirit. And what was I
thinking when I asked Cook to make dinner? Our
meal was overcooked and tasteless. How can a
mediocre dinner in our old dining room compete
with the banquets Joy has been attending?

Again, I have to tell you she looks good. She's
been taken to the best seamstress in the city. This
woman is no Madame Garnett, but what she's
made for Joy is far more elegant than the usual

233

clothing I see on the street. Maybe she can still experience a little of the Shanghai we loved, or at least what's left of it.

It's only been a little over a month, but I keep waiting for the moment Joy will say, "Mom, take me home." We're a long way from that, I'm afraid. It doesn't help that I think she's in love. She hasn't told me much about this Tao, but when she speaks of him a pretty pinkness comes to her cheeks and her eyes shine. The best I can say is that Joy and I have come to an uneasy truce.

Love, Pearl

Again, I don't write about Z.G. I don't tell May how carefully he held on to Joy's elbow as he walked her through my house. A couple of times, she looked like she was going to flee — when she saw the grime in the kitchen I haven't yet had a chance to clean, when she saw the posters of my sister and me in our bedroom, when she met Cook. I saw Z.G.'s knuckles turn white as he held her in place. I wonder what he said to her before and then after they left.

I don't receive a response from May to my last two letters. Have they been held up? Am I to be arrested? Has May been too busy to write? Or has she been worn down by grief, mourning, and guilt? I know what that's like. I wait a month and then write a short note:

Is everything all right? Have you received my letters? In case you haven't, I found Joy and I'm sorry about Vern. Please write as soon as possible.

And then I wait for a response. I don't receive one, which means I don't have to write to May about the poster of Joy, which would, in turn, lead back to Z.G. I don't have to write about the day when Joy visited unannounced and by herself for the first time either. I looked out the window and there she was, staring at the first rose to bloom along the fence. I was extremely pleased to see her, convinced that Joy had experienced a sea change. I made tea, and we sat in the salon. Joy's coming here was her way of reaching out, I'm sure of it, and yet she only made small talk. She told me that she'd reported to the police station and the block committee in Z.G.'s neighborhood. "It wasn't a big deal," she said. She'd also gone to the Overseas Chinese Affairs Commission and had been given the same special coupons that I'm entitled to receive. "But I don't need them," she said with a shrug. "I can get whatever I want at Z.G.'s house."

As she spoke, I wanted to cry, because sometimes it's just so damn hard to be a mother. We have to wait and wait and wait for our children to open their hearts to us. And if that doesn't work, we have to bide our time and look for the moment of weakness when we can sneak back into their lives and they will see us and remember us for the people who love them unconditionally.

I have my worries, but life continues elsewhere. Z.G. has a new poster, which shows Mao — as the Chairman himself asked to be painted, according to Joy — in simple trousers and a white shirt unbuttoned at the neck against a plain background. He looks like a

235

benevolent god — of and for the people. I honestly can't go anywhere or do anything without seeing his face. He's literally everywhere — on the sides of buildings, in restaurants, in private homes. I'm told that 40 million copies of this poster have been sold across the country. In any other part of the world, this would make Z.G. an extremely wealthy man. Here, it earns him privilege and party (Party!) invitations for him and Joy.

And still no letter from May. Do I write another note to her or stop writing completely for a while? I don't know where or what the problem is. In case there's been an issue with the content of my letters, I decide to write something pro-political about the Great Leap Forward. I'm still careful, but that's easy. All I have to do is echo the enthusiasm I hear on loudspeakers, see on posters, or read in the newspapers. May and I are sisters. I expect her to look for hidden meanings in my words.

May 15, 1958

Dear May,

Chairman Mao, our Supreme Leader, is leading us into wonderful times. He has come up with a slogan that we all joyously repeat: Hard work for a few years, happiness for a thousand. You remember how people used to starve in China? Now China will be a land of abundance and wealth. Other nations will no longer look down on us. We will accomplish this with help from "two generals": agriculture and steel. If we all work hard, soon everyone will dress in satins and silks. We'll live in skyscrapers — with heating, air-conditioning, telephones, and elevators. We'll have leisure time to spend with our families.

I can't grow grain, but every day before and after work I join my neighbors in creating steel. We are happy not to be paid, because we are building the nation. Each block has at least one blast furnace made from gray brick. The comrades in our old house all agreed to take our last radiator to our street's furnace. Oh, May, you should see me. Three nights a week I work the bellows to keep the furnace going. Can you imagine me smelting iron? That's how strong I am for the People's Republic of China. When I'm not at the bellows, I walk the streets with my eyes down, looking for old nails, rusty cogs, and any piece of metal that has been overlooked by others. Chairman Mao says steel is the marshal of industry!

I don't write that when it comes time to pour what we've melted onto pallets it doesn't look at all like the steel I've seen being made in newsreels. Instead, it comes out in dull, red, sandy blobs. When it dries, it looks like cakes of *nui-shi-ge-da* — cow turds. I can't imagine what anyone will use it for. Certainly not to make tractors, girders, or textile machines, because it won't be strong enough. So, as far as I can tell, it's all a waste of time, energy, and sweat — and all without remuneration, which, if I said that aloud, would cause

237

me to be struggled against by the boarders and the block committee for being too capitalistic in my thinking.

> The biggest news is that last month the first people's commune opened. It has 40,000 people! Chairman Mao says, "The people's commune is great!" I have not been to the countryside and can only rely on Chairman Mao's mouth to tell me what his eyes have seen. He says that in the countryside bags of grain reach the sky. Yes, we are on the way to outgrowing the United States. Soon China will be exporting grain to you!

> Love, Pearl

Finally a letter arrives, and it's not in response to my news about the Great Leap Forward. It's dated March 1, and May must have sent it upon receiving my letter saying that Joy had returned to Shanghai. A good part of it has been blacked out. What's left are mostly questions for which not only May but apparently the censors and Superintendent Wu would like to know the answers. "Where has Joy been all this time? If Joy isn't staying with you, then where is she living? Who bought her clothes? Was it this Tao you mentioned? I don't like the sound of that. She is not a girl to be bought for a few yards of fabric." This line more than any other tells me May has no understanding of what's happening behind the Bamboo Curtain. There are no bad girls anymore. Then she asks the question I've been expecting for some time. "Have you found Z.G.? It will be difficult for you, but you must try to find him. We were all good friends once. He must help us."

I read this last part several times. Pathetic jealousy burbles in me, but how can I be jealous — now, after all these years? I'm here to do whatever I can to get my daughter to remember who and what she is, but a part of me still dwells on petty things from twenty years ago. I think back on all the letters I've received from May since I arrived in Shanghai. Has she asked about Z.G. before? No, but his presence has been in every letter she's written: "Do you see anyone from the past? What of the friends we knew back then?" How many times have I ignored her questions, blocking them out even more blackly than the censors? Sure, I've written back here and there: so-and-so died during the war, was a hero, was shot, or escaped . . . But never once have I written about Z.G. Why? A bitter place inside me kept that secret. Has this been my revenge for May's part in Sam's death? How can it be, when I now know she was not at fault?

None of us is perfect. I'm not the good woman I always believed myself to be. I'm ashamed to say that I don't write back, because I could say things that would really hurt her. Ever since Joy came to visit me by herself, she and Z.G. have been taking me out to dinner once a week. I could tell May that just last night Z.G., Joy, and I had a meal of stewed crab with clear soup, duck triplet, and Mandarin fish — all Shanghai delicacies — at a restaurant on the Bund. I could write about how beautiful Joy looked and how the tension between us seems to be lifting, but that Z.G. stared at

239

me in my red dress that May herself loved so long ago. I could write that sometimes the three of us go for walks in the Yu Yuan Garden. Or that we've worked together at the backyard furnaces either in my neighborhood or in Z.G.'s. We've been having a nice time, and I don't want to break the spell by sharing it with my sister. But while I may not be perfect, I can't *not* write to my sister. That would be brutal and unnecessary, and she would worry too much. Again, though, I stick to politics.

June 20, 1958

Dear May,

It's been almost three months since the first people's commune opened. A commune is made when several collectives or villages are brought together to share in the work and the profits. Now communes are everywhere! Some have 4,000 members, some as many as 50,000. We Shanghainese are helping our comrades in the countryside. We've always sent our nightsoil on barges to farmers. Now we all wait for those moments in the day when we can add what comes out of our bodies to the building of socialism and the attainment of our targets. What indescribable happiness, excitement, and pride we feel when the nightsoil barges leave the Bund and head upriver to the communes.

The steel the people have produced has given Chairman Mao great confidence in our abilities.

First we were to overtake Britain in steel production in fifteen, then seven, then five years. Now we're to do it in two years! At the same time, he's announced we'll double our grain harvest. Chairman Mao says that communes are the gateway to Heaven. China will be able to leapfrog over socialism and go straight to communism. I wish you were here to see all the changes. You'd be laughing and crying with happiness at the same time.

How fortunate Joy never feels homesick for the land of her birth. She relishes the land of her blood. She understands that true free thought comes when everyone obeys the commune. Her heart brims with idealism.

You should remember your motherland and send remittances to help build the nation.

Love, Pearl

I'm sure May will understand my not-so-hidden messages about the craziness of these communes, the ridiculousness of the Great Leap Forward targets, and the fear I feel for Joy.

On July 28, I receive a package from Wah Hong. Inside I find a skirt and a blouse. I cut through the stitching on the collar and find twenty dollars and a short note from May.

I have great faith in my sister, but you must work harder to convince Joy to come home. And you still haven't told me about Z.G. Has Joy found him?

If I've been sending her coded messages — and leaving out things that surely she would notice — then she has sent a note she must have known would upset me. I must "work harder to convince Joy" to leave China, as though I haven't given up my life to be here, as though I'm not struggling every single day to keep myself strong for the moment I can break through to her? And, of course, there's the part about Z.G.

I hide the letter with the others I've received and write back what I consider to be a chatty missive.

Often when I come home from work, Dun — do you remember the student boarder who lived in the second-floor pavilion? — makes tea for me and we sit in the salon and talk about books. The other day I went to a pawnshop and found one of Mama's etched glass vases. I bought it, and now it sits on our dressing table. I filled it with roses I cut from our garden and their aroma scents the room.

I don't write any of the things that would mean nothing to the censors but would wound my sister. She, however, has become impatient with me. Her next note is her shortest:

Have you seen Z.G.? Are you *seeing* him? Just tell me, because we've hurt each other enough.

I stare at the words. I have a feeling my sister wrote this late at night, because otherwise she wouldn't have been so blunt. This makes me wonder if she's moved inside, off the screened porch. Is she sleeping in Vern's bed? In Father Louie's bed? In my bed? Our house was not large, but it must seem enormous to her now that she's alone.

Three days later, Z.G. and Joy come to my house with news. The Great Leap Forward is not just about steel and grain, they tell me. All 600 million Chinese must "go all out, aim high, and achieve greater, faster, better, and more economical results in building socialism." As part of that mandate, Z.G. is being sent back to the countryside to visit several villages. Alarmed, I ask the obvious question.

"Is Joy going with you?"

"Yes, we're going to the countryside," Joy answers for him.

I don't want her going back to the countryside. She can't go if Z.G. doesn't go. I turn to him. "You're famous. You don't have to do this, do you?"

Z.G. gives me a hard look. "I have a choice," he says. "All art students and artists must spend three to six months in the countryside, getting the masses to produce art, or spend three to six months working in a factory."

He goes on to explain that factories have given themselves challenges to manufacture more flashlights, radios, or thermoses in a week than in the usual month. Cotton mills have upped the amount of cloth they will make for the year. Z.G. would rather create art —

something that's at the very core of his being — than lose himself in a factory, where he might never get out.

"I'm trying to look at this as an honor and a privilege, really. The government wants to see a lot of art produced," Z.G. explains. "To do that, we'll need extra hands. Those hands are where they've always been. In the countryside."

"But peasants aren't artists."

I'm trying to use logic as a way for him not to go to the countryside — and take my daughter with him — but Joy thinks this is a political argument.

"You haven't seen Z.G. teach," she says. Her eyes have that same glittering look they get whenever she talks about revolution. She more or less quotes Mao, saying, "As long as we have enthusiasm and determination, we can achieve anything!"

Z.G., as he has since we were young, takes a more pragmatic view. "Taiwan and the United States are allies. They're trying to create an alliance with Japan and South Korea. Chairman Mao doesn't like that, and he's trying to show our power to the world."

"But how does making a bunch of bad paintings — let alone thousands of cheap flashlights — prove anything to the outside world?"

"Redness, as it has for years now, takes precedence over expertise," Z.G. answers. "We must think quantity, not quality, if we are to meet this new challenge. As for Joy and me, we'll start in Green Dragon, where we went last summer. It's now part of a commune. When we're done there, we'll head south to other communes. Then, at the beginning of November, the Artists'

244

Association wants me to visit this year's commodities fair in Canton. After that, we'll come home." He pauses before adding, "I hope."

That's a long time, and I don't want to be separated from my daughter again.

"Are you sure you want to be away so long?" I ask Joy carefully.

"Oh, Mom, don't you get it? We're here to ask you to come with us. Z.G. has received permission for all of us to go."

Mom. She called me Mom.

"I want to show you everything," Joy continues. "You should bring your camera so you can take pictures. Please say yes."

This is the first time Joy has asked me to do something since I've been here. (Those dinners for the three of us have all been Z.G.'s idea.) I can tell she really wants me to come. And that, even though I'm nervous about going to the countryside, convinces me to join them.

After a lengthy interview, Superintendent Wu gives me a travel permit. I break down and change some of my dollars into special certificates at the Overseas Chinese Affairs Commission. Before I leave Shanghai, I write a last short note to my sister. I know it will hurt her. I was going to tell her the truth sometime, but I didn't think it would come out like this.

Z.G. and I are taking Joy to the countryside.

I imagine May in our home as she reads that line. She'll think the worst of me. I know she will, because that's what I would do. (And, if I'm honest, she'll be right. This is the chance I've never had to be with him. Yes, Joy will be there, but who knows what could happen . . . I shouldn't get ahead of myself.) May has always been easy with tears. This time I imagine them coming from a deeply scarred and tragic place. Her older sister has gotten revenge. No thrust into the heart is greater or more harmful than that from one who says she loves you the most. I know, because my sister drove that knife into my heart many times.

I'm sorry I haven't told you about Z.G. before. Forgive me. *Nothing* has happened. I'm still just your *jie jie*, wishing I could have something of yours that I could never have and certainly don't deserve. I will write from Green Dragon Village, our first stop, but I don't know how good the mail service will be. I love you very much, May. Always remember that.

Joy

A Small Radish

We're on the bus taking us from Tun-hsi to the drop-off point for Green Dragon Village. Baskets of produce and pots of cooked food have been placed by the side of the road, sending the message that the Great Leap Forward has been so beneficial that people can give away food to anyone who passes. *Eat! We have plenty!* I see lots of small children — another of Chairman Mao's gifts. *Have babies! Have more and more babies!*

Z.G. and my mother share a bench across the aisle from me. My mother has pulled her body into something small and taut, as though that will protect her from the other passengers, the chickens and ducks, the smells, and the cigarette smoke. Every once in a while, she fingers the little leather pouch that hangs around her neck. It's identical to the one that Aunt May gave me before I went to college and that I wore when I came to China. I hope my mother isn't going to keep grasping the pouch and acting like the end is near. I won't let her take away my happiness, because . . .

247

We're going back to Green Dragon and I'm going to see Tao again!

Shanghai has not been at all like what my mother and aunt described, but there's a vitality that can't be resisted. I loved Z.G.'s house. I liked his three servants, although they sometimes looked at me strangely and argued among themselves about things I couldn't figure out. But apart from that tiny unpleasantness — which Z.G. told me to accept because you can't stop servants from gossiping — this was the good life, better than anything I'd experienced in Chinatown.

My father is very important. His position — plus a few packs of cigarettes passed to the right person — got me to the front of the line at the doctor's office when I had a sore throat in the spring, and it's placed us at the best tables at banquets. I've listened to jazz bands play familiar tunes: "You Are My Sunshine," "My Old Kentucky Home," and "My Darling Clementine." Yes, it doesn't sound very communist or socialist. And yes, everything I've been doing since Z.G. and I left Green Dragon months ago is a betrayal of my ideals, but to help China I had to know more about it. The meals — whether cooked at home by Z.G.'s servants or at a banquet — have been delicious. Food in Shanghai is sweet. I remember my mom always liked sugar and she put it on the craziest things, like sliced tomatoes. Now I understand where she got that. Even the fanciest banquet comes with a platter of French fries sprinkled with fine white sugar. There have been so many things to taste, see, and learn. It's been fun.

Except I could never escape the fact that Shanghai was once my mother and aunt's home. I don't want to be them, like them, or reminded of them, and yet I couldn't avoid any of those things. Just look at the way Z.G. wanted me to wear the clothes from his attic. They were beautiful and all, but the whole thing was kind of creepy. And, of course, my mother was in Shanghai. Z.G. insisted that we see her once a week. I can't believe how often I had to listen to Mom and Auntie May go on and on about how big and elegant their home was, but I didn't think it was so great. It was big all right, but dirty and filled with too many people. And what about Cook and the way he kept calling my mom Little Miss? No one's supposed to talk like that anymore, but he did.

My mother? She's tried her best — I know she has — but I came to China to get away from her. I don't want to be reminded of the past. I don't want to think about my father Sam. When my mother looks at me with her sad eyes, when I hear the reproach in her voice, when I feel her tentative touch on my arm, when I glimpse her hiding in the shadows watching me, I want to get as far away from her as possible. Then a way out of Shanghai happened, but not as I'd hoped, because Z.G. insisted that we ask my mother to join us. But then, the more she balked, the more I wanted her to come. I want to prove her thinking is wrong. I want her to see the glory of the Great Leap Forward. If she can see how happy I am in Green Dragon, then maybe she'll let me go — release me, like she did when I went away to college.

249

I stare out the window as the bus nears the drop-off for Green Dragon. Up ahead, several people cluster together, cradling sheaves of rice or carrying welcome signs. From a distance, Kumei waves. Her little boy stands at her side. Ta-ming has grown a lot this past year. Party Secretary Feng Jin and Sung-ling strike straight and dignified poses. There are others as well, but I'm not sure who they are. The one I'm looking for — Tao — has placed himself in front of the group to make sure I see him.

The bus wobbles to a stop. Someone helps my mother down. She says thank you, smoothes her hair, and then clasps her hands and waits. People unload our bags. I grin like a fool. Tao looks just as handsome as when I left — strong, brown from the sun, with a radiant smile. I want to hug him, but of course I can't.

An unfamiliar bald man steps forward. "I am Brigade Leader Lai," he says. "I've been sent by the district to run the Dandelion Number Eight People's Commune."

He's a one-pen cadre, which is only so-so for someone who looks to be about forty. On the other hand, he's already bald, which is considered a sign of wisdom. All in all, the commune is lucky to have someone of his stature to make sure it meets the goals of the Great Leap Forward.

"Come," he says. "We've prepared a tour and dinner for you."

He leads the way and we follow. The heat is harsh and white hot. We have a few miles to walk. My mother pulls out an umbrella to shield herself from the sun, and the others look at her in amusement. Eventually, we come to the hill that serves as the natural barrier to Green Dragon. My mother sets her face, adjusts her suitcase in her hand, and determinedly trudges forward. At the crest of the hill, Green Dragon spreads out below us. A new sign has been mounted by the side of the path.

WELCOME TO GREEN DRAGON VILLAGE

MEMBER OF THE DANDELION NUMBER EIGHT PEOPLE'S COMMUNE

1. PLANT MORE.
2. PRODUCE MORE.
3. WORK POINTS WILL BE AWARDED ACCORD-ING TO PHYSICAL STRENGTH AND HEALTH.
4. ALL PRIVATE HANDICRAFTS AND PRIVATE ENTERPRISES ARE FORBIDDEN.
5. EAT THREE MEALS A DAY FOR FREE.

Brigade Leader Lai babbles about all the changes that have happened in Green Dragon in the last year. "A generator supplies power to loudspeakers that are hung in the trees," he says, "and in every house not only in this village but in all thirteen villages that make up the Dandelion Number Eight People's Commune. Ours is a small commune — a little over four thousand members. I have a telephone in the leadership hall."

"I've not only seen the telephone," Kumei brags, "but also heard Brigade Leader Lai speak into it. He's staying in the villa, and he let me see it one day."

251

We pass blast furnaces, and I recognize several women who used to come to Z.G.'s art classes stoking the fires.

"Kumei, tell our guests about women in our village," the brigade leader orders.

"We women have been emancipated from the narrow confines of our homes." Her voice is filled with as much enthusiasm as ever. "With the Great Leap Forward, we no longer have the drudgery of being wives and mothers. We no longer hold parasitical positions in the home. We've been freed from our frustrating and self-centered lives."

"Everything the people were promised when I was last here has come to pass — from the telephone to food for everyone to the true liberation of women," I say.

The brigade leader gives me an appreciative smile, but leave it to my mother to see the hair in the glass of milk.

"Excuse me, but may I ask who takes care of the children?" she asks. "Who washes the clothes? Who makes the meals? Who cares for the old and the sick?"

My mother can be such a pain, but the brigade leader responds with jovial laughter.

"It must be hard for you, a woman of your age, to accept that things have changed," he says. (This does not go over well with my mom.) "The people's commune offers child care, a laundry, and a canteen —"

"Wonderful," my mother says. "I'd like to see them. Are men running those enterprises?"

The brigade leader starts to bluster. "The canteen sets women free. They are untethered from the grindstone and the wok —"

"Things certainly are happier now," Sung-ling says, stepping between my mother and the brigade leader. She takes my mother's elbow and leads her to the villa. We drop our bags in the front courtyard, just as I did my first night here. Then we leave again, walking along the path that abuts the villa's wall. Huge posters depicting commune life, steel and iron production, fishing, and new roads in the countryside have been pasted to the wall. We cross the little bridge and continue, walking on the path that runs parallel to the stream. I wish Tao and I could detour to the Charity Pavilion, but he's up ahead with Z.G. The two of them have their heads together, talking animatedly.

"At last we can do the same work and enjoy the same food as our fathers, husbands, sons, and brothers," Sung-ling continues. "No more leftovers for us. We're each paid according to our work. The more work we do, the more we're paid. Now I can spend my money as I please. No man can tell me what to do. Every woman is the boss — and owner — of herself. This is a good thing, don't you agree?"

"Yes," my mother admits. "These are all good things."

I smile. Finally, Mom has heard something she likes.

"The people's commune is truly fine," Sung-ling adds. "No single list can tabulate all its advantages."

"The people's commune is great!" Kumei practically shouts. When people look her way, she blushes, looks down, and then covers her scar with her hand.

"Kumei is right." This comes from Tao. "Fortune smiles on us all!"

Even though it's blisteringly hot, a shiver of excitement runs down my spine. I'm happy to be back here. These are my friends and this is my place.

After about ten minutes, we cross over another stone bridge. Rice paddies spread out to our right. We veer left past squash, corn, and sweet potato fields. Just ahead is a series of buildings, of which all but one are constructed with dried cornstalks lashed together as walls and roofs over bamboo frames.

Brigade Leader Lai thrusts out his arm dramatically. "The Dandelion Number Eight People's Commune! That building houses our kindergarten. We have the Happiness Garden — a home for the aged —"

"Is it made of cornstalks too?" my mother asks.

Brigade Leader Lai ignores her. "We've built a maternity courtyard in another village, but here we have a clinic and a nursery for children too young for school. That building over there is the canteen. Yes, it's made out of cornstalks. Nothing is wasted."

"Where will I hold my classes?" Z.G. asks. "We have a lot of art to create for Chairman Mao."

Party Secretary Feng Jin's brow furrows. "I thought you'd still want to do that in Green Dragon's ancestral hall."

"No, this must be a commune-wide enterprise. Everyone must create art. That is the mandate."

"What about producing steel?" the brigade leader asks. "We have a quota to fill —"

"More important, what about the harvest?" The Party secretary continues to wear a worried look.

"These are my orders," Z.G. says, not without sympathy. "We all must do our best to fulfill Chairman Mao's wishes."

"Then that's what we'll do! You will lead us right here in this field." Brigade Leader Lai makes a fist and raises it in the air. This causes Sung-ling, Tao, Kumei, and the others who've been following us to break into rhythmic shouts: "The people's commune is great! Long live Chairman Mao!" I copy them, raising my clenched fist and shouting too. With everyone staring at them, Z.G. and my mom join in. I'm so glad we brought my mother, because she's finally starting to *see* what I see and *feel* what I feel.

Brigade Leader Lai pulls Z.G., my mom, and me aside, and leads us to a cinder-block building. He calls it the leadership hall, although he doesn't invite Feng Jin or Sung-ling to join us. I glance back to see Kumei, Tao, Feng Jin, and Sung-ling drop to their haunches in the shade of a ginkgo tree. Inside the leadership hall are three spacious rooms — a dining room, a kitchen, and a large storeroom — plus another five rooms that look like they could be bedrooms or barracks. A table has been set for four people. Peasant women hurry from the kitchen to lay out an elaborate lunch of eight dishes. The meal is perfect — the vegetables are fresh on the tongue, the chilies give a wonderful bite, the flesh falls delicately from the bones of the whole fish, and the cured pork with salted black beans is properly tasty — but I want to eat with Tao and my other friends. Even if this meal is only for very important persons, why haven't Feng Jin and Sung-ling been invited?

After lunch, we go back into the bright sunlight. I blink, trying to clear the black spots from my eyes. Tao, Kumei, and the others jump up when they see us. On the way back to Green Dragon and the villa, Tao and I lag behind. When we reach the turnoff to the Charity Pavilion, Tao dips onto it. I don't hesitate for a moment. I run after him, scampering up the path as fast as I can. I reach the pavilion and throw myself into his arms. Our kisses are sweet yet frantic. So many months have passed. Instead of my feelings for Tao cooling, they have only grown. I can tell his have grown for me as well.

I wake at five the next morning to the sound of announcements being read over a background of military music blaring from a loudspeaker in the villa: "Bring your woks. Bring your griddles. Bring your locks." I dress quickly and go out to the sitting room that's shared by the four bedrooms in this part of the villa. My mom sits at the table. Her eyes are shut and she massages her temples.

"Are you all right?" I remember my first morning here a year ago, when I was sicker than the village dog.

She opens her eyes, which are dulled by pain. "I'm fine," she says. "I'll be fine. It's just —"

256

She doesn't have a chance to finish, because Z.G. comes out of his room, looking cross. "What's that noise?"

We head to the kitchen and find Kumei, Ta-ming, and Yong searching through cupboards. Brigade Leader Lai is already gone. He must go to the leadership hall very early each morning. The table in the center of the room, which has always been used for food preparation, has no vegetables or jars of pickles. Instead, cooking utensils and other metal items are laid out in a straight line from the smallest to the largest.

I introduce — or try to anyway, since I have to compete with the racket from the loudspeaker, which hangs from a rafter — Yong to my mother. She takes in Yong's bound feet and then stares into her face.

"I'm honored to meet you," my mom says.

"It's been a long time since I met a real lady from Shanghai," Yong responds.

"You know the city?" my mother asks.

"I was born there," Yong answers, slipping into the Wu dialect. Kumei and I glance at each other. Yong never spoke to me in the Wu dialect when I was here before. I wonder if she spoke to Z.G. in the language of their shared city when I wasn't around.

My mother and Yong share a look. *How did we end up here?*

"Bring your cleavers," the loudspeaker continues to trumpet. "Bring your door hinges. Bring your scissors."

"We must hurry," Kumei says. She gestures to the objects on the table. "You may take the wok, if you'd like."

"For the blast furnace?" my mother asks.

Kumei nods.

"But a wok? Don't you need it?"

"It's our last one," Kumei answers. "We had to give the others to the canteen."

"But what will you use to cook?" my mother asks, appalled.

"We get all our meals in the canteen."

"That's a long way from here." Then my mother gestures to Yong's feet. "How can you go there for your meals?"

"They let Kumei and the boy bring me food," Yong answers.

"Come on," Kumei implores. "Grab something. We have to go."

I pick up a soup ladle. I watch the others pick the smallest items possible — a Western-style spoon, a metal basket for fishing tidbits out of a hot pot, some hairpins. With our donations in hand, we troop to the village square. Everyone holds something made from metal — an old farm tool, the business end of a hatchet, some spikes, and more kitchen utensils. We give our pieces to a woman, who passes them to someone else, who feeds them into the blast furnace.

"This reminds me of when we used to gather tinfoil, bacon grease, and rubber bands during the war," I say to my mom. "We had fun collecting those things, remember? What we did helped us win the war."

My mother stares into the middle distance. I can tell her head still aches, but what she thinks remains a mystery. Then she pulls her shoulders back, steps forward, and says to the woman collecting metal, "In Shanghai, I worked the bellows for my street's backyard furnace. May I help here?"

"Everybody works so everybody eats," the woman replies. "We welcome your help, comrade."

Just then, a few people pull out red flags and raise them above their heads. The villagers systematically fall in behind those with the flags. Military music bursts again from the loudspeakers. Tao grabs the hem of my blouse — careful not to touch my skin in public — and pulls me into the line led by Z.G. Then everyone except those working at the furnace marches behind the red flags, flowing out in different directions like streams of ants.

Our group heads to the main part of the commune, stopping outside the leadership hall, where we had lunch yesterday. Our project is simple but ambitious. We have one week to create seven thousand posters. Even though it's easy and fast to print posters, Mao wants to show the world what the communes can do if people use their hands to work together in the Great Leap Forward. The content has been approved by the Artists' Association. The image will show the masses harvesting a cornfield. Identical couplets will decorate the left- and right-hand borders. One side will read, "The longer the communes exist, the more prosperous they will be." The other side will read, "The higher the sun rises, the brighter it will shine." Although four thousand people live in the commune, not all of them can participate in our project. Each of the commune's thirteen villages has sent about thirty people to help us.

Every person on our team will need to produce about twenty posters in seven days. And, except for a few people I recognize from last summer, most of our helpers have had no art training and almost none of them are literate.

Z.G. hangs the sample poster on the cinder-block building's wall. I distribute paper, brushes, and paint. The villagers do their best to copy the image on the sample poster, and I write the couplet when they're done. We work until eleven, when we break for breakfast in the canteen, which is the largest of the cornstalk buildings, covering a huge piece of cleared land. The meal is plentiful and filling — porridge, dumplings stuffed with meat, and a hearty soup. Then we're back outside for the worst heat of the day. Still, we work as hard and as fast as we can. We cheer each other on. We laugh. We're contributing the best way we know how. At three, we break for lunch, sitting on long benches in the dappled shade under the dried cornstalk roof. Then we go back to work until the military music sends the message from the trees that it's time to go home.

I gather the posters and give them to Z.G., who flips through them and observes drily, "A bumper crop of such works is nothing different from a harvest of misshapen trees and ugly weeds in a garden where not one rare plant or beautiful flower can be found." What can I possibly say to that? He's right.

I walk to the villa to pick up my mother and take her to dinner. When she says she wants to stay with Yong, I go back to the center of the commune and join everyone in the canteen. Families are encouraged to split up for their meals. Children sit with children. Women sit with women. Young men also like to group together. Some gather by work teams — the rice sowers, hullers, and packers; the tea planters, pickers, and curers; the women who run the nursery; the butchers; the animal breeders; the clothes and shoe makers; and the artists like us. The sounds of a good meal being shared — gossip, laughter, chatter — fill the air. Again, it's a bounteous meal — oxtail soup, cured pork with vegetables, pickled bamboo shoots, and giant bins of steamed rice on every table. For dessert, we have slices of watermelon. After dinner, we pack up containers of food for my mother and Yong, and then Tao, Kumei, Z.G., and I retrace our steps to the villa.

"Why don't your mother and father share a room?" Kumei whispers as Z.G. strides out ahead of us. "Do they do *things* differently in the cities?"

Tao looks at me curiously too. I wonder how many people in the commune know about my mother and Z.G.'s sleeping arrangements after just one night. Why didn't we consider this before we arrived? Everyone must think my mother and Z.G. are married. I have to come up with an explanation to answer Kumei's question in a way that will satisfy not only her but everyone in the commune. I can't say they're too old, because Tao's parents are still making babies.

"In some communes, Chairman Mao has asked husbands and wives to sleep in separate dormitories," I answer lightly. It's true, but it has nothing to do with why my mother and Z.G. are in separate rooms.

"I hope that rule never comes here," Tao says so somberly that Kumei breaks into giggles.

Z.G. waits for us at the villa's front gate. Tao waves goodbye and then bounds up the hill towards his house. I'm tired but happy. As we near the kitchen, we hear Yong and my mother laughing conspiratorially.

"That man is a small radish — an insignificant person," comes my mother's voice. "A brigade leader! How ridiculous. He doesn't look like he could lead anything."

I'll have to tell my mother to be more careful. Brigade Leader Lai lives in the villa, and sound travels.

"He's better than Feng Jin and his wife." Yong sniffs disdainfully. "Those two have been running the village since Liberation. She was once one of my husband's servants. He was a peasant, who used to come begging at our door."

"Illiterate too, I suppose."

"Of course, and in charge."

"Oh, but that Tao!" This again from my mother. I hear the humor, but it's tinged with contempt. *"Hsin yan,"* she spits out just as Z.G. and I enter the kitchen.

Yong quashes her laughter. Kumei gives me a sideways look. Z.G. sets the food containers on the table. The silence is awkward and I know my cheeks are beet red. The literal translation for *hsin yan* is *heart eye,* but it means *mind* or *intention.* It can have a good interpretation — *kindhearted* — or a negative one, meaning that someone has done something nasty or is *tricky.* I know my mother, so I know which interpretation she's using, and so does everyone else.

"We brought you dinner," I say with what I'm sure is a very stiff smile on my face. "I hope you enjoy your meal." Then I nod to everyone and step out of the kitchen and into the corridor. I breathe in the humid air and let it out slowly.

The next three days follow the same pattern: waking before dawn to the sound of announcements accompanied by military music, taking something to the blast furnace, following our red-flag leader, painting all day, eating in the canteen, and stealing secret moments with Tao that have become more and more intense. Throughout the fourth day, I'm aware of him watching me. That night, after dinner, Tao helps pack up the food containers for my mother and Yong. He hands them to Kumei, who sets off with Ta-ming and Z.G. We follow behind them, and then we veer off the path and climb the hill to our secret spot. We kiss. We do other things. We kiss some more, and then we turn to the view. The glow from backyard furnaces glitters on the landscape as far as we can see — a galaxy of red stars.

I know what's coming next, and I'm ready for it. I've turned twenty. I know myself and I know what I want. But going all the way is not what Tao desires, at least not right this second.

"Comrade Joy," he says, "I asked you last summer and now I ask you again. Will you go with me to Party Secretary Feng and his wife to ask permission to marry?"

This time I don't hesitate. "Yes!" It's a yes to everything — the New China, the commune, Green Dragon, Tao, and doing the husband-wife thing — as my mom has always so delicately called it — without having to worry about getting in trouble.

Tao takes me straight to the Fengs' house.

"It's about time!" Sung-ling exclaims.

She and her husband are delighted. We meet all the criteria, so they immediately fill out the forms for us, which they'll turn in to the district office.

"Do you want me to pronounce you married right now?" Feng Jin asks.

We'd both love that, but Tao wants to tell his family and I need to tell my mother and Z.G. We walk to the villa hand in hand. Never again will we have to worry about someone seeing us, though public shows of affection are discouraged, even between married couples. Tao says goodnight at the front gate. I pass through the various courtyards, making my way to the building where I'm staying with my mother and Z.G. They're awake and sitting in the shared living space. The light from the oil lamp flickers. Shadows dance on the walls. Z.G. wears the same expression he had when he confronted me last summer about my visits with Tao. My mother has her hands folded tightly in her lap and her back is rigid, but I can tell she's trying to hide her emotions, as she usually does.

"Where have you been?" she asks calmly. The stillness in her voice shows me just how upset she is.

"I've been with Tao. He asked me to marry him and I said yes."

She nods almost imperceptibly. "Yes, I thought this might be coming."

"It's out of the question," Z.G. says to my mother. "You must tell her no."

She doesn't acknowledge him in any way. "Of course, all I've ever wanted is your happiness," she goes on in that same even voice. "You understand that, Joy, don't you?"

"Yes," I answer, uncertain.

"Will it be all right if I ask you a few questions?" she asks.

I know what she wants to do. She wants to guide me to a point where I'll see I've made a mistake, but I haven't made a mistake. I'm happy and this is the right thing to do. Nothing she says or asks will change my mind.

"Don't you think you're better than this village? Don't you see that you're better than this boy? You went to university and he's illiterate. You don't need to settle for a small radish. You've already made enough mistakes in your life. Don't make another."

"Dad was illiterate," I say, homing in on something I can fight her on.

My mom cringes at that. I've hurt her, but she knows exactly what to say to wound me right back. "That's correct. Your father was illiterate. He was a peasant. Do you remember how you used to make fun of him for his greasy food, his bad English, and his backward ways? Do you remember when you taunted him for not knowing the names of American presidents? Do you think Tao knows the names of the emperors?"

I doubt it, but I don't worry about that, because I've hit on another argument. "Grandpa Louie always wanted me to come back to China. He wanted all of us to return. You sent me to Chinese school to learn traditions, rules, and the language. You wanted me to be a proper Chinese girl, because you longed to come back here too. How many times did you tell me that life was better in China?"

"In Shanghai —"

"Right, Shanghai. Well, I've been there. I prefer Green Dragon Village."

"You mean the Dandelion Number Eight People's Commune," she corrects me, but to what end? Then, "Your skin has always been as translucent as rice milk. Do you want to ruin your fortune?"

Is she speaking for May when she asks that question? I don't know, but I answer, "I was here before, and my skin was fine."

"You're still young, and you were here only a few weeks. Think what a year, a lifetime, will do to you. An inch of gold won't buy an inch of time."

"I don't care about things like that. I'm not Auntie May."

"But you're as stubborn as she is," she responds. "If you stay here, you'll be living from dirt to mouth."

"You've always been prejudiced against country people and the countryside."

My mother doesn't deny that.

"What about the special coupons you collect as an Overseas Chinese?" she asks. "And the special treatment you've received as Z.G.'s daughter?"

266

"I don't want special treatment," I respond. "I want to be a real Chinese, not an Overseas Chinese. And I don't need special coupons either. I'll have all the food I could ever want. We grow it here."

"The only reason Tao wants to marry you is that he yearns to leave the village," Z.G. suddenly injects. "He may look like a bumpkin, but he's ambitious. He wants to go to Shanghai, to Peking. But that's not going to work."

"I know. You told me yourself that he can't leave the village, and neither can I, if I marry him. What you don't understand is that I *want* to stay here. I love Tao."

My mother leans forward. A small, knowing — all right, I'll say it, malicious — smile plays on her lips. "Isn't the real problem that you're pregnant?"

Pearl

Riding a Flowered Palanquin

I shouldn't have said that. I told myself I was going to be different on this trip. I told myself that coming out here was an opportunity to reclaim my daughter and to spend time with Z.G. I told myself I would be agreeable, not pick any arguments, and show Joy that I could see her side and give whatever she's looking for a chance. I know all the things I *should* and *shouldn't* have done, but those words just popped out of my mouth, because what Joy wants to do is unacceptable. I've tried hard these past few days — no, these past months — to be alert and vigilant when speaking to my daughter so I wouldn't hurt her feelings or drive her away. Just now I tried to guide her with questions to help her see her mistake. I never should have let her glimpse what I really thought or felt. Like all mothers, I needed to hide my sadness, anger, and grief, but what I thought — she must have gotten pregnant (*just like her mother*) — sneaked right out of my mouth.

"Of course I'm not pregnant," Joy says, her eyes flashing. "How could I be pregnant? We've only been here a week."

"A woman can know —"

"But I haven't done anything like that!"

That's something anyway, I think but don't say. Instead, I ask, "But marriage, Joy? Why?"

"Because we love each other."

And she does love him. I see it in her eyes. I hear it in her voice. In fact, I've known since the first time she said Tao's name back in Shanghai, but that doesn't mean marriage is a good idea. My life has been filled with bad choices, and I've been living with the consequences for too long. I can't bear another heartbreak, and I burn with the shame of having failed as a mother. I take a deep breath, hoping that an angel will sit on my shoulder and settle me into the mother I should be. Z.G. isn't helping, that's for sure. I guess that's to be expected. Yes, it's been nice having him sleep in the room next to mine. I've been comforted hearing the weight of his footsteps, his whistling when he thinks no one is listening, his deep sighs, the sloughing and dropping of his clothes as he gets undressed, and his belching and other man sounds, but I know that a Rabbit will never go all out for you, defend you, or do battle for you. On top of that, Z.G. honestly and truly doesn't know what it means to be a parent. What would Sam say to Joy?

I clear my throat. "Your father believed in perfect matches," I begin. "My mother believed in them too. So did Yen-yen and Grandpa Louie. Your father and I were

269

very happy, even though an Ox and a Dragon aren't a perfect match. Still, a Dragon and an Ox have great respect for each other. They work together for common goals. Even I, as a Dragon, could never complain about an Ox's worthiness. You're a Tiger. You've never mentioned what sign rules Tao."

"He's a Dog," Joy replies.

"Of course," I respond. "A Dog is the most likable of all the signs." Joy smiles at that, but she shouldn't be so sure of my sentiments; I'm not done. "A Dog can put on a smiling face, but by nature he's a pessimist. He doesn't care about money —"

"And neither do I," Joy exclaims.

"A Dog can be violent —"

"Not Tao —"

"Is he the kind of Dog you can trust and love, or will he bite you? Is he a lazy Dog, who likes to lie by the fire and do nothing?"

"You're listing only negative attributes," Joy says. "You say these things because you're a Dragon. A Dog will never bow to your self-importance."

"Your auntie May would say that a Dog and a Tiger always act on impulse —"

"Auntie May is a Sheep," Joy cuts me off. "Tao would be too practical to indulge her selfish views." She seems desperate as she appeals to Z.G., trying to get him on her side. "Tell her that the Dog and the Tiger are among the best matches possible. We believe in strong bonds with other people. That means we both share in our love of the masses and what's happening here in the commune."

270

"Yes, you're both motivated by idealism," Z.G. agrees. "These are hallmarks of both your signs."

God, but men — fathers — can be weak and sentimental.

"Fine, but this isn't a good idea," I say to him. "You know that. You just said it was out of the question."

"I know, but think how much sorrow would have been prevented if May and I had followed our hearts," he says.

Will I forever feel like I was the one betrayed? Will he ever understand that things would have been very different if he had followed *my* heart?

"But you and May loved each other." (How it hurts me to say that, even after all these years.) "Joy can't possibly love Tao. Sympathy is often mistaken for love. It snares people into unhappy marriages and lives. How do we know Tao isn't a blind Dog, who just stumbled on a good meal by accident?"

"Is that how you felt about your husband?" Z.G. asks. Before I have a chance to respond, he adds, "In any case, Joy doesn't feel sympathy for Tao." He turns to Joy. "Do you?"

"I love him," she says, and I still can't help being reminded of May at that age — stubborn, dumb, and romantic.

Z.G. once again addresses me. "A woman is like a vine. She can't survive without the support of a tree. Isn't that what you had in your marriage?"

"Tao is not a tree," I snap, but Z.G.'s words are hard on me. I thought Sam was so sturdy. I thought he could support me, Joy, all of us, forever.

271

"Besides," Z.G. goes on, "Joy admires Tao as an artist."

That stuns me. "You said he isn't very good."

"He's still an artist," Z.G. says with a shrug.

That's such an egotistical comment, and so like Z.G., but his earlier words about my marriage still sting. Who am I to say how the heart works? Sam was just a rickshaw puller when we first met, and I loved him deeply.

I realize I can't win the fight against this marriage, but I try to delay things by suggesting we hold a proper wedding in Shanghai. "I'll hire a flowered palanquin to carry you to the ceremony. I'll arrange a banquet with all the best dishes. You can have the wedding I didn't have."

"Mom, I don't want that kind of wedding. We're in the New China. You fill out some forms and you're married. That's all."

"You won't be able to leave here. You'll be stuck," I say, repeating what I consider the greatest reason against this match.

"I don't want to go back to Shanghai," Joy insists.

"Honey, you aren't from Shanghai, but you don't belong in Green Dragon Village either. You're from Los Angeles," I remind her. "That's your home."

That's greeted by sighs from Z.G. and Joy. Apparently, mothers of the bride know absolutely nothing.

As a girl, I dreamed of my wedding — the dress, the veil, the banquet, the gifts — and none of it turned out the way I imagined. As a mother, I've dreamed of my daughter's wedding — a ceremony in the Methodist church in Chinatown attended by all our friends, Joy's dress, my dress, the flowers, the reception at Soochow Restaurant — but this is nothing like that either. Joy was right that there isn't supposed to be any kind of ceremony or celebration, but as a stranger and as someone who has some money to spend, I can bend the rules. Brigade Leader Lai is more than happy to take a bribe — some of my special Overseas Chinese certificates, worth less than twenty dollars — so I can give my daughter a wedding that pays homage to the past and is still true to the New China.

The ceremony takes place two days later at dusk on a hillside overlooking Green Dragon's verdant fields. Scent from tea bushes planted on terraces wafts on the breeze. The bride is in wedding red — an outfit Yong found in a dowry chest in the villa. She wears the pouch May gave her, and I wear mine — symbols of the ways that Joy is linked to my sister and me and the three of us to my mother. Joy's hair, which has grown a good six inches this year, hangs in two braids just past her shoulders. Strips of red wool have been woven through the plaits and are tied in heavy bows. Her cheeks shine with happiness and the heat. Her nails have been stained a reddish color with balsam juice. The groom is as dressed up as I've ever seen him — a blue tunic, loose blue pants, and sandals. His hair has been combed and he looks clean.

Brigade Leader Lai says a few words: "Communism is paradise. The people's communes will take us to it.

273

Tao and Joy — comrades first and always — will help the country climb to the highest heights. If Tao sails the seas, then Joy will row in the same boat. If Joy climbs a mountain, then Tao will be at her heels."

Z.G. takes my hand. His touch — his kindness — at this moment makes me want to weep. Until now, I had thought that my daughter had made the greatest mistake possible in coming to China, but that was nothing compared with this marriage. Mothers suffer; children do what they want. I look over at Tao's family. They don't look particularly happy either. The mother must be about my age, although she looks closer to sixty or even older. That happens when you have nine living children, who knows how many dead children, and are as poor as can be. The father is just an older version of his son — thin, wiry, but as dried out and wrinkled as my father-in-law was just before the cancer took him.

Brigade Leader Lai comes to the end of the ceremony. Tao turns to everyone and announces, "Comrades, I am happy."

"I too am happy," Joy echoes.

"In hard times, we will share the same piece of pickled turnip," Tao promises.

"We will drink from the same cup," Joy adds. "I will work by my husband's side in the commune. I will work with all of you."

I take a few snapshots of the wedding couple while Tao's young male friends set off strings of firecrackers. Then we walk to the canteen. Big wedding banquets aren't allowed in the New China — even the ceremony was more than what is considered acceptable — but if I look hard I can find ingredients with fortuitous meanings in our meal. We're served chicken, which symbolizes a good marriage and family unity, but we receive no chicken feet or lobster, which are typically served together to represent the dragon and phoenix. Instead of the many-tiered, Western-style wedding cake I'd always wanted for Joy, one of the servers brings out a plate of sliced pomelo for abundance, prosperity, and having many children. After dinner — and we can't linger or dance because other members of the commune still need to eat — we head to Joy's new home. More firecrackers pop and crack. In olden days, firecrackers scared off fox spirits, ghosts, and demons. In the New China, where we aren't supposed to have superstitious beliefs, the firecrackers symbolize good luck.

Joy's new home — which with her arrival will house twelve people — is a crude two-room shack made from mud and straw. It faces north. Everyone — except my daughter apparently — understands that only the poorest of the poor build their houses in places where they can't be heated by the sun in winter. Piles of bedding lie stacked to the left of the door. Tao's parents and all those brothers and sisters must be planning on sleeping either outside or in the main room tonight.

People celebrate around me, making toasts with rice wine, but I can barely breathe because in entering the room I've been tossed back in time to a shack outside Shanghai on the way to the Grand Canal. My sister is hiding in the other room, and my mother and I are

275

being repeatedly raped and beaten by Japanese soldiers. I tremble, and my breath comes out in shallow pants. The smell of the firecrackers and all those scraggly, dirty little brothers and sisters is making me physically ill.

I step outside to get some fresh air. My chest feels heavy, and my heart feels like it's breaking apart. Even when I was a little girl, long before the rape and my mother's death, I hated the countryside. When my father sent May and me to summer camp in Kuling, I saw evil in the way paths and dirt roads wove through the land like slithering snakes. I've never seen the charm of squalor, filth, or poverty either. Now the countryside is dealing me another cruel blow.

Joy steps outside to find me. Her cheeks are flushed with triumph and elation. Her words come out like frothy bubbles. "Mom, don't you want to be inside with everyone?"

My daughter and I truly are like *yin* and *yang* — one dark, sad, and closed, the other bright, happy, and open to her new life. But no matter how dejected I am at what's happened, I still love her very much.

"Of course I want to be a part of the celebration," I say. "I just wanted to take a minute to look at the beautiful night. Look at it, Joy. The sky, the moon, the fireflies. Remember it always."

Joy hugs me. I hold her tight, trying to memorize the warmth of her body, the beat of her heart, the crush of her young breasts against mine. "I know I haven't always been the mother you wanted —"

"Don't say that —"

276

"And I know I've handled this badly, but I hope you know that all I've ever wanted is for you to be happy."

"Oh, Mom." She gives me another hug.

I should tell Joy what to expect on the wedding night, but all I have time to do is whisper, "Always show the greatest kindness to the ones you like the least. If you show kindness to your mother-in-law, who like all women has been bred to hate her daughter-in-law, then you will create an obligation she will never be able to repay."

Joy pulls away and looks at me in surprise. I draw her close again. "Remember what you learned in church too. No matter what you're feeling or how desperate you become, always take a moral position. If you do that, God will watch over you."

People file out of the house, coming to get the bride, sweeping her away. I follow right behind, determined to be a proper mother of the bride, no matter what I feel inside or what memories the shack stirs up in me. Jie Jie, Tao's fourteen-year-old sister, hangs red couplets outside the door to what for this night has been designated the wedding chamber. One side reads: SONGS FLY THROUGH THE AIR. The other side reads: HAPPINESS FILLS THE ROOM. People step forward with gifts. Some have brought red azaleas picked in the surrounding hills. Others give packets of tea grown on Green Dragon's slopes, a jar of pickles, a piece of embroidery. Brigade Leader Lai presents a gift from the Dandelion Number Eight People's Commune: a hundred feet of cotton cloth for Joy to make wedding quilts.

277

"When your children are born, you'll get another fifteen feet," he proclaims.

Yong offers the bride and groom a Golden Cock alarm clock. Tao and Joy won't need an alarm clock, not with the loudspeaker and all the small children in this house, but the gift is both generous and mysterious. How did Yong acquire it? Was it preserved from happier days with her husband?

The time arrives for us to enter the bridal chamber. The room has been decorated with red paper cutouts: carp for harmony and connubial bliss, orchids for numerous progeny and the superior man, and peaches for marriage and immortality. In contrast, a couplet has been pasted over the single lattice window, which reads WITH MEN AND WOMEN EQUAL, WORK GOES WELL. FREE MARRIAGES ARE HAPPY MARRIAGES. Another large sheet of red paper has been pasted over the platform that serves as the bed for this family. In the old days, the paper would have been painted with the character for *double happiness*. Instead, Z.G. has written in his elegant calligraphy something to match the times: THE MANDARIN DUCK AND HIS MATE SWIM IN THE REVOLUTIONARY OCEAN. MARRIED COUPLES ARE COMRADES.

Two red candles flicker, sending shadows dancing on the walls. A couple of young men give speeches, making the usual suggestive comments about Tao's prowess in the bedroom and the bride's blushing ways. No one asks me or Z.G. to speak, but Kumei addresses the crowd with her customary cheerfulness.

"Why did we love weddings? We went to weddings to rejoice in the happiness of others and to swell our own joy."

Then Yong sways forward. "Heaven created the world," she says, "but it forgot to make happiness. This is especially true for women. When I married, my father hired people to cry. He wanted so many people to cry that the Yangtze would overflow its banks. For seven days, broth was my only sustenance, so I would be weak and obedient. A veil covered my face. When my husband lifted it, I saw a stern face. This was to make me understand that I needed to be compliant. Only since Chairman Mao came have we found happiness. I wish all gladness for Tao and Joy."

A few more bawdy jokes, unrefined quips, and rowdy laughs erupt from the guests. More cups of rice wine are drunk. Then it's time. Everyone but Tao and Joy backs out of the room. The door is closed. The young men go outside. They clap their hands, whoop, and bang together whatever they can find to make noise — all in an effort to break their friend's concentration and prolong the duration of the husband-wife thing. The young women, with Kumei and Jie Jie as their leaders, linger by the door to the wedding chamber to eavesdrop. They begin to giggle. Have they heard something already?

The next day is the end of Z.G.'s assignment. Today we'll be going south to another commune. We pack our bags. I wrap a scarf around my camera and the few rolls of film I brought with me. I walk up the hill to where

Joy lives. It's early, and the bamboo mats and bedding for most of the family still cover the floor of the main room. The children stand around in their birthday suits. They seem even grimier with their clothes off.

The door to the other room is still closed. My mind shies away from the thought of Joy in there with Tao and what they did last night. Joy emerges. She has a look on her face I don't understand. Doubt? Confusion? Disgust? I wonder if Joy's father-in-law is going to examine the wedding sheets for bloodstains as my father-in-law did so many years ago. At least that doesn't happen. Either the tradition is gone in the New China or this family owns no sheets.

Tonight will Joy and Tao sleep in the main room with the other children? In the future, when Joy and Tao want to do the husband-wife thing, will they sneak out of the house and find a spot in a field? I catch Joy's eyes. The gleaming light that shone from them last night has disappeared. I remember the feeling of disappointment I had after my wedding night — is that what all the fuss is about? — but my circumstances were very different. Joy insisted she was in love. So maybe the husband-wife thing isn't the problem. Maybe she woke up this morning in a small village in the middle of nowhere in the second room of a shack that's home to twelve people and finally realized what she's done.

I want to ask her what's wrong, but I don't feel like I can. Instead I say softly to her in English, "One last time, I ask you to come home with me. It's not too late . . ."

My daughter — tremulous and uncertain — stares out the open door. A sheen of sweat glistens on her upper lip. She stands very still.

"Walk out of here with me, Joy," I continue in English — a language that seems so open and free to me in this claustrophobic place. "Please."

When she shakes her head, I give her my wedding presents — my camera, film, and the scarf. "Take some photographs," I say. "Send me the film and I'll get it developed. I'll send some of those pictures to May. She'll want to see you here."

Joy walks me down the hill to the villa. Z.G. and I pick up our bags. Then she escorts us up the hill that leads out of the village. Above us, clouds like fish scales drift across the sky. Cicadas screech. We say our goodbyes at the welcome sign. My girl doesn't cry and neither do I, but looking into her face I see not the gloriously strong bride of last night but someone unsure. Z.G. and I are halfway down the other side of the hill when I glance back. I expect to see my daughter still standing there, but she's already started her journey to her husband and her new life.

Z.G. continues along the path. He's loaded down with his suitcase and various other satchels. The art supplies and all the posters that were done in the commune were sent ahead of us in a caravan of wheelbarrows earlier this morning. I want to say that I'm torn between my daughter and going off alone with Z.G. for the next several weeks, but this decision is easy.

"Z.G.," I call. He stops and looks back at me. I set my bag in the dirt and hurry to him. "I'm staying here." He unburdens himself of his bags, preparing for an argument. "I can't leave Joy," I rush on. "I've come this far, and I love her too much."

He regards me, clear-eyed. What I've learned these past five months is that, while he may not be the best father or give the best advice, he feels some connection to Joy.

"I wish I could stay here with you," he says at last, "but my status is too unstable."

"You don't have to explain. Dog today, cat tomorrow," I recite, quoting his servant from when I first arrived in Shanghai. The success he's had with his New Year's poster and his recent Mao portraits helped get him out of the political trouble he was in, but that could change on a whim.

"I'll return in three months to take you to the trade fair in Canton. I used my *guan-hsi* to get permission to bring both you and Joy with me. Joy probably won't want to come. In any case, she can't because she's married into the countryside. You'll need to attend the fair with me though."

Or else he'll be in trouble again.

"I understand," I say, "but I may not want to leave."

"You say that now, but by then you'll know if Joy is happy. If she can show you that, then you'll be able to come with me."

For the first time, I feel something like admiration for Z.G. He's finally beginning to understand the kind of woman I am. He puts his hands on my upper arms and squeezes them. He stares into my eyes. I hold his gaze.

"Pearl."

"Yes?"

"You're a good mother. I can never thank you enough for that."

He lets go of my arms, picks up his satchels, and heads down the path toward the road, where he'll catch the bus. I watch for a few moments, then turn, walk back to my suitcase, and continue on to Green Dragon Village.

Part Three

THE DOG GRINS

Pearl

A Smiling Face

Bang, bang, bang, bang.

I roll over and pull the pillow over my head. I had another restless night, getting woken up a couple of times by the sound of someone prowling through the corridor outside the building where I sleep in the villa. I could use a little extra sleep.

Bang, bang, bang, bang.

It's no use. The loudspeaker hasn't even come on yet to tell us to get up, but the Campaign Against the Four Evils — sparrows, rats, insects, and flies (which, for some reason, have their own special category) — isn't for lazybones. The worst of the evils are sparrows. They're said to devour seeds and grain, and now they must be eliminated. If the masses make enough noise — beating drums, clapping sticks, clanging pots and any cooking utensils that haven't already been fed to the blast furnace — then the sparrows will keep flying, never landing, until they fall from the sky, dead from exhaustion. I put on a smiling face and leave my room.

Kumei and her little boy are in the kitchen. Ta-ming holds a small slingshot, and he bounces from foot to foot eagerly. Kumei smiles.

"Do you want to walk with us this morning?"

She always asks the same question, and I always answer the same way.

"Of course!"

We leave the villa, turn left down a cobblestone path, cross a moss-covered footbridge, turn left again, and then follow the shaded creek. After about a half mile, we veer down a new path lined with poplar trees. It's barely dawn, yet from the hills around us we hear banging. Apart from the noise, which is as unsettling as it's supposed to be, these early morning walks along the stream are pleasant. Kumei is a nice young lady, and her son is quite dear. He's only five years old but earnest. He stoops to pick up a small rock, which he loads into his slingshot and shoots into the trees, hoping to hit a sparrow.

"I missed again, Auntie Pearl!"

"Don't worry. You'll get one eventually. You just have to keep trying."

We pick up food at the canteen and then hurry back to the villa, where Kumei dashes inside to drop off breakfast for Yong and Brigade Leader Lai. She returns a moment later, and we wait for Joy, Tao, his parents, and his eight siblings to make their way down the hill. Together we walk from the village to the main part of the commune to receive the day's work assignments.

Mothers drop off babies and toddlers at the nursery. Older children grab younger brothers' and sisters' hands to go to school. Ta-ming puts his slingshot in his pocket and joins his classmates. Everyone else separates to follow their red-flag leaders, marching with their knees thrown high and singing Great Leap Forward songs as they head off to their workstations: some to the sewing room to make blankets, trousers, and blouses; some to the leadership hall, where letters, telephone calls, and telegrams are processed; and some to the fields. Today the farmers' assignment is one I hardly believe: crushing glass sent from Shanghai and then working it into the soil as a "nutrient." It's ridiculous to me, but the farmers do it because the Great Helmsman can't be wrong.

All mothers and grandmothers must now come out to work. Tao's mother may no longer stay at home to wash, sew, and clean for her too-large family. Even Yong may no longer remain hidden in the villa. Most women — and I include myself in this — are ordered back to jobs in their own villages. I stop by the villa to get Yong and take her elbow as she totters to our workstation.

Brigade Leader Lai has assigned "old" people — like Yong, Tao's mother, and me — to the nation's Overtake Britain Battalion. Some days those of us on the gray-power team work at the blast furnaces — stoking the fires, feeding whatever metal is left in the commune to the smelter, or carrying the cooled pig iron to the central square, where men with wheelbarrows load the blocks and push them the few miles to the main road. Other days we shuck corn, sort rice, or lay out sweet potatoes for drying. I'm not old and I don't have any gray hair, but I put on my smiling face and do as I'm told. Many of the tasks remind me of the things I did with my mother-in-law when I first arrived in Chinatown years ago. Those chores brought me closer to her, just as these chores have brought me closer to Joy's mother-in-law. (I say "Joy's mother-in-law" because she doesn't have what I would consider a proper name. She was born into the Fu family. She went by No Name until she married out at age fourteen. Then *shee* was added to her natal family name to indicate that she was now a married woman from the Fu clan — Fu-shee.) We're a small group — all women of a certain age, but again, not *that* old. Today we sit together to tie garlands of garlic, share stories, and complain about husbands, housework, and the visit from the little red sister as mothers, sisters, and friends have done for millennia.

"We're lucky we live where we do, where we can use sand to catch the blood," one of the women says. "Do you remember when I joined the Eighth Route Army after they came through our county? We used dirt wrapped in cloth between our legs. Sometimes we used soft flowers and other plants. When we went to the tundra in the far north, the local women showed us how to use dried grass."

"When I was a girl and still lived in my natal village, we used a leaf from a tree that grew by the river," Fu-shee recalls. "My mother gave me ten dried leaves to use for my entire life. Each month, the blood goes in. It dries, and then you use the same leaf the following month. Every month throughout your life those leaves get harder and harder. I was happy to marry into this village."

I worry that someone will ask what I use. Would they believe that I bought sanitary supplies in Hong Kong or that my sister sent me some from America? That I throw the napkins out after every use? It wouldn't sound good. It might even be a bad reflection on my daughter. But there's someone even more suspect to question than me.

"What about you, Yong?" someone asks. "You lived in the villa. We always heard you used something special."

"I regret those days and I admit my mistakes," Yong responds contritely. In other communes, women with bound feet are going through a process of slowly unbinding their feet, preventing emotional and physical trauma — which would leave them completely crippled — and allowing the feet to regain their original shape gradually so the women can work in the fields. We have only one bound-footed woman in our commune, and so far her feet have been left alone. Still, they are a visible reminder of her privileged past. The others lean forward, ready for her confession. "The women in the villa used the scented ash from incense burned in the ancestral hall."

"Aiya! From the ancestral hall?"

"Bah!"

The women shake their heads in disbelief. If this weren't a matter for women alone, Yong would probably be attacked during one of the political-study sessions or be forced to make a public self-criticism.

291

"You were of the landowner class," someone says. "You could do whatever you wanted."

"It may have looked that way to you," Yong responds, "but I had to obey not just my husband but also the first, second, and third wives. How cruel they were — worse than the worst mother-in-law."

It's awkward for me to hear about bad mothers-in-law, since Fu-shee has not been as welcoming to my daughter as Joy would like. But then Joy doesn't understand how some relationships are so deep and fundamental that they cannot change just because Chairman Mao says they must. She knows, but doesn't understand, that on a bone-and-blood level mothers-in-law don't get along with daughters-in-law. I've told her that the written character for *quarrel* is two women under a roof. I've recited the old saying — "a bitter wife endures until she becomes a mother-in-law," meaning that a wife must slowly climb the ladder of position in a family before she can command respect. According to Joy, however, this kind of thinking has no place in the new social order. She can say what she wants, but mothers-in-law will be the same long after I'm dead, Joy's dead, and that Chairman Mao is only a bad memory.

At eleven, we recess for breakfast in the canteen, which is one thing I absolutely love. In the New Society, women no longer have the burdens of cooking for their families. Everything is prepared for us. Some people grumble that communal dining halls are destroying the heart of the Chinese family. After all, the family is built around breakfast, lunch, and dinner. I say we're still eating together, aren't we? Since I've been here, the canteen has been expanded (which didn't take much — just more cornstalks tied together to form walls and a flimsy roof over bamboo framing) so that it can hold about a thousand people at a time. This morning, as at every meal, children run between the tables, old women gossip, and everyone else talks about the weather and the coming harvest. In this way, every meal is like a banquet, except that, over the chatter and laughter, loudspeakers blast news from the capital, patriotic music, and encouragements to keep building a better China.

I find Joy, kneeling before her husband and father-in-law, tending their badly cut feet. I sit on the floor beside her to help. They have no leather shoes. They rarely even wear sandals. Their feet are tough, but not tough enough to walk through fields filled with glass shards. I look sideways at Joy. Her lips are set in a determined line as she picks slivers of glass out of her father-in-law's callused, cracked, and bleeding foot. Doesn't she see how insane this is? Doesn't anyone here see the mistakes that are being made? Sensing me staring at her, she glances my way. Her mouth spreads into a smile, and I automatically smile in return. Is her smile an apology or an expression of embarrassment? I tell myself I'm not here to criticize, even though I want to very badly. I tell myself that Joy looks happier than the morning after her wedding. I tell myself she'll confide in me, if I give her time.

★   ★   ★

Bang, bang, bang. A new week, a new month. I put on my same clothes and my same smiling face.

In the canteen, people *ooh* and *aah* about reports of extraordinary activities in other communes that come to us over the loudspeaker. "Go all out, aim high, and achieve greater, faster, better, and more economical results in building socialism," the announcer reads enthusiastically. "In Hunan, they've produced radishes as big as babies. In Hopei, they've grown melons larger than pigs. In Kwangtung, schoolchildren have crossed a pumpkin with a papaya, farmers have crossed a sunflower with an artichoke, and government scientists have crossed tomatoes with cotton to produce red cotton!" These accomplishments can't possibly be real, but everyone loves hearing them. We need to find inspiration wherever we can, if we're to bring in what everyone says will be the best harvest in years.

Today the commune holds a contest. Which village — Moon Pond, Black Bridge, or Green Dragon — can harvest crops the fastest? I'll be putting in my first full day in the fields, since every hand is needed if Green Dragon is going to win.

"Drink plenty of water," Joy recommends. "When we break, eat some pickled vegetables. They'll help with the loss of salt. Oh, and empty your shoes at every chance, because you don't want to get blisters. I learned that the hard way!" She grins happily. "Stay with me. I'll show you what to do."

She ties a kerchief over my hair and places a big straw hat on my head. She gives me a scythe. I've never held one before. Joy swishes hers back and forth to show me the motion. Then she picks up a basket and we take positions with others from the Green Dragon work teams in a field of golden rice stalks. Brigade Leader Lai blows a whistle. Joy and I work side by side as fast as we can. *Slash, slash, slash.* There's nothing neat about what we do, and a lot of stalks aren't cut.

"What about the grain that falls to the ground?" I ask.

"Don't worry about it," Joy answers. "Just hurry."

It doesn't make sense, but I'm with my daughter and she's speaking to me. Every step brings me closer to her, doesn't it?

Moon Pond Village wins the rice-cutting contest. Next, three small cornfields need to be harvested. Moon Pond rushes through their field — claiming another win, even though Green Dragon and Black Bridge fill more baskets with corn. And on it goes. We stop for lunch. The mood in the canteen is ebullient. I see sweaty faces streaked with dirt. I hear laughter and good-natured goading. We're all hungry, and the meal is plentiful: melon soup, stewed beef in red sauce, tofu with cured ham, sautéed water greens with garlic and chilies, and shredded fresh baby bamboo shoots.

"You did really well, Mom," Joy whispers to me in English. I hear the pride in her voice. This time when I smile, I actually mean it.

Then it's back to the fields for another series of contests: more corn, more rice, and then a quick change of pace to pull old and tough leaves from tea plants. The morning's enthusiasm dissipates as the afternoon wears on. We're tired but still determined.

295

The Black Bridge teams fall out of contention, but Moon Pond and Green Dragon win an equal number of contests.

"For the last challenge, you will harvest sweet potatoes," Brigade Leader Lai announces.

It hardly seems fair to put this at the end of the day. It hardly seems fair to include this type of challenge at all! Sweet potatoes? These aren't like the sweet potatoes we had in Los Angeles — big, fat, and orange. Even there I didn't like them all that much, making them only once with mini-marshmallows, because Joy said that's what we were supposed to eat on Thanksgiving. Here, sweet potatoes are grown as fodder for water buffalo and other livestock. Why should I be bending and digging under the sun for them? But I want to make Joy happy, so we race from one end of the field to the other, digging, pulling, and throwing sweet potatoes in our baskets but leaving plenty behind in the soil. We learned our lesson earlier today. Speed over quantity. Our Green Dragon team finishes first, winning the Dandelion Number Eight People's Commune award for fastest and best harvesters. Our prize? Extra coupons to use for rice, which we already receive in plenty. I don't understand it, but my daughter's delighted. She hugs me and I hug her back. Over her shoulder, faces register disapproval at our affectionate display. I stare back at them, a big smile on my face. What can they do to me?

"Would you like to come back to the villa for a bath?" I whisper in Joy's ear.

She pulls away and gives me one of those looks I'm hopeless to interpret. Then she says, "Yes, I'd like that. I'd like that a lot." She lowers her voice to add in English, "Thanks, Mom."

My muscles ache and I'm exhausted, but I go back to the villa, haul water, set a fire in the stove, and heat the water in our last big pot. Kumei helps me pull an old washtub into the kitchen, and then she steps out of the room. We may all be women, but naked flesh is too private to share even among ourselves. Joy strips and steps into the tub. I notice she no longer wears the pouch around her neck. She sits with her knees drawn up under her chin. Her enthusiasm drains into the hot water. She seems unaware she's let down her guard, as that low spirit I saw the morning after her wedding reappears.

"Do you remember when you were young and I used to wash you in the kitchen sink?" I ask. When she shakes her head, I say, "I guess you were *too* little — just a baby really. Your dad would sit at the table and watch us. Your grandparents too."

I pick up a cloth, dip it in the water, lather it with soap, and wash my daughter's back in long, rhythmic strokes.

"The way you giggled! I loved that sound and I'll never forget it. You used to slap the water with your hands until I was soaked and the kitchen floor was a mess!" I laugh at the memory.

"Grandpa Louie didn't mind?"

"You know how he was — Pan-di this, Pan-di that. He made a lot of noise, but he loved you. Your yen-yen

297

loved you. Your baba loved you. I loved you most of all."

A tremor shivers through her body. *Stop before you go too far*, I tell myself.

"As long as we're here, let me wash your hair." I ladle the warm water into Joy's hair. I wash and rinse it, letting the water cascade down her back.

"I'm not saying we didn't have hard times," I go on. "We did. But, Joy, when I took you out of the sink all pink and slippery, wrapped you in a towel, and put you in your baba's lap, no one in the world was happier than we were in those moments."

I wish I had clean clothes to give Joy. Instead, she puts on the same dirty, sweaty clothes she wore today and will again tomorrow. We walk together to the front gate.

"Will you come again?" I ask, almost as though she's an acquaintance, knowing enough as Joy's mother to keep a little distance.

She gives a slight nod.

In my fourth week at the commune, during lunch one day in the canteen, Brigade Leader Lai asks a group of farmers how much wheat they can produce per *mu*.

"We don't grow wheat," Tao's father answers. Several of the other men nod their heads in agreement. "We've never grown wheat. We grow rice in the paddies, tea on the terraces, and cotton, rapeseed, and vegetable crops elsewhere."

"Yes, but this fall how much winter wheat will you grow per *mu*?" Brigade Leader Lai still wants to know.

Tao's father consults with the other farmers before answering. "Maybe three hundred *jin*."

"Three hundred *jin*? Make that eight hundred or a thousand *jin*!"

"That's impossible," observes Party Secretary Feng Jin, who's resistant to the city cadre's ideas even though it's risky to go against him.

"Nothing's impossible in the Great Leap Forward!" Sensing the farmers aren't with him, the brigade leader asks, "How much grain do you need to eat?"

"We've always had at least one and a half *jin* of starch a day."

That's not a lot. A single *jin* of grain makes one steamed bun, a bowl of rice porridge, plus rice for lunch and dinner.

"You're eating far more than that now," Brigade Leader Lai points out.

And it's true. Every meal has more than enough rice. In fact, I'm sure I've gained weight since coming to the commune.

"Here's what we're going to do with our first winter wheat crop," the brigade leader continues. "It's called close planting. You plant six times the normal grain in a single field."

The men groan.

"It won't work," one of them says. "If you sow seeds too close, then the plants will die from a lack of sun and not enough nutrients."

"You're wrong there," the brigade leader replies. "Chairman Mao says that close planting will be like getting the masses to form a solid flank in the war against the advances of imperialism. Think how much wheat we will grow! More than seven hundred *jin* per *mu*." (At least he's dropped his estimate.) "We'll have so much wheat we'll have to give it away. We'll be a model commune!"

"Where are we going to plant this wheat?"

"You'll tear out some of the tea plants and change over the vegetable fields," Brigade Leader Lai snaps. "Our great Chairman says he wants wheat. Wheat we will give him."

The radio announcer broadcasts the time. The farmers slowly rise, shaking their heads. How can you reason with someone who's lived in a city his entire life about the crops and soil that you and your ancestors have worked for generations? Even I know, from my little garden in Los Angeles, that what the brigade leader suggested won't work, but everyone is afraid to voice too much criticism or skepticism. No one wants to get in trouble. No one wants to be singled out. Those who have little to lose don't want to lose what little they have. We all put on smiling faces as we go back into the sun to rejoin our work teams.

This afternoon, the women on the gray-power team share stories of giving birth. I hear one harrowing story after another. I tell them about losing my son during his delivery. To lose a daughter is sad, they tell me. To lose a son is tragic. They weep with me, and I feel part of a community in a way I've never experienced before.

As the end of the day approaches, people straggle into the village from the jobs they've been assigned. Joy and Kumei enter the village square together. Joy's shoulders are hunched, and she has a hunted look.

"I have a letter from Father Louie's village," Joy says, holding out an unopened envelope and pointing to the return address. "Why would anyone there write to me?"

"It probably contains a letter from May," I say. "I wrote to her and told her we were here."

Joy thinks about that.

"Why don't you open it?" I suggest.

Joy rips open the envelope. A photograph flutters to the ground. I pick it up, and there's May, standing in our backyard. Cecile Brunner roses cascade around her in an abundant display of Southern California fertility. She holds a small, fluffy dog, what I would call a yappity-yap dog.

"Let me see," Joy says.

I give her the photograph, and the others crowd around to look too. The gray-power women gaze incredulously at the image. They point at May's clothes — a skirt made extra full with a big petticoat, tiny belt cinched at her waist, and silk stilettos dyed to match her blouse. They comment on her make-up and touch her hairstyle with their fingers.

"Why is she holding a dog?" Fu-shee inquires.

"Why would she have a dog?" Kumei asks.

"It's a pet," Yong, the onetime Shanghai girl, answers.

"A pet? What's that?"

"An animal you keep for fun," Yong explains, sounding worldly. "You play with it." Seeing the looks

301

of disbelief on the other women's faces, she adds, "For fun?"

Snorts of disapproval greet that response.

"What did Auntie May write?" I ask.

Joy releases the photograph to the women, who continue to comment and stare in a combination of disgust, wonder, and excitement. It's as though they're looking at a movie star from olden times, except that these people (apart from perhaps Yong) have never seen a movie, let alone a movie star. Joy holds the letter close to her chest, and it's not because she doesn't want the village women to see what's written there. May was never good at Chinese characters, so I'm sure the letter is in English. Joy doesn't want *me* to see what's written.

"Dear Joy," my daughter reads, slowly translating, "I understand congratulations are in order. I hope you are deeply in love. That is the only reason for marriage." Joy's brow draws into tight little lines. These are hardly wholehearted good wishes. "I've enclosed a photograph. The dog's name is Martin. My friend Violet gave him to me. She says the dog will help me with my loneliness. She doesn't know that I named the dog after one of my special friends."

Oh, May. I shake my head. She mentions *her* friend Violet. Violet is *my* friend! She's been my *only* friend apart from my sister. And then there's the bit about the dog. I tell myself that Violet was just being kind to my sister, and that I can bear. But who is this Martin — the special friend, not the damn dog? Doesn't May realize she's a widow?

I know the real reason for these words. They're to get back at me. I've been writing May regularly and she's been deliberately silent. I don't blame her. I'm here with Z.G. and she isn't.

"You must write to me of your new life," Joy continues reading. "Tell me about your father. I long to hear of your time together." Joy doesn't have to read this part aloud, but she does. It seems this letter has brought back some of her anger at May and me, and she's always known how to drive a wedge between us. "Please write to me . . ." Joy looks up from the letter, glances at the faces around her, and says, "It ends with congratulations on our bumper harvest."

I have no idea what May wrote, but I'm positive it wasn't that. Joy's eyes remain hooded as we walk to the canteen, and she's quiet throughout dinner. After the meal, Joy comes back to the villa for her bath. These evenings have become a ritual I look forward to. Some nights Kumei and Yong — having gotten over their initial reticence — sit on stools in the kitchen near us, and we all chat, drink tea, and let the hard work of the day ease out of our bones. Ta-ming sits on the floor plucking the strings of a violin. From what I've learned, his father was educated. The violin — one of only a few of the landlord's personal possessions not destroyed or confiscated during Liberation — belongs to Ta-ming now. Sometimes he picks at the violin strings, as he is now, or he'll hold it like an *erhu* — upright in his lap — and run the bow across the strings. It sounds terrible but not as bad as some of the military marches we hear over the loudspeakers.

303

Usually when we're together Joy lets down the walls that surround her. That blue part is still at her core, but some nights she laughs, tells jokes, even gossips. It's times like those that I feel closer than I ever have to my daughter — as though we've made the transition from mother and daughter to friends — but tonight she's unsettled. I shoo Yong, Kumei, and Ta-ming out the door. I sit on a stool a short distance from the tub and watch as Joy scrubs her skin as though somehow that will cleanse her soul. If I can talk about my mistakes and failures, maybe she'll start to understand she has to forgive herself. My biggest failures have to do with May, and Joy has always been right in the middle of that.

"I haven't always been the best sister," I say, trying to sound as conversational as possible. "I've often been impatient with May. I wasn't as understanding as I could have been. Z.G. has also been between us for twenty years. I look back and see how blind I was. I loved him, but he loved May."

"You're here now," Joy says in benign resignation. "He's coming back for you. The two of you can still be together."

Waa! I've thought this myself. Z.G. will come for me, we'll go to Canton, we'll stay in a hotel, we'll . . . But for Joy to say that?

"I haven't been a good sister," I repeat. "Since returning to China, I've had a lot of time to think about how hard it must have been for May all those years —"

Joy shakes her head, not wanting to hear this.

"You don't have to like it, but it's the truth. I love you and you'll always be my daughter. That must have been very hard for May. You can see that, can't you?"

"I can, but why would either of you want me? Why would anyone want me?"

She really is still such a child, needing proof of my love and her value.

"Because you're smart. You're beautiful. You have many talents —"

"Like what?"

"You were able to act from a very young age. You were good at Chinese language and calligraphy. Now I see you were born with a talent I didn't recognize until recently — your skill with a paintbrush. It's like I see you in the strokes."

"You're just saying those things because you have to. Nothing can change the fact that my birth parents didn't want me. They knew even before I was born that I wasn't worthy of love. That's why they gave me away."

"How can you possibly think that?" I ask. This is worse than her guilt over Sam's suicide, because it goes to the core of who she is and her value in our family and in the world. "Z.G. didn't know May was pregnant. May loved you so much that she gave you to me so that she'd always be with you. And, if we're honest, who did you spend more time with when you were a little girl — your aunt or me?"

"Auntie May."

"That's because she loved you. And I love you too."

"But don't you see? That's one of the reasons I ran away. You've always fought over me. If I'd stayed, I would have finally had to choose between you."

"Choose between us? Oh, sweet one, your saying that just proves how much we loved you."

"But I didn't deserve it."

"Of course you did! Your grandparents loved you. The courtesy uncles loved you. May and Vern loved you. Your dad loved you. You were a pearl in his palm. And I . . ."

Can she really not tell how much I love her? My daughter and I stare at each other. What I see is a cracking of Joy's hard shell and beneath that the softness of understanding. She was and is loved. Tears run down her cheeks.

"I've failed in so many ways," she says. "I failed Dad. I failed you and Auntie May. And I'm not a very good wife."

"You can't blame yourself for everything," I say, but inside I berate myself. How can she have lost such confidence? Is this what May's and my secret did to her? She has to realize none of us is perfect. "I wasn't the best wife, sister, or daughter either."

"You looked perfect to me."

"You *know* I failed at many things. I lied to you. May and I both did. I didn't do enough to help your dad." I hesitate. This subject is still painful for both of us, but I'm not going to lie to her, not even if it would make her feel better right this moment. She deserves more than that. "We're all partly responsible for what happened to your father. None of us is innocent, but we aren't evil or bad or beyond redemption either."

I pull my stool over to the tub, dip a cup into the water, and pour it over my daughter's hair. I lather soap into her scalp. I let all the love I have radiate out of my fingers and into the aching body of flesh and bones that is my daughter, hoping she'll release her sorrows, wash away the past, and finally forgive herself. And after this night, Joy's spirit is lighter, which makes me thankful.

Pearl

A Perfect Circle

Birth, growth, decline, death. All Chinese festivals remind us that we are a part of that cycle. It's the fifteenth day of the eighth lunar month, around mid-September in the Western calendar. The bumper crop has been harvested, but, in the effort to make steel or compete in contests, whole fields have been ignored, with melons, cabbages, and turnips literally rotting on vines, on stems, and in the earth. The rice has been brought in, although even this most precious grain was left on stalks in the paddies or can be found in the dirt on the main square, where we did the threshing, sorting, and drying. We've been encouraged to eat, eat, eat. This is contrary to just about everyone's way of thinking, because you never know when hard times will come, but we obey and enjoy ourselves in the process.

I'm told this is the usual time of quiet and celebration, but this year is different. Brigade Leader Lai has ordered teams to plow under what's left in the fields so the farmers can get the winter wheat planted.

308

The seeds are going in as densely as possible — forty to fifty *jin* of seed per *mu* instead of eighteen. Some of us are sent back into the cornfields to harvest the stalks to add heft to the existing walls and roof of the canteen before winter comes. Trees still need to be cut and brought down from the hills to keep the blast furnaces going. It seems like most metal has been fed into those furnaces, and yet the *bang, bang, bang* of metal utensils can still be heard from before dawn until long after dark, driving what remains of the sparrows to their insane deaths.

These may not be traditional times, yet some things are still fixed and certain. Tonight the moon is closer to earth than at any time of the year. They may call it Mid-Autumn Festival now, but it will always be the Moon Festival to me. Tao's family has invited Kumei, Ta-ming, and me to join them to celebrate family togetherness, the harvest, and the moon. The canteen has made moon cakes filled with a sugary paste of dates, nuts, and candied apricots. The tops are embossed with images of a three-legged toad and a rabbit. I take a box of cakes to Joy's house. *Tuanyuan,* the word for *reunion,* literally means *a perfect circle,* and that is what the moon, the moon cakes, and our family are on this night. Jie Jie and some of the children stretch out on the ground or sit on their haunches, staring up at the moon. I hand out the cakes. The children aren't old enough to have bittersweet memories, but the adults are. We see the cakes and we remember the past — people now gone, happy holidays.

"This year I hope we can create new memories for the future," Joy says.

I've been here six weeks. Joy still comes for her nightly bath in the villa. She's stopped complaining about her mother-in-law and never seems upset about living in such cramped quarters with so many people, most of whom are children. I've watched her paint and discovered a part of my daughter I never knew existed. I've seen her work in the fields — with a smile on her face even as her skin burns. She's turned a corner. Even though she's had her tragedies, she can laugh, be content in her marriage, and work happily and with enthusiasm at something that truly is bigger than she is. So, as much as I love Joy, I'll go with Z.G. to the Chinese Export Commodities Fair in Canton when he comes for me. My daughter is a married woman now. She's chosen a life I wouldn't pick, but it is her life and she's going to have to figure things out for herself — as a woman. It kills me to let her go, but it's the best and only thing I can do as her mother.

When it's time to place some of the moon cakes on the ground as offerings, we sit together — mother and daughter — with a bunch of wiggling children gathered around us. There's no need for bean-oil lamps tonight. Illumination comes from the moon. It's bright, and moon shadows dance around us. Joy takes my hand in hers and balances it on her knee.

"This is a special night," she tells the children. "The Moon Lady will hear your wishes and grant your requests, but only if they are one of a kind and never heard by anyone else."

310

Joy looks up to the moon, and so do the children. I too stare at the rabbit in the moon, forever pounding out the elixir of immortality. My wish is simple. *Let my daughter continue to be happy.*

At the end of October, Z.G. walks back into the village. That night, I pack my bags, thank Yong and Kumei for their hospitality, and promise Ta-ming I'll send him books and paper. In the morning, Joy escorts us to the top of the hill. "Write to me," I say. "When the fair in Canton ends, we'll go right back to Shanghai. I'll be close by, if you need me." Then Joy watches as Z.G. and I make our way down the dusty path toward the main road. I keep looking back and waving, until finally I don't see her anymore.

This is one of the few times in my life that I've been completely alone with Z.G. In the past, May was always with us. Since I've come back to China, we've almost always been accompanied by Joy. During these past months, Z.G. and I have gotten to know each other again. He is Joy's father and I am her mother, and that links us on a deep level. Now that we're by ourselves, I think we both feel anxious about what could happen. I've told myself I don't want *anything* to happen. I love my sister too much, and I don't want to upset the balance Z.G. and I have found with Joy, but I'd be lying if I didn't say there is the awkwardness of expectation between us — first on the bus and then later on the boat to Canton. I don't know what to say, and he doesn't know where to look.

When we reach Canton, we check into a hotel — separate rooms, of course. We have a casual dinner with the rest of the Shanghai delegation — all strangers to both Z.G. and me. Toasts are made with *mao tai*, a fiery liquor. We eat bowls of noodles and then drink more toasts. Everyone laughs and tells jokes, and I'm reminded of when Z.G. and I were young and every night was like this. When it comes time to disband, I'm surprised by how woozy and light-headed I am. Z.G. is in even worse shape, weaving unsteadily down the hall to our rooms. We reach his door first. When he pulls me into his room, I don't resist. I tell myself the *mao tai* is making me incautious and that I'll leave in a minute. But the next thing I know, I'm in his arms and we're kissing, fumbling at each other's clothes, and pushing each other toward the bed.

I know, I know. A widow should never go with another man. She's expected to spend the rest of her life in chastity. But I've loved two men in my life — Sam and Z.G. The love I felt for Sam stemmed out of gratitude, reliance, and respect. My love for Z.G. began when I was just a girl. He has been the big love of my life — the big *passion* of my life. May called it infatuation and maybe that's true, but here I am and here is Z.G., and we're both a little more than tipsy and we're lonely for the people we really love. And, if we're honest, men are attracted to women who are crazy about them, as I was for Z.G. in the past. Suddenly, it's all so easy — the hotel room, our defenses down because of the alcohol, and the opportunity. No one knows us here. No one will ever know. And besides, wouldn't it be strange if it *didn't* happen? Still, we have enough wits about us to take precautions.

"I don't want you to get pregnant," Z.G. says.

"I can't get pregnant," I reply. Fortunately, he doesn't ask why.

He has the sense to get up and get a towel from the bathroom. And that gives me a second to think. *What am I doing?* Then I watch him walk back to the bed. He's naked and, you know, *ready.* A proper woman would look away, but I stare right at him, looking at everything. His body is beautiful. He slides the towel under me on the mattress so any fluids that escape will be caught there instead of on the sheets, which the chambermaids might report to the floor monitor, who, in turn, might push this knowledge to higher-ups. And then . . . And then . . .

He knows exactly where to touch me, saying, "I know the shape of your body because I painted it so many times." I feel safe, forgetting for the first time what happened to me during my rape. I have no sense of duty or obligation, which I often felt with Sam even though he was kindness itself. I'm not going to say everything is perfect in that low-down area, but I feel something I've never felt before.

Afterward, as we lie naked, Z.G. touches the pouch I wear around my neck.

"Joy wears something just like this," he says. "What is it?"

"My mother gave one to May and one to me." As I say the words, I feel my connection to Z.G. slipping away. "May gave hers to Joy when she was born."

I sit up and pull the sheet over my breasts, abruptly shy and embarrassed. I love my sister and what I've just done may not be the worst thing in the world, but it wasn't very good either.

"We have to think about May," I say.

"I agree," he says, sounding much more sober.

"You've lived a long time without May, but I'm certainly not the only other woman you've had in your life." Why am I saying that? To make myself less culpable?

"I'm a man, and it's been more than twenty years," he says.

I silently take that in.

Then he asks, "Have you heard of Ku Hung-ming? He lived at the end of the Ch'ing dynasty. He said, 'One man is best suited to four women, as a teapot is best suited to four cups.'" He laughs sheepishly. "I always thought that if that philosophy was good enough for Chairman Mao, it was good enough for me."

"But it wasn't. You love May." Finally, after all these years, I seem to have made peace with that.

"Pearl —"

"You don't have to apologize for anything." I put a hand on his arm. "You'll never know how much this" — I motion to our rumpled bedclothes — "meant to me, but it can never happen again."

I pull the sheet with me as I get out of bed. Z.G. tugs the quilt over himself, but I'm careful not to glance his way. I pick up my clothes off the floor, go in the bathroom, and get dressed. I catch sight of myself in the mirror. My cheeks are still flushed from the *mao tai*

314

and the husband-wife thing, but to my eyes I look different. I'm finally over Z.G. and my fear of sex. Those two circles have closed. It's unclear what this will mean for me — a widow — but I feel possibilities are now open to me that I haven't had since I was a young woman.

I give Z.G. a rueful wave, check to see if the hall is deserted, and then sneak out of his room and make my way to my own. In the morning, we meet for breakfast, as though we're good comrades, and then go to the fair. We will never speak of what happened again, but before we leave Canton I write a letter to May. I can't erase what I did with Z.G., but I can soothe her mind. I'm so close to Hong Kong, I wish I could go there, fly home, and tell her myself. Instead, my letter will go to nearby Wah Hong, be put in a new envelope, and make the usual journey across the border and on to Los Angeles Chinatown.

There is something you should know. Z.G. is a Rabbit and you are a Sheep. Z.G. loves you and only you.

Joy

Between the Yellow
and the Green

"How many flies did you kill today?" Brigade Leader Lai inquires as he walks between our two rooms as part of his newly instituted cleanliness inspection. Tao's little brothers and sisters show him a cup where they've saved their dead flies. "That's good," he praises them, "but did you kill any rats or mice?" We haven't, which is not good. "How about sparrows?" he asks.

"There aren't many left," Tao's father answers.

"I hear this from others in the commune," Brigade Leader Lai acknowledges. "But why do I still see them flying in the sky? You must try harder! Now, what has your family done to eradicate other insects?"

"It's winter," Tao's father says. "Look." He points to the paper we've pasted over the window openings with rice paste to keep out the cold. "We don't get many insects now."

"Take down the paper," the brigade leader recommends. "Keep a lantern going on the table in the main room. In the morning, you'll have many dead insects."

I'd be more upset about this, except that rice paper isn't exactly the same as a windproof glass windowpane.

"Shall we keep what we kill to show you?" Tao's father asks.

"Absolutely. It won't be an inspection if I don't see what you catch."

When Brigade Leader Lai leaves, the children roll out their sleeping mats on the floor. Tao's mother and father go to the other room. They're trying to make another baby. As Chairman Mao says and as my mother-in-law reminds me every day, "With every stomach comes another pair of hands." As soon as my in-laws are done, Tao and I will take our turn.

Is marriage what I expected? Not at all. That first night? It wasn't romantic, and Tao wasn't very gentle either. I realize that who he is and how he acts are partially determined by being raised in this place, but also making out with him was very different from actually going all the way. But what bothers me isn't limited to sex. I hadn't entered Tao's house until that day, so I hadn't realized how dirt poor his family is. I didn't have a marriage bed like I did in the villa. I didn't have a suite of bedroom furniture brought to my home piled on the back of a bicycle like I'd seen traveling through the streets of Shanghai, Canton, and Peking. I had enjoyed roughing it in the villa, but here I didn't have privacy to use the nightstool, not with twelve people living in two rooms. That night when I undressed, Tao told me to take off the pouch Aunt May gave me. He said I was safe and didn't need it to protect me anymore. I obeyed because he was my husband. I told myself I didn't require money, furniture, or a talisman to love and make love. Still, none of it was what I expected. It's one thing to have a sort of camping adventure in a villa for a couple of weeks and quite another to realize that I'm going to have to live like this for the rest of my life.

Here's what I've learned in three months of marriage: Even in the New Society, women must care for the husband, children, and older members of the family. They must look after the house, clean, make and wash clothes. All this they do and work outside too. Since the inauguration of the communes, a few adjustments have been made. Three rules now apply to working women: No women may labor in wet places during the visit from the little red sister. Expectant mothers will have light physical tasks. Mothers will toil near their homes. There are some unwritten rules too. At the end of the day, women should be ready to make another baby for the great socialist nation. In return, we are to be happy with a few words of praise or a pat on the arm. I grasp at these things and hold them to my heart as proof of Tao's love and my worth.

The alternative isn't so great. "Criticism and self-criticism should apply in marriage," Tao tells me almost every day. "Unity is possible only when one side wages the essential and proper struggle against errors committed by the other." Now that we're married, I commit a lot of blunders in Tao's eyes.

I was once enamored of Tao, but sex is a huge disappointment. Even if Tao touched me in the right places and wasn't so rough and fast, how could I feel anything but nervous and uncomfortable with ten people in the other room? Sometimes I ask if we can go to the Charity Pavilion. I want to feel what I felt before we got married. I imagine all the things we could do there if we had that privacy. I've even whispered some of them to Tao. I can feel his response in my hand, but he says, "It's not necessary to go there now. We're married. You shouldn't be so self-concerned." In other words, I'm trying, but so what? He doesn't care.

Sex is one thing, happiness is another. I hate this place, and I'm not even sure I *like* Tao now that I've gotten to know him.

Does this seem sudden? Not at all. I knew the morning after I married Tao and every morning since that this was a mistake, but in my own stubborn Tiger way I've accepted it as the punishment I believe I deserve. On the other hand, I constantly castigate myself for being so easily deceived and swayed. Yes, I'm still as mixed up as always.

I couldn't talk about these things with my mother when she was here, because I didn't want her to worry. I tried to act happy in front of her after that night we talked in the villa. I told her what I thought she wanted to hear. I needed her to *believe* I was happy so she could go back to Shanghai. But the truth is I'm heartbroken. I've ruined not just my life but hers as well. My actions have only made things worse, and I'm unable to change or fix them. And now that she's gone, the dark feelings that have plagued me since my father's death wrap their oily blackness around me.

All through November, I stay peasant busy — mending clothes, making pickles, storing dried vegetables. Pigs are killed — which is disgusting to begin with — and then soaked in salt water for a couple of weeks, and finally covered with chilies to keep the flies away. Since we're part of a commune now, the body parts are hung outside the leadership hall instead of individual houses as they once were. We keep eating as much as we want in the canteen, but when December arrives and the temperature drops below freezing — and those cornstalks added to the canteen walls are not much of a barrier against the weather — Brigade Leader Lai introduces rationing.

Tao tells me not to worry. "This always happens between the yellow and the green. The fields are bare of crops, the harvest begins to run out, and the planting that starts at Spring Festival hasn't happened yet."

"But I thought we had a bumper harvest," I say. "How can the commune run out of food?"

"Don't concern yourself with these matters," my husband responds, trying to act like a grown-up, but I learn from others that the brigade leader pledged a huge amount of grain to be delivered to the government based on our bumper harvest. He made good on his promise by handing over the inflated

320

amount, told us to eat as much as we liked, and now the granary in the leadership hall is dangerously low.

As the month progresses, it gets colder and damper. Tao's family home faces north, so we don't get much warmth from the winter sun. Frost whitens the ground. Standing water freezes overnight. Snow falls sometimes, but it melts quickly. Frigid air blows through cracks around the door and roof. And as far as I'm concerned, the window — we've reglued the rice paper over the opening — does absolutely nothing to keep cold air out or warm air in. I can see my breath inside the house all day. Tao's family has had a long time to learn how to make do. They dress in layer upon layer of padded clothes. I do too, but I never get warm.

I write to my mother every Sunday, since it's the one day I don't have to work for the commune. I tell her about Yong, Kumei, and Ta-ming. I tell her about the weather. I tell her that I'm learning how to be a wife. Then, on Monday, I walk down to the pond and wait for the mailman, who visits the different villages that make up the commune on his bicycle. I give him my letter, which he'll take to be sorted, read, and processed in the leadership hall. Today he hands me a letter, which I read to the entire family:

"Z.G. and I went to a tea party at Madame Sun Yat-sen's home. She has a beautiful garden with thirty camphor trees. Did you know that she writes all her speeches in English? If you were here, I bet your father could get you a job helping her, since you went to college in America, just like she did. Anyway, representatives from Burma, Nepal, Pakistan, and India also came to the party. You should have seen the women in their saris. They were very elegant compared with the Russian women. Your father talked me into wearing a red silk *cheongsam* with yellow piping from the old days. Everyone said your father and I were the most handsome guests in attendance. I believe they were right, if I say so myself."

A week later, she sends Christmas presents — a red scarf, a tin of cookies, and cloth purchased with her cotton coupons. I give the cookies to Tao's brothers and sisters and the cotton to my mother-in-law so she can make clothes for the children. I keep the scarf for myself. I don't explain Christmas to them.

Two weeks later, my mother writes with news we've also heard over the loudspeaker. Officials in Peking have announced the construction of ten projects in the capital to celebrate the tenth anniversary of the People's Republic of China next year on October 1, 1959. "The greatest of these will be called the Great Hall of the People," I read to Tao and the others. "It will be bigger and grander than anything China has built before, except perhaps the Great Wall. Most important, the Great Hall of the People is being built with volunteer labor. Your father promises to take me to the celebration. That will be something to see!" Here's what I think she means by her false enthusiasm: *Volunteer labor? I'm happy I don't live in Peking and won't have to work on this or any of the other nine ostentatious shrines to Mao's ego.* Censors can't black out what isn't written.

But to my husband and in-laws it all sounds glamorous, and the main room is filled with their excited exclamations. Madame Sun Yat-sen! The Great Hall of the People! They've been less impressed by May's letters, because they don't understand anything about television sets, cars, or movie stars. Still, they look at the photographs she sends and ask questions like "Why is she wearing that? Isn't she cold with her naked shoulders?" Sometimes they look at the photos in which May wears make-up and teased hair, and they don't say a word. They may never have seen a prostitute, but they know a broken-shoe when they see one.

My mother and aunt always ask me the same questions: *Are you happy? Are you painting?* I'm not happy, but I don't want to tell them that. I'm not painting either, but Tao is. Knowing of Z.G.'s success with his New Year's poster, Tao now wants to enter the national competition. "If I win, we could move to Shanghai or maybe even Peking," he often says. He works at the table, bundled in padded clothes, with a quilt over his shoulders and another over his legs. He's taken a traditional subject — door gods — and transformed them into two peasants bringing in an abundant harvest. He doesn't use me as a subject or as inspiration as Z.G. did, which hurts my feelings something awful. Whenever I say anything about it, Tao says, "Quit complaining and do your own painting. No one's stopping you." That's easy for him to say. I wish I could put brush to paper with as much confidence as my father and husband do. I have something in my mind — I know I do — but I haven't yet been able to reach it and I have no one to encourage me.

At night, Tao and I lie on mats in the main room. The clothes we'll wear tomorrow are under our mats, so they'll be warm when we put them on in the morning. The older children curl around us. Tao nuzzles my neck. He puts a hand under my sleeping shirt. If we're really quiet we can make the night pass in a way that will bring warmth of its own.

"Next time you write to your mother and father," Tao says as his fingers slip into my wetness, "ask if they can get permits for us to visit them in Shanghai."

Beginning in February, I wake up and go to bed hungry. I tell myself that I'm not as hungry as I think I am, that I have a bad Western attitude, and that what I'm seeing and sensing is not real. But some people say this is the worst between the yellow and the green ever. A few want to break up the commune, claiming they were better off when they were responsible for their own land, grain, and families. I keep my mouth shut, but I begin to think that the canteen is no longer there to encourage us to eat for free; it's there to restrict what we're given to eat.

All this leads to new inspections.

"Are you hiding grain?" Brigade Leader Lai demands, as Party Secretary Feng Jin and Sung-ling look through our cupboards.

Tao's mother is small but tough. She looks him straight in the face. "Where could we hide anything?"

That momentarily stumps him.

324

"Have you turned in all your cooking utensils?" Sung-ling asks — woman to woman. "You shouldn't have *any* cooking utensils. By now, they should have been either given to the canteen or melted in the blast furnace."

"Are you asking if we've been cooking?" Fu-shee retorts sharply. "We couldn't cook even if we wanted to. All we have left is our teapot."

I thought my mother and aunt were good liars, but my mother-in-law may be the best, and she knows how to take care of her family. She's been going out to the fields with the younger children and scavenging rice, turnips, and peanuts that were ignored during the hurried harvest. She also saved enough utensils — all hidden in a hole in the floor — to make cornflour buns, which we eat with pieces of dried peppers.

"I smelled food when I came in," Sung-ling continues accusingly.

"You must be smelling the hot water we make to drink, since we no longer have leaves to make tea."

That night I write to my mother:

They say mothers-in-law are awful creatures put on earth to torture their daughters-in-law, but Fu-shee isn't so bad. She's pregnant again. I'm not. I'd like to have a baby. A son, of course. It would make Tao happy. It would please my in-laws. I hope it would make you happy too.

In Chinese, the word *womb* is made up of characters for *palace* and *children*. At night, lying next to Tao, I

325

send propitious wishes to my womb. If marriage doesn't cure my sadness, maybe a baby will.

At Chinese new year, food is found in a neighbor's house during an inspection. The house is torn down. The family has nowhere to go, so they sleep in the ancestral hall. Also, as a result of our neighbors' sloppiness, all the locks in the commune are taken away.

"If you don't give up your locks," Brigade Leader Lai tells us, "we'll take away your doors."

He doesn't stop there. In a flurry of activity, gates and courtyards that separate property are taken down to prevent the hiding or hoarding of food — and to keep everyone and everything visible. If clear lines of sight still aren't available, then the entire house is destroyed. "Our new policy benefits the motherland," Brigade Leader Lai remarks, "since the last remaining metal from hinges and locks can now be smelted and we can use the wood from houses and furniture to stoke the fires in the furnaces." The villa, where he lives, remains untouched.

Three days later, we come home from the fields and find Fu-shee squatting in the corner, a bucket filled with blood and little bits of tissue under her. I'm told to clean the bucket, which is sickening and revolting. I try to be helpful in other ways too, but whatever gains I've made with my mother-in-law disappear. Now she looks at me reproachfully. Soon other pregnant women in the commune walk the other way if they see me or turn their backs on me. Women who haven't given birth are believed to bring bad luck to unborn and newborn babies.

My only friends are Yong and Kumei, who repeatedly tell me not to be concerned. "We're between the yellow and the green," they say, as though that will make me less hungry, pregnant women less likely to ignore me, or my mother-in-law less upset with me. "It's worse than usual, but it happens every year."

I have an American perspective: Should we accept something just because it's always happened that way? I come up with ideas to help ourselves.

"Let's buy a few chicks to raise, so we'll have chickens to lay eggs," I suggest to my husband's family.

"Where would we hide them?" my father-in-law asks. "What would happen when the brigade leader comes for his inspection?"

"We could make tofu," I say. "When I was a little girl, my grandfather made tofu in our bathtub."

"Where will we get soy milk?" my husband asks.

"What's a bathtub?" Fu-shee asks.

"Maybe we could start a wheelbarrow business," I try again. "People always need things hauled to the main road."

"Where will we get money to buy them?" my father-in-law asks.

"I have some money," I say. "We're a family. I want to help in any way I can."

I buy three wheelbarrows. We earn four *yuan* — a little less than two dollars — a day carrying coal, bricks, and grain, until we're told we have to stop. The village cadres criticize us and remind us that no private enterprise is allowed. The next time I make a suggestion to improve our situation, Fu-shee snaps, "Instead of bragging about your money, why don't you buy us some food?"

But I can't buy food, because there's no food to buy. Even if there were, where would I change my American dollars? I'd have to go to Tunhsi, maybe even Hangchow, to do that. The brigade leader would never give me permission.

I could write to my mother about all this, but I don't. How can I? I don't want to hear her say, "I told you so," when even worse recriminations run through my brain.

Joy

Glass Clothes

I wake just after dawn on a Sunday morning in late March. The first thing I see is our new poster of Chairman Mao pasted to the wall. Every house in the commune has the identical poster — Mao floating above a sea of red clouds. I imagine this same poster in every house throughout the country. Nothing can hang above him (which would be insulting), and nothing can mar the surface of the poster (which would prove that the household is not showing the proper respect). I shift my weight, causing the babies and small children snuggled around me to wiggle and squirm. I put a hand on my stomach, trying to calm my nausea. Something I ate or drank has caused me to feel low. I quietly get up off my sleeping mat and go outside.

The spring air is crisp and the sky is bright blue. Standing on the terrace, I see out over several fields of rapeseed. The plants are in full yellow flower, reminding me of the wild mustard that grows in Southern California at this time of year. Plumes of smoke curl into the air from chimneys throughout Green Dragon. I chop wood and start the fire in the outdoor stove. Then I grab a couple of buckets, walk down to the stream for water, haul them back up the hill, and put some of the water on to boil.

My mother-in-law joins me outside. "You still brush your teeth with boiled water?" she asks with false incredulity. "You'll never be one of us until you can drink the water. Here, let me make you some tea with ginger in it to help your stomach. It's always calmed mine."

Since it's Sunday and we have no work to do for the commune, everyone's slow getting dressed. I tell Tao I'm going on ahead to the canteen. He doesn't mind. Spring is all around me — more rapeseed fields, trees in extravagant flower, pink and white petals drifting through the air like snow, and fresh new greenery on the precious few tea bushes that have been spared Brigade Leader Lai's insistence that all land be converted to growing grain. Although we had a tough winter, I'm eagerly anticipating the harvest of the commune's first winter wheat crop in June. We've been close-planting other crops — tomatoes, bok choy, corn, and onions — as we've been instructed by Brigade Leader Lai, putting in two or three times the usual amount of seed per *mu*. We tell ourselves Chairman Mao wouldn't steer us in the wrong direction. Yes, the longer days and warmer weather have done a lot for my mood. Maybe this hasn't been a mistake. Maybe I was just a girl from Los Angeles who truly was suffering from too many years of comfort and waste.

Now, looking at the bright green of the fields against the sky, I wish I could spend the day perched somewhere, painting and drawing. Instead, I eat a small breakfast, go home, and pass the rest of the morning writing letters to my mother and aunt. "Life is OK. The weather is better." Tomorrow I'll wait by the pond for the mailman to arrive. I'll give him my letters and hope he brings some for me.

In late afternoon, the loudspeaker in the main room crackles to life.

"All comrades come to the canteen immediately!" It's the brigade leader's voice. "All comrades come to the canteen immediately!"

No political rally is scheduled, but we do as we're told. As we near the area where the canteen, nursery, and leadership hall are located, we see this will be a commune-wide meeting. It's rare that we're all together at one time, but here we are — nearly four thousand of us. Maybe we're going to "launch a Sputnik" — a twenty-four-hour project inspired by Old Big Brother that will require the participation of the entire commune. Earlier this year, the whole country launched a Sputnik, spending twenty-four hours making more iron than the United States does in a month — or so we were told — but not only was the result worthless but it left communes like ours without many scythes, hammers, or buckets. But no, we haven't been called here to launch a Sputnik.

Brigade Leader Lai stands on a raised platform with his hands clasped behind his back, rocking on his heels, a fierce look on his face. My stomach tightens when I see Yong on her knees next to him, her bound feet hidden under her. A white ribbon has been pinned to her tunic, showing that she's been denounced. Kumei and Ta-ming stand on the edge of the platform. Kumei can smile in any situation, but not now. Her face is pale and her scars have turned lavender with what I take to be fear. What could Yong and Kumei have done to so upset the man who's been living with them in the villa these past months? Party Secretary Feng Jin and Sung-ling also have spots on the platform. They look invigorated and alive with excitement. This isn't a small performance for just Green Dragon Village. This time thousands of faces stare back at them in anticipation.

Brigade Leader Lai raises a bullhorn to his mouth. "Chairman Mao has said there will be no parasites in the New Society," he recites. "Everybody works so everybody eats."

We've heard these things before, but what he says next sounds ominous.

"These three are black elements. Two shared a bed with the landlord. One is the landlord's black spawn. Once this label is affixed, it is passed from generation to generation. They and their descendants will never escape their black labels."

A shudder ripples through me.

He motions to Kumei and Ta-ming. "These two do their best." Then he nudges Yong with his shoe. "But this one is a daily reminder of all that was bad in the old society. Years ago, Chairman Mao ordered all women to unbind their feet. Did the landowner's fourth wife obey?"

Shouts of no come from the crowd. Yong doesn't react. She keeps her eyes cast down.

"We all work in the fields, but what about this one?" the brigade leader asks.

Disgruntled mumbles ripple around me. Everyone seems to have forgotten that Yong came out of the villa to work in the Overtake Britain Battalion with my mother, mother-in-law, and some of the other older women in Green Dragon.

"It's time you remove your bindings and join us. Do it now!" Brigade Leader Lai orders.

Without a word of resistance, Yong shifts to a sitting position, accepting insult and humility in a way that everyone here understands, for in the past only slaves, condemned criminals, those captured in battle, and servants sat on the ground. The crowd falls silent, and people strain their necks as the long bindings come off in loop after loop. The commune's members may have been too poor to have bound-footed women in their families, but everyone knows that a woman's bound feet are her most private parts. "Even more private than that place low down," my mother once said to me when she was telling me about my grandmother's bound feet.

"Now get up!" Brigade Leader Lai yells at Yong.

How can she when her feet have been broken and crushed, held together in their tiny shape for more than forty years? But an order is an order, and the crowd is raw with hatred. Yong wobbles to her feet. Her face remains stoic, but her body sways uncertainly. Ta-ming moves to help her, but Kumei wisely holds him back. As the brigade leader said, the boy is and will always be a black element. How he acts now will save him from harassment in the future.

"Walk!" Brigade Leader Lai shouts. When Yong doesn't move, he yells even louder. "Walk!"

I'm horrified, terrified, and thrust to that place I never want to visit — what happened to my father and my part in his death. The nausea I've been feeling the last few days comes up and burns the back of my throat. I feel sure I'm going to faint.

"Walk!" Red fury infuses the brigade leader's face. "And tomorrow you will join the other comrades in the fields. It's planting time, and we need all hands . . . and feet."

Is he joking? Yong can't possibly work in the fields. She wouldn't last an hour, let alone a day.

"Walk!" he bellows. "Walk all the way back to your villa!"

The crowd takes up the chant. "Walk, walk, walk."

This is much worse than when Comrade Ping-li's husband was struggled against because his wife killed herself by throwing herself in front of the hay cutter. I willingly joined in when the mob attacked him, but Yong, Kumei, and Ta-ming are my friends. They didn't do anything wrong. And maybe, I'm shocked to think now, Ping-li's husband didn't either.

Kumei and Ta-ming are permitted to help Yong down the platform's steps, then they move aside so she can proceed on her own. The crowd parts to let her pass. Tears roll down her cheeks, but she refuses to cry out. I look everywhere, trying to find Tao, but I've gotten separated from him and his family. I need him. Where is he? I try to calculate how far it is to the villa. Yong will have to walk on the footpath next to the stream, past the turnoff to the Charity Pavilion, and then continue to the villa. I can make that trip in about ten minutes, but I don't see how Yong will be able to do it at all.

The people from the other villages that make up the commune begin to disperse to spend the rest of their Sunday in peace with their own families, but the villagers from Green Dragon stay close to Yong, taunting her, spitting on her. I see Tao and grab his arm. He shakes me off as he turns to me. His face is filled with rage and hate. How could I have married him?

I push past a few more people. Up ahead, Yong staggers. When I reach Brigade Leader Lai, Party Secretary Feng Jin, and Sung-ling, I plead with them to end this, but they continue their chants. "Walk! Walk! Walk!" Their faces are as twisted and frenzied as my husband's. An image of my mother comes to my mind. It was on the day the FBI and INS agents accused my father of so many terrible things. My mother showed no fear. She was Dragon strong. The realization that truth, forgiveness, and goodness are more important than revenge, condemnation, and cruelty gives me courage and certainty. I'm dizzy and sick to my stomach, but I straighten my back, walk forward, and take Yong's arm. Seeing what I've done, Kumei takes Yong's other arm. Epithets are hurled our way. I recognize the voices of my husband, his mother and father, his brothers and sisters. Finally, I give in fully to what I've known for months now. I don't belong here. As soon as this is over, I'll go home, tear up the letter I wrote to my mother earlier today, and write a new one, asking her to come and get me. I want to go home to Los Angeles. If I can't go all the way home, then at least I can be with her in Shanghai.

Kumei and I help Yong over the villa's raised stone threshold and into the first courtyard. I fear the villagers will follow us, but they don't. They stay outside, still chanting. We pull Yong through the courtyards and corridors to the kitchen, where she collapses on the ground. I'm going to be sick and I look around frantically, trying to find a bowl or pot, but all those have been given either to the canteen or to the blast furnace. Usually there's a washbasin on the floor, but it isn't here today. In desperation, I run to the low wall that divides the kitchen and the stall where this family once kept their pigs. I lean my head over it and throw up. Once my stomach is empty, I sink to the floor, turn, and look at the others. Yong is white with pain, Kumei looks terrified, and Ta-ming shivers from shock.

"Why?" I manage to ask.

"Food," Kumei answers weakly, leaving me even more confused. "We needed food. We're black elements, so I knew we'd receive less food when rationing began. We live in the villa with the brigade leader. He brought home extra food, but there's been a price."

"You've been . . ." I glance at Ta-ming, not sure how blunt I can be.

"It's a price I've paid before," Kumei says. "It's not as bad as you think, but last night the brigade leader and I had a disagreement. I needed to take care of Ta-ming, but the brigade leader wanted me to *take care of him*."

I close my eyes. Of course, this had to be true. The brigade leader didn't need to live in the villa when he already had the leadership hall — the most secure and comfortable building in the commune. I lived in the villa with Brigade Leader Lai only a few days after I returned to Green Dragon and before I married Tao, but I remember my mother complaining a couple of times about how she kept getting woken up at night by the sound of someone creeping around. That must have been the brigade leader going to and from Kumei's room, or vice versa. There are no secrets in China, not even in a house this large, but why hadn't I understood what was going on before? Because I'm an idiot.

"Have you eaten?" Yong says, her voice barely a whisper. "Do you drink tea?"

These are the two most common questions asked when a guest enters your home. Even in her agony, Yong is a woman far above the barbarians outside the villa's walls.

Kumei, remembering she is also a hostess, gets to her feet and puts water on for tea.

Later, after the peasants leave, I fetch water from the stream. The cold water will help sooth Yong's feet, which are about the most disturbing things I've ever seen. Her toes and midfeet have been broken and rolled over until the toes meet the heels. They've been wrapped in that position for decades. Now they've uncoiled, but only so far. They look like camelback bridges — just the toes and backs of the heels touch the ground. The cadres made her walk barefoot, so her flesh, which looks baby soft from being hidden from the world all these years, is ripped and torn. The color? It does not belong on a living creature. I'm trying to be brave and helpful, but my stomach churns. I wish whatever it was I ate or drank would hurry up and pass through me, just as it did when I first arrived here with Z.G.

I've had questions about Yong and Kumei for a long time. In the past, I made up romantic stories, for Kumei especially. Now that I've helped them in front of everyone, I suppose I'll have a black mark against me too. Since that's the case, I need to know what they did to earn such antipathy from everyone in the commune.

"Why do they hate you so?" I ask.

That's about as direct and American as I can make it. I expect them to shrink from my rudeness, but instead they look at me as if I'm stupid.

"My master was the landowner," Yong answers, fingering the white ribbon she'll wear as a stigma for the rest of her life. "Didn't you know that?"

"I did, but I still don't understand what they have against you."

"Because we're all that's left of his household," Kumei says. "The people think we lived privileged lives, but he was a bad man and we had to endure a lot —"

"I know you feel that way," Yong interrupts. "But I thought he was a good man. He cared for the people here. When the Eighth Route Army came and the soldiers asked him to redistribute his land, he did so without argument."

"I never even heard the word *landowner* before the army came," Kumei says.

"That's because the word didn't exist," Yong explains, her voice warped by pain. "Everyone always called the master *en ren*, which means *benefactor*. But the soldiers gave him a new title — *dichu* — landowner. When the soldiers left, we thought everything would be fine. Instead, the villagers' hidden anger and resentments surfaced."

Kumei holds one of Yong's feet in her hand and with her other hand dribbles cold water over the purple and green skin. Washing bound feet is something that should always be done in complete privacy. Yong should be mortally embarrassed, but she's already been so humiliated in front of the commune that having me here for this most intimate moment is nothing.

"All wars are brutal, especially for women," Yong continues haltingly. "But our lives were not so wonderful even before the War of Liberation and land reform. We entered this house as wives, playthings, entertainment, and servants —"

"My parents were poor," Kumei cuts in. "Poorer than your husband's family." She doesn't wait for me to comment on that. "We had a bad famine when I was little. You think this winter was difficult? It wasn't nearly as terrible as when I was five. When my brother

339

died, I was told I was being given to the master to help pay the death tax. They said I was "going to the benefactor," but I didn't know what they meant or what was required. I was brought into the second courtyard and told to put my forehead on his feet and those of the bound-footed women in the household. He was fifty."

I put a hand over my mouth to cover my surprise as I realize why Sung-ling chose Kumei to play the maiden in our propaganda play and why the cadre was so tolerant of my friend for ignoring the set script. Comrade Ping-li's husband wasn't the only one being struggled against that night. Kumei was also being made to tell her story. How many times has she been forced to do that in one form or another since Liberation? Other moments come to mind too: when we first arrived and I asked Kumei why more people didn't live in the villa and she was so evasive, and the night my mother came to Z.G.'s house and he said that we'd been housed in the villa as punishment. Even when people were telling me things, I wasn't *hearing* them.

I tune back in to Kumei's tale as she says, "I waited on the wives and concubines and took care of their bound feet. Yong was the youngest and prettiest wife —"

"I was also the meanest," Yong confesses. "I was from Shanghai and spoke Shanghainese. The villa was beautiful, but Green Dragon wasn't Shanghai. Our master was never satisfied either. He had many wives and concubines. He had plenty of children. Sons, even.

340

But he wanted to prove his strength to the village. He was the headman, see?"

I don't see, but Kumei goes on to explain it to me. "He had control over us, but as the headman he also needed to prove his strength to everyone in Green Dragon. What better way to do that than to have me in his bed and show that he could give me a son. By then, I was eleven. After the first night, I ran to my uncle and aunt's house in Black Bridge Village. I begged them to let me live with them, but they turned away from me, stepped back into their house, and shut the door. I walked back to Green Dragon, to the house where I'd been born. I sat outside and cried. I rubbed dirt over my face and arms, into my clothes, and into my mouth. And then I stood up and walked back to the villa."

"Why didn't your parents help you?" I ask.

"They starved to death the winter they gave me away," she answers. Then, after a moment, she continues. "I didn't understand the things that went on in the villa. I was a servant, but I was also a concubine."

"You were a little girl!"

Yong has been saying that the landowner was a good man, but how could he have been?

"We treated Kumei worse than the lowest servant, because she was the master's favorite in the bedchamber," Yong admits. Then she addresses Kumei directly. "You had no proper status in the household, and you could never enjoy the luxury that the other wives and concubines did. I remember Third Wife used to poke you with the sharp end of her brooch. She

341

insisted that the kitchen servants feed you only melon rinds and rotten vegetable leaves."

"At least I got something to eat —"

Are they teasing each other?

"And what about that concubine from Hangchow?" Yong rolls right over Kumei, laughing. Despite her pain and humiliation, Yong is managing to find humor in what I think is a ghastly story. "She thought she was so special — one of the great beauties! If her tea was too cold, she threw it on the floor and made you mop it with your clothes."

"If it was too hot, she threw it in my face!" Kumei giggles at the memory. This must be how she got her scars, but before I can ask this, she exclaims, "Oh, I would have gladly traded places with any of you! The things he did! The things he made me do! I don't know how real husbands and wives do this thing, and I will never find out."

Now Yong and I exchange glances. Was what Kumei did then any different than what she's been doing with the brigade leader? Kumei, as far as I can tell, has had sex only out of duty or necessity. Wouldn't that color the experience, especially if she wasn't in love the way I once loved Tao?

"I did many chores," she goes on. "I washed the feet of the wives and concubines. I listened to their bickering. I watched them put on face powder, silks, and jade jewelry. The more I endured, the more beautiful the master said I was. I got pregnant when I was thirteen. I didn't understand what was happening. I was sleepy and sick."

342

"We thought you were lazy," Yong says. "But now I can say you led an animal's existence in those days."

"Finally, a kitchen slave told me what was wrong." Kumei's face pales with her memories. "Pretty soon I felt this thing growing inside me, moving, like I was invaded by a demon. I wanted to disappear into the black depths of death. I would kill myself by swallowing the gold ring the master had given me or by eating food that had turned bad, but these methods didn't promise a sure result. Then I realized the best way to do it. I would drink lye. But my master slapped it away from my lips, which is how I ended up looking like this." Her fingers trail over the scars that run down her neck and under her clothes.

"She has as many scars in her heart as she has on her body," Yong says. "Her life has been dark without a glimmer of light."

"But your life couldn't have been easy either," I say to Yong.

"I was supposed to have a happy life," she concedes. "My mother told me that if I had my feet bound, my swaying walk would look like the drifting mist and I would marry into a good family with at least five other women with bound feet. She promised that, when I married, I would wear a headdress weighing more than a dozen pounds. She said I would never have to leave my home, but if I wanted to for some reason, I'd be carried in a palanquin so no one would see me. She said I would always have four maids to help me, and for a while I had even more than that. She said I would never have to work in the fields —"

"You won't have to do that," Kumei promises. "I'll make sure that doesn't happen."

We know the price Kumei is willing to pay. Yong grabs Kumei's hand in gratitude. We wait for Yong to continue. When she doesn't, Kumei picks up where she left off in her story.

"The master didn't want me to die, but by then what had happened to me was insignificant. The War of Liberation had been won and things were changing."

"Two concubines ran away with soldiers," Yong says. "Number One wife died from an infection. Second Wife, who'd been disgraced by the birth of three daughters, took them to visit relatives in Macau and never came back. Third Wife sneaked away in the middle of the night. Those last days were very hard, very sad . . ."

"Once the soldiers moved on, the villagers looted the villa, looking for gold, jade, and money," Kumei continues. "They carried away furniture and burned most of the books. Then they dug up the family's tombs, so the master's ancestors would have no peace in the afterworld. They let us keep our beds, the master's musical instruments, some quilts, cooking utensils, and a few other things. But the villagers were not done. They dragged the master's sons to the square and used a chopper to lop open their heads until their brains spilled out. The only ones left in these twenty-nine bedrooms were the master, Yong, and me."

"What happened to your master?" I ask, once again letting my American side show.

"After they let him suffer in heartbreak for another four years, they came for him," Kumei recounts. "It was winter. They had him strip down to a thin cotton garment. Then they tied him to the scholar's tree and poured cold water on him. They left him outside all night. By morning he was dead, his clothes frozen into ice on his body. The villagers laughed and said he was wearing glass clothes." She pauses for a moment before going on. "To tell the truth, in some ways he was already on his way to the afterworld, having said goodbye to all that he'd known and cherished. Some nights when we were alone in his room, he had me dress in old clothes. Remember the costume Sung-ling made me wear for the play? That was one of the things the master put on me. The clothes were soft, shiny, and in beautiful colors."

"They were silks, satins, and brocades," Yong translates for her.

It occurs to me that this is not unlike Z.G., my mother, and my aunt — always remembering the past, dressing up, dressing *me* up. But I have to admit that there've been times this winter when I've thought longingly of my Levi's, the fancy clothes Auntie May bought for me, the costumes I wore on movie sets, and the cowgirl outfit I loved as a little girl.

"He would stare at me, play his instrument, and weep," Kumei continues.

"The violin," Yong clarifies, using the English word.

"It was not our Chinese music. I didn't like it, but it always calmed my baby." Kumei pauses, dwelling in the past. Finally, she resumes. "Even when I saw so much bloodshed, even when common sense told me to run away, I couldn't leave my master."

"I couldn't leave him either," Yong adds. "We two had been treated the worst by the other women in the villa, but we were the most loyal."

Kumei sighs.

"The master wasn't a bad man," Yong says again, and this time Kumei nods in agreement.

Maybe the two of you didn't know any better, I think.

"The master could trace his family back thirty generations," Yong says. "He had imperial scholars in his family, which is how he came to own so much land. He took care of the people in Green Dragon. He truly was a benefactor. He was also a fine musician. When I was a girl in Shanghai, my parents gave me piano lessons. Not so easy with bound feet! I met the master at a recital." She turns to Kumei. "Did I ever tell you that?"

Kumei shakes her head, but I'm pretty sure she doesn't know what a recital is anyway.

"The master and I used to play together," Yong adds wistfully. "We were educated, like your mother," she says to me.

Now I understand why Yong and my mother got along so well. Their lives have been different yet similar. Yong has bound feet; my mother was born just four years after footbinding was outlawed. Yong married a wealthy man who brought her to the countryside; my mother married a poor man from the countryside who took her away from the city she loved. Neither had children of her own, yet Yong has Kumei and my mother has me. Both had their lives shattered by political circumstances. Both, for whatever reasons, loved the men they married. But wait . . .

"At my wedding, you talked about how hard the day of your wedding was and how stern the master was when he lifted your veil," I say. "But it sounds like you wanted to get married."

"It wasn't an arranged marriage," Yong replies. "My parents insisted I bind my feet, but in other ways they were very modern. They wanted me to marry for love —"

"But at my wedding you said —"

"*Aiya!* Do you need to have everything explained? I was married to the master and I'm from Shanghai. I can read and play the piano. I'm not like Kumei. I'm not from here. No one will ever have sympathy for me. I say and do what is necessary to survive. If that means lying to a room full of small radishes . . ."

She drifts off, and I allow what she said to sink in. I'm not from here. I come from imperialist America. I can read and write. I express my opinions too freely. I haven't been careful enough . . .

"After the master was killed, new soldiers arrived," Kumei says suddenly. "They asked if I wanted anything. Why would they do that, when no one was supposed to want *things*? So I said I didn't want anything. But the captain looked at my baby and he gave him the violin."

"And you survived. All three of you are still alive." After everything I've heard, I ask, "How can that be?"

"There came a time when all I could think about was how to save myself and Ta-ming," Kumei admits. "I thought I could turn on Yong. I thought about joining others when they taunted her. I thought about running away from this place, but where could I go? What could I do? Beg? Sell my body? Who would buy it? And what about Ta-ming? Didn't I have a duty to him? He was born here. His father was born here. This is Ta-ming's ancestral village. And Yong?" Kumei juts her chin.

"She had too much goodness in her heart to desert me," Yong tells me, as though I didn't understand this already.

"I told myself to look clearly," Kumei says. "The soldiers were simple and polite. They didn't steal from us. They didn't kill the master. It was the villagers who had blood in their hearts, but through it all they hadn't hurt me or my baby. You see, I may have a black label, but I'm from this village, and for years everyone had seen how I was treated. I was one of them. I'd never demanded special foods or expected people to kowtow to me when I walked through the village. Why would anyone kowtow to me? I was emptying and cleaning the villa's nightstools in the fields just like other women. But mostly I couldn't leave, because this was my son's home. Just as this will be your son's home."

"I don't have a son," I say, startled.

Kumei and Yong once again glance at each other.

"You're going to have a baby," Yong says. "Don't you know that?"

I wave my hand back and forth. "Not at all! Not possible!"

Yong's eyes widen. "Didn't your mother teach you about these things before she went back to Shanghai?"

"My mother didn't have to tell me anything," I respond indignantly. "I know how babies are made." But I have a bad feeling, because yes, I do know how babies are made.

"Have you had the visit from the little red sister lately?" Kumei asks, trying to be helpful. "Your mother-in-law says you haven't."

I flush in embarrassment to have what I consider a private subject gossiped about so broadly by my mother-in-law that even Yong and Kumei know about my periods, but it does explain why she's been kinder to me lately.

"I haven't had the visit," I admit. "But I bet you — and even my mother-in-law — haven't had it either. We haven't been eating properly or enough."

"Comrade Joy, you haven't had the visit because you've been doing the husband-wife thing."

And if I didn't already know she's right, I prove it by leaping up, running to the low wall, and throwing up again into what was once the pigsty.

Kumei comes back to her cheerful self. "You're very lucky. Having a baby changes you. Having a son is even better. It gives you value and worth. Sung-ling is going to have a baby too. Have you heard?"

I hadn't heard this piece of gossip either. This leads me to suspect that people in Green Dragon truly must consider me an outsider — and that was before I helped Yong.

349

"You and Sung-ling should become friends, since you're both pregnant," Kumei suggests. Then, as if reading my mind, she adds conspiratorially, "She'll be able to help you after what you did today."

It starts to sink in. A baby. How can I leave Green Dragon now? I cover my face with my hands.

"Make yourself some ginger tea," Yong recommends, confirming that my mother-in-law has known about my condition. "It will settle your stomach."

"You'll need to eat plenty of fish," Kumei advises, "because that's important for the growth of a baby's hair."

"And forgive your husband and his family for their actions earlier," Yong adds. "They were just pulling at the roots of their poverty and hardship. Remind yourself that once they had no rights as human beings."

I reluctantly leave the villa and walk up the hill to my husband's home. *I'm pregnant.* It shouldn't be a surprise, but it is. I suddenly understand something about my mother and aunt that I never did before. They stayed in arranged marriages to men who were not of their social class — and, in Uncle Vern's case, not all there. They stayed in Chinatown, a place they didn't like. They stayed because of me. This, more than anything, shows me the depth of their mother love. They loved me very much and sacrificed for me, just as I'm finding myself filled with love — and fear — and am determined to sacrifice whatever's necessary for my child. Not two hours ago, I wanted to leave this place, but how can I now? My son — every Chinese mother wishes for a son — belongs here. His family is here and

350

his father is here. This is his ancestral village. I must stay here to show my son the depth of my mother love. But how can I do that, after what I saw in Tao's face during the struggle session, after the black mark I earned today helping Yong, after realizing the terrible misjudgments I've made about communism, communes, and the ideals of village life?

I pause on the terrace of my husband's home and look out over the fields. What is it about impending motherhood that causes me to see things with such fresh eyes? I don't know, but how much more rapturous the yellow of the rapeseed looks than it did this morning. For me to survive here — as a wife and mother — I'm going to have to do something for myself, as Auntie May did with her work in Hollywood and my mom did in her care of our home, the café, and all of us. I need to take the images that have been flitting through my brain and put them down. A photograph is too small. A poster is too common. In my mind I see something as big and expansive as the rapeseed fields. While I can't have a canvas that large, I know of the perfect place to paint what I'm feeling: the walls of the leadership hall where Brigade Leader Lai has his meals and stores the grain for the commune. I'm going to have a baby, I'm going to launch a Sputnik, I'm going to right things with my husband, and along the way I hope to protect myself from the peasants and find my true self.

Pearl

The Ladder of Life

It's April — twenty months since I left Los Angeles and five months since Z.G. and I returned from Canton. I've gone back to being a paper collector; Z.G. has gone back to his studio. I'm ignored for the street cleaner I am; he's watched closely to make sure he doesn't stray from mandated subjects. We follow our daily and weekly routines: painting, parties, and political meetings for Z.G.; working, participating in the life of my house, visiting Superintendent Wu at the police station, political re-education, and a little time in my garden for me. Z.G. and I still see each other quite a bit. We've finally become what we always should have been — good friends, brother-and-sister close.

Right now I sit on the front steps of my family home, letting the last of the day's sun warm my face. The season's first roses are in bloom. I hear Dun and the other boarders inside, laughing. I hold two letters in my hand: one from May, one from Joy. I open May's letter first and find twenty dollars. Nothing in her letter has been censored, and obviously no one took the money. We seem to be in a period of openness, but that could change tomorrow. I put the bill in my pocket and open the letter from Joy — my treat for the day.

I'm pregnant.

I take this news with decidedly mixed feelings. I'm thrilled that I'm going to be a grandmother — who wouldn't be? — but I worry about my daughter. Is she healthy? Will she be all right having a baby in the commune? But most of all, is she happy? I hope with all my heart that she is. But that's not enough for me. I want to see her. I want to be part of this miraculous moment. I want to bring gifts, and already I start thinking of things I can make and buy for Joy, the baby, and even all those other children in her household. I'll visit Superintendent Wu tomorrow and see if I can get a travel permit, but first I need to tell Z.G. the news.

I go to my room, change clothes, and then take the bus to his house. I'm prepared to wait for him to return from some party or other, but he's home, which is a nice surprise.

"Joy's going to have a baby," I announce. "I'm going to be a grandma and you're going to be a grandpa."

I try to interpret the emotions that ripple across his features, but I'm unsuccessful.

"I have just stepped up a rung on the ladder of my life," I go on. "So have you."

"A grandfather? I haven't been a father all that long." He's trying to be humorous. Or maybe this news makes him uncomfortable. Being a grandfather may not mesh with his view of himself as a bachelor about town. Then, "It's wonderful! A grandfather!" Then he laughs and I laugh with him.

Later, Z.G.'s driver takes me home in the Red Flag limousine. I say goodbye and enter my house. I get some stationery and find a spot in the salon to sit. Dun is across from me, reading student papers. I'm struck, as I always am, by his dignity during these difficult times. He has a tranquil and orderly way about him, which I find reassuring. The two former dancing girls listen to an evening broadcast on the radio, unaware that their feet move in time to the music. Cook dozes in another chair. I hear the cobbler rummaging in his space under the stairs. The policeman's widow sits cross-legged on the floor, knitting a sweater for one of her daughters.

I write to Joy, telling her how delighted and excited I am. I ask if she needs anything and when it would be good for me to visit. I seal the letter and lean back in my chair to think before I write to May. I recently turned forty-three. I've had many terrible days in my life, experienced many woes, and changed a lot along the way, but now I'm going to be a grandma. I let that word sink in and fill my heart. Grandma! I smile to myself, and then I put my pen to paper.

Dear May,

I'm going to be a yen-yen. That means you're going to be a yen-yen too. Tomorrow I'll go to the shops to see what's available for me to send Joy in preparation. I'll try to buy some powdered baby milk like the kind we gave Joy when she was born, and maybe you can send some to her directly too, as well as a baby thermometer, diaper pins, and bottles.

Will May realize what I'm saying? Even after Joy married, a part of me believed she would eventually see the light and want to go home. Now, she'll never leave, which means I can never leave either. My daughter is here. My grandchild will be born here in the fall. The people in this house will be my companions from now on. For the first time, the prospect of remaining in China for the rest of my life doesn't seem so bad.

I fold the letter and put it in an envelope. I clear my throat, and the boarders look up. "My daughter's going to have a baby. I'm going to be a grandmother."

I let their good wishes and congratulations wash over me. I'm very happy.

The next day, I go to the police station. After a long wait, I'm shown into Superintendent Wu's office. "This is not the day for your regular appointment," he says when he sees me.

"I know, but I'm hoping you can help me. I'd like to visit my daughter."

He rocks back in his chair. "Ah, yes, the daughter you neglected to tell me about when you first arrived in Shanghai."

"I've told you before that I'm sorry about that, but I didn't know where she was, so there was nothing for me to report."

"And now you want to see her. Unfortunately for you, the government isn't issuing travel permits to the countryside right now."

"What if I go to the Overseas Chinese Affairs Commission? You've told me before that as a returning Overseas Chinese I'm allowed to travel wherever I want as long as I asked you first."

He throws up his hands. "Things change."

"My daughter is going to have a baby —"

"Congratulations. I hope you get a grandson."

I've known this man for some time now. He's been promoted from superintendent third class to superintendent second class. He's warmed up a bit since we first met, but he's still a stickler for the rules. He'll never accept a bribe and he'll make sure I'm punished if I offer one. So when I ask my question, he knows I'm looking for a practical answer.

"What will I need to do to get a travel permit?"

"Go to your block committee. If they give you a written endorsement, I might be able to help you. But, comrade, hear what I'm saying. *Might*."

Despite his caution, I leave the police station feeling optimistic. Cook is the director of our home and is very powerful on the block committee. He'll make sure I get a positive recommendation.

Except it doesn't turn out that way. The two former dancing girls accuse me of being a secret capitalist. "She keeps vestiges of her decadent past in her room," one of them tells our neighbors. "She brings home posters of herself and her sister from former times."

"Even little pieces — an eye or a finger," adds her roommate.

This is startling news, because it means they've been in my room when I'm not there. What else have they found?

"She wears clothes from before Liberation." This comes from the cobbler. "She puts them on to teach one of our boarders English!"

"And she hides food," the widow chimes in. "She only shares with us when it suits her."

In my mind, I haven't done anything wrong. After all, I strip posters off walls as part of my job, I wear my old clothes so I won't be wasteful, I teach Dun because he asked me to, and I share food to be a good comrade. I've heard of others who fight back when they're criticized, believing they're innocent or morally, ethically, or politically right, and I want to fight back, but that won't help me get a travel permit to visit my daughter.

Following the slogan "Leniency to those who confess," I rush to make full disclosure: "I lived in an imperialist country, I'm too accustomed to weak Western ways, and my family was bad." They seem fairly satisfied with that, but I'm sure I'll be accused again. As worried as I am about Joy, I'm thankful she's in the countryside, where she's liked for who she is and not under suspicion for where she came from.

Of course, all this is reported to Superintendent Wu. "You have no hope of getting a travel permit right now," he tells me when I see him. "Just wait. Behave. And maybe you'll be able to get one in time for your grandchild's birth."

I'm horribly upset, but what can I do?

I was foolish to keep the scraps of May and me I'd stripped off walls in the box under my bed, and I need to get rid of them in a way that won't draw more attention to me. I used to knit and sew for Joy when she was a girl, and now I've hit on a project — making homemade shoes for her and her family — that will also prove to the boarders who complained about me that I was actually being a good and frugal socialist in gathering this particular paper and that I am arm in arm with our comrades in the communes. I have two friends in the house, and I decide to ask for their help. The following Sunday, I first approach Dun. I've come to rely on him for many things, and he is, as always, happy to see me at his door.

"We have a good time together, you and I," I begin. "You've shown me all the places I can go for tastes of the past."

And truly he has: to the last White Russian café in the city to serve borscht, to a little place to buy cream so I can make butter, to a flea market to buy bread pans so I can make my own bread for toast.

"I enjoy spending time with you," he says. "I'd like us to do more things together, if you'd like."

"I'd like that very much," I respond. Then I tell him about my project.

"That's perfect!" Dun says. "But do you know how to make shoes?"

"No, but Cook does."

Even though Cook let me be attacked by the block committee, I know he loves me very much. In fact, as I think about it, he may have let the criticism against me be voiced so that I wouldn't be attacked in a harsher or more dangerous way sometime down the line. Maybe Cook was planning ahead to the baby's birth. After all, how many travel permits can one person get?

I go to my room, get my box out from under the bed, and then Dun and I go downstairs to the kitchen. Since it's Sunday afternoon, most of the boarders are out — window-shopping, visiting friends and relatives, strolling along the Bund — but Cook is home, too old and frail for excursions. He gives me a toothless grin and rises to put on water for tea for his Little Miss.

"Director Cook," I say, addressing him formally, "when I was a little girl you used to make soles for shoes right here on the kitchen table. Do you remember that?"

"Remember? *Aiya!* I remember how mad your mama used to get at me. She didn't like the mess. She said she'd give me a pair of the master's shoes if I'd stop mixing rice paste in her kitchen —"

"Do you think you could show us how to make soles? I'd like to make shoes to send to Joy and the children in her family. Most of them don't have any shoes."

I open the box and dump the scraps of May and me on the table. Cook gives me another toothless grin. "Smart, Little Miss, very smart."

Cook gets up and makes a paste from rice. Then he shows Dun and me how to glue sheet upon sheet of paper in a time-consuming process to build a sole. The final step involves sewing cloth onto the soles, which I'll do later in my room. What could be tedious work becomes a bit of a game as we try to guess which mouths, eyes, ears, and fingers are May's and which are mine. Dun is particularly adept at singling out pieces of me in the pile, which pleases me greatly.

"Paper collectors from the feudal era would have been very upset to see us doing this," Dun says. I watch his fingers as he picks up another of my noses, brushes it with glue, and applies it to the sole he's been making for Jie Jie, the oldest of Tao's sisters.

I smile and shake my head. He can't help himself. He's such a professor. "Which part?" I ask. "That we're making shoes or that we're using these funny pieces of paper?"

"Both," he replies. "Does a paper sole show reverence for lettered paper? Not at all! You should never tread on lettered paper."

"But not all of this is lettered," I point out. And it's true. While there's writing on some of the slivers of May and me, most of the writing was at the bottom or along the sides of beautiful-girl posters.

"Nevertheless, the whole piece of paper was an advertisement," Dun responds. "In olden days, this would have been considered a deliberate act of disrespect. Our lives could have been shortened by five years —"

"Ten years!" Cook corrects.

"Because we'd go to jail?" I ask.

"Nothing so simple," Dun replies. "Maybe lightning would find you. Maybe you'd develop runny eyes or go blind or be born blind in your next life —"

"I remember a woman in my village who hid coins in her socks," Cook says. "The coins had words on them. She tripped, fell in a well, and died."

"And I remember a warning my mother gave me as a boy," Dun adds. "She said, 'If you use lettered paper to kindle the fire, then you will receive ten demerits in the underworld and you will be given itchy sons.'"

"As a paper *collector*, I should be eligible for an incredible reward then," I say.

Dun nods. "My mother always said that he who roams the streets, collecting, storing, ritually burning, and then depositing lettered paper into the sea will receive five thousand merits, add twelve years to his life, and become honored and wealthy. His children, grandchildren, and great-grandchildren will be virtuous and filial too."

I apply several paper fingers along what I think will be the arch of a shoe for Joy. "All I do is strip paper from walls and clean alleyways," I admit. "So maybe I don't have reverence for lettered paper. Even so, I think what we're doing right now is good. Joy may never know what's layered here, but I hope she'll feel my love."

We work companionably for a while, until Dun bursts out, "I have an idea! What is paper for? Advertising, of course." His hand sweeps across the table where May's and my eyes, mouths, noses, fingers, and earlobes lie in little piles. "But what else?"

"It can be burned, to keep us warm," Cook offers tentatively. "You can sleep under it. Or on top of it." He really is red through and through. "You can eat it, if you're hungry enough —"

"You can use it to make cigarettes," Dun jumps in, and then he turns to me expectantly.

"For books," I say hesitantly. "To make Bibles. To print money." I'm still unsure where he's going with all this.

"But what's the most important thing?" he asks. "Why even have reverence for lettered paper? It's because the words themselves have reverence. The things my mother taught me are what made me want to read books, become a professor, and teach others to love the written word. She considered words to be magical —"

"Like prayers that were written and then burned," I say. "My mother believed that was the most effective way to communicate with her gods. Of course, at the mission we were taught that this kind of thinking was just another form of idolatry."

"You made your mother very sad by visiting those people," Cook reminds me.

It's true. My going to the Methodist mission upset my mother and father, but I did it anyway. I learned English and manners, but what I learned most of all was faith. I don't regret that for a minute.

Dun bunches a hand into a loose fist and taps it lightly on his lips, thinking. Then, "But don't you think that we *still* believe in the efficacy of written characters? We still write *peace, wealth,* and *happiness* on red paper to hang on doors at the New Year. Pearl, you said you hoped Joy would feel your love, but what if you wrote that to her and then glued it in her shoes?"

"For what purpose? She'll never know it's there."

"But you will." Dun gets up, opens a drawer, and pulls out paper and ballpoint pens so the words won't smear when they get wet. "Let's send messages to everyone for whom we're making shoes. You said the shoes I'm making are for Joy's oldest sister-in-law, a girl of about fourteen or fifteen." He starts to write, reading aloud his message. "You are very pretty. I hope you get married and have a happy life."

Since Cook is illiterate, I help him with his note. Then I write a secret message to Joy and paste it into the middle of the sole. I feel the warmth from Dun's gaze as I quickly paper over my words with a pair of my eyes.

Joy

Launching a Sputnik

I've prepared everything as best as I can: I've rehearsed my request. I've made drawings and mixed pigment samples. I've washed my hair and put on clean clothes. I wish I could go to the leadership hall to speak to the village cadres about my idea now, while it's still cool and I'm still clean, but that's not possible. I pack my satchel and then join my husband and his family as they leave the house and walk down the hill. It's summer again. It's already porridge hot and with about as much visibility. I swat at the mosquitoes that buzz around my head and land on my arms, but what's the use? There are more of them than I could ever kill.

As the others continue along the path toward our new work site, I stop at the villa to pick up Kumei. Yong, thankfully, won't be coming with us. After Brigade Leader Lai made a fuss in front of the whole commune, he confiscated Yong's bindings and hung them outside the villa, where they flutter like streamers in the breeze. He also took her bound-foot shoes — all tiny, all in brilliant colors, all with fine embroidery — and nailed them to the main gate, where they're fading from the sun and rain. Now Yong is reduced to crawling on her hands and knees to get from room to room. The good life in the commune is not good for everyone, which has helped me focus more strongly on my plan.

Kumei doesn't have much to say this morning as we walk together, and I'm too nervous about my plan to make small talk. We reach the work site and go our separate ways. A few weeks ago, when Brigade Leader Lai announced we would be building something together — as a commune — I hoped it would be a proper canteen. Instead, he ordered us to construct a road from the place where the bus lets people off several miles from here to the center of the commune. Weeding, aerating furrows, and picking away the pests that attack the crops have been abandoned so we can dig out boulders, shovel dirt, and compact earth. All this work is done by hand, and we're still getting by on reduced rations, so the sun makes me woozy, and my shoulders, back, and legs quickly tire from the labor. I'm luckier than most. As a pregnant woman, I'm given extra food. Fortunately, I'm over the worst of my morning sickness and have been able to keep my meals in my stomach. My belly is slowly swelling, but it's not terribly noticeable under my loose cotton blouse. Everyone knows everything in the commune, though, so I get plenty of advice.

"Don't attend magic shows," a woman struggling to lift a basket of dirt next to me recommends, "because if

365

you see through any of the magician's tricks he'll cast a spell on you out of embarrassment."

"Don't climb any fruit trees," another counsels, "because if you do, they won't bear fruit in the coming year."

And on it goes. I shouldn't quarrel with anyone (but I should accept criticism), go on any journeys (which I can't do anyway since I don't have an internal passport), or step on any goose droppings (I tried not to do that even before I got pregnant).

A whistle announces the lunch break. While the others line up for rice and vegetables served by the side of the new road, I hurriedly grab my satchel and set out for the leadership hall. How different everything looks from when I first came here two summers ago. This year's corn crop should be shoulder high, with the kernels filling the air with a warm and fragrant scent, but what I see is short, stubby, and patchy, as though the fields have severe cases of mange. The reasons are simple and all tied together.

First, although scientists have announced that sparrows eat more insects than seeds, Chairman Mao has insisted we continue to kill the birds. Now the only things getting fat around here are the swarms of locusts and other insects that eat contentedly at the free canteen that our fields have become. Second, close planting. When any of the farmers who grew up in this area ask Brigade Leader Lai about the wisdom of this practice, he says, "Trust in the people's commune." Third, when we inquire what he's promised the government this year, he answers, "We'll deliver ten times the normal grain yield!" That's where our fear comes in. How can we possibly give that much grain when our yield has gone down not up? If we turn over our harvest to meet the brigade leader's "exaggeration wind," then this winter will be far worse than last. To protect ourselves, we deliberately left as much in and on the ground as we could when we brought in the early crops, in case we need to rely on gleaning the fields for food next winter.

I reach the center of the commune. I take a breath to calm my nerves and give me courage. Then I stride purposefully to the leadership hall in the cinder-block building. A guard stands before the door.

"May I see Brigade Leader Lai?" I ask.

"Why?" the guard, a young peasant from Moon Pond Village, asks in response.

"I'd like to present something to the brigade leader as well as to Party Secretary Feng Jin and his honorable wife."

I haven't answered the guard's question, only expanded my request. His jaw muscles tighten. Give a low man one ounce of power and he'll throw ten thousand pounds of bricks on your head. He yells at me. When he loses steam, I state my request again. He gets angrier. Brigade Leader Lai comes to the door. He wears a cloth napkin tucked into his shirt.

"What's this noise? Don't you know I'm eating?"

"Brigade Leader, I want to launch a Sputnik," I announce.

"You?"

I give a sharp nod, exuding confidence.

"No," he says.

"Please hear me," I persist. "My idea will bring important cadres to the Dandelion Number Eight People's Commune."

This is a bold claim, but one I hope will elicit a good response from the brigade leader. In the New China, no one is supposed to seek personal glory, but individual recognition is something all cadres desire. He looks me up and down, calculating: she's a backsliding imperialist, but she's also the daughter of a famous artist, she looks professional, she has a satchel slung over her shoulder that contains . . . what?

"Let me finish my lunch," he says, having made his decision. He orders the guard to fetch Party Secretary Feng Jin and Sung-ling. "Have them come here in fifteen minutes." To me, he adds, "Wait here." Then the brigade leader closes the door and goes back to his meal.

Fifteen minutes later, the guard escorts the three of us into the building's private dining room. The smell of food — meat — is tantalizing and painful at the same time. I glance at Sung-ling. As Kumei suggested, Sung-ling and I have become friends. When Sung-ling says her baby likes to kick, I tell her my baby kicks even more. When I say I'm going to have a son, she tells me she's going to have twin boys. I've worked hard to establish this good-natured banter, because I need Sung-ling to help me. But now, as I look at her, I wonder if she can. She was plump when we first met. Now she's pregnant and losing weight. As village cadres, she and her husband should have the same benefits as the brigade leader. Instead, they've decided to continue eating with the rest of us in the canteen.

The brigade leader motions for them to sit. I'm meant to stand before them as the supplicant I am.

"All right then," Brigade Leader Lai says in his rough voice. "What do you want?"

"We should launch a Sputnik by painting a mural to show our pride in our new road," I begin. They stare at me, sure I have more to say. "Chairman Mao says murals can teach people. They're visible reminders of what the masses should and shouldn't do."

"We don't have money to buy supplies," Brigade Leader Lai says.

What a strange response. Is he fishing for a bribe?

"That's all right, because we're going to make our own pigments." I open my satchel and pull out little jars of color. "This yellow I made using the flowers from the scholar's tree in Green Dragon's main courtyard. This red comes from the red soil in the hills. The black comes from the soot left over from the blast furnaces. We can use lime for white. I made blue and purple from flowers. Green is easy. I soaked some of our tea leaves to extract the color."

Sung-ling smiles appreciatively. "You're using what we have around us."

But it's not because I've embraced some Communist lesson or other. Rather, I'm doing exactly what my frugal mother and practical father taught me to do in

Chinatown: conserve, manipulate, and utilize what others consider worthless.

"Yes, yes, but what is the subject?" Brigade Leader Lai asks. "This comrade has many black marks against her. How can we trust her to paint something that will not be reactionary?"

"I want to show the glories of the Dandelion Number Eight People's Commune. Here, let me show you." I hand him my drawings. "Look, here is our magnificent harvest with the road leading right to it. And I want to do a portrait of you, Brigade Leader. Our dreams of socialism wouldn't be coming true if not for your leadership."

The brigade leader's chest expands, but the Party secretary has lived in Green Dragon his entire life. He knows who's who and what's what.

"Tao is the artist in your family," he notes. "Why isn't he here?"

The short answer is because he doesn't know what I'm doing. I've been working alone, sneaking up to the Charity Pavilion when I should have been washing clothes in the river or doing other chores. My announcement that I was pregnant didn't bring the happy change in attitude toward me that I was anticipating. My husband and my in-laws have an interest in me now that I'm pregnant with what we all hope will be a son, but they've also been wary of me since the struggle session against Yong. They've been walking a fine line between possession of me and the baby and absolute distrust and distance. But I've thought about this and know how to respond.

"My husband asked me to come here. He's the better artist, but he's also the harder worker. That's why he's building the road and I'm here before you."

The three nod approvingly, but how will Tao react to what I've just said? What I wish is that he'll regard me as a good wife who supports him. Maybe that will happen, and maybe he'll happily take credit for the mural, especially if he thinks word of it will reach others even higher than those in this room. Oh, but I do sound bitter.

"Where will this mural go?" Brigade Leader Lai asks.

"There's only one place," I answer. "On the outside of this building. You have four walls that will now sing the praises of our commune."

"Think of the effect it could have on members of the commune," Sung-ling says tentatively. "They'll pass it every day when they come to eat, visit the clinic, leave their children at school —"

"More than just people in our commune!" I interrupt. "Everyone in the county will come to see it! They'll walk on our new road and see what good jobs our cadres have done."

The looks on their faces! I once respected and feared them. Now I see them — even Sung-ling, my supposed friend — as clowns.

"Launching a Sputnik is a very specific program," Party Secretary Feng Jin, the most cautious of the three, observes. "Twenty-four hours is not very long to create such an extraordinary amount of work. We want to launch a Sputnik" — he glances at the others uncertainly — "not an oxcart."

He doesn't have to tell us this. Everyone in the room knows how pointless the launching a Sputnik projects have been — building a well in twenty-four hours only to see it collapse in the first rain or sewing pants for everyone in the commune in twenty-four hours only to see mismatched pant legs sewn together.

Reminded of the potential traps, Brigade Leader Lai adds a new concern. "This can't be an individual project. There's no place for individual thinking or acting in the New Society."

I don't smile, but I surely want to because they've said exactly the things I predicted they would.

"That's why I came to you," I say. "Launching a Sputnik means improvising with what we have around us, but it also requires many hands. I respectfully ask that you assign a work team to the project. I propose we launch four Sputniks — one for each side of the building."

"That's four days!" the brigade leader exclaims. "And you're pregnant. The Party says that expectant mothers will have light work."

What a joke! Does he think painting a mural is harder than building a road under the blistering sun? Does he think it's worse than having my shoulders swell from carrying heavy loads of rocks and dirt in buckets strung from poles in the struggle to remake nature, with little to eat? I've gone from optimism to disillusion very quickly. The Tiger leaps, but this time I keep my head on straight.

"Night and day, we make revolution!" I shout. "We will work longer than four days if necessary! We want to honor our commune cadres!"

"You're sure it won't cost us anything?" This comes from the brigade leader, who sleeps in the villa and eats wonderful meals by himself here in this building.

"Even if I buy a few materials," I say, "they won't cost more than two *yuan*. Remember, 'More, faster, better, and cheaper!'"

The brigade leader grins. He'll be getting what he thinks is a paean to his accomplishments, just like Chairman Mao has all over the country with his giant posters, for under a dollar.

Four walls, four Sputniks. We'll do one mural each Tuesday during the month of July to cover the leadership hall's four walls.

"My comrade-wife has been very helpful to me in planning my Sputnik," Tao tells Kumei, Sung-ling, and the rest of the work team assigned to us. He smiles with his big white teeth, and everyone smiles back at him. Naturally, he thinks this is his project and he takes over all planning. He sketches some new ideas, which follow the five accepted themes for murals: the natural beauty of the motherland, scientific advances, technical knowledge and production, babies to promote population growth, and happy families. Everyone likes them, except for Sung-ling.

"These are festive pictures," she says, "but this is not what the committee approved." She gives me a

373

questioning look. She may not know much about art, but apparently she can tell the difference between what Tao and I have drawn. I make my face as bland as possible. I may be a comrade with a questionable background, but I'm a wife first. Sung-ling understands that. After all, although she is a cadre in her own right, her husband is the Party secretary. Mao may say that women hold up half the sky, but it is the lesser half. Still, Tao must tread carefully. In an effort to show his socialist spirit, he graciously divides the walls between the two of us. We will each get one small wall and one long wall to paint as we wish.

In the first twenty-four-hour period, we paint the first of Tao's murals. The hours during the day are brutal. Powdery dust rises from the scorched dirt. The air is oppressively hot. It feels as though we're laboring inside a brick oven, but at least we aren't building the road. We work with people who have little sense of perspective, shading, or proper dimensions. That's all right, because the Great Leap Forward has lost these sensitivities too. In Tao's mural, fishermen row on the sea in peanut shells the size of sampans (to show how great the peanuts are in the New Society) and pull in huge nets filled with gigantic leaping fish.

"Hurry up, hurry up," Tao shouts at us. "We can't fall behind. We have only four hours left!"

I did not know he had such ambition.

The following week, I lead the team to paint a pond on my small wall. On the surface, at the center of the mural, is a giant lotus. No one can complain about the size, which is in keeping with the exaggerations of the Great Leap Forward. The lotus symbolizes purity, because it rises out of the mud but looks pristine. The one I paint, however, is spattered and bruised. Flying above it all is Chang E, the moon goddess, looking down with tears in her eyes. When people ask why she weeps, I explain that her tears of happiness are filling the pond and cleansing the lotus. In my heart I believe she weeps for the people of China.

I'm pregnant, living in a depressing place, trying to make the best of a bad situation, and hoping that working together will help change things between Tao and me. It's unrealistic, I know, but so are Tao's dreams. He's looking at the mural as a way to leave the commune and go to Peking or Shanghai. "People will want to meet the artist," he tells the pretty girls who gather around him when he paints. "Not everyone will come here. I will need to go to them." He flirts with the girls, but he treats me with increasing formality — as a woman with black marks against her who happens to be the mother of his unborn son. I try to pretend I don't care.

During the third week, Tao paints his long side of the leadership hall. The subject is one we all wish we could see: rice paddies stretching to the horizon, fat children climbing ladders to reach wheat heads, and babies sitting next to tomatoes larger than they are. Tao does a good job with the brigade leader's portrait, placing him amid the happiness.

A week later, inspired by our project, Brigade Leader Lai decides to launch a whole new Sputnik.

On the night of the full moon, while some of us paint the last mural — my painting — the rest of the commune works on the road, trying to reach the leadership hall by dawn.

People say there is poetry in painting and painting in poetry. I want my mural to stand on its own, yet be read differently by different viewers. I've been thinking about something Z.G. once said to me: People are shaped by the earth and water around them. I want my painting to reflect this idea. I outline the central figure in black and then ask my husband to fill it in: Chairman Mao as a god towering over the land and the people, removed from the masses, challenging nature itself. This is my secret criticism, but I'm sure the brigade leader, Party secretary, and other members of the commune will take it at face value. I assign groups of two and three to work on the sky and on the background, where figures rise up out of China's earth — made from this land's red mud to be molded into obedient peasants. I give Kumei the important job of leading a team as they paint humungous radishes, which again will make my painting recognizable to the members of the commune as a piece of Great Leap Forward art. Corncob spaceships filled with laughing astronaut babies — a supposed tribute to China's agricultural and technical advances meant for the people of the Dandelion Number Eight People's Commune, who have never seen an airplane let alone a spaceship like Sputnik — fly through the sky.

That night, a full moon illuminates the fields around us. The road comes closer and closer. My mother-in-law brings more red paint made hastily from the soil. We can never use too much red, and it feels as if it glows in the moonlight.

On the left side of the mural, I paint a tree with its branches spread to form a cross. In the twists of the bark hangs an abstract Jesus, his head low, a slash of green representing the crown of thorns. On the right side, I paint another tree, so that the whole mural is framed by branches, roots, and leaves. An owl sits on an upper branch with one eye shut.

What is my message, if anyone asks? I will say that China's best people come from this good earth, while the owl gazes at the world, offering its wisdom. But to me there are deeper meanings about blame, tolerance, and forgiveness. Yes, I've used too much black in contrast to the false bright red of the rest of the mural. Yes, I've painted an owl, which sees everything and is fooled by nothing. And yes, I have used a cross and Jesus upon it to show the suffering of the people. As far as I know, no missionaries ever came to this area. So if anyone asks, I will say that I've painted a tree god.

I think the mural will magically change my life. It doesn't. No dignitaries come to the Dandelion Number Eight People's Commune, Brigade Leader Lai doesn't win any prizes for being a model leader, Tao doesn't like me any more than he did before, and the people on the work teams quickly forget that I got them off the road crew for a few days.

Pearl

A Rose-Petal Cake

National Day — China's Independence Day — takes place on October 1. This year — 1959 — is also the tenth anniversary of the People's Republic of China, so the holiday is going to be the biggest and best yet. People labor day and night to beautify Shanghai. The city thrums with shoveling, hammering, and military music. Flags, lanterns, colored lights, and drapery festoon buildings, lamp poles, and bridges. Everything is in red, of course. An enormous arch is being built on the Bund, flanked by trees and flower beds. My work unit doubles its time on the streets, cleaning, stripping, and collecting every piece of paper we can find. I'm swept up by the enthusiasm around me and genuinely excited for and proud of my home country.

But as they say, everything always turns to the opposite. Just as I'm feeling truly good about being in China, we start to have food shortages in the city. In my household, we're each allotted nineteen pounds of rice, a few tablespoons of cooking oil, and half a pork chop each month, which means, among other things, that the bickering in my family home is even worse than usual. I try to keep jealousies from boiling over by bringing home the occasional bag of rice or brown sugar bought at an exorbitant price on the black market or at the store for Overseas Chinese, where I can use my special certificates, for which I'm very grateful these days.

All this makes me worry about Joy. Could she be suffering from the same food shortages that we're experiencing in Shanghai? I tell myself not to fret, because how could the members of a commune not have food? They grow it! But I'm a mother and I agonize. I write to Joy to ask how she is. "How are you feeling?" I send candies and dried fruit. "Tao's brothers and sisters might like these." But I don't hear back from my daughter. In fact, I haven't heard anything since she wrote to tell me she was pregnant, nearly five months ago. This causes me great apprehension and keeps me up late at night with anxiety. I tell myself she's busy with Tao and preparing to have the baby. I tell myself to be calm, but I'm not calm. I have to see her. To see her, I'll need a travel permit, but I'm still not having any luck with that.

I go to Z.G.'s house to see if he can help me, but even he can't get a travel permit. I write to May about my concerns. She writes back two weeks later that she's heard from Joy and that she sounds fine. I relax a bit, but I don't lose my desire to see my child during this special time in her life. In the coming weeks, I return several times to Superintendent Wu's office. I tell him I still haven't heard from my daughter and I ask again for

379

a travel permit. During one of my visits, he informs me that almost no permits are being issued for travel.

"It's as though they don't want anyone to go to the countryside," he says.

"Why would that be?"

Superintendent Wu doesn't know. But eventually he makes some inquiries — refusing to tell me where — and reports back that Joy is fine.

"Fine?" That's what May said too, but I'm Joy's mother, and something doesn't feel right. "If she's fine, why hasn't she written to me?"

He doesn't have an answer. I begin to mark time by how many more days until the baby's due.

October 1 — national day — finally arrives. It's a golden autumn day, and I try to imagine what my daughter looks like in her eighth month of pregnancy. I imagine the commune commemorating the occasion with firecrackers, a big banquet, and the speeches in Peking broadcast over the loudspeakers. And then I tuck those images into my heart and get ready for the celebration here. Months ago, Z.G. invited me to go with him to Peking to see the festivities. He said we'd have a place with Mao on the dais to watch the parade and hear the speeches outside the Forbidden City. I admit it would have been a once-in-a-lifetime experience, but I stay in Shanghai to be closer to Joy in case I'm suddenly awarded a travel permit. I'll celebrate with Dun, the other boarders, and Auntie Hu.

Our entire household dresses in matching red shirts and blouses, and then we head into the streets. We wave little red flags as the parade passes us. We see seas of children in white shirts, blue pants or skirts, and red bandannas tied around their necks. Brigades of the People's Red Army march in brisk formation. The entire membership of one commune after another proceeds along the route, fists raised or waving red flags. Floats highlighting the country's economic and military achievements move with a dignified air. For everything that's bad here, for every moment I miss my home in Los Angeles, there are times like this when I feel great pride for what China has accomplished in ten years.

Dun and I leave before the local speeches begin and meet Auntie Hu at her house, since she can't be on crowded streets on her bound feet. We sit in her salon, and she serves us rose-petal cake.

"Auntie Hu, you always have the best pastry," I say after taking a bite. "How do you get something like this with the shortages?"

Auntie Hu's eyes crinkle with pleasure. "I'm always trying to find the good old days in these bad new days. Come, lean close, and I'll tell you." I do as I'm told, and Madame Hu whispers, "Do you remember the Russian bakery on the Avenue Joffre, where your mother always bought your birthday cakes? One of the Chinese helpers now uses those recipes to make cakes in his apartment. He sells them only to the best people, those who can keep a secret. Shall we get one for Dun's birthday? Do you know when it is?"

She relaxes back into her chair and stares affectionately at Dun, who sits on one of the salon's velvet sofas, reading a book and feigning indifference to the big secret. Dun started accompanying me to Auntie Hu's a few weeks ago after I told him about her collection of books in English. Auntie Hu took an instant liking to Dun, treating him like the son she lost years ago. The way she's embraced Dun has made me surprisingly happy, as though I'm receiving approval from my own mother.

"Do you like chocolate cake or do you prefer vanilla?" she innocently asks Dun. "Or do you prefer more exotic cakes — grapefruit, butter cream, or rum?"

"I never tasted cake until I came here, Madame Hu," Dun answers. "Even a single bite is a treat for me."

These days a bite of anything made with sugar, eggs, milk, and flour is something beyond a "treat."

"I wonder if we could send one of these cakes to Joy," Auntie Hu says. "Wouldn't a pregnant woman love a rose-petal cake?"

"I'm sure she'd love it," I say, but do I tell her how worried I am about Joy?

"Pearl-ah, I know you too well," Auntie Hu observes. "Don't keep things from me. Is something wrong with Joy?"

"Everything's fine," I answer brightly, trying to hide my concern. "May wrote to me just the other day to say that Joy has been writing to her and asking for the strangest things."

"May writes to Joy?"

"Of course, all the time. And Joy answers." And the knowledge of this is painful (why is Joy writing to May instead of to me?) and reassuring (Joy really must be all right). "Joy has asked her auntie to send Oreos, Hershey's milk chocolate almond bars, and Bit-O-Honey. Do you know those sweets?" Auntie Hu remembers Hershey's from the old days but not the others. "Well, this — more than anything — tells me Joy is pregnant and happy." I'm practically quoting May's last letter, in which she wrote, "Oh, the cravings we women have!" "May also sent a layette she bought at Bullock's Wilshire. That's one of the finest stores in Los Angeles," I explain. "My grandchild will be the most stylish baby in the commune!"

Dun and Auntie Hu laugh with me. What is a peasant baby going to do with a sleeping gown, booties, cap, and receiving blanket?

"May." Auntie Hu lets out her breath in a tolerant sigh. "She always liked to shop. What else? Tell me more."

"May's been taking care of my café," I answer, happy to shift the conversation away from Joy. "She just got a beer and wine license. She says we have more customers now."

"That's good. You'll go home to a successful business."

"I've told you before I'm not leaving China. My life is here now, with my daughter and her baby."

Auntie Hu frowns, and I rush on. "But May's biggest news has to do with her own business. She's still renting props and costumes to movie productions, but television shows are now coming to her too. You'll never guess what happened. They want Chinese faces in their shows too! May got a job, playing a housekeeper on a doctor show. If only they knew what a bad housekeeper she is in real life!"

We all chuckle. Then Auntie Hu gets up to turn on the radio so we can listen to the speeches being broadcast from the capital. "The Chinese have changed from slaves living in a hell on earth into fearless masters of their fates," Premier Chou En-lai tells the country. "The imperialists ridicule our Great Leap Forward as a big leap backward. But let me tell you this: The European imperialists tried to carve us up. The Japanese aggressors wanted to devour us. Now the United States is trying to isolate and exclude us from international affairs. That policy is more of a failure with every passing day. We have full diplomatic relations with thirty-three countries, economic relations with ninety-three countries, and cultural contacts and exchanges with one hundred and four countries. How is all this swift, flying progress to be explained?"

Auntie Hu doesn't care to hear the answer and gets right back up to turn off the radio, saying, "I'd much rather have Dun read to us."

We spend the rest of the afternoon drinking tea, chatting, and listening as Dun reads to us from *Wuthering Heights* — Auntie Hu's favorite. It's so peaceful here, and it makes me happy that Dun and I can share this time together without Cook or the other boarders watching and listening to us.

Later, even though Auntie Hu has servants, I take our tray of cups and saucers to the kitchen. Auntie Hu follows, swaying on her tiny feet. She shoos her servants out of the kitchen and then she turns to me, her gentle features filled with concern. "How worried are you about Joy?"

"Very worried. I don't understand why I haven't received a letter from her. Even one in which the censors crossed out every word would be better than nothing."

"You went through this silence before when you were waiting for Joy to return to Shanghai with Z.G.," she tries to reassure me.

"That was different. She didn't know I was in China."

When Auntie Hu nods sympathetically, I ask her the question that's been gnawing at me lately. "Do you think Joy suddenly prefers May — who gave birth to her — over me now that she's approaching birth herself? Is that why Joy isn't writing to me?"

"You are such a silly girl! Of course not!"

"Well, then, what's the reason? Why haven't I received a letter?"

"Who knows? This is China. Things run smoothly one day and go crazy the next."

"I just . . . I just have a bad feeling —"

"Then write to May and ask her advice —"

"She doesn't know anything about what it's like here. She doesn't understand."

"May is your sister. She may not know China anymore, but she knows you. And you worry too much. Your head goes to too many dark places. She'll say, 'Calm down, Pearl-ah!'"

"It's hard for me to say what I feel in a letter."

"Then you should see each other. Why don't you meet her in Hong Kong?"

"May actually suggested that in her last letter," I say.

"Well?"

"If I can't get a travel permit to see Joy, then how am I going to get an exit permit to see May?"

"These are two different things. One is to the countryside —"

"And one is out of the country."

"What if you meet your sister at the fair in Canton?"

"May suggested that too. She thought she might be able to get a day permit to visit the fair to buy costumes for her movie rental business and canned goods for the café. I don't think she'd be able to get that kind of permit, but even if she did, I'd still have to get a travel permit. If Superintendent Wu ever gave me one, I'd use it to see Joy."

"Then try for a one-day exit permit. See what happens."

"I'd love to see May, and maybe sometime in the future I'll try to get a one-day exit permit. But not now, not when the baby is due next month."

We go back to the salon. Then Auntie Hu walks Dun and me to the front door, where she holds us back.

"I've been thinking about it," she says to Dun. "The two of you should try to leave China. I lost my husband and my son, but if they were alive, I'd be telling them we should get out of here."

It's strange that she suddenly feels so adamant about this and is pushing so hard when she knows I won't leave China permanently without Joy.

"You're the one who should go abroad, Madame Hu," Dun says.

"Yes, I've thought about it, and I'm trying," she confides in a low voice. "I have a sister in Singapore. I haven't seen her since she married out more than forty years ago."

I'm startled by her revelation. "You've never mentioned this before. How can you leave?"

"How can I not leave? Your mother was the smart one. She got you and your sister out in time."

I don't add that, yes, she did, but she died horribly in the process.

"I started going to the police station and the Foreign Affairs Bureau to apply for an exit permit more than a year ago," Auntie Hu goes on.

I'm surprised by how much this hurts me. "Why didn't you tell me?"

"I didn't have anything to tell in the beginning. I didn't think I had a chance. Some people wait forever to get an exit permit. Others can get a permit to go to Hong Kong for a day very quickly. I thought I'd be in the forever category. Now they say they may give me an exit permit because they're sure I'll return. They think I can't live without servants!" She lets out a wicked cackle. "They don't know me very well."

I think they know her better than she knows herself. Auntie Hu has never lived without servants. She has bound feet and is in many ways as isolated as Yong is in Green Dragon Village. She doesn't know about housecleaning, laying out her own clothes (let alone washing, ironing, or putting them on by herself),

387

cooking (let alone grocery shopping, doing anything beyond boiling water, or scrubbing pots and pans), or working to make ends meet.

"The real reason they'll let me go," she continues, "is that they've already sucked everything from me except this house. If I ever leave, they'll take it." Auntie Hu touches Dun's arm. "You'll come back next Sunday, won't you?" (This, after all her talk about leaving.)

He puts his hands together and bows. It's old-fashioned, completely out of style these days, but it makes Auntie Hu happy. Even with all the changes, we have to remember our humanity, and it pleases me that Dun is so kind, but I'm subdued on the way home. The city would feel very empty without Auntie Hu, but I tell myself I shouldn't worry. No matter what she says, she'll never get an exit permit.

The other boarders still haven't returned, so Dun opens some plum wine and we take our glasses outside to wait for the fireworks to begin. He sits on the steps, while I putter in the garden. I cut the last roses of the season and I bring them back to the steps, where I sit down next to Dun. In the distance, we hear the celebration. When Dun reaches over and puts a hand on top of mine, I'm not startled or scared. I smile, and my heart thumps in my chest.

"Pearl Chin," he says, addressing me by my maiden name, "I have known you a long time. When I first moved into your house, I don't think you saw me, but I saw you. I hope it will not upset you if I tell you I loved you from afar even then. I knew there was no hope for me, but perhaps now you will consider me."

"I'm a widow," I remind him.

I don't have to explain anything else. He's a Chinese man of a certain age. He knows all the old restrictions on widows. But as the first volley of fireworks explodes above us, he squeezes my hand.

"I don't believe in arranged marriages," he says, "but I don't believe in the kind of marriage we have in the New China either. You know my background. You know I've read many English books. What I want is a courtship — a *Western* courtship."

I am forty-three years old, and I've never been courted before.

Joy

Living an Abundant Year

Everyone worried that this winter would be worse than last year's, but we didn't realize just how much more dire it would be. It's only November — the worst of the between the yellow and the green hasn't come yet — and Fu-shee and I are already gleaning. The close planting didn't work. Most of the seedlings died. What survived produced very weak and small crops. Then we launched Sputniks, racing to harvest an entire crop of turnips, corn, or cabbage in a single day. We worked without food or much water until we were dazed and disoriented. Those women who had their periods were not allowed to take care of themselves, and their pants soaked through with blood. And still there remained the problem of harvesting an entire crop in just twenty-four hours. The only way to do that was to lop the top parts of the turnip plants and leave the bulbs in the ground, ignore ears of corn, or carelessly drop cabbage leaves on the soil. All that was scavenged months ago, so my mother-in-law and I have moved on

390

to one of the failed wheat fields, looking for a piece of grain here, a piece of grain there. We've been told to value quantity over quality, but we have neither. Our rice rations have been reduced to half a *jin* per person — enough for a single bowl of rice porridge a day. I pick up a piece of grain, put it in my pocket, and walk over to Fu-shee.

"I think the baby will be coming soon," I say. "My contractions started early this morning. They're strong now. I think we should go home."

Fu-shee's given birth to all her children on the floor in the corner of the main room in the family house. If she can do it, then I can too, especially if she's there to help me. But she shakes her head.

"You're better off going to the maternity courtyard," she says. "You'll get extra food if you have your baby there."

In the New China, new mothers are entitled to eight weeks' maternity leave, fifteen yards of cotton cloth, twenty *jin* of white flour, and three *jin* of sugar. Those things are important, but to get them I'll have to deliver my baby in the maternity courtyard.

"I'm afraid to go there," I admit.

With the hunger, too many babies are stillborn. The feeling throughout the commune is that the maternity courtyard is inhabited by demons, looking to steal a baby's first breath.

"Don't be swayed by feudal beliefs about fox spirits and things like that," Fu-shee cautions, not realizing my reasons are practical. "Sung-ling had her baby girl in the maternity courtyard last week. The two of them are still alive. Now the four of you can be together."

She leans over, scratches at the dirt, and picks up a few more kernels. She puts them in her palm, blows on them to clean them, and then holds them out for me to see as a reminder that these little bits of grain are what are keeping our household of twelve alive. The promise of flour and sugar cannot be rejected lightly.

Fu-shee walks me to the maternity courtyard, which is located in Moon Pond Village. The contractions are closer now and so fierce that sometimes we have to stop so I can brace myself against the pain. I wish my mother were here, and I don't understand why she isn't. I wish the letters she sends me were in response to the ones I send her. I don't understand what that means either. I've been careful not to write overtly about the famine, sure that would never get past the censors. Instead, I've written about how much I miss my dad's cooking. I've even mentioned particular dishes from our family's restaurant and the way the rice always smelled, hoping that she'll send ingredients or a bag of rice. Maybe even those hints are too much and the censors are blacking out those lines. Maybe my letters aren't getting through at all. Another contraction. I want my mother, and all I have is Fu-shee.

We reach the maternity courtyard — a large house that was confiscated and converted to its new use when the commune was formed. My mother-in-law explains to the midwife that I'm from a city and that I've never seen a baby come out. The midwife gives me a pitying look, guides me to a room, tells me to take off my pants, and directs me to a corner where she's spread a piece of cloth. I squat in the proper position and support myself against the walls. The contractions come faster and harder. I want to scream, but that's considered inappropriate. But even with my jaw clenched, moans come from somewhere deep inside me. My mother-in-law and the midwife stare at me disapprovingly. I look down and see a bulge between my legs. Just when I feel like things are going to rip apart down there, the midwife reaches under me and snips the skin.

When she finally orders me to push, I gladly obey. This is the easiest part, at least for me. I haven't had much to eat these past months and the baby is small, slipping out like an oily fish. It's a girl, which means I receive no tears of happiness or words of congratulations. The midwife hands me the baby. She makes little jerky motions with her arms. She has tufts of black hair on top of her head. Her nose is perfect. Her lips are pretty. She's tiny, thin really, but I can tell she's strong by the way she grips my pinkie. She's been born in the Year of the Boar, just like my uncle Vern. I remember something my mother said about him: "Like all Boars, he was born with a remarkably strong body. He can withstand a great deal of pain and suffering without complaint." I hang on to those words now. I hope my baby will be like my uncle — courageous in the face of great odds. Blessing and worry, happiness and fear — this is a mother's love.

Once the baby and I are cleaned up, we're moved to the dormitory. I get a bed next to Sung-ling, who

393

regards me sympathetically. She also had a daughter, so she too has felt disappointment from those around her. My mother-in-law goes home and comes back the next morning with special mother's soup fortified with peanuts, ginger, and liquor to bring in my milk, shrink my womb, and help me regain my strength. I don't know where she got the ingredients, but the soup works and the baby greedily sucks from my breast. For the first time, I have real compassion for what my aunt May went through when she gave me away right after my birth. Her breasts, her womb, her whole body must have ached for me.

It's good I have Sung-ling next to me, because otherwise I'd be miserable. How many movies and television shows have I seen where a wife gives birth and the husband arrives with flowers and kisses? Too many to count. But Tao doesn't come to see me. Now I know there's nothing I can do to please him, and it's heartbreaking. This is not my only failure or source of sadness. Sung-ling, the other new mothers, and I are supposed to be fed extra rations, but the commune's food stores are small. We receive no brown sugar and ginseng to restore blood, and no chicken and fruit to help rebuild our constitutions. I anticipate that no red eggs will be made to celebrate my baby's one-month birthday either. Still, three neighbor women give me eggs: one egg is rotten, the second is so old the yolk can't be distinguished from the white, and the third has a dead chick inside. I think about the risk they took to hide the eggs. If someone is caught hoarding or hiding food, Brigade Leader Lai will have him or her beaten.

When I'm sent home, I'm not given any of the food or cotton I was promised. My father-in-law refuses to look at me. My mother-in-law ignores me. I ask Tao if he'd like to hold our daughter, but he won't touch her because she's a girl. Any chance that Tao and I might get along better has been ruined by her birth. I say we should give her a name.

"Stupid," suggests my husband.

"Pig," my mother-in-law spits out.

"Dog," one of Tao's brothers says with a smirk.

"Jie Jie," offers Jie Jie, the oldest of Tao's sisters. This is clearly the kindest and most generous suggestion, since it suggests that in naming my baby Oldest Sister I'll have more children. It also gives me the feeling that Jie Jie will help me with the baby and look out for her.

"No Name would be best," my father-in-law says, simultaneously offending the mother of his children, my baby, and me.

"I want to name her Samantha. I will call her Sam for short." I'm thinking of my father Sam and that this little baby deserves to be named for someone who was honorable and kind. Samantha Feng. I'm a new mother and I'm in bad circumstances, but already I know I'll fight for her. Of course, Sam means nothing in the local dialect, which turns out to be a good thing.

"You can call her whatever you want," my husband says dismissively. "We will call her Ah Fu."

It means Good Fortune, but it's actually a terrible insult, because every girl baby is considered a misfortune. That's all right. My grandfather always called me Pan-di — Hope-for-a-Brother. His name for me only made me stronger.

I write letters to my mother and aunt, telling them of my baby's birth and giving them her name. Then I wrap Sam in a piece of cloth and tie her to my chest. Together we walk down the hill and wait by the pond for the mailman to arrive. Today he brings a package from my mother. I take it home, excited, hoping it will be filled with food. But the package has already been opened and it's half empty, so I know someone in the leadership hall has taken whatever he or she wanted. What's left is some powdered baby formula and some home-made shoes. I hide the formula with the carton of formula Aunt May sent. (Hers came with a note saying I should protect my breasts from early aging and sagging by giving Samantha a bottle.) As for the homemade shoes, Fu-shee won't let the children wear them even though it's cold, saying they should be saved for special occasions.

What's worse, I wonder, to freeze or to starve to death? I'm a long way from starving, but a relentless cold draft comes through the window that must be stopped, especially with a newborn in the house. I ask one of Tao's siblings to get water from the stream and another to add fuel to the fire outside. Once the water comes to a boil, they come and get me. Tao's little brothers and sisters watch wide-eyed as I pour the water in a basin, bring it inside, and put one of the shoes my mother made for me in to soak. Very quickly the shoe begins to fall apart.

The loudspeaker in the house is rarely quiet. Right now the announcer talks about natural calamities — drought, floods, typhoons, and monsoons. As I peel off each layer of paper from the soles, I realize we've seen none of these calamities. But if the loudspeaker says it's true, then it must be. I take the layers of paper from the shoes and smooth them across the thin rice paper that's already been pasted over the window opening, hoping to block the wind from entering through any cracks and create extra layers as a barrier from the elements. Maybe the dark paper will attract more of the sun's warmth too. As I work, I understand what my mother has done. She's sent little pieces of herself and Auntie May: their eyes, their lips, their fingers. Then, about halfway through the sole of the second shoe, I come across a different kind of paper. I carefully lift it off the sole, unfold it, and see six words written in my mother's delicate calligraphy.

My heart is with you always.

I glance at the collage I've made over the window opening. I take the baby out of her sling and hold her up so she can see. "Look, it's your yen-yen and your great-aunt. See how much they love us?"

Then I put Sam back in her sling and return to my pasting. Tao's little brothers and sisters rush out to tell our neighbors what I'm doing. They come, they look, they shake their heads.

★   ★   ★

In early December, Brigade Leader Lai brings militiamen from Tun-hsi to search our houses, because he no longer wants to do his own dirty work. "Where have you hidden your grain?" the men demand gruffly. "We know you stole it."

The amount we've hidden is small — just cupfuls — but we've spread it widely throughout the two-room house. We've slit open our padded jackets and sewn little packets of gleaned rice and wheat in with the cotton bunting. We buried some millet in a jar under the sleeping platform. We wrapped foraged peanut shells in an old rice sack and tucked it between a rafter and the roof. We'll grind the shells to mix into porridge. Party officials have told us to "live an abundant year as if it were a frugal one." To me, we're living in a frugal year, doing everything we can to get by, and it still isn't enough.

Brigade Leader Lai's men come to Green Dragon Village every day for two weeks. (I'll say this: it's easy to tell who's been eating just by looking at their bodies. The brigade leader and his militiamen don't show signs of starvation. They haven't lost weight, developed concave stomachs, or had any of their limbs swell from edema.) People hope that if Lai's men find a stash it will divert them from searching other houses in the village and that the punishment won't be too harsh. The lucky are beaten with sticks, or have their hands tied behind their backs and then are hung from a tree by their wrists until they scream from the agony. Those less lucky are forbidden to eat at the canteen. The least lucky are sent to a distant irrigation project, but no one can work in icy water in this weather and survive. Those who've been sent away have not returned, but many who've been beaten have died, and not getting to eat in the canteen is also a way to die, only slower. The village, the fields, and the canteen begin to look like movie sets — just façades. The people around me seem fake too, putting on their smiling faces and shouting slogans about things they don't believe. Everyone still pretends to be open, welcoming, and enthusiastic about the Great Leap Forward, but there's a furtiveness to them that reminds me of rats slinking along the edges of walls.

Even though our first winter wheat crop was paltry, Brigade Leader Lai hasn't given up on the idea of converting still more of our rice paddies, vegetable fields, and tea terraces to wheat. Now he wants us to deep-plow too. We're to dig ten feet under to make our furrows richer than ever before — or so he says. The farmers know that topsoil is precious and that what lies beneath it is useless, but the brigade leader won't take no for an answer. Even though it's winter, we're ordered back to the fields. One man pulls a plow and two men push it, while the rest of us dig even deeper with shovels and hoes. The slogan is "Plow deep to bury the American aggressor!" When we aren't reciting the slogan, we're encouraged to chant, "We work all day! We work all night! We work all day! We work all night!" And we do, sometimes stopping only to nap by the side of the field or slurp down our single bowl of rice porridge. When someone asks the brigade leader why we have to use our own bodies to do what draft animals have always done, he responds, "An ox or a water buffalo can't dig as deep as humans."

I remember the story Tao told me about the water buffalo and why it wore blinders. He said the animal's suffering in this life was punishment for things it had done in a past life. Now I think of a different reason. To make an ox or water buffalo work so hard, it needs to be blinded and uninformed. That's what the government is doing to the masses now. Why? Because peasants are China's true beasts of burden. Still, no one blames Chairman Mao. "The Great Helmsman wouldn't hurt us," my neighbors say. "The people around him just aren't telling him the truth. It's not his fault." They spout this even as they develop dark patches on their lips and limbs that quickly turn into running sores. They feel sick to their stomachs, yet hungry, dizzy, and unable to stop walking. It seems we're all paying for things we did either in this or in our past lives. The only good news — if it can be called that — is that sometimes we're given dried sweet potatoes, as draft animals once were, to supplement our half *jin* of rice.

At the end of December, Brigade Leader Lai cuts our grain ration to one-quarter *jin* per person. That's barely four ounces of starch — about half a bowl of rice porridge a day when we're still working like animals, deep-plowing the bitterly cold fields.

"There's plenty of grain," he assures us, "but you people have an ideological problem."

400

No, the real reason is that he delivered too much of our small harvest to the government. Model communes are the ones where the leaders lie the best and the biggest. Now even Brigade Leader Lai understands that doubling the grain harvest in a single year can be achieved only on paper. But to keep his promise, our rice, wheat, millet, and sorghum have been shipped to national silos so people in cities can be fed, leaving the Dandelion Number Eight People's Commune with almost nothing. Our meals in the canteen have strange ingredients — cornstalks, corn roots, dried sweet potato leaves, and wild grasses cooked into soup, or dried pea powder, sawdust, acorns, elm bark, and pumice stone ground into flour to make into heavy cakes cooked on a griddle. Those labeled black elements — like Kumei, Ta-ming, and Yong — are allowed even less than the scant allotment of food. My mother and aunt don't seem to understand what's happening here. They continue to send packages with goodies for the children instead of real food. (My aunt's letters arrive just fine, but entire paragraphs in my mother's letters are completely blacked out.) Cookies and candies are more than other people have, so I suppose we're fortunate. Still, not a day goes by when I don't remember how cavalier I was about the special food coupons I was entitled to as an Overseas Chinese. What I wouldn't do for those now.

We stop shrinking and losing weight. We develop what everyone calls the swelling disease as our arms, legs, necks, and faces swell from edema caused by a lack of protein. Our new diet is terrible going in and

401

worse coming out. Some of us are constipated; others have diarrhea. This isn't so bad for the babies and smallest children who can't make it to the nightstool. The slats in the floor are wide enough for the diarrhea to slip through. But things are more awkward for those of us who are older. This is a two-room house and we use a nightstool. Naturally, what leaves our bodies is as much of a concern for Brigade Leader Lai as what goes into them. Our house is not the only one with intestinal problems, so now he sends his men on cleanliness inspections.

"Are you still brushing your teeth and washing your hands? Are you emptying and cleaning your nightstool every morning? What is this mess in the corner? Why do you have flies when it's winter?"

Things are happening very quickly. The members of the commune are moving from hunger to starving and from starving to death. Few die from a lack of food, however. Instead, they drop dead from heart attacks, get fevers and colds that bring on pneumonia, receive small cuts that become infected and lead to blood poisoning, or they eat the wrong thing and then lose all their water through diarrhea. Baby girls are the first to die, followed by young girls and grandmothers. Sons, fathers, and grandfathers don't die. An old saying reminds us that there are thirty-six virtues, but to be without a son negates them all. That means all food must go to males first.

"Otherwise who will take care of the family?" Tao asks.

402

I want to say, "I was raised to believe that women and children should be saved first. My father was Chinese, but even he believed that." But I know better than to argue with my husband, and I don't want to talk about my father Sam. His sacrifice makes my hunger feel meager.

Some of our neighbors try to sell their daughters, but no one wants to buy girls. Other families — ours included — send small children into the fields at night to cut unripe shoots from the new winter wheat crop. No one is supposed to leave the commune, but Brigade Leader Lai issues certificates permitting men — including my father-in-law — to leave the Dandelion Number Eight People's Commune to beg or find work. We don't know what will happen to them, but one thing is certain: fewer mouths mean more food for us.

I don't know what finally sends me to the leadership hall to ask for a divorce — that my husband has done everything possible to take credit for my mural, that he won't touch our baby, that he ignores me completely, that he takes food from my bowl in the canteen and gives it to his brothers, or that he's begun "sharing his time," meaning he's fooling around with some of the young women in the commune. When I was in school, girls had a name for boys and men like my husband: a dog. Tao is a dog — with all the worst characteristics of a Dog. If I were in a city, I'd go to the People's District Court and plead my case before a judge, a prosecutor, a recorder, and a policeman, but I'm on a remote commune, which is one reason divorce is so uncommon in the countryside. Brigade Leader Lai, Party Secretary Feng Jin, and Sung-ling compose the tribunal, but this is not to be a private matter. I arrive at the canteen just as dinner ends. The members of the tribunal sit at one of the food-service tables, reminding those in our vast cornstalk room of all we lack. Without television, movies, books, magazines, or newspapers, the winter can be long. At the very least, my application for divorce is a break from the loudspeaker. I stand a few feet before the tribunal. Samantha sleeps in a cloth sling tied across my chest. Tao and our audience sit behind me.

"What is the nature of your complaint?" Sung-ling, the only woman on the panel, asks.

"I married Tao for the wrong reason," I begin, gesturing to him. "To see if I was worthy of love —"

"Love has no place in the New Society," Sung-ling states.

All right then.

"When we first married, we got along all right," I say. "Then we began to quarrel. Now he rarely speaks to me."

"These things happen in marriage," Sung-ling says. "You need to try harder."

"My husband won't touch our daughter," I confess, sure this will show Tao for the kind of man he is.

When people in the canteen titter, Party Secretary Feng shushes the crowd and then addresses me. "No one is glad when a girl is born." He may be illiterate, but feelings about female children are so deep that even he can quote from Fu Hsüan's famous poem that begins, "How sad it is to be a woman! Nothing on earth is held so cheap." He must have learned to recite the poem from his father, who learned it from his father, as have probably all the men — and women — in the commune and perhaps the country.

"Baby girls are equal too, aren't they?" I argue back.

But I get no sympathy on that point.

"You aren't doing your duty as a comrade," Sung-ling scolds me. "Anything that doesn't have to do with the revolution is a waste of time. Arms should be put to the work of improving the country, not to carrying babies."

And yet I've seen Sung-ling cuddle her daughter. We've often sat together to nurse our infants. We've walked with them in the late afternoons when they've cried. We've even plotted, as mothers do, about the two girls growing up to be best friends for life.

I don't want to accuse Tao directly of fooling around, so I list my other reasons. "He criticizes me all the time. He suspects me when I'm late. He rarely speaks to me, even though we live in two rooms. A woman shouldn't have to suffer in marriage."

"You have serious complaints, but a divorce is not a trifle," Brigade Leader Lai comments. "If we grant you a divorce, what will you do about your baby? Will you leave her with your husband? How will you support yourself? Where will you live? A woman is like a vine needing the support of a tree. What will you do?"

I remember Z.G. saying something like this when I announced I wanted to marry Tao. I don't like it any more now than I did then.

"A woman is like a vine? We've been told that women hold up half the sky," I respond.

Before I can continue, Party Secretary Feng Jin jumps in. "Women are like water; men are like mountains."

"*Bah!*" Sung-ling snorts. "If a man is a mountain and a woman is water, then it is the woman who confirms the mountain's existence. As water, a woman can go anywhere. It gives life. It nurtures life. A man is reflected in her water."

Could Sung-ling be alluding to my mural? I came up with the idea, mixed the paints, and allowed Tao to take the credit. The other judges — both men — look as though they've just swallowed cod-liver oil. When I first came here, I saw how the people of Green Dragon loved Tao for his artistic talents and took pride in him. I piggybacked on their good feelings to get my mural made. This won't go well if they think I'm now trying to steal credit from him.

"A hurried marriage is not a basis for a good marriage," I stumble on before the two men can compose their thoughts. "We didn't know each other well enough to know if we could get along. We do not treat each other as equals," I add, hoping that, if I accept some of the blame, then they'll be more compassionate in their deliberations.

"Let us hear from the husband," the brigade leader says.

I sit down and Tao gets up. I don't expect him to hold back. I embarrassed him by coming here, and his only hope is to make me look bad. But I haven't prepared myself for the slipperiness of his honeyed words as he picks up where Sung-ling left off.

"It is natural for a man to go to a higher place, just as it is natural for water to flow to a lower place. When my wife came here, she was a broken-down shoe."

He just called me a low prostitute! Behind me, people mumble and shift their weight. I don't turn around, but I imagine hundreds of bodies suddenly leaning forward, eager to hear what Tao will say next. Yes, this is most definitely more entertaining than the loudspeaker, but I'm worried and scared. I wrap my arms around Samantha, protecting her, protecting myself.

"If you give her a divorce," he continues, "no man will want her, because they only want fresh brides. And she'll have to leave the baby with me. Ah Fu is mine until she marries out."

The brigade leader is not at all interested in my baby's future, not when there's something more titillating to pursue. "This is a serious accusation," he says. "What proof do you have of your wife's bad behavior?"

"She kissed me in the Charity Pavilion before we married," Tao answers truthfully. Again, the people in the canteen grumble and whisper among themselves. The brigade leader asks for quiet and Tao continues. "She touched me with her naked feet in the stream." This elicits shocked *ohs*. "Once we were married, she wanted to do the husband-wife thing right next to my brothers and sisters." He turns and addresses me directly. "Now you won't do it at all."

I jump to my feet. All eyes turn to me, but what can I say? Everything he said is true. I can't get mad, but I can't let this go either.

"When Tao and I first met, I was a virgin," I say. "Now he insults me by saying I was a broken-down shoe —"

"A baby — even a girl — should not be with a mother such as this." Tao speaks right over me. "Ah Fu belongs to my family and our village, not to an outsider. My wife puts on a red face, but I've seen her bourgeois ways. I've encouraged her to open her heart to the Party. I've told her she needs to be a cog in the revolutionary machine, but she refuses to perform ritual self-examination and self-criticism."

Everything my mother said about Tao is true. He is *hsin yan* — heart eye, tricky. He's using the safety of his background to denounce me as a way of diverting attention from his having sex with girls on the work teams.

"She is *not* red," he emphasizes. "She is black and she has tried to spread her blackness to all of us by painting a black mural! There are rules for paintings. They must be *hong, guang, liang* — red, bright, and shining — but what did she choose for her subject on one of the walls? An owl. The whole world knows that the owl is a symbol of bad omens, darkness, and evil."

"You are suffering from *hong yen bing* — red eye disease — envy," I shoot back. But I'm frightened by his comments, because in my mural I *was* trying to send the message that the Great Leap Forward is a disaster.

Then Tao says something even worse, proving to everyone I'm not only a bad wife but also a traitor to Green Dragon Village and the commune.

"She's always encouraging me to leave the village. She says I can have a better life if I go elsewhere."

"That's a lie!" I exclaim. "You're the one who's always asking me to write to my father to see if he can get you a travel permit or an internal passport. You've made it very clear that I'm a weight around your neck, preventing you from leaving the village. You're the one who's seeking praise and recognition. You've tried to claim the mural as your own."

But who are the people in the canteen going to believe — someone they've known their entire lives or me? I've always thought of Party Secretary Feng Jin as an honest and straightforward man. I turn to him now, my hands outstretched in supplication.

"You must try to work this out," he says. "A divorced woman is like a dried-up silkworm — ugly and totally useless to anyone."

"But Tao has been sharing his time —"

"Enough!" Brigade Leader Lai orders. "Sit down, and let us hear from your comrades."

Like that, my divorce turns into a struggle session as one after another person gets up to denounce me as a rightist element. They speak in low voices, as though they haven't had a decent meal in a long time, and they haven't. Then a young woman I recognize from one of the work teams walks to the area before the tribunal. The way she looks at Tao tells me she's one of his girls.

409

Seeing her causes my body to tense. Samantha wakes and begins to squirm.

"You wanted to be the star in the play the propaganda team mounted when you first came here," the girl accuses. "You were always singling yourself out for special treatment. Ever since then, you've chosen to work in an individualistic way."

"I came here to help the People's Republic of China," I say staunchly. "I wanted to serve the people, and I have."

"You use the word *I* too often," someone calls out. "*I, I, I* — that sounds like self-exaggeration, self-expression, and self-glorification of the individual."

"You speak too frankly," another states.

"And you brag —"

"Like a foreigner."

"And your arm movements are too extravagant and expressive." (This is true. I am more American than Chinese in this regard.)

The brigade leader gestures to the audience to quiet down, and then he addresses me directly. "Your comrades are telling you that your individualism has not yet been washed clean. You've also refused to open your heart to the Party. Understand, our criticism is meant to help you."

Two pairs of arms reach under my armpits and lift me onto a table where people can see me better. More insults and accusations are hurled my way. It's time for Samantha to eat, and she begins to cry. She's a tiny little thing, but the sound that comes from her is both angry and desperate. My breasts respond, filling with milk. If I don't feed her soon, my nipples will begin to leak. My situation should bring some sympathy, but it doesn't.

"You're concealing more serious defects by hiding behind trivial flaws," Brigade Leader Lai says after another half hour of criticisms. "Let us hear more from the people who know you."

Tao's mother rises. Our relationship has been uneven at best and Tao is her son, but what she says isn't as bad as it could be.

"You wanted a wedding ceremony and celebration, but these things aren't necessary in the New China. You were crowing even then!"

One of Tao's brothers steps forward. "Sometimes my sister-in-law gets a letter. She says it's from her mother or aunt, but we can see it's written in code." He's talking about the alphabet. "We have to rely on what she says is written there. She comes from our most ultra-rightist imperialist enemy. How do we know she isn't a spy?"

"What is there to spy on?" I ask, indignant. This boy has benefited from me in so many ways — from the packages of treats my mother and aunt have sent to the food that's literally been taken from my bowl and put into his. Still, I have to be careful. Asking for a divorce is one thing, being labeled a spy is quite another.

"We sleep together in the main room," Tao's brother continues. "She doesn't do enough to keep the baby from making noise. Just listen to her now." Samantha helps his case with her cries. "None of us can sleep. My

411

poor brother is so tired he no longer has the strength to paint."

I want to say Tao's tired because he's hungry, working too hard in the fields, and playing around with too many young women, but I don't because I'm grateful the accusations have turned back to something far less threatening than my being a spy.

He sits down and elbows Jie Jie, urging her to get up and say a few words against me. But she shakes her head no. I wish she had the courage to say something in my favor, but she doesn't do that either. Still, I take her silence as a small victory.

A few more people criticize me. I didn't work hard enough during the harvest. I wanted to win the corn-picking contest not for the glory of the team and the country but so I could boast about how important I was. I let my mother hug me in front of everyone.

I stand there, feeling bitter and angry. This is a great way to take people's minds off their hunger and fatigue — work all day with no food, then come to a struggle session at night. Then someone kicks the leg of the table. It tips, and the baby and I fall. I turn my body so I can land on my back, protecting Samantha. I look up and see Kumei. I reach a hand out to her, believing she's come to help me as I helped Yong. Instead, Kumei points a finger at me accusingly.

"You took baths — naked — in the villa's kitchen," she says. It breaks my heart that Kumei feels she must speak against me. But I understand. She has to protect herself, her son, and Yong. Still, this is stunning — shocking — information. The mood shifts yet again, turning ugly. I think of Yong's struggle session. Fortunately no one has brought up how I helped her that day. Not yet anyway. But everyone's hungry, everyone's tired, and this could get violent.

I get up off the floor. Samantha is what my aunt May would call screaming bloody murder. I look directly at Sung-ling. *Please help me.* Sung-ling stands and raises her hands for silence. The audience quiets, which makes Samantha's cries all the more pathetic. The village cadre's voice is strident and harsh as she addresses me, but her eyes are not. Another show of kindness.

"We all agree you are too soft," she says. "You complain too much. But Chairman Mao says, do not fear hardship. Do not fear death."

I don't fear hardship, but I do fear death. Few choices are open to those who are struggled against: hold to your morals and risk further punishment; admit guilt and accept punishment; admit guilt, offer thanks for everyone's comradely help, and hope for leniency. My father Sam comes clearly to me now. I feel as though he is standing next to me, his hand on my shoulder, reminding me not only what a parent should do but also how he might have done it differently. I turn and face my accusers.

"I'm grateful for your criticisms, for I know you'd not have said them if they weren't true," I say. "I'll take them to heart and I'll improve. I thank my comrades."

"Good!" Sung-ling says. "The tribunal will take a few minutes to discuss the case. Everyone remain in your seats. We will return shortly."

Brigade Leader Lai, Party Secretary Feng, and Sung-ling walk down the center aisle and out the door. I sit on my bench and face forward, aware of the restlessness of those behind me. I unbutton my blouse, and Samantha's mouth grabs my nipple. My shoulders relax. Everyone around me calms at the sudden quiet. Tao comes and sits next to me. He doesn't look at me or check on Samantha. Why is he being so difficult? Why doesn't he just let me go? He doesn't love me. He doesn't even like me. Have I harmed him in some way? Does he want something from me? The only thing I can think of is just what Z.G. said. Tao wants me to help him leave this place. How many times has he asked me to write to Z.G. for a travel permit? Too many to count. And yet this was one of Tao's biggest complaints about me.

The tribunal returns.

"You have quarreled over minor differences," Brigade Leader Lai says. "Comrade Joy, you will not be made to wear a white ribbon of denunciation, but you must abstain from capitalist thoughts and make sure your husband receives his prerogatives. Comrade Tao, remember that children — whether sons or daughters — do not belong to you. Your daughter belongs to Chairman Mao." He pauses to create the greatest effect, and then announces, "This divorce is not granted."

The entertainment is over and people get up to leave. I catch Kumei's eye, and she turns away in embarrassment. My mother-in-law, Jie Jie, and the other children group together, waiting. Tao flicks his

414

finger, motioning me to follow him. I have nowhere to go and no other options at this time, but as soon as I get home I pull out paper and a pen. I write a letter to Z.G. begging for travel permits. Tao watches me the entire time.

The next day I come home from work, feed the baby, and leave her with Jie Jie. Then I take my letter to the pond and wait for the mailman. It's the beginning of January in the Western calendar. I've missed Christmas and New Year's again. It's cold and dreary. When the mailman doesn't come, I walk up the hill that leads out of the village. From here, I can look far across the desolate fields. In the distance, I see a man bicycling toward me. It's not the regular mailman, which tells me he must be dead. Will this new one be reliable? All I can do is trust and hope, but I know with sinking certainty that my letter will never go through. Brigade Leader Lai will read my request for travel permits, and that will be that. Word of what's happening here cannot be allowed to leak out from the commune. The only way I'll be free of Tao is to help him leave the village, and the only way I know to do that is going to fail.

After handing my letter to the mailman, I turn to walk back to Green Dragon Village. A new welcome sign has been posted by the side of the path:

1. ALL CORPSES MUST BE BURIED.
2. ALL BODIES MUST BE BURIED AT LEAST THREE FEET DEEP WITH CROPS GROWN ON TOP. NO SUPERSTITIOUS TRADITIONS WILL BE TOLERATED.

3. THERE WILL BE NO CRYING OR WAILING.

4. THERE WILL BE NO BEGGING, HOARDING, OR STEALING.

5. ALL VIOLATIONS WILL BE PUNISHABLE BY BEATING, LOSS OF FOOD PRIVILEGES IN THE CANTEEN, OR IMMEDIATE DISPATCH FOR RE-EDUCATION THROUGH LABOR.

Pearl

A Brave Heart

"Where were you born?" Superintendent Wu asks again.

"Yin Bo Village in Kwangtung province," I answer.

"Do you have relatives still living there? Can you name them?"

"I'm related to everyone in the village, but I left when I was three. I don't remember anyone."

After twenty-nine months of meetings, I wouldn't say that Superintendent Wu and I are friends, but we get along all right.

"Are your relatives workers, peasants, or soldiers?"

"I guess peasants, but I really don't know."

"Let's turn to your daughter. Is she still on the Dandelion Number Eight People's Commune?"

"Yes, she is. As you know, I finally heard from her. I have a granddaughter now. She's ten weeks old. I'd still like to visit —"

"Tell me about your family in America."

"I have a sister. I hope one day for family reunification."

And on it goes. The exact same questions.

After two hours, I'm allowed to leave. The February air is bitingly cold. I pull my hat down and my muffler up. When I get home, I hear arguing coming from the kitchen. I glance in the salon and see Dun reading a book. He wears a coffee-colored sweater and loose brown pants. He's lost weight; we all have. He sees me and smiles.

"I have something for you," he says.

I glance around to make sure no one is looking, and then I slip into the salon. He reaches down on the other side of his chair and pulls up a bouquet of pink flowers.

I kneel by his chair and kiss his cheek. "Thank you, but where did you get them?"

It's now against the law to sell anything privately. Unauthorized peddlers are sent to jail. All the selling songs and trills I used to hear on the street have disappeared.

"There are ways to buy things," he says, "if you know where to look."

"I don't want you to get in trouble."

"Don't worry," Dun says. "Just enjoy them."

But I do worry.

"Are we visiting Madame Hu tonight?" Dun asks. "I bought flowers for her too. They're the first of the season."

"She'll like that," I say.

How is it that his doing something nice for an old woman can make me feel such open-hearted affection for Dun? His thoughtfulness and kindness to my mother's closest friend have been more meaningful

418

than all the gentle caresses he's given me. I blush and look down. Dun puts a finger under my chin and lifts my face. He looks into my eyes. Somehow he understands what I'm feeling and thinking. He moves his hand to my cheek, and I rest it there for a moment, soaking in his tenderness.

On my way to the kitchen to get a vase for the flowers, I stop to straighten a painting — something I bought from a woman in the old French Concession last week. Lots of people are selling treasures, family heirlooms, and porcelain these days in back alleys and from their kitchen doors. Other people's hunger has been a way for me to slowly bring my home back to what it was. Again, no one is supposed to be selling — or buying — privately, but we all do it to one extent or another.

Entering the kitchen is like stepping into a typhoon. The arguing never stops. Dinner tonight is rice, wilted cabbage, and two six-inch-long fish steamed with a little soy sauce. Our food must be divided among six people who've lived together for over twenty years but are not family and me. The biggest fights have to do with our main staple — rice — its scarcity something unheard of in a country that won the hearts of the people on the promise of an iron rice bowl, meaning reliable and promised food for life. Our other starch comes from flours made from sweet potatoes, sorghum, and corn. Meat and eggs are impossible to find. We've been told that Premier Chou En-lai's wife, to show solidarity with the people during what the government is calling "these years of bad weather," now serves tea made from fallen leaves to her guests. Other leaders plan to plant vegetable gardens as soon as the weather warms. Even the Great Helmsman says he'll turn his flower beds into a vegetable plot — or so it's been reported. This news and our constant hunger make us jittery and on edge. What's coming next?

"You aren't putting your fair share of rice into the cooking pot," one of the former dancing girls complains to the cobbler. Two weeks ago, she caught him sneaking rice in the middle of the night and she hasn't been able to shake her mistrust of him.

The cobbler shrugs off the accusation. "You don't count out portions fairly."

Cook, who is the reddest among us and has the ability to report any one of us to the block committee, doesn't like the bickering. "Stop fighting. I'm too old to listen to all this noise," he orders, trying to muster the command he had when I was a little girl. "I've told you before to use this scale to make sure everyone gets an equal amount of food." It's a good idea, except that Cook's eyes are bad, which only causes more squabbling.

Otherwise, life goes on. I continue to collect paper, Dun teaches at the university, the dancing girls go to their factory, the cobbler labors at his stand, the widow collects her stipend and knits for her grandchildren, and Cook sleeps for most of the day. Every morning and every evening — out of habit and wishful thinking — I still walk along the Bund, plotting a way out of China. I've come to the conclusion that escape down the Whangpoo and out to sea would be impossible.

Over a thousand vessels come and go from Shanghai every day, and the waters are filled with inspection cruisers. Inspection Cruiser Number Five won a "model" prize last year for most stowaways caught trying to leave the mainland. According to the local newspaper, the crew has vowed to top those numbers this year. The river and the sea are just too risky.

But people *are* leaving, just not by choice. The city isn't as crowded as when I first arrived. The police have done a good job keeping country bumpkins outside city limits. Those who managed to enter two years ago, when new factories were opening, have been sent home, relinquishing that work to the locals. Troublemakers have been sent to labor camps. At the same time, the People's Government, which has been anxious to expand trade with Hong Kong, has granted some exit permits for family reunification for those who have relatives there. People lucky enough to receive those permits are allowed the equivalent of five dollars to take on their trip, ensuring they have only enough money to visit their families and then come home. If Joy were with me, I'd be going to the police station every day to ask Superintendent Wu for permits. May would be waiting for us in Hong Kong with the money to take us all the way to Los Angeles. What's that American saying? Hope springs eternal?

At five, Cook calls everyone in for dinner. To show camaraderie with the masses in communes — but what is really a way to make sure no one gets more food than he or she deserves — we eat together in the dining

421

room. We've all lost weight. We all look pale. We simply don't have enough to eat.

Ten minutes later, after dinner is over, the others go to their rooms, too weak to do much else. I go upstairs to change into clothes more appropriate for visiting Auntie Hu. I meet Dun downstairs; we put on our jackets, boots, hats, and gloves, and then step out into the freezing air. We take the bus across town to the Hu residence. Usually lights brighten the front windows, but tonight all we can see is a single light flickering from a back room. Dun holds up his bouquet. I ring the bell and wait. I peer through a window, but I don't see anyone. I ring the bell again and knock a few times. Finally, I see someone coming down the hall through the shadows. It's not Auntie Hu. I would recognize her lily gait. It's not one of her servants either.

A tall, surly man opens the door. "What do you want?"

"I'm looking for Madame Hu," I say.

"No one here by that name. Go away."

I glance at Dun. Could we have the wrong house? Then I peer down the hall. I see Auntie Hu's favorite etched glass vase with flowers past their prime in it, her furniture, and the pictures on the walls. No, this is the right place. I look back at Dun and watch as cold steeliness comes over his features.

"Madame Hu lives here," Dun says in a hard voice. He pushes past the man and into the house. I follow. Dun and I call out for her. People emerge from darkened rooms, some carrying oil lamps, some carrying candles. Nails — squatters — have somehow gotten in the house. I catch a glimpse of one of Auntie Hu's servants peeking out from around the edge of a doorjamb.

"You! Come here!" I haven't used that tone since I had servants of my own. The girl steps from her hiding place. She has enough shame to keep her eyes lowered. "Where is she?" It's less a question than an order.

The girl sucks her lips between her teeth as though that will somehow keep me from getting an answer. She doesn't know how many people I've lost. I raise my hand, ready to hit her.

"Where is she?"

"She left five days ago," the girl whimpers. "She has not come back."

"Did she get an exit permit?" Dun inquires. "Is she visiting her sister?"

The girl shakes her head. "Madame Hu didn't tell me anything. But the next day, the gas and electricity were turned off."

The surly man who opened the door jabs a finger in my shoulder. "You have no rights here. Get out!"

Dun takes a step, but I put a hand on his arm.

"Let's go. There's nothing here for us."

We go back into the frigid night. We walk almost to the end of the block before I let Dun take me in his arms. I bury my face in his padded jacket, fighting tears.

"Auntie Hu wouldn't have left without telling me," I say.

"She would have if she didn't plan on coming back or if she didn't have an exit permit. She wouldn't have wanted you to get in trouble."

"But she left flowers —"

"A decoy, don't you think, to protect you and her servants? You can tell the police you didn't suspect anything."

This can't be. "Do you really think she's tried to escape? She's an old woman."

"She's just sixty, maybe a little older, maybe a little younger."

"But if she's caught, she'll go to prison for a long time. She'll never survive that."

"She has a brave heart, just as you have a brave heart, Pearl. We must pray that she is safe and that she gets out."

A brave heart? It feels like a swollen and aching thing in my chest.

"Let's get some tea," Dun says. "You'll feel better."

He takes me to a government-run teahouse. We sit as close as we can to the charcoal brazier, but even here cold air whistles through cracks and swirls around our feet. We sip our tea in silence. I stare into my cup, but I'm aware of Dun watching me. I'm surprised by the depth of my sadness. My mother and father are both dead. My sister is far away. My daughter and granddaughter are physically near but could just as easily be a million miles away, since they can't come to Shanghai and I can't go to the commune. Auntie Hu was one of only a few links to my past, and now she's gone.

"Pearl." I look up and see concern in Dun's eyes. His expression makes me want to cry. "We don't know what will happen in life. This is why it's important for us to move forward, to live, to buy flowers, to —"

"What are you saying?"

"Look at Auntie Hu. She lost everyone, but she acted. Wherever she is, she's trying to find a better life." He pauses to let me think about that. Then, after a few moments, he slips off his stool to one knee. The tea-house's proprietor hurries to our table in concern, but Dun waves him away. "We are not so young, you and I, and things will not always be easy, but would you do me the honor of marrying me?"

The tears that have been threatening finally come, but the drops that fall contain not sadness and loss but great joy.

"Absolutely," I say.

Dun pays for our tea, and then we're once again on the street. We're too happy to go straight back to the house, where we'll have no privacy. Our best way to be alone is right here, strolling among hundreds of people along Huaihai Road. But we don't go far before a limousine pulls to a stop just ahead of us. The door opens, and Z.G. gets out.

"I saw you walking," he says. "I had to say hello."

Dun puts a hand on the small of my back — a gesture of reassurance or possession? Z.G. gives us an amused smile.

"I'm on my way to a dinner," he goes on. "They'll be showing a movie too. Would you like to come? You're just the kind of people they want, probably more so than me."

425

"We've already eaten," I say, even though it was a small meal.

"And we're on our way home," Dun adds.

"I won't hear of it." Z.G. steps between us, loops his arms through ours — just as he used to do with May and me years ago when we walked together down the street — and leads us to the limousine. "Come, come. Get in the car."

Z.G. has always had the ability to sweep people along with him, and soon we're speeding through the streets, the driver honking at pedestrians and people on bicycles.

"Where are we going? What's the occasion?" I ask.

"There's a delegation here from Hong Kong," Z.G. replies. "We're to show them that China is doing well, that no one is starving, and that they should do more business with us."

"A delegation from Hong Kong?" Dun asks, perplexed. "That's a British colony."

"I know," Z.G. responds, world-weary. "It's to be one of those events that's so vexing in the New China. On the one hand, England is considered an ultra-imperialist country, since it was the first foreign power to invade China and it still occupies Hong Kong. On the other hand, England is one of the few countries that recognizes the People's Republic of China . . . even though it still aligns itself with the United States — the most ultra-imperialist of all countries — in the United Nations to keep China from membership. We must do what we can to win over the few capitalists we've got. Ah, here we are."

426

The car pulls into the grounds of the Garden Hotel, what used to be the French Club. The brightly lit façade and the walled garden bring back memories of parties I attended here with my sister. It feels strange to walk up the steps and enter the lobby with its crystal chandeliers, sweeping staircase, and marble walls and floors. The art deco grandeur looks dilapidated and musty, but young men and women dressed in old hotel uniforms take our coats, usher us through the lobby, and guide us upstairs to one of the banquet rooms. Inside, the people are divided into three groups: those in the usual gray suits of Communist China's elite, those in colorful Hong Kong-made *cheongsams*, and some — like Dun and me — who wear Western-style clothes of twenty years ago.

Dun and I accept glasses of French champagne. As Z.G. scans the room, looking to see who's important, Dun and I tip our glasses in a silent toast. He smiles. I smile. It seems we have a way to celebrate our engagement after all.

We sit down to an elaborate banquet. It's more food than I've seen since I came to China, and it's fabulous: whole roast squab served with fresh lemon slices and little bowls of salt for dipping; sweet sticky rice stuffed into the holes of lotus root and braised to bring out the greatest sugariness; thin slices of tofu as fresh and light as custard topped by fresh scallops; whole crab sprinkled with chopped scallions, fresh coriander, and chilies; pork belly in honey; soft-boiled eggs topped with caviar and garnished with tiny slivers of pickled vegetable; deep-fried greens coated with sweet syrup, and a whole steamed fish. Our table host tells the Hong Kong guests there's so much food in China that it's not necessary to serve rice. "That would be redundant," he says, and the guests laugh in merry agreement.

Dun and I eat every delicacy designed to impress "our Hong Kong friends," and we savor every bite. I speak in my best British English to a gentleman who owns a textile factory in Kowloon. He's hoping to open a factory on the mainland. I listen to Dun practice his English with a woman on his left. He's deft and humorous. Every once in a while, I glance over at Z.G. He looks good. He hasn't lost any weight, and I can see why, if he's been coming to banquets like this.

When dinner ends, we go to an adjoining room with a small stage, where we're treated to a short program of provincial dances and songs. Then a screen is lowered, the lights dimmed, and a projector begins to whir. I expect a newsreel on the Great Leap Forward. Instead, we get a Laurel and Hardy short followed by *Top Hat*, starring Fred Astaire and Ginger Rogers. I saw it at the Metropole with May a year before we left Shanghai. After the film, the people from our table come up and ask questions.

"Do all Americans drive cars?"

"Do they all own airplanes?"

"Do all people live in houses like that?"

None of them are from Hong Kong.

Joy

A Good Mother

I wake on a Sunday morning in March to unnatural silence. The roosters and chickens in Green Dragon have all been eaten. The oxen, water buffalo, and village dogs have also been eaten. I don't hear the scratching of mice or rats in the rafters and walls, because they've been eaten too. There are no birds in the trees, children playing between houses, or people going about their daily chores.

Tao's brothers and sisters still sleep around us. They need the rest. Last night, they ran out to steal pubescent wheat heads, rub them between their fingers to separate the grain from the husks, and then eat the still-green kernels. It's completely against the rules, and if you're caught by the night patrols, punishment is swift and harsh. People have been tied to the scholar's tree in the square to have their ears, noses, or scalps sliced off or the hair on their faces, heads, or private parts burned. Others have had their eldest sons killed to cut the roots of a family or been deprived of all food

429

until the only thing they can eat is the cotton stuffing in their padded jackets, so they die full but naked.

I was seven years old when World War II ended. Later, in school, we often debated why Germans didn't revolt against their leadership and why Jews didn't fight harder for their lives. Now I understand how that happened, because there have been no riots, protests, or uprisings here either. We're too weak, tired, and scared to do those things. We've been brainwashed through hunger, and people still believe in Chairman Mao and the Communist Party.

We're told no one can leave the commune without written permission. Even if we ran away, what would we find? It's not as though cafés, restaurants, or wealthy homes pepper the landscape. There'd be no point in begging. We live in constant fear and with constant hunger. We're trapped by fate, and our destiny looks bleak. Still, we try to be optimistic, but in the darkest way, by reciting a variation of an old proverb. Instead of "It takes more than one cold day for a river to freeze three feet deep," we tell each other it will take more than five months to starve to death. We don't know if that's true.

I've been receiving packages from my aunt sent through the family association in Hong Kong and from my mother in Shanghai. Whenever the officials in the leadership hall see the stamps on the packages, they open them, hoping to find officially sanctioned food remittances. They take all my food — except for the powdered baby formula, which no one here understands or wants. Even so, Brigade Leader Lai's thugs still search our house — and those throughout the commune — looking for food. Anyone found with hidden food is sent away for re-education through labor. This is certain death, but worse things can happen.

The children's fearful looks tell it all. They aren't deaf or blind. They've heard about — or maybe even seen — our neighbors who sneak out late at night to cut the flesh from the dead or yank apart the limbs of babies that have been put outside to die. They've heard about children who've been boiled alive in other villages that make up the commune. They've heard about classmates who've been strangled by their mothers before being cut up and put into the cooking pot. They've heard of fathers trying to convince their wives to eat their little ones, saying, "We're still young. We can have other children." It's all horrifying, but my mind — so dulled by hunger — has a hard time absorbing any of it. I tell myself these things could never happen in our house. Fu-shee is a good mother and she loves her children too much.

Samantha sleeps in the crook of my arm. I peel the blanket away from her face. Her lips and tongue move in a sucking motion. Even in sleep, she's hungry. She's five months old but looks more like two months. My milk has dried up, but at least I have formula to give her. That's more than Tao's brothers and sisters have. Last night, when the younger ones cried from their hunger pangs, Fu-shee gave them hot water to drink and told them to sleep on their bellies so they'd feel full. They didn't fall asleep though. Their stomachs can never acclimate to eating green crops, rotting tubers, dried sweet potato vines, or other scavenged leaves, bark, and roots, and one after another child ran to use the nightstool. The stench in the main room was beyond putrid.

I didn't get much sleep either. Tao and I did the husband-wife thing last night. We had sex because it reaffirmed we'd be fine and reminded us that we're still alive, but I was disgusted with myself as soon as it was over.

I want to visit Kumei and Yong to take my mind off my hunger and off what I did with Tao. I place the baby next to Jie Jie. I'll be away only a few minutes. They'll probably still be asleep when I return. I leave them snuggled on the floor, tiptoe out of the house, and plod down the hill through the village toward the villa.

Many of the houses and other buildings are crumbling, because either the metal that held them together was taken to make steel or the wood was seized to make fires for the blast furnaces. Even a wall in the old ancestral hall, where Z.G. gave his art lessons two and a half years ago, has collapsed. The people sent to live there as punishment died. The scholar's tree that once stood so proud in the center of the main square has been stripped of its bark and leaves. The ground beneath it is bloody. The willows are as naked as they are in winter. The elm trees that once provided shade along the path out of the village have also been reduced to bare skeletons. The people? We drag ourselves from place to place, vacant looks in our eyes, thinking constantly of food, our legs, stomachs, and foreheads strangely bloated.

A week ago, Brigade Leader Lai made a new announcement over the loudspeaker. "Meals will no longer be served in the canteen. The masses may now pick up food from the canteen and take it back to their homes. You said you missed eating at home. Now you can be with your families again."

What he meant was he didn't want to hear people talk about food, which has become more dangerous than discussing politics. He also didn't want to see any more people collapse from hunger, die right on the canteen floor, or — even more distressing — watch relatives weep over the dead. Now we send one family member to pick up our daily grain ration of a quarter of a *jin* of rice or some other starch — less than a fourth of what's needed for survival — at the leadership hall and bring it home, without everyone having to expend extra energy walking to the canteen, so we can die with our families without others having to witness another death scene.

This isn't like last year, when a few elders and babies died. *A lot* of people are dying. Two weeks ago, we received word that my father-in-law died from a fever after working in freezing water on an irrigation project a long distance from here. Brigade Leader Lai doesn't want anyone to know how many of their neighbors have perished, so we couldn't tack yellow paper outside the house to announce my father-in-law's death. We were forbidden to mourn him in public. We weren't allowed to make offerings to help him on his way to the afterworld. So, buried far from home, he is consigned to becoming a hungry ghost, forever wandering and lost. And we can seek no solace in Buddhism or Daoism for fear of being labeled reactionaries.

Every day Fu-shee, the smaller children, and I fan out in the hills around Green Dragon to strip trees of their bark and leaves, dig up roots, and search for wild grass. We'll eat anything, and we have. But you can't eat a leather belt like it's a crisp cucumber. You soak it, boil it, and chew on it for days. Once we tried eating Kwan Yin soil — named after the Goddess of Mercy. You take dirt, mix in dried grass, boil it, and then eat it. You can imagine how it tasted, and none of us ate very much. That turned out to be a good thing, because a family up the hill ate it three days in a row. The mud hardened in their stomachs and they died painfully.

I know I should be crippled from the horrors I've witnessed, but I'm too hungry for emotions. My hunger is all I can feel or think about. It's like a snake slithering through my brain, down to my stomach, out to my fingers, then down my legs and back up to my brain. It never stops.

I reach the villa and go straight to the kitchen, knowing I'll find Kumei there. We speak in clipped sentences to save energy.

"Yong died," she announces.

"What are you going to do?" I ask.

"Hide her. Hope she isn't found."

"But the brigade leader lives here."

"He moved out of the villa a few days ago. He's gone to the leadership hall." This is more than I've heard

Kumei say in ages, and I can see the toll it takes. "He says he needs to protect what's left of the commune's grain supply."

I think he had a different reason. The villa has twenty-nine bedrooms, but the leadership hall gives him total privacy. People will do anything for food. Many women in the commune have walked or crawled to the villa to prostitute themselves to the brigade leader in exchange for a single bun. Now they'll go to the leadership hall, where Brigade Leader Lai won't have to worry about anyone watching him. It's a long way, and I wonder how many women will die either going or coming.

"The villa has lots of places to hide a body," Kumei continues. "Yong's too withered to stink. I hope I have the strength to keep moving her and still collect her food ration."

Many families are doing this, hiding the corpse of mother, father, brother, sister, wife, husband, grandma, or grandpa in the house, so an extra ration can be picked up each day at the canteen.

I bite my lower lip, thinking of the old woman. She suffered so many indignities in the last ten years of her life. I swallow, and then say, "I'll help move her, if you want."

Starving is a grim business, but Kumei nods, grateful.

"Ta-ming is very weak," she informs me. "He hasn't gotten off his mat in two days."

"Do you have anything to give him?"

She doesn't respond. We both know the answer: no. And now that Brigade Leader Lai is gone, she can't give his scraps to her son.

Kumei takes me to see Yong, who lies curled like a baby. Even in death she wears the white ribbon of denunciation. Kumei and I sit on the edge of the bed. I put a hand on Yong's ankle, and then tell my two friends about having sex with Tao. Yong doesn't respond, of course. Kumei tries to look sympathetic, but I know what she's thinking: *I need food.*

We're caught in the jaws of hunger, and our minds are tortured by this thought. And as hungry and weak as we are, we know that tomorrow and for the next six days, until next Sunday, we'll have to work, pulling plows, digging wells, planting, and weeding from 6a.m. until 6p.m., followed by a political meeting or struggle session, with just a bowl of mirror soup — so thin you can see your reflection in it — to sustain us.

I catch a glimpse of myself in Yong's mirror. My body is as thin as a ginseng root. My hands are as bony as dried twigs. My skin looks translucent. My hair hangs lifeless. My lips, which were soft and full, have shrunk to almost nothing. I'll turn twenty-two on the twentieth of this month, but hunger has turned me into an old woman nearing death. I think of my friends Hazel and Leon back in Chinatown. Hazel's probably gotten married, and Leon will have graduated from Yale by now. If I'd stayed home . . . What would be happening? Maybe I'd have a job, my own apartment, my first car . . .

Later, I take the long, slow walk back up the hill to my house. There's still no activity on the terrace, but I can see my mother-in-law has put a pot of water on the outdoor stove: breakfast.

Inside, Tao, Fu-shee, Jie Jie, and some of the children are up and dressed. They sit on stools and boxes around the table. They don't talk or make sounds. They don't squirm or push each other. Their concentration is totally focused on something in the middle of the table. They're waiting and watching. Their eyes somehow manage to gleam like those of animals and yet be dull as dirt.

I peer over their shoulders to see what they're looking at. It's something small and wrapped in a blanket.

"Samantha!" I scream.

Could she have died in the few minutes I was away? The bundle moves. As I reach forward to pick up my baby, I hear a strange barking sound. My hands draw back. It's not Sam. I know her cry.

All the while, my husband has not moved. His eyes are like coal — dead and opaque. My body shakes as I reach over one of the children and pick up the bundle. I open the blanket. It's Sung-ling's baby, who looks hours, maybe minutes, from death.

"Where is Sam?" I ask.

They look at me, hungry, desperate, as though I'm holding their last meal. I step back in horror. I am holding their last meal! I've heard whispers about something the villagers have been doing in Black Bridge Village. They call it *I Tzu, Erh Shih* — Swap Child, Make Food — when mothers trade infants, let them die, and then feed them to their families.

"Where is Sam?" I shriek in terror, but no one responds.

I hold Sung-ling's daughter close to my chest and run to her parents' home. I push through the door and find a scene similar to the one I just left. Party Secretary Feng Jin and Sung-ling — who once were portly but now are wasted and waxy looking — stare at Sam. At least they have the decency to weep.

I hand Sung-ling her infant and swoop up my daughter. I hold her so tightly, she cries. I don't think I've ever heard a happier sound. I begin to back out of the house.

"Please don't report us," Feng Jin says weakly. "If you do, we'll be sent away for re-education through labor."

"What does it matter?" I ask. "You're going to die anyway."

It's a curse, but it's also a pronouncement of truth. My heart is racing and I feel more weak and terrified than I thought imaginable, but I manage to step back into the morning air. It's spring. I can see the day is beautiful. We should be out planting, but we're dying and becoming animals in the process. I may have failed as a daughter, but I can't fail as a mother. My mother used to tell me that Heaven never seals off all exits. There has to be a way out of here. I return to Tao's hut. Fu-shee and the children have gone back to the mats on the floor. The children have coiled into little clumps against their mother, waiting to die. I don't care. Tao still sits at the table, his legs spread, one arm dangling, his jaw slack.

I get a piece of cloth and tie Samantha to my body. I won't let her leave my touch again. I step over and around those on the floor. Their eyes look up at me like sea creatures. I pack the last of the baby formula, get my American money and a few clothes for Sam and me. I go outside and pour some of the boiling water into bottles. Then, without looking back, I walk down the hill, past the villa, up the next hill, and down again. I don't have written permission to leave, but no one stops me. Eventually, I'll reach the main road. From there, I'll walk to Tun-hsi. It's not a big town, but I'm sure I'll find someone desperate enough or dumb enough to change some of my American dollars into *yuan*. Then I'll take a boat to Shanghai and my mom.

Many times during the last few weeks, I've wondered if only the Dandelion Number Eight People's Commune has suffered and if our food shortages were merely a matter of bad leadership. I don't walk very far before I get answers. I just left what I thought was the ultimate horror, but I pass many other frightening sights on the road. A man offers to sell me "rabbit" meat. His wife sits a few feet away, her eyes blank, two large, wet splotches on her blouse from the milk that drips from her breasts. Others pull themselves hand over hand along the road, through the fields, and around dead bodies. Are they looking for food? Are they trying to escape? Are they so deranged and weak from hunger that they don't know what they're doing? How can the dead and dying be out here at all when we've been told runaways will be caught and sent away for re-education? Maybe the number of people fighting razor-sharp hunger is too great for local authorities to do anything

439

about. Maybe the famine has spread across the country. If so, then millions of people must be dead and dying.

When I can walk no farther, I sleep by the side of the road with Sam tied tightly to my body. In the morning, I continue on to Tun-hsi, where I go straight to the river landing to buy a boat ticket for Shanghai. I'm turned away at a checkpoint by a guard, who tells me that the schedules have been cut in half because there's no fuel. But even if a boat were scheduled, I wouldn't be allowed to board.

"You're a country woman," he says brusquely. "You don't have an internal passport or a travel permit. You aren't allowed to go to a city. Forget about Shanghai. Go home."

I'm not going to do that. I hire a pedicab to take me to the bus station, where again I'm not allowed past the entry checkpoint. I take another pedicab to the train terminal. A train is not the easiest or fastest way to Shanghai, but it's my last option. A checkpoint is set up here too, but I find a way around it by waiting until the guards are distracted by an entire starving family making a ruckus and then ducking around them. Inside the station, I'm told, once again, that the schedules have been curtailed, but this time I'm lucky. I only have to wait three hours for the train. I buy more hot water and mix some formula for Samantha. Once aboard, I hold my baby to my breast, cover her with a blanket, and surreptitiously feed her the bottle. I'm still hours from Shanghai, but already I feel tremendous relief. How could I have not done this sooner?

440

But before we can pull out of the station, uniformed guards enter the car and demand to see everyone's papers. In truth, it's not hard to pick out those who shouldn't be on the train. We're the ones dressed in rags, our bodies artificially bloated or our arms, legs, and faces just skin over bones. Still, the guards follow a process, going from person to person, checking documents and identification cards. I look around. Is there a place to hide? No. Is there anything I can do to prevent myself from being kicked off the train? Maybe offer a bribe, but the risk is great. I could be arrested.

The oldest of the guards approaches.

"Please," I say, folding back the blanket to reveal Samantha's face.

"You're a runaway. You have to get off the train," the guard says, not without sympathy. "You have to go back to your village."

I pull out a hundred-dollar bill, hoping he's old enough to recognize American money. He looks around to see how close the other guards are.

"Put that away before they see you," he whispers. "Besides, it won't do any good. The authorities don't want anyone to know how bad things are in the countryside, so even if I let you stay on the train, you'll be turned back later. And those guards might not be so understanding."

I start to cry as he lifts me up by the elbow and guides me to the exit. After he helps me down to the platform, he opens a satchel slung over his shoulder, pulls out two wheat buns, and tucks them in the blanket between the baby and me.

"Go home," he says. "That's the best thing."

I've never felt such despair. I walk out of the station, sit on the steps, and eat half a bun. The taste is amazing and I'm very hungry, but I have to be careful. After being on a starvation diet, my stomach has shrunk. Plus all the food substitutes I've eaten have ruined my digestion. I'm unsure how much food my stomach will hold or my intestines can handle, but this little bit of sustenance gives me more energy — physical and mental — than I've had in weeks. I walk down alleys, looking for a safe place to sleep.

The next morning, I fill Sam's bottles at a hot water store, feed her, and eat the other half of my first bun, making sure I catch every crumb. I consider whether I have the strength to walk to Shanghai. Impossible. I still have money, but it's hard to spend. I don't have the necessary coupons, and I'm turned away at store after store, café after café. Finally, I'm able to buy some dried sweet potato flour. When I get back to Green Dragon, I'll make a batter with water and grill small cakes. If I share them with my husband and his family, we may live a few more days.

On my way back to Green Dragon, I sleep again by the side of the road. Only three nights have passed, but there are more bodies, including those of the man and woman who were trying to sell their dead baby as rabbit meat. I enter Green Dragon in a state of utter defeat. Every time I think things can get no lower, something worse happens. I walk into the house and discover Tao sitting alone almost as I left him four days ago. The house is eerily quiet. The children are gone. Tao's mother is gone.

"You shouldn't have come back," he says.

"I have nowhere to go." I sit on the floor, hold Samantha to my shoulder, and pat her back. "Where is everyone?"

"After you left, I went to work in the fields." He squeezes his eyes shut. "When I came home, Brigade Leader Lai's men were burying . . ." He opens his eyes and stares at me.

My stomach, which for the first time in weeks is not rumbling and crying out with hunger, sinks in fear and apprehension. "What happened?"

"They dug a pit. They put my mother and the little children in it. Then they threw dirt on top of them. They buried them alive."

This is dreadful, sickening news, but I think, maybe they're the lucky ones. They're out of their suffering now.

"You said the little children. What about Jie Jie and your other older brothers and sisters?"

"Brigade Leader Lai had them marched out of the village along with Party Secretary Feng Jin and Sung-ling."

"To where?"

Tao shakes his head. "No one will tell me."

"What about you?"

I always thought he had such a beautiful smile. Now his face sets into the death mask I've seen on so many corpses on the road — emaciated lips pulled back, too much gum exposed, and teeth looking like dried bones.

"I'm a lesson to others in the village."

I should ask how the brigade leader found out about Tao's family's plan to Swap Child, Make Food, but I really don't care. I want to weep for the children, but I have no tears. For the others, maybe I should feel more compassion, but I don't. These people were willing to trade my baby to eat. Beyond that, I'm already calculating how much farther my sweet potato flour will go with only two of us to feed instead of eleven. Because I'm not going to give up. *Heaven never seals off all exits*. I have to believe that.

I force myself to stand. I pull out everything I own, almost all of it things either my mother or aunt have given or sent me: sanitary napkins, but my system has been so weakened that I haven't had a period since Samantha was born; the pouch with three sesame seeds, three beans, and three coppers that was supposed to protect me but may become my last meal; the pretty baby clothes from Bullock's Wilshire that I doubt Sam will live long enough to wear; and my mother's camera, which she left along with the film to inspire me to take photographs of my new life but which, until this moment, has seemed a useless instrument.

I put together one last, desperate plan. I take out a piece of paper and write a letter to my mother. I have to couch my words in a way that will encourage Brigade Leader Lai to let my letter go through and that my mother will still understand what I'm telling her. I read the letter again and put it in a padded envelope stitched from a piece of cloth. Then I tie Samantha to my chest, pick up the camera and the unsealed letter, and leave the house.

I pass the villa and keep going along the path that borders the stream. I stop at the turnoff to the Charity Pavilion. This has always been a lonely stretch, which is why it was so easy for Tao and me to duck onto it without many people seeing us. I sit on a rock, pull out the other bun the guard on the train gave me, and eat it. My mind needs to be powerful and quick. I drink from the stream, and then I continue on to the leadership hall. I walk all the way around the building, praying I'll find what I need. Just outside the door to the brigade leader's private kitchen, I spot a few chicken feathers. None of us have seen an egg, let alone had a bite of chicken, in months, but the brigade leader has had live chickens specially brought in and slaughtered for his meals. I take a few of the feathers and carefully slip them into the bottom of my cloth envelope. I don't think my mother will know what they mean, but I hope she'll ask someone. Then I walk around to the front of the building, knock on the door, and ask to see the brigade leader. The smell of cooked food permeates the halls as I'm led to his office. Of everyone in the Dandelion Number Eight People's Commune, Brigade Leader Lai alone has not lost weight. A pistol lies in plain view on his desk. People are too weak to rebel, so is it here to remind those who come begging of his dominance?

"Comrade," he says, "how can I help you?"

I raise my voice in an effort to project full Great Leap Forward enthusiasm (and not seduction!). "My mother and father must see the mural our commune produced."

"You want to invite them to visit?" His grimace lets me know that this is not even a remote possibility.

"I'm not inviting them to return." (*But, oh, God, please make them understand I need them to come here.*) "I want my father to show our mural to the authorities at the Artists' Association. I'm sure this organization, the most important for artists in the country, will recognize Tao as a model comrade —"

"You want that after what he and his family just did?"

"Please let me finish. I want the Artists' Association to recognize the Dandelion Number Eight People's Commune as a model commune. And, of course, it must also recognize our farsighted brigade leader," I add deferentially. "We never could have created the mural without your guidance."

He taps a fingernail on his desk, considering. His first comment is the very one I expect.

"Your husband said the mural's content was black."

"He only said that because he was angry with me. I embarrassed him with my request for a divorce. But now, if I help him get recognized as a model artist, he'll forgive me, as both of us should forgive him. He has lost almost his entire family. The baby and I are all he has left. Besides, your leniency can bring you great honors. As you can see yourself, the mural is very patriotic. Have you not seen the spaceships, the giant radishes, the . . . Oh, you'll receive much acclaim!"

446

The brigade leader likes my explanation, especially since he has so much to gain from it. Still, he doesn't want any outsiders coming to the Dandelion Number Eight People's Commune. He feigns indifference, although his desire is quite clear.

"You said you wanted your father to see the mural. How can he do that if he doesn't come in person?"

I pull out my mother's camera. "If you help me take some photographs, I'll send the film to Shanghai. Again, all praise belongs to you and the commune. There will be many honors. No one will come here, but the masses will hear your name over loudspeakers in houses and communes all across the country." I pause to let him conjure that image. "As you know, all it takes are connections, and my father —"

"Has good *guan-hsi*," he finishes for me. He pushes his chair from his desk. "Come. Let's do this quickly."

We go outside. I take a few shots to show Brigade Leader Lai how to use the camera.

"You're doing fine by yourself. You don't need my help," he says, stating the obvious.

"I need to be in some of the photographs," I respond. "Otherwise how will my parents know the mural's from our commune? Anyone could be sending the film. You don't want credit to go to the wrong commune, do you?"

"Right, right, absolutely," he agrees.

I back up, stand next to a part of the mural that shows chickens pecking at the ground, with eggs the size of footballs in nests nearby. Snap. Snap. Slowly we move around the building until we reach the figure of Jesus hidden in the branches and bark of the tree. Snap. Snap.

"Excuse me, Brigade Leader, but could you wait one second? I need to do something."

He pulls the camera from his eye. I peel off my jacket, take Sam out of her sling, and then hold her up.

"My parents haven't seen my baby yet," I say. "I think they'd like to see their granddaughter, don't you? That will make them feel even closer ties to our commune."

The brigade leader nods again and holds up the camera.

"Oh, please, Brigade Leader, step a little closer. Yes, a little closer still."

I'm exhausted from fear and concentration, but I smile for the camera. I know exactly the message this photograph will send. *Samantha and I are starving. We may be days from death. If you get this, please help us. If you come too late, at least you've seen your granddaughter.* If Brigade Leader Lai doesn't send the film, then there's nothing to be done.

The brigade leader hands me the camera. I follow him back inside the leadership hall. He sits behind his desk. I keep standing as I take the film out of the camera. I start to put the roll in the envelope with my letter and the chicken feathers.

"What's that?" he asks.

"The film has to go in an envelope, doesn't it?"

The brigade leader's eyes narrow. "What else is in there? Are you trying to communicate with the outside? This is against the rules."

"I can't send the film without a letter," I say.

"You may not send a letter."

"All right." I remove the film and put it in my pocket. I turn to leave.

"Wait! What does your letter say?"

I remove the piece of paper, careful not to disturb the feathers, and hand it to him. He quickly scans the lines with their abundant praise of Brigade Leader Lai for his foresight and guidance, and an explanation of what's on the film, noting that the mural is certainly the best in the county, that it was painted by Tao and other comrades, and that it sends a Great Leap Forward message to the masses. At the end, I added that, although we eat chicken every night, I hope my mother will send more of her special treats. (I asked for food knowing that the brigade leader has confiscated it before.) But all these are just words. The real message is in the film and with the chicken feathers. When the brigade leader finishes reading, he looks up. I'm pretty confident he'll send the letter, but to make sure I hold out the camera.

"You can keep this," I say.

He puts the letter in my hand as I put the camera in his. I tuck the letter and the film inside the cloth envelope. The brigade leader watches as I stitch it closed, making sure I don't add or subtract anything. When I'm done, I give it to him.

"The sooner they receive this, the sooner you'll have your acclaim," I say. I bow and then back out of his office, like I'm a lowly servant from feudal times.

I go home, rummage through my belongings again, and pull out the pouch my aunt gave me. I lay Sam on one of the sleeping mats, put the pouch over her head, and then push it down around her distended belly like a belt so there'll be no chance of strangulation. Then I lie down next to her. I don't know how quickly my package will leave here or what will happen to it when it passes through the censors' hands in Shanghai. Will my mom receive what I've sent in a few days, a week, never? I've done what I can, but the end is coming. I have only a little baby formula left. If I take the bits and pieces of my mother and aunt that I pasted over the window and boil them, I might be able to extract enough rice paste to make a weak milk to keep Sam alive for a while. For now, she sucks at my empty breast, too weak to complain. *The Boar always suffers in silence.*

I close my eyes. I hear the voices of the past in the wind and in the beating of my heart. My two mothers, my two fathers, and my dear uncle all tried to tell me I was wrong about the People's Republic of China. In the beginning, going all the way back to the University of Chicago, I thought socialism and communism were good, that people should share equally, that it wasn't fair that my family had suffered in America when others drove fancy cars, lived in big houses, and shopped in Beverly Hills. I ran away and came here in hopes of finding an ideal world, to find my birth father, to avoid my mother and aunt, and to crush my guilt. None of that worked the way I expected. The ideal world was filled with hypocrisy and with people like Z.G., who went to parties while the masses suffered. In finding my birth father, I only remembered how wonderful my father Sam was. He loved me unconditionally, while Z.G. wanted me as a muse, as a pretty daughter to show off, as a physical manifestation of his love for Auntie May, as an artist who would reflect how great an artist he is. I thought I could use idealism to solve my inner conflicts, but in healing my inner conflicts I destroyed my idealism.

As I gaze into my daughter's face, everything becomes very clear. My mother and aunt loved me, stood by me, and supported me, no matter what. They were both good mothers. My greatest misery and grief is that I have not been a good mother and I can't save my daughter. I pray that in our finals days and hours Samantha will know how much I love her.

Part IV

THE DRAGON RISES

Pearl

Separated by a Thread

At the beginning of April, I come home from a day of paper collecting to find a package from Joy. Finally! I hurry upstairs to my room and close the door. The package is in pristine condition, which means that no one has opened it or read the contents. I'm so excited that my hands are clumsy as I snip open the hand-sewn seams with scissors. A roll of film and a few feathers fall on the bed. I pick up one of the feathers and examine it closely. Why would Joy send these? Then I push the lot of them aside. But how happy I am for the film. At last I'll get to see my granddaughter. The letter dated from two weeks ago is filled with information that raises my spirits: "See the kind of plenty we have here? We eat chicken every night." (Which may explain the chicken feathers.) She writes about the baby. She describes the mural Sputnik the commune created and goes overboard in her gratitude to Brigade Leader Lai for his role in seeing the project completed. She ends with a request for me to send special treats. It's just as I've

455

dared to hope. Things are better in the countryside. I'm relieved and delighted she's doing so well.

I go to the pavilion and knock on Dun's door. I read him the letter and show him the film.

"Anything else?" he asks.

"That's it. Why do you ask?"

"She seems so positive. Do you think these are positive times?"

"She has a baby and a husband. She's where she wants to be."

He nods slowly, thinking about that.

"There were some chicken feathers in the package," I add. "I didn't think —"

"Let me see them."

We go back to my room and I show him the feathers. Dun stares at them gravely.

"Pearl, maybe it's nothing and I don't want you to get upset, but where my family was from a chicken feather was an urgent distress signal."

I know nothing of country ways, but Joy must have learned them. My mood instantly turns to anxiety and fear.

I hold up the film. "She may have sent a message here as well. If there's a message, a camera shop might not give me the prints." My voice trembles. I cannot be afraid. I hear a Dragon's strength when I next speak. "Let's go to Z.G. He's an artist. He'll know a photographer who can develop the film."

It's seven o'clock by the time we reach Z.G.'s house. The servant girls let us in. Of course, Z.G. isn't here.

"The master is at a banquet," the girl with the bob volunteers.

The older servant sighs. She's never going to be able to train her subordinates, but soon enough we've been served tea and the girls have backed out of the room. Dun sits in an overstuffed chair, and I pace impatiently. It's after eleven before Z.G. arrives. He's suave — like a movie star — showing no surprise that Dun and I are here so late at night.

"Have my girls been treating you well?" he asks. "Have you eaten yet? Can they pour you more tea?"

Here I am, in a desperate moment, and he's thinking about manners.

"We think Joy's in trouble. She sent a roll of film. Do you know anyone who can develop it?"

Dun explains about the chicken feathers, and Z.G. instantly recognizes their significance from a tale his grandmother used to tell. The concern on the two men's faces terrifies me, but I try to stay calm. Z.G. motions to us, and we follow him back outside. We walk quickly through the deserted streets. It's nearly midnight. In the New China, there are no late night strollers, people on their way to nightclubs or teahouses for final drinks, no prostitutes waiting to amuse. It's just the three of us, skirting down one alley after another. We dip into a courtyard and climb four flights of stairs. Z.G. bangs on a door. A man in a gray undershirt and baggy drawers answers.

"Hey, Z.G., it's been a long time. But it's late. What are you doing here?" He rubs his eyes to get the sleep out of them.

457

"Old friend, you need to do me a favor," Z.G. says, pushing the man back into his apartment.

Within minutes, the four of us are packed into a tiny darkroom illuminated by the glow of a bare red lightbulb that dangles from a cord. The photographer mixes chemicals and develops the film. He hangs the negatives on a line, and we wait impatiently for them to dry. Then he makes contact prints, which are put in a tray with a solution. The first image that comes into focus in its chemical bath shows an owl painted on the side of the leadership hall. The photographer sucks air through his teeth. "Bad," he mumbles. The other two men nod their heads somberly.

"What's wrong?" I ask.

"Owls are always taken as criticism," Dun explains. "Add that to the message of distress from the chicken feathers."

Z.G.'s friend hangs the first print on the line and then proceeds to develop a series of images showing the mural from each side of the leadership hall, with some details thrown in for good measure. Spaceships, giant corn, and even more chickens. How easy it is to spot my daughter's work as opposed to what Tao or the other people who must have helped painted. Then come photographs with Joy standing in front of the mural, her face thin, dressed in layers of padded clothes, and holding Samantha, who is equally bundled.

"Why doesn't she show the baby?" I ask. "I'm the grandmother. I want to see her."

Despite my impatience, Z.G.'s friend hangs each of these prints on the line. The next photograph shows Joy standing before what looks to me like Jesus on the cross, but maybe I'm seeing things. Once again, the photographer shakes his head. Is he worried for my daughter's safety or his own? Then he places the last photograph in its chemical bath. He swishes the paper with a pair of tongs. The image that comes into focus is one I won't forget as long as I live. Joy has taken off her jacket and unwrapped the baby. The person taking the photograph has come close so I can see my daughter and granddaughter. If I didn't know this was Joy, I wouldn't recognize her. She looks more like a ghost than a human. We stand in silence for a long moment, each of us absorbing what this means. Dun is the first to speak.

"We have to get her. We have to get her now."

"He's right," Z.G. says. "We have to go out there. We have to get her."

"But how?" I ask.

"We could submit applications for travel permits, but . . ." Dun hesitates, not wanting to state the obvious. Even if we applied for travel permits, there's no guarantee we'd get them. If we did get them, it would probably be too late.

"We could walk," I suggest.

"It's a long way," Z.G. says. "About four hundred kilometers."

I won't let that stop me. "My mother, my sister, and I walked out of Shanghai." I hear the desperation in my voice. But even if I could walk the 250 miles or so, we'd never get there in time. I stare at the photographs, despair creeping over me. Then

459

it hits me. "She's also sent a hint for how to get her in an official way."

The others eye me questioningly.

I gesture to the photographs of the mural hanging around us. "Joy said it is a 'model project made by a model commune.'"

Z.G. pinches his chin, slowly nodding, deep in thought. "We'll get permission to see it," he says at last. "We'll go to the Artists' Association as soon as it opens. We'll make them send us."

That seems unlikely, but I have to trust Z.G. or else I'll go crazy. He pulls the photographs off the line and hands them to me.

"Go home," he continues. "Get some clothes and —"

"Food," I finish for him.

"We have some rice," Dun says.

"And I'll get more," I add. Dun frowns. He knows about the special coupons I get from the Overseas Chinese Affairs Commission, but I haven't told him how much American money I have or that I use it to buy food on the black market. "May has also sent some food. I'll bring that and what I've saved — brown sugar and —"

"You're a mother," Z.G. cuts me off. "You know what Joy and the baby will need." He looks at his watch and frowns. "It's one now."

Which means no buses are running. We've already hit our first obstacle.

"We'll go back to your house now," I say. "We'll leave at five, when the city buses start running, gather everything, and be back at your house by eight."

We thank the photographer and retrace our steps to Z.G.'s house. We should sleep, but we can't. When Dun and I go back to my neighborhood a few hours later, the early morning rhythms are in full swing. We purchase what foodstuffs we can find. We'll buy ginger and soy milk when we get closer to Green Dragon.

The boarders are suspicious, as well they should be.

"Why are you taking rice from the bin?" the widow asks. "You aren't allowed to do that."

"Are you running away together?" Cook inquires. "That kind of thing will not be tolerated in the New China —"

"You're going to get us all in trouble," one of the dancing girls complains.

I can't and won't listen to them.

We're back at Z.G.'s by eight. We leave our bundles in the entry and the three of us walk to the Artists' Association. When the doors open, Z.G. asks to see the director and we're shown into his office. This man was pudgy when I first came here looking for Joy and Z.G.; now he's gaunt and gray. Z.G. lays photographs of the mural — minus the ones showing the owl, the Christ figure, and Joy and the baby — on the desk. I read Joy's letter praising the commune and in particular her husband's role in launching this particular Sputnik.

When I'm done, Z.G. says, "You should bring Feng Tao and his wife to Shanghai."

"Why would I want to do that?" the director asks, skeptical.

"Because the boy is one of Chairman Mao's favorites," Z.G. answers. "His work was submitted to the New Year's poster contest two years ago."

"The contest *you* won," the director notes.

"Yes, but Feng Tao was my student, and this is a model project from a model peasant," Z.G. goes on. "If you bring him to Shanghai, then our branch of the Artists' Association will get the credit, since what he's accomplished is an outgrowth of your wisdom."

"Your punishment, you mean," the director observes wryly, not giving an inch.

"I'll spend even more time in the countryside teaching the masses," Z.G. offers, "if that's what it takes."

I have a different idea. I open my bag and hold out American dollars. The director takes them, just as he did when I came here the last time.

"You and the woman will go to the countryside to deliver the good news that the mural will be submitted to Peking under the Shanghai Artists' Association's auspices," the director announces. "Bring the boy and his family here. I will send word ahead to the commune cadres, so they'll know you're coming. But only four travel permits. This one" — he points to Dun — "has no reason to go."

I want Dun — I *need* him — to come with us, but the director won't be persuaded otherwise.

It's not going to be easy to get to Green Dragon. All boat and train travel has been curtailed. Z.G. has a car but he doesn't know how to drive, and we can't ask the chauffeur to take us because he doesn't have a travel permit. After some discussion, Z.G.'s servant girls dress me in one of their uniforms so I'll look more like a chauffeur and our appearance won't be questioned. By noon, Z.G.'s Red Flag limousine is packed and we're ready to go.

"Be careful," Dun says. "Come back to me."

"I will," I tell him. As we embrace, I whisper in his ear, "I love you."

Then Z.G.'s chauffeur hands me the car keys. I open the backseat door for Z.G. Once he's inside with the blue curtains drawn, I walk around to the driver's side, get in, start the ignition, and put my foot on the gas pedal. At the corner, I look in the rear-view mirror for one last glimpse of Dun.

On the outskirts of Shanghai, we pass a camp that's been set up to hold peasants who've been captured trying to enter the city illegally. From here, the drive is extremely slow. The roads are terrible — at times almost impassable with mud and ruts — but roadblocks are our biggest problem. We're stopped every few miles to have our papers checked. We're going against the tide. The roadblocks are to prevent even more peasants from leaving their villages to come to cities — and how many people we see being turned away and sent home. Even though we're going in the opposite direction, my hands sweat and my heart races at every checkpoint.

We reach Tun-hsi around midnight. We check into a guesthouse, but how can we sleep? The next morning, we go downstairs for a meal. It's a crisp spring morning

463

and we sit outside at a table under a tree. The innkeeper won't accept our city rice coupons, so we can't have porridge. Instead, we're served a soup made with water greens and water. Then it's like one of those scary movies Joy liked to watch on television. People — walking skeletons, zombies — begin to emerge from corners, alleys, and homes. They stare at us as we eat. The minute we stand, a couple of them bolt from the crowd, grab our bowls, and lick them clean.

A few miles out of Tun-hsi, a nightmare landscape appears before us. People dressed in rags crawl by the side of the road. Dead bodies lie splayed in the fields and dot the road. The smell should be atrocious, but the corpses have no blood or meat left to decay. They're like mummies — gray and emaciated. Wild dogs are plentiful, and they feast on the dead. I drive slowly, swerving from one side of the road to the other in an effort to miss the gruesome obstacles. Z.G. sits behind me. We could still be pulled over, and the master would never ride next to the driver. I keep glancing in the rear-view mirror. Z.G.'s eyes are wide with shock. We're both terrified for Joy.

I come around a corner and brake as hard as I can. A couple lie in the center of the road. I can't drive around them. We sit in the car, the engine idling.

"What should we do?" I ask, my hands gripping the steering wheel.

"Let's give them something to eat. Maybe we can move them that way."

464

I don't want to get out of the car, but I do. Z.G. and I look in the trunk and pull out some crackers. We walk tentatively toward the couple, both of us holding our crackers at arm's length. The man reaches forward to grab Z.G.'s cracker and then collapses, dead. The woman takes the cracker from my hand, clutches it to her chest, and curls into a little ball to protect it.

"You should try to eat it," I say softly. The woman stares at her dead companion, her eyes unseeing, her treasure protected. It's as though I've given her the most precious Christmas gift possible, something that should be saved and cherished — never broken, let alone eaten.

Z.G., showing nerve I didn't know he had, grabs the dead man's heels and pulls him to the side of the road. Then I help him move the woman. As soon as we're done, he gruffly says, "Come on. We need to keep moving."

Several more times, we have to stop to move the dead or dying from the road. The sun shines resplendently overhead. Always I expect silence when I get out of the car — no singing, no sounds of working in the fields, no braying of animals, no birds trilling — but cicadas, immune to the concerns of humanity, drone steadily. Then, at one of our stops, cutting right through the cicadas — and piercing into my soul — children and babies yelp, sob, and whimper. Z.G. and I scan the fields, searching for the source of these sounds that seem to come at us from every direction.

Ahead of us something moves — bouncing angrily — not far from the side of the road. It's a small girl's head

465

and shoulders. The parents have dug a hole deep enough to prevent escape and abandoned their daughter in it. They must have hoped someone would stop and take her home. I take a few steps forward so I can see down into the hole. The girl's naked. Her skin hangs like wrinkled tofu skin, and her belly is swollen and purple. Then Z.G. grabs my shoulders.

"Look." He points to different spots in the field.

Other children and babies have been abandoned in these pits too. They're everywhere. I think I'm going to be sick.

"This is horrible, but we have to go," Z.G. says.

"But —" I gesture to the field.

"We can't help them. We have to get Joy and her baby."

I'm overcome with despair. If I save even one of these children, then I might be too late for my own flesh and blood. I close my ears and my heart, get back in the car, and continue driving.

Finally, we reach the old drop-off point for Green Dragon Village. Since the director of the Artists' Association called ahead, I expect to see a welcome party, as we had the last time we came. Instead, the road is ominously empty and quiet, while the footpath we used to take to Green Dragon has been blocked with sawhorses and other junk. A sign with an arrow to the Dandelion Number Eight People's Commune points to a new road that cuts through the fields and veers around Green Dragon's enveloping hills. The commune's cadres wouldn't have done this unless they

466

wanted us to see Joy and the baby there — at the site of the mural.

I take the road to the center of the commune. Here's the Happiness Garden for the aged, the nursery, and the clinic. The canteen's cornstalk walls, however, have broken apart and the roof has collapsed. And there, just as in the photographs Joy sent, is the leadership hall with its critical but stunningly colorful mural. Next to the hall, small children jump and play on piles of what looks to be freshly cut hay. They clap their hands and cry out, "Welcome! Welcome!" They perform as though their lives depend on it, and maybe they do, because their stomachs are distended from hunger and the look in their eyes is not something anyone should see. A group of adults, clean but grotesquely thin, hold signs with words of gracious salutation and sing the usual Great Leap Forward songs, but there's no honest enthusiasm — or energy — from them either.

Brigade Leader Lai steps forward. He looks the same as when I last saw him. He greets us and gestures for us to enter the building. I hurry inside, expecting to see Joy. After all, she wrote the letter. It could only have come with the brigade leader's knowledge. In fact, now that I think about it, he probably took the photographs of her and the baby. A round table is set for a banquet.

"We have prepared a twenty-course banquet for our honorable guests," Brigade Leader Lai announces.

The table is set for three.

"Where is my daughter?" I ask.

"She and the artist are at home. There is no need to see them. Enjoy! Enjoy!" He clasps his hands expectantly. "After dinner, Li Zhi-ge can present his award." He bows his head deferentially. "I hope I'm not presuming too much —"

I run back outside. The men, women, and children, who moments before were jumping, waving, and singing, sit on their haunches, shoving small balls of rice — presumably a reward for their performance — into their mouths, while a guard keeps watch. I can reach Green Dragon on foot in about ten minutes. If I drive back to the original crossroads and then walk, it's a few miles.

Z.G. takes my arm. "Let's go."

We hurry along the path that runs next to the stream. In minutes, we cross the little stone bridge and enter Green Dragon. Bodies lie everywhere. The smell wasn't so bad on the road, but here the odor of death and decay is noxious. I look up the hill to Tao's family home. I don't see any signs of life, but then the whole village is deathly quiet.

Z.G. dashes up the hill. I follow close behind. The door to the house stands open. The outdoor kitchen looks like it hasn't been used in some time. Three rusty wheelbarrows tilt against the wall. That same broken ladder still lies at a haphazard angle. No one has righted it since the first time I came here.

Z.G. stares at me. His daughter, my daughter — she's inside. I take a breath to steady my heart and prepare myself for the worst thing a mother can imagine.

We enter the house. The room is dark, cold, and dank. Shredded paper hangs from the windows.

Sleeping mats stretch across the floor, but no one is on them. Then, in a corner, I see a slight movement. It's Tao. He looks bad.

"Where is Joy?" I ask.

I follow the direction of his eyes and see a heap of padded clothes in another corner. I run across the room and kneel next to the pile. I pull gently on it, and it falls forward. It's Joy. Her skin looks like old parchment. Her cheeks are hollow and her lips have a bluish tint. I suck in air, sure we're too late, but the sound causes her eyes to open. They burn bright — staring in an unseeing, feverish way. Her mouth moves, but no sound comes out. "Mama."

I swallow my terror and fear. I can't be too late.

"Z.G., boil some water. Hurry."

While he goes back outside, I peel away more of Joy's clothes, and there tucked against her naked but shriveled breasts is my granddaughter. She too is alive. I open my bag and bring out the packet of brown sugar I brought with me. I take a few granules and drop them into Joy's mouth. Then I do the same to the baby.

Z.G. returns with a pot of hot water. I make a weak tea of brown sugar and some slices of fresh ginger. While Z.G. stirs the concoction, I look for a knife. I slice open my arm and let the blood drip into a cup. For millennia, daughters-in-law have done this for their mothers-in-law out of respect and reverence during times of famine. I do it because I love my daughter. Z.G. wordlessly pours the tea over the blood. I spoon a bit into Joy's mouth while Z.G. blows on another spoonful to give to the baby. Our eyes meet. *What now?*

I'm torn. Should we stay here and build their strength or try to get them back to Shanghai as quickly as possible? What will happen when the brigade leader realizes we want to go back to Shanghai? It's clear he's been hoarding food while the people in the commune have been dying. What would the punishment be for that, and what would the brigade leader be willing to do to keep his activities a secret? We have to get out of here and we have to hurry.

I feel hopeless. Z.G. is just an artist, a Rabbit artist at that. He's not good in an emergency, but then I realize with sudden clarity that I'm not either. My sister always got us out of trouble. What would May do? After I was raped and my mother died, May put me in a wheelbarrow and pushed me to safety.

"Can you push a wheelbarrow?" I ask Z.G.

We grab some quilts and tuck them into two of the wheelbarrows to provide cushioning. Then Z.G. carries Joy and the baby outside and lays them on the quilts. While he goes back to get Tao, I give Joy more of the blood tea and half a cracker that I've pre-chewed. Z.G. reemerges from the house, supporting Tao, who has just enough strength to walk. Joy sees him and begins to mutter and shake her head. "No, no, no." She must be delirious.

I smooth hair from her forehead. "Everything's going to be fine now."

Joy turns her head and closes her eyes. Z.G. and I heft our wheelbarrows and begin to walk. The first part is easy. Joy barely weighs anything and we're going

470

downhill. We turn right at the villa. When we reach the front gate, I stop.

"Wait," I call ahead to Z.G. I run inside the villa. Kumei, Yong, and Ta-ming aren't in the kitchen. I hurry through the courtyards to Kumei's bedroom. She lies on the bed. Ta-ming sits cross-legged next to her. Flies feast in the corners of his mouth and eyes. He's a bundle of protruding and crooked bones. His eyes are vacant.

"Ta-ming," I beckon softly.

He continues to stare at his mother, unable, it seems, to expend the energy to turn his head. I slowly approach so as not to frighten him. The truth is, he may be beyond frightening. I try to rouse Kumei, calling her name and shaking her. She doesn't open her eyes and her body remains limp. It's too late to do anything for her, but I can't leave Ta-ming — not after leaving all those other children and babies in the pits by the side of the road. As for Yong, there's no way she could still be alive. I take Ta-ming's hand, and he looks up at me.

"Can you walk?" I ask.

He moves like an ancient — brittle, deliberate, and slow. I go to the chest in the corner, grab some clothes, the boy's violin — about all that's left from his inheritance from his father — and some drawings that Kumei did in class with Z.G. Then we walk back through the silence of the villa's courtyards and corridors. Once he and his worldly goods are stowed in the wheelbarrow next to Joy, I pick up the handles and we begin to walk back to the center of the commune.

471

I'm terrified about what will happen when we reach the car. Miraculously, the brigade leader and his guards are nowhere in sight. We don't have time to wonder where they are or what they're planning. Z.G. and I quickly pile the four nearly lifeless bodies in the backseat. Z.G. joins me in the front seat, I gun the motor, and we begin the long and grisly journey back through the death roads toward Shanghai.

I wish we could drive straight out of the country. Go north to the Soviet Union? That might be worse than where we are now. Go south to Canton and hope we can cross the border? That would be a brutally hard and long journey, taking weeks of travel over dirt roads and through numerous guard posts. Joy and the others wouldn't make it. We have to go back to Shanghai for them to build strength (if they live), gather money and food (if I can find them), and make an escape plan (if we survive that long).

We stop where we can to buy a bit of food, doling it out to Joy, Tao, and Ta-ming in one or two bites at a time so their stomachs will adapt and accept the sustenance. We give the baby bottles of watered-down soy milk, trying not to overwhelm her weakened system. The boy hasn't spoken and the baby's cries are weak. Neither Joy nor Tao has much to say. Talking takes too much effort. At night, I pull the car far from the side of the road. Z.G. helps Joy to the front seat, where she sleeps with her head in my lap. I'm exhausted, but I stay awake, watching my daughter's chest rise and fall with each breath.

472

When we near the roadblocks preventing the masses from entering cities like Hangchow and Soochow, Z.G. returns to the backseat and pulls the curtains. Much to my relief, we pass through most of the security posts without difficulty. We were here a couple of days ago, and the young men with their machine guns still remember the limousine with the blue curtains. Additional questions are unnecessary.

It takes us five days to reach the outskirts of Shanghai. A little food, plenty of water, tea, and soy milk have considerably revived our bunch. Looking in the rear-view mirror, I see Joy staring out one window while Tao leans on the other side of the seat, staring out the other. Ta-ming sits between them, eyes straight forward, seeing nothing.

Remembering the last big checkpoint with the camp for those who've tried to enter the city illegally, I pull off the main road and drive to a secluded area. Z.G. and I do what we can to make Tao and Joy presentable. I brush Joy's hair and pin it into a bun at the nape of her neck. Z.G. dresses Tao in one of his shirts and buttons it. We have only four travel permits. The sentries outside Shanghai are bound to be more inquisitive than those in the countryside. The baby can easily be hidden under Joy's blouse, but what can we do about Ta-ming? I take him to the back of the car and open the trunk. He grips my hand tightly.

I kneel down so we're eye to eye. I hold his shoulders and speak directly to him. "You have to get in here. It's going to be very dark and very scary. You'll need to stay silent. But it won't last long. I promise."

473

I tuck him in the trunk, put his violin case in his arms for comfort, close the lid, and drive back to the main road. Coming from this direction, we can see into the camp, where bodies have been dumped in a big pit. I brake at the final roadblock and hand the guard four sets of papers. He leafs through them suspiciously. When he peers over my shoulder to see into the backseat, Z.G. snarls at him. "We're on important business. Step aside and let us through or I'll report you!" It sounds tough, and the guard obeys. I'm the only one who hears the fear in Z.G.'s voice. As soon as we pass into the city proper, I drive down an alley and get Ta-ming out of the trunk.

"You're a good boy. A brave boy."

He doesn't acknowledge me. I understand his numbness. I went through it myself twenty-three years ago, when I fled Shanghai.

Two hours later, Z.G. and I sit at his dining room table. Joy and Tao rest on separate couches in the salon, where we can see them. They're too weak to walk upstairs to the bedrooms. Z.G.'s servants have made a clear soup. I still won't allow Joy and Tao to feed themselves. Their temptation to gorge would be too great. Fortunately, they don't have the strength to fight and lie there docilely as two of the servants spoon broth into their mouths. Ta-ming, young yet remarkably resilient, sits at the table with Z.G. and me. The third servant brings a tray with dishes, chopsticks, napkins, a teapot, and teacups. The tray just has room for a small bowl of rice, which fills the room with a homey and safe fragrance. She sets the bowl in front of Ta-ming before

474

returning to the kitchen for the rest of the meal. The boy stares at the rice. Then Z.G. and I watch as he counts out one grain of rice at a time — one to Z.G., one to me, one for himself — setting them on the table in three small piles. This is how hungry they once were. Life and death are separated by a thread or, these days, by a few kernels of rice.

Joy

This is Joy

The kite dips and whirls. Ta-ming holds the controls, but the pull of the wind against the kite is so strong that Z.G. stands behind the boy, steadying his shoulders. This isn't just one kite at the end of a string. Z.G. and Ta-ming have put up a whole school of goldfish, each one with unique tails and fins. Next, it might be a flock of butterflies with wings that flutter or maybe a flock of cranes against the brisk fall sky, soaring and diving on the breeze.

It's the beginning of November and it's been seven months since my mother and Z.G. rescued us. We are ghosts brought back from the dead, and today is a vision of what life can be. We have a need to forget, if only for a few hours. When I leave China — if we're able to get out — what I'll remember most are Sundays, the one day of the week when we're free to do more or less as we please. We've come to the Lunghua Pagoda. I've been told that Z.G., my mother, and my aunt used to fly kites here years ago. Back then, the pagoda stood in empty land taken over by young Chinese soldiers, waiting for battle. Later, the Japanese had a detention camp here for British citizens. Now it's a park. Elm, ginkgo, and camphor trees — green and lush — breathe life. Peddlers sell little toys — paper lions for good luck and dragons mounted on sticks that dance and writhe. A musician plays an *erhu*, singers warble folk songs, and jugglers, contortionists, and magicians awe with their mysterious ways. Old men shuffle along with their hands behind their backs. Old women sit on stone benches with their legs spread wide, their hands on their knees. If you have enough money, and we do, you can buy a little treat — a toffee, a chocolate bar, or an ice sucker. The Great Leap Forward continues elsewhere. Vast numbers of people are dying, but here we are happy . . . and healthy.

I glance at my mother, who stands by my side. She shields her eyes as she stares up at Z.G.'s kites. Then she looks at me and smiles.

"True suffering has taken away my taste for brooding about the past," she says. "Look at what I have here on earth. My daughter, my granddaughter, Z.G., Dun, and Ta-ming are all right here with me. We're a family. More than that, maybe we're the family . . ." She stops to laugh. "Maybe we're the *families* we were supposed to be all along."

She raises her arms as though embracing the world. What she calls out tells me just how American she's become — and remained here in China — with her open expression not only of her feelings and physical demonstrativeness but also her desire for happiness, as

477

though it's her right. "This is joy, and I want to hang on to it for as long as possible!"

I do too.

Nursing Tao, Ta-ming, Samantha, and me back to life must have been agonizingly slow and terrifying for my mom. Ta-ming was the first to regain energy, although he still doesn't say much and his bones are crooked and weak from undernourishment. Maybe that will be permanent, but I hope not. The baby responded quickly to bottles of formula and fresh soy milk, although none of us know what the consequences of malnutrition will be for her down the line. If she has problems, well, then . . . My uncle Vern had problems too, and we all loved him. I presented the most worrisome case. I ate little and said little. I wouldn't release the baby to anyone but my mother. How could I with Tao nearby? Z.G. and my mom thought they were doing the right thing by bringing Tao back to Shanghai, and for a while I was too weak to tell them otherwise. Even so, several times I asked my mother to take me to her family home.

"But there's so much more room here," she always answered. "When you're well enough to climb the stairs, you, Tao, and the baby can go to your room. You'll have servants here. It will be more comfortable for you."

We had variations of this conversation several times, but she never caught my hints and I wouldn't say anything in front of Tao out of fear of what he might do. It wasn't until Tao got up from his couch in Z.G.'s living room and volunteered to wash the rice for dinner

— what my mother, Z.G., and Dun considered a huge turning point in his recuperation — that I had my chance. As my husband wandered off, I motioned for my mother to come to me. Just then, Tao called for help. Dun, Z.G., and my mother followed Tao's voice and found him in the downstairs bathroom.

"I'm having trouble washing rice in the rice washer," he said.

I'll say he was. He was washing rice in the toilet! I could hear them all laughing like crazy. When my mom returned to the salon, leaving the men to clean up the toilet, I told her about Swap Child, Make Food. Mom had the baby, Ta-ming, and me out of Z.G.'s house and in her childhood room within an hour.

"Let Z.G. deal with Tao!" she fumed. "But tomorrow, I'll —"

It was all I could do to keep her from reporting him to the police. That's when I told her what I really wanted.

"Forget about him," I said. "Let's go home."

That night, in the room my mother once shared with my aunt, we began to plot. Obviously, the first thing to do was contact Auntie May.

"I've waited a long time to write this letter," Mom said as she put pen to paper. "Joy and the baby have returned to Shanghai," she read to me as she wrote. "How wonderful it would be if we would have a family reunification visit at our old home in Hong Kong." She looked up and explained. "She'll know I'm talking about the hotel we stayed in twenty-three years ago."

I had to trust my mother's judgment on this, because it didn't seem all that clear to me, but then my mother and aunt have always communicated in a way I've never fully understood.

"From our Hong Kong home, please send an official invitation for family reunification," Mom continued. "Ask for a twenty-four-hour visit. As soon as I receive it, I'll take it to the police station and Foreign Affairs Bureau to request travel permits. And one more thing . . ."

My mother put down her pen, put her hands together, and laid them in her lap in such a prim and decorous way I was tempted to laugh.

"I'm going to ask my sister to include Dun in her invitation. He's asked me to marry him, and I've accepted."

"Mom!" I was totally surprised.

"I don't want to leave here without him."

I could have been upset — why wasn't she more loyal to my father? — but her face radiated happiness in a way I'd never seen before, which in turn gave me the purest feeling of joy. So one of the first things that would need to be done as part of our escape plan would be for my mother and Dun, whom I'd met only a few times, to start filing the papers for permission to get married — a process far more difficult in the city than in the countryside.

"What about Z.G.?" I asked. "Won't he want to come too?"

Here's how much my mom loves Dun: she didn't even flinch at the idea that May and Z.G. might be reunited.

480

"Let's ask him," she responded. "But I don't think he'll want to come, do you?"

I didn't think so either, not when he's so famous here. In America, he'd have to start at the bottom. Maybe my mom would give him a job as a dishwasher in the café. I didn't see that at all. And even though he clearly still loves May, a Rabbit is not born to fight for what he wants. He'll choose what's easy, comfortable, and familiar every time. Which is exactly what Z.G. did.

"It's better if I help you with your plan," he said.

In fact, he'd be playing a pivotal role, but we didn't know that at the time, and my mom, who was writing the letter, said, "Let's not bring it up to May just yet. I don't want her to be disappointed."

Later, after she finished her letter, my mother tucked the baby and me into Auntie May's bed. Never could I have imagined how she would look at us right then. She glowed with love and happiness. Nor could I have imagined the way she allowed Ta-ming to snuggle close to her in her own twin bed. I saw that my mother — somehow, and at last — had found solace and comfort in physical affection, whether hugging me, comforting the baby, protecting Ta-ming from the dark, or looking forward to her new life with her professor.

Happiness out of horror, that's what I felt. When I tried to explain that to my mom, she said from her bed, "I look at you and I see a double rose — two beautiful colors, one in soft yellow, the other in bright pink. You are part me and part May, and I'm so happy for that." She regarded me again with her surprisingly open and tender eyes of love. "What else can make a woman happy?"

"A husband who loves her, will support her, and encourage her to be a whole human being — like you had with Dad," I answered. "And will have with Dun too."

My mother had found two men to love her, and I . . .

"I'm really sorry your marriage didn't work out," she said sympathetically. "You couldn't have known the kind of person Tao was."

The response to that was, *But you and Z.G. did!*

Before I married Tao, Z.G. said he was using me to try to escape village life, while Tao's mother often insinuated that I wanted to steal him and take him to Shanghai. We now know who was right. Tao's wish has been fulfilled: Shanghai. And it's worked out very well for him. Once we recovered some of our strength, the Artists' Association held a ceremony to give Tao a prize as a model artist. Z.G. and my mom told me I had to attend, because the Artists' Association had also sponsored my return to the city and because I added interest to Tao's story. What a pathetic pair Tao and I made. Our clothes drooped. Our eyes were still dark and hollow shells. But now my husband is a bit of a celebrity. He tells us, and anyone who will listen, that he came up with the idea of the mural and then painted it with "a little help" from some members of the commune. Fortunately, he's often out of town, touring the country as a model peasant artist. In July and August, he went to the Third National Congress of Literary and Art Workers in Peking. "I was one of twenty-three hundred cultural delegates," he boasted when he returned. "The people's life is rich and varied. Art should reflect this. It's going to be a new period of blooming!" This is nothing to get excited about, since the last blooming period ended with the Campaign Against Rightists. But that's my husband: a small radish who thinks he knows something.

But long before any of these other things happened, and my mom and I were in her bedroom, she said, "Remember, Joy, you still have your whole life ahead of you. You're only twenty-two. You're going to find a good man. Or maybe he'll find you. For all you know, you're already acquainted. I'm sure Violet's son is still waiting for you —"

"Leon?" I giggled. My mother and her friend Violet have been trying to set the two of us up since forever.

"Well, why not?" she asked, all innocence. "Happiness, Joy, that's all I'm trying to tell you." She paused to let that sink in. "Another thing that makes a woman happy is to find work that will make her life bigger — whether hiring your neighbors to work as extras in the movies as May does or working at her husband's side as I did with Sam in the café. For you, I think it's going to be your art."

Memories of Tao, the mural, and the commune had ruined art for me. "I don't want to paint again," I told her, and I meant it.

"You say that now, but things will change."

And, of course, my mother was right about that too.

It took nearly a month to hear back from May. We received a letter and a package, both of which were sent through the regular route from Grandfather Louie's family in Wah Hong Village. The letter was May's formal invitation for us to take to the police station. The package had some dried bread and crisp rice — most welcome — and a frilly white dress for Samantha with smocking done in pink, a matching bonnet, and bloomers to cover her diaper. Before I could stop her, my mother had ripped apart the bonnet.

"May knows to hide things for me in hats," she explained.

All I could think was, *Those two sisters!* But there, lying flat against the sizing for the bonnet's visor, was an additional letter from Auntie May:

I've arrived in Hong Kong. I've left the café in the care of Uncle Charley. Mariko is taking care of my business. As for my acting job, I told the producers what I was going to do. They said I was nuts, but the cast all got together and gave me $1,000. Look elsewhere in this and other packages to find it.

You must hurry, but you must also be careful. The man at the family association tells me that many people are leaving China. Officials here and in the U.S. don't believe the stories refugees are telling about the famine. At the same time, the PRC is inviting people in Hong Kong to send food and money to their relatives on the mainland. The lines at the post office are terrible. Those who are generous are rewarded with a banquet. Do they not see the irony in that?

I don't think the Chinese government sees the irony in much of anything.

I'm so close to you now. Please tell me what else I can do.

We continued to correspond and we found all the cash, but we were careful about transmitting the details of our plan, feeling it would be safer that way.

"Just stay in our old home," my mother wrote back, meaning the hotel. "One day soon we will arrive."

So here I am today, months later, flying kites on a blustery afternoon with this improvised family. At a very deep level, I'm no longer afraid and no longer pinched by guilt. Is it possible to be happy in the People's Republic of China? Absolutely, because I am happy right now.

Our escape plan has evolved into something very simple, with just two components. First: travel permits. Z.G., having gone to the Chinese Export Commodities Fair in Canton at the beginning of November the last couple of years, has asked for and received permission to attend and bring with him Tao (a model artist) to give a joint painting demonstration — showing the old and new styles of art in China. Accompanying them will be a baby, her amah (my mother), and me (the wife of the model artist). Second: exit permits and passports. My mother and Dun will get married tomorrow, and then we'll go to the police station and the Foreign Affairs Bureau to pick up passports for those of us who need them, travel permits to Canton for Dun and Ta-ming, and exit permits for my mother, Dun, Ta-ming, Samantha, and me to go to Hong Kong for a family reunification visit. (We've been going to interviews for six months now, pushing and begging everyone to get things done in time for our departure date. Tomorrow we have just one more set of appointments. If we don't get our papers, then none of this will work.) Once we reach Canton, Z.G. will keep Tao occupied at the fair, allowing the rest of us to slip away and take the train to Hong Kong. Once there, we'll go to May's hotel.

It sounds simple, but many obstacles still need to be overcome. What if someone suspects something — at my mother's work unit, at the Artists' Association, in our house or Z.G.'s house. So, we must try to stay focused, not let fear overwhelm us, and keep moving forward.

As the others help Z.G. reel in his kites, I pick leaves from the poplars and gather some grass. They will be nice additions to tomorrow's meals.

Joy

The Heartbeat of the Artist

Monday morning, my mother's wedding day. My mom and Dun help me prepare breakfast for the household. The boarders sit around the kitchen table, arguing and gossiping. My position in the house has changed since I first came to live here. Back then, the boarders were frightened by my presence. I didn't have a residency permit, a work unit, or food coupons. I was half dead and brought with me two additional mouths to feed. I wasn't shown sympathy or kindness, except by Cook, who clearly loves my mother and therefore loves her daughter and granddaughter. Fortunately, he was the only one who mattered, since he was in charge of the household and made all reports to the block committee, which then passed information on to the neighborhood committee, and on up the chain. Now he holds Samantha, giving her a bottle. Soon he'll pass her to someone else at the table. She'll have her first birthday in a couple of weeks, but she's still frightfully small — a constant reminder that something isn't right in the country.

The majority of city dwellers don't fully understand what's happening in the countryside. They've heard rumors, but they can't reconcile them with being told crops grow to the sky on communes, hearing government officials report on the so-called years of bad weather that have destroyed fields of plenty, and what they see on the streets of Shanghai, where there's no avoiding or covering up how people look as they wait in long lines to buy food with their coupons. They're just moving past the first sign of starvation — losing weight — to the second stage — edema. They've begun to swell around their necks and in their faces. When people greet, they press thumbs into each other's foreheads to see how deep the impression and how long it will last until the flesh resumes its normal shape. Everyone seems to walk in a listless haze. Still, no one complains, no one revolts. Only when people are truly hungry can you make them submit to you.

But the people in this house have seen starvation and its effects with their own eyes. Now they're glad I'm here, because I understand what's coming and I know how to survive. So does my mother. Her money and her special Overseas Chinese certificates have protected us, allowing us to buy provisions at exorbitant prices. In Shanghai, where the food is traditionally sweet, sugar is precious. Meat is hard to find and very expensive. My mom buys one quarter of a pork chop for fifty *yuan* or twenty-five dollars. Foodstuffs that once cost two or three *yuan* she now purchases at the equivalent of about thirty-five dollars. She procures wilted cabbages and other vegetables of inferior quality from farmers who've somehow skirted the checkpoints and sell their wares in dark alleys. She once paid a ridiculous price for a chicken, saying, "You need to be strong for our plan to work." But none of this is enough to feed the ten people now living in the house.

I stand at the stove making "bitter cakes" from the grass I gathered at the Lunghua Pagoda yesterday. Later, when everyone goes to their jobs, I'll soak the poplar leaves in water to get rid of their sour taste so I can make leaf pancakes tonight. I know how to make food out of almost nothing, and for this everyone not only tolerates but welcomes my presence.

"First, they tell us to kill sparrows, but now we have a campaign against bedbugs," one of the dancing girls complains. "We don't have bedbugs, so how are we going to prove we're doing our part?"

"We'll blame our lack of bedbugs on Old Big Brother," the cobbler quips slyly. "We'll say they took the bedbugs home with them."

In July, Soviet experts pulled out of China, taking with them their machines, equipment, and technological expertise. Since then, the government has blamed Old Big Brother for everything.

"Yes, yes, yes! I've already heard that," the widow chimes in. "We'll say that's why we don't have bedbugs."

"Now we have two enemies," the cobbler continues, reaching out his arms so he can have a turn to hold the baby. "We must fight Soviet revisionism while continuing to fight American imperialism."

489

Their logic makes no sense for many reasons, including that we've already been told the Soviets brought bedbugs with them and then left the pests to torture us, but then little makes sense anymore. The announcer on the radio tells us many things: that the USSR may join forces with the USA in the UN to further ostracize and diminish the PRC. (I was born in America and lived there for nineteen years. My family was victimized by red-scare tactics. I cannot imagine a single way that what we're being told could ever come to pass.) In the meantime, other things are happening. Foreigners from countries other than the USSR have also been sent home. In fact, this is the smallest number of foreigners in China in centuries. All publications — except for two propaganda papers — have been barred from leaving the country. In other words, China has cut itself off from the rest of the world. What word escapes our borders, no one believes, as May pointed out in her letter. People *inside* China, including those right here at the breakfast table, try to look behind what we're told to find the truth. Right now, the gossip turns to Mao Tse-tung, who recently relinquished his position as chairman of the People's Republic of China to Liu Shao-ch'i.

"It's said that Mao made his own self-criticism in front of a gathering of seven thousand Party officials," one of the dancing girls whispers conspiratorially.

"Maybe he stepped aside to avoid blame for the Great Leap Forward," the cobbler counters.

Samantha starts to fuss, and he hands her off to the widow. As the mother of two daughters, she knows exactly how to calm a baby, putting Samantha on her shoulder, swaying, and rhythmically patting her back. I set a platter of bitter cakes on the table, and the boarders quickly snap them up, all the while chattering.

"So what if Mao's retired as head of state?" the widow asks. "He still maintains supreme command. Nothing has changed."

"Except that we're hungry." This comes from Cook. The boarders still don't fully realize how lucky they are.

"Who could have guessed that rats would disappear from Shanghai?" The dancing girl leans forward, and everyone edges in to listen as she reveals in an awed tone, "People have eaten them!" Then she turns to the widow. "It's my turn. Give me the baby." She holds Samantha under her arms, so she can practice standing. Samantha's still weak, but she's surprisingly stubborn and persistent. Her little legs wobble, but she flaps her arms excitedly, a big smile on her face. The dancing girl steadies Samantha and then turns to me. "We'll come with you to the Lunghua Pagoda to collect leaves the next time you go, if you'd like."

"I'd like that very much." (Except I'll be gone.)

Dun and my mother duck out of the kitchen first, taking Ta-ming with them. The dancing girl hands me the baby. As the others file out, they chuck her chin or give her a delicate pinch. Everyone leaves their dishes for me to clean. I pour Cook another cup of tea.

"You should rest," I tell him. "Little Miss doesn't want you to be too tired for your duties later today."

He nods, takes his cup, and shuffles toward the stairs. I hurry past him to the room I share with my mother. She stands before the mirror, staring at herself critically. She wears her work trousers and an ironed white blouse. Her hair has been brushed and tucked behind her ears.

"You look beautiful," I say. "A perfect bride."

"Little in my life is how I imagined it," she says as she turns to me. These are not the words of regret that were always so much a part of my mother's make-up. Although she's longed for a big wedding with the dress and banquet — first for herself and then for me — she's still not going to get it, yet she's smiling and happy. Life is what it is, and she's living it as a Dragon should — never accepting defeat.

As she puts on her paper collector's jacket, I go to the window, open it, and bring in the box we've stored on the sill to keep the contents cool and safe. I sit on May's bed and carefully lift the lid. Inside are a dozen eggs given to us by Z.G. Today my mother will go to her work unit and tell her supervisor that she wants to marry a professor. She will promise her supervisor a dozen fresh eggs if he will accompany her to the government office at one o'clock, where they'll meet Dun, who'll be coming from his morning classes. Her supervisor needs to approve the marriage: verify that she doesn't suffer from disease, that she's a helpful member of the proletariat, and that she and Dun are not blood relatives up to the third degree of relationship. The officer will have my mother and Dun sign some papers, and then they'll be given a marriage certificate. My mother will hang on to the eggs, however, unless her supervisor also agrees to let her have the afternoon off for her honeymoon. We're sure he'll accept this bribe, since none of us have seen eggs in months and their protein is a good safeguard against the swelling disease.

I rotate the eggs so they'll look perfect, replace the lid, and hand the box to my mother. I give her a kiss and a hug. "I wish I could be there with you."

"I wish you could be too, but everything must appear as matter-of-fact as possible. I learned that from Auntie Hu," she tells me.

Then she's out the door with her dozen eggs.

Keeping to our usual schedule is important, so at nine I pack up the baby and Ta-ming and we take a bus to Z.G.'s, as we've done every day for the last two months. Tao is still living with Z.G. I wish more than anything that I didn't have to see Tao, because I hate him and because nothing is more dangerous than an uneducated peasant — someone who can claim redness while painting black the people who helped him — but I have to see him to make our actions seem normal. "You just have to tolerate him awhile longer," my mother often reminds me. I have, but it's hard.

One of the servants lets me in, and I go straight upstairs to a bedroom Z.G. recently converted to a studio. Light streams through the window. Easels with canvases or watercolors in progress painted by Tao, Z.G., and me are propped around the room to take advantage of the natural light. Tao is here already. He's still handsome, no doubt about that, but he doesn't

493

smile to show me his beautiful teeth or even turn to acknowledge my presence. He waits until I put Samantha in a baby tender — a wooden box that allows her to move around but not escape — and then he wanders over to pat his Ah Fu's head.

Ta-ming goes to the window seat, where he can look out on the walk street below. The poor boy is not the same happy child I first met in Green Dragon. He doesn't talk about his mother, the villa, being hungry, or that terrible time he spent in the dark by himself in the trunk of Z.G.'s car. He rarely smiles, but I guess that's to be expected. Dun asked a friend of his, who teaches Western music at the university, to give the boy some simple violin lessons. He says the landowner's violin is quite old and quite valuable. Now the things that make Ta-ming happy are his violin lessons and the time he gets to practice in our room at night. The rest of the time he's quiet and pensive.

Z.G. enters the room. "Good morning," he says. "Is everyone ready to paint?" He strides over to Tao, and they talk about what he's working on. "I like the way the fields look so raw and cold . . ."

In many ways, our time together reminds me of when Tao and I had our private lessons with Z.G. in the villa, minus our crazy love, of course. Z.G. still treats Tao and me differently. He admires Tao's work, praising him for the model artist he's become. It's a charade that helps to build my husband's inflated opinion of himself. Z.G. teaches me the rub-and-paint technique he once used to paint the beautiful-girl posters of my mother and aunt — working carbon powder over an image and then applying watercolors to get the warmth and depth for cheeks, fabric, hair, furniture, and sky.

In my work, I've been trying to achieve what Z.G. told me when I first arrived on his doorstep is the true essence of Chinese artistic striving: depict the inner world of the mind and heart. I was physically saved by my mother and Z.G., but in my most hopeless moment I found my true voice, which saved my heart and soul. Art for art's sake is not what motivates me. Certainly politics are not what motivate me anymore. Emotions are what motivate me. Of those emotions, the strongest is love — love for my two mothers, my two fathers, and my baby. During the days of my recovery, I began to see something. I remembered moments from my childhood: stringing peas with my grandmother, walking with my grandfather through China City, playing dress-up on movie sets with my aunt. And, of course, anything and everything my mother did with me: pinning me into a jumper she'd sewn, helping me spell the names of all the kids in my class on my Valentine's Day cards, taking me to church, to the beach, to Chinese school, doing all those things that helped turn me into the person I am.

It's the New Year's poster — where beautiful girls once and still reside — that has become my art form and the way for me to realize my vision. The painting I'm working on shows my two mothers — the one who gave birth to me and the one who cared so much for me that she chased me all the way here. I'm between them — the link, the secret, the one who was loved. We've gathered together to stare at a baby girl,

Samantha, who's just learned to sit on her own. We're three generations of women who've suffered and laughed, struggled and triumphed. My New Year's poster is my heart's thank-you for the gift of life. That I've painted it in the style perfected by Z.G. during the beautiful-girl days makes me happy. My two mothers have creamy complexions, tinted lips, eyebrows like willow leaves — all unmarred by time, worry, or Socialist Realism. They are as they are meant to be — forever beautiful.

My watercolor will never leave this house. We decided it had to stay here, along with all my other work, as proof to the authorities that Z.G. and Tao never suspected I was going to escape. When others do see it, I'll probably be accused of worshipping foreign things, of being bourgeois — referring to the United States — or revisionist — referring to the Soviet Union. But it won't matter, because I'll be gone, gone, gone.

Z.G. comes to my side. "In the West, they say beauty is in the eye of the beholder," he says. "Here, in China, beauty is defined by politics and realism. But what are the most beautiful things I know? They are the emotions of the heart — the love you feel for Samantha, the love you feel for Pearl and May. These things are pure, true, and unchanging."

His words seep into me. I loved my father Sam, and that will never change, but Z.G. is my father too. The time, patience, technique, and color sense he has given me have changed my life in ways I haven't even begun to understand.

496

"I used to believe that *ai kuo* — love for China and our people — was the most important thing in life," I say. "Then I thought being able to call someone *ai jen* — beloved — was the most important." I glance at Tao. His back stiffens at my words, but he doesn't turn my way. "Now I realize love is something much bigger. *Kung ai* — encompassing love — is most important."

"You've shown that in your painting," Z.G. observes. "Art is the heartbeat of the artist, and you've found your heartbeat."

My father continues to praise me, saying my painting is the best he's seen in years. After he leaves the studio, Tao and I work silently. At one thirty, I gather up the baby and Ta-ming. Tao begins crating his and Z.G.'s paintings to take to the trade fair. At the door, I take one last look at my painting. Yes, I most definitely feel my heartbeat.

At two-thirty, we meet back at my mother's house. We pull together the various documents, photographs, and other papers we've been required to fill out. Then we take a bus to the Foreign Affairs Bureau to pick up our passports. We approach the window and are greeted by Comrade Yikai, a wiry woman with a surprisingly pleasant manner, who's been meeting with us weekly for nearly six months. We show her our documents, which she's seen dozens of times, but now she has our last requirement in her hands. She beams when she sees my mother and Dun's marriage certificate. "Finally!" she exclaims. "All good wishes!" She leafs through the other papers, barely glancing at Ta-ming's and Samantha's recently issued birth certificates. How did we get those? I was able to claim, accurately, that I never received papers for Samantha from the Dandelion Number Eight People's Commune. My mother lied, saying she adopted Ta-ming after she found him abandoned in a pit by the side of the road.

"You are a good comrade to help the child," Comrade Yikai praises my mother, as she does every time we come here. "And besides, every woman should have a son." But one issue still vexes her. "China is the best country in the whole world. Why would you want to leave, even if it's just for a visit?"

"You're so right, Comrade Yikai," my mother agrees. "Chairman Mao is our mother and father, but don't you think it's important for blood relatives to see each other too? I want my sister — long lost to the capitalist West — to observe our good family." She motions to Dun, Ta-ming, the baby, and me. "Once she does, surely she'll want to return to the motherland."

Comrade Yikai nods her head solemnly. She stamps five passports and slips them to us under the window.

"Everyone on your block will be proud if you bring back your sister," she says. "Have a good trip."

As planned, we return to the house to get Cook, because Superintendent Wu has asked that someone vouch for us. Together we walk to the police station, where we bypass the line of people hoping to get travel and exit permits. We go straight in for our appointment with Superintendent Wu, who's been questioning my mother since she first arrived in Shanghai. He treats

Director Cook deferentially, offering him a chair and tea. Then he gets right to business.

"We've been considering this travel request for several months. We have just a few more questions, which I'm sure you can answer." He nods to Cook, who nods back, understanding the seriousness of the situation. "Would you say that Comrade Pearl has joined with the workers, soldiers, and peasants to help build a better society?"

"She has cleaned her own nightstool and washed her own clothes," Cook answers, his voice quavering with age.

It was a gamble bringing Cook here. No one knew exactly what he would say, but this is perfect. I could kiss the old man, but that would be unseemly.

Superintendent Wu turns to my mother. "For a long time, I was suspicious of you. You answered my questions the same way every time we met. How can that be? I asked myself. You responded to the call to return to the motherland, but you had nothing to offer since you weren't a scientist or an engineer. I told the higher-ups that we shouldn't feed, house, or tolerate American imperialists like you, but you've proved me wrong. Now my superiors ask me if they think you'll use this opportunity to return to America."

"I'd never go back there," my mother says.

"This is exactly what I told my superiors." Superintendent Wu grins. "I told them you're too smart for that. The Americans would never accept you. They'd take you out and shoot you."

We've heard all kinds of things like this these past months. It's the same sort of propaganda my mother and I were told before we came to China.

"A one-day trip to Hong Kong?" The policeman sneers and then adds staunchly, "In a few more years, Hong Kong will be part of China again. We just need to know that you'll be welcomed there. We have no wish to place burdens on our little cousin."

As we have for the last six months, my mother hands him Auntie May's letter of invitation. Then she shows him her new marriage certificate and the passports.

"What about this marriage?" Superintendent Wu asks, even though he's known it's been coming for a while.

"This is to be expected," Cook volunteers. "They are two people of the same age, living under the same roof. They have known each other for more than twenty years. The girl's mother was quite fond of the professor. I'd say it's about time."

Superintendent Wu stares at the marriage certificate with a bemused look. "A bachelor marrying a widow." He chuckles and then addresses Cook. "The widow will show him what's what, no?"

Cook bristles. Worried that he'll start to say things to protect Little Miss's reputation, I quickly put Samantha on his lap to distract him.

With no one to join in the traditional wedding banter, Superintendent Wu shakes his head in disappointment. "Everything is in order," he says. He slides five exit permits across the desk, ruffles Ta-ming's hair, and makes a few unprompted bawdy comments about the nuptial couple and what Dun might expect tonight. As we leave his office, he calls out to my mother, "See you at our usual time next month!"

The hardest and most dangerous part of our trip is behind us. Standing on the front steps, we're ecstatic but careful not to show it. Still, the people waiting in line regard us enviously. At least we got in the door.

When we reach home, my mother stops in the garden, as she always does. If all goes well, this will be the last time she'll ever pinch dead blooms, trim scraggly twigs, or rearrange the pots in her family's garden.

The cobbler comes through the gate. "Are you picking flowers for us to eat or for one of your vases?" he asks.

"I want to get the last flowers before the first frost," Mom answers lightly. "I think these might look nice in the salon, don't you?"

The cobbler doesn't respond, but I know my mother's thoughts on this. She's talked about visiting her friend's house and seeing the dead flowers in a vase on a table. They made her believe that Madame Hu was coming back. Mom hopes her actions now will make everyone think we'll be gone just a few days. As with Z.G., we don't want anyone to get in trouble after we're gone. When the police come to question the boarders, they'll be able to answer truthfully that they didn't suspect a thing. They'll point to my mother's flowers as proof.

I make dinner. Everyone sits around the table in the dining room. We listen to the day's gossip. One of the former dancing girls got a promotion at the textile factory. This has infuriated her roommate. The two bicker as only two women who have shared the same small room for twenty-three years can. Yes, everything is exactly as it should be. Even when Cook announces the marriage between Little Miss and the professor, no one seems particularly surprised.

"There are no secrets in this house," the cobbler says, as he raises his cup of hot water for a toast.

My mother looks from face to face. She takes in the faded wallpaper and the art deco sconces she bought at a pawnshop. Her fingers glide along the surface of the dining table, memorizing it. I can see she's fighting back tears. I have a momentary fear she'll give away everything, but then she blinks, clears her throat, and picks up her chopsticks.

Pearl

A Place of Memory

I leave my family home almost as I arrived. The boarders crowd around me in the hall, offering words of advice. They part when Cook enters. The knowledge that I'll never see him again burns in my chest, but I say, "Take care of things until next Tuesday." Then I address everyone. "Don't forget the cleanliness campaign. I don't want to come back and find —"

"We know, we know," the others sing in chorus. Then I pick up the bag I brought into China and walk out the door and down the steps into the garden. Joy carries the baby. Dun holds Ta-ming's hand. I open the front gate for the others to pass. I don't look back. Then together we go to the corner and board the first of a series of buses that will take us to the airport.

As a paper collector, I spent a lot of time on the Bund, watching ships go up and down the river, trying to figure out if there was a way to leave Shanghai on the Whangpoo. Even now, I would have guessed we'd take a boat or train to Canton, but Z.G.'s superiors at the

Artists' Association insisted that he, Tao, Joy, the baby, and her amah fly to Canton. Plane tickets are expensive, they told Z.G., but we'd be gone for a shorter time and they wouldn't have to provide us with as many rice coupons. I used my money to buy additional seats for Dun and Ta-ming.

We wait six hours in the terminal. Some of us exchange worried glances. Z.G. and Tao are to give their demonstration at the fair's opening festivities first thing tomorrow morning. What if the plane doesn't take off today? If we can't be in Canton by tomorrow morning, then there'll be no reason for Z.G. and Tao — and therefore the rest of us — to go to Canton. We wait and wait. Babies wail, children fuss. People huddle together in layers of padded clothes — taking extra clothes in a way that won't look suspicious, except it does. The acrid smell of damp humans, dirty diapers, cigarette smoke, and pickled turnips is sticky at the back of my throat. The linoleum floor is a mess of spit, nicotine-flecked phlegm, bags, baskets, and satchels. Soldiers patrol the aisles, stopping occasionally to check papers and photo identifications. The wait, the anxiety, the worry every time the armed soldiers pass is nerve-racking. Even so, pallid faces and hollow looks have been replaced by glimmers of hope. Maybe things will be better in the south.

Finally the aircraft is ready for departure, but flying on a Chinese propeller plane is not at all like my transpacific Pan Am flight. Samantha screams the entire way. Ta-ming holds his father's violin case in his lap, handing it to me just before he leans over and throws up in the aisle. Tao and Z.G. smoke nonstop, as do most people on the plane. It's a long and bumpy ride. I stare out the window, watching China's mainland pass below.

When we step off the plane in Canton, the first thing I notice is how much warmer it is than Shanghai. It feels like Los Angeles, and I love that. Then I hear Cantonese. I look at Joy. This is the sound of Chinatown. We're still in China, but we're getting closer to home. We both grin and then just as quickly compose our faces, remembering we must seem as though there's no particular reason for us to be happy.

We take double-seat pedicabs to the hotel. Refugees are everywhere on the streets, with their bundles, children, and treasured goods. Everyone wants to get out. But the hotel is just as I remember it. I remember as well the things I did with Z.G. here. When he catches my eye, I know he's recalling those things too. Embarrassed, I look away and edge closer to Dun. We're given three rooms: one for Z.G., one for Tao and Joy (poor thing), and one for the children, Dun, and me, since I'm here as the amah.

Tao barely reacts to the lobby. He's come a long way from washing rice in the toilet. However, I can see, for the first time, a trace of nervousness in him. Everyone speaks Cantonese. He's become relatively proficient in the Shanghai dialect, but Cantonese is nothing like Mandarin, the Wu dialect of Shanghai, or his home dialect from Green Dragon Village. We all have to remind ourselves that Tao cannot suspect a thing, but I

505

just can't express how exciting it is to be only one hundred miles from Hong Kong.

In the morning, Joy comes to our room, and together with Dun we go over our plan one last time. We wear clothes appropriate for the opening festivities. Joy — wife of the model peasant artist — in the simple cotton blouse and pants she wore when I pushed her in a wheelbarrow out of Green Dragon Village; Dun in an ill-fitting Western-style dark suit, which we hope will give the impression that he is a Hong Kong Chinese visiting the fair; the children in matching black outfits to show they're from the countryside; and I wear what I wore out of China, back into China, and, we hope, back out of China later today — the peasant clothes May bought for me many years ago.

"I'll carry the baby," Joy recites.

"I'm responsible for Ta-ming, and I have our money in my pants," I say.

"I have our papers right here." Dun pats his jacket. Then, "We all have to be present when the painting exhibition opens at nine."

We agreed we had to do this, but it will be hard when we're so anxious to flee. However, it would look strange to Tao if we didn't show up and stranger still to the fair organizers, who invited Tao, his wife, and their baby girl to this special event.

"Once Z.G. and Tao's demonstration begins, we'll sneak out of the hall and go to the train station," Joy picks up. We're talking about something terribly

506

dangerous, but she sounds calm and determined. My Tiger daughter is leaping yet again.

"And then it's just two hours to Hong Kong," I say, gathering courage from Joy.

We head downstairs to the dining room, where we join Z.G. and Tao. Z.G. wears one of his most elegant Mao suits, befitting his status. Tao also wears a Mao suit, but of inferior fabric and cut. Unlike Joy, who still must appear a peasant wife, Tao is showing the world that he is Z.G.'s protégé. He walks proudly erect with a big smile on his face.

The fair is international, and so is the buffet: hard-boiled eggs, yogurt, and savory flatbreads for attendees from India and Pakistan; stewed tomatoes, bangers, limp bacon, and toast with butter and jam for the English; and porridge, pickles, and piles of dumplings for the Chinese. It's crucial for the government to project that nothing is wrong in the country; the Great Leap Forward is great! Ta-ming loads his plate with more food than he could ever eat, but then so do we all.

Just before nine we walk to the fair entrance, where we're greeted by the organizer, an officious man with a shiny, round face. He escorts us into the great hall. On the stage at the front of the room are several easels draped with red silk.

"As soon as the doors open, we'll make the introductions, and then your paintings will be revealed," the organizer explains in Mandarin, a cigarette dangling from his lips. He pauses and frowns, concerned. "Members of the Canton branch of the

Artists' Association will give you proclamations, and then you'll do your demonstration. But please make all of this fast. People have come here to buy our products, and they'll want to go on to the exhibition floor quickly."

Hundreds of attendees are let in. Tao sticks close to the organizer, probably hoping to make connections, while the rest of us wait for the program to begin. Naturally, there's a little more to it than we were told. A dragon dance with clanging cymbals, banging drums, and colorful costumes sets a celebratory tone. Then the organizer, with Tao still trailing him — not for the first time do I look at my son-in-law and think what a greedy, foolish man — steps up to the podium.

"Welcome all guests to the People's Republic of China's Export Commodities Fair," the organizer begins in Cantonese. He repeats his welcome in Mandarin and then continues using Mandarin, the official language of China. "This year you will see — and we hope buy — even more of our wonderful tractors, textile machines, alarm clocks, and flashlights. You'll see we make the best and cheapest merchandise in the world. There is nothing the masses can't do!"

The audience applauds. The organizer holds up his hands for silence.

"I know you're all eager to get inside, but first we have a special treat for you. We open today by unveiling a major art exhibition," he continues. "From here it will travel to Peking for the annual New Year's poster competition. Then it will go on tour to cities around the country. If you've been here before, you're already familiar with Li Zhi-ge, one of our nation's best artists. He's come again, and in a moment I'll bring him up here, but let me first introduce Feng Tao."

More applause as Tao waves, smiles, and bows several times as he's learned to do at other events since he recovered.

"Feng Tao is red through and through," the organizer goes on. "But he's more than that! He is what we call both red and expert." This is the highest compliment that can be given these days, and it refers to peasants like Tao, who are "red" through their millennia of suffering and "expert" through their ignorance. "He's here to show the world that anyone can be an artist. Surely he'll win the award in Peking for the best New Year's poster."

I glance at Z.G. to see how he's taking this. How hard it must be to have listened to this kind of nonsense for the past several months, but he keeps his expression bland and indifferent. I feel Joy shifting impatiently at my side. She knows she's about to be called up there to be displayed as Tao's model-comrade wife, who came to the motherland from imperialist America.

The organizer asks the delegation from the Canton branch of the Artists' Association to join him onstage. They begin to pull the red silk from each of the easels, revealing several of Z.G.'s recent works — glorious round-faced women driving tractors, robust women waving red flags and smiling at a column of tanks on Chang'an Boulevard during the People's Republic of China's tenth anniversary parade, and Chairman Mao striding through the countryside, appearing taller than

509

the mountains, greater than the sea. Tao's paintings couldn't be more different. They show village life in clean but simple strokes, all rendered in bright colors.

People applaud appreciatively. Then one of the men from the Artists' Association pulls one of the red cloths off an easel and I hear Joy's sharp intake of breath. I peer around the heads to see what has upset her, and there on the stage is something so beautiful I can't fully absorb it. It's a watercolor of my sister, Joy, Samantha, and me rendered in the old-fashioned beautiful-girl style. My first thought is that Z.G. must have painted it.

"That's mine!" Joy says loud enough for a few people to turn her way and stare. Z.G. puts a restraining hand on her arm. She looks up at him, her face flushed in anger. "He stole my painting. He's going to take credit for this too."

Those around us from other countries don't seem all that impressed by anything that's happened so far, and they carry resignation in their bodies — this is China and we have to tolerate the greetings, proclamations, and demonstration before we can enter the exhibition hall — but the Chinese listen to this exchange with great interest, edging closer, drawing attention our way.

"He must have crated it with the other paintings when I wasn't looking," Z.G. says quietly. "But you can't worry about that now."

That's right, because there's something much worse to worry about. Onstage the members of the Artists' Association speak animatedly among themselves and gesture furiously at the organizer and Tao. I understand

510

why — Joy's painting recalls the beauty of the past and the deep emotions of mother love in a style that's been deemed bourgeois and ultra-rightist — but I'm very proud of her. I'm happy and honored too. She might never be able to express her feelings in words, but through her brushstrokes she's given me indisputable proof that she has forgiven my sister and me.

The organizer moves again to the microphone. He's flustered and clearly trying to make the best of a disastrous situation. "We're sorry that this piece of black art has been put before your eyes. Fortunately, in the New Society, even the worst criminals are given an opportunity to confess." He motions to Tao with a flick of his hand. "Please step forward and explain yourself to our guests. Let them see our great country at work building socialism and communism."

As Tao saunters to the podium, I sense what he's going to do. This won't be like the mural, where he took credit for Joy's work. Instead, he's going to name the artist and accuse Joy — and maybe Z.G. too — for trying to lead him down a black path. By targeting them, he'll raise his status in the government as a model artist, who is red, expert, pure, and a brave defender against and accuser of hooligans, who should and will be punished.

"We've got to go," I say. "We've got to go now!"

As I start pushing the others toward the door, I hear Tao's voice. "I did not paint this evil atrocity, but I saw it being birthed. My wife was criticized in our commune for being a right opportunist. My father-in-law has a decadent past. They are the ones to blame —"

511

"Hurry!" I exclaim.

"Where is the real artist?" Tao calls out. "Step forward! Accept criticism!"

I disliked Tao from the first moment I saw him. I've despised him since Joy told me about Swap Child, Make Food. He's a country bumpkin, and I wish with all my heart, Christian though I am, that he would just die.

"Where is the artist?" Tao demands again.

"I am the artist," Z.G. suddenly shouts. We're so close to the door, but we stop, horrified at what he's done. "You can recognize my technique from years ago."

"Dad!" This surprising word comes out of my daughter's mouth. "You can't —"

But onstage, Tao doesn't make the correction.

"My father-in-law taught me that art should serve workers, peasants, and soldiers, but you can see he is only concerned with beautiful women," Tao prattles, relishing his role as accuser.

I see it now: Tao would much rather target Z.G. than Joy. If Tao can push Z.G. aside, then he'll become more than just a model peasant artist. He'll take Z.G.'s place.

"It's not too late for you to confess your many crimes," Tao proclaims. "You are a poisonous weed. Step forward! Show your face!"

Someone up front shouts, "Where is this rightist?"

"There he is," Tao says, pointing to our group.

Dun turns to me. "You have to save the children. Go!"

"What are you saying?" I ask.

In the chaos around us, Chinese faces move closer.

"Where is the traitor?" another voice calls.

Suddenly, Dun shoves me into Z.G.'s arms.

"Go now!" Dun implores urgently. I look up into Z.G.'s face and watch his reaction as I hear my husband, who's behind me, call out, "I'm right here. I'm the artist."

As Z.G. pulls me from the room, I look back to see people close in around Dun, enveloping and trapping him. I can't possibly leave him. I fight Z.G. as hard as I can, but he drags me out the door and into the center's lobby. Joy, holding the baby and looking terrified, is there already. Ta-ming is at her side, white faced.

"Come on!" Z.G. says.

Again, I try to yank my arm loose. "I'm not going!"

Z.G. looks at Joy. She nods and grabs my other arm. Together they pull me through the lobby, out the door, and into a Russian-made car converted to a taxi for foreigners at the fair.

"Drive!" Z.G. demands in Mandarin.

The driver stares at us in his rear-view mirror. He doesn't seem to understand what Z.G. said, plus he has three out-of-breath adults, a baby, and a frightened little boy in his backseat.

Joy, who grew up speaking Cantonese, says, "Take us to the train station." The car pulls away from the curb and drifts into bicycle traffic, then Joy turns to me. "Mom, we have to keep going," she says, switching to Mandarin so the driver won't understand. "If we don't go now, we'll never get out."

"What about Dun?" I ask.

"We can't go back," Joy answers. "You know that. He saved us. Don't you understand?"

"They won't do anything to him," Z.G. promises.

"Your promise means nothing, if we leave," I say. "You know *that*!"

"They've probably already discovered he's not me," Z.G. counters. "That means they're already looking for us. The authorities will want me, and Tao will want Samantha."

"Tao doesn't want the baby," Joy says. "She's a girl. Tao doesn't even like her. He calls her Ah Fu."

"He's her father, of course he wants her," Z.G. responds.

"Nothing is more precious than when you might lose it," I add.

I bend over and bury my face in my hands. The others will do as I say, leaving me with a horrible choice. My husband, or my daughter, granddaughter, and the little boy I've just adopted? Dun said I have to save the children, and I do. I push my emotions down into a little ball, and then I sit back up.

"Dun has our papers," I remind the others. "We can't leave by train now."

In all the excitement, apparently Joy forgot this, and now her body deflates. "What will we do?" she asks, panicked.

I put a hand on her arm to calm her as I speak to the driver. "Please take us to Wah Hong Village."

He gives me a contemptuous look in the rear-view mirror: don't you know what you want? I give him the directions I remember from my visit three years ago.

The driver nods, makes a U-turn, and continues down the crowded roadway.

"I told Tao that Wah Hong was Grandfather Louie's home village," Joy says nervously in Mandarin. "That's the first place the authorities will look for us."

"Yes, it is," I agree. "But it will take them a while to get that information. Tao doesn't speak Cantonese, after all. So yes, the police will go to Wah Hong, but we'll be gone by then."

"What are we —"

"We're going to stop in Wah Hong for a few minutes, so we can get some provisions and leave a false trail," I explain before she can complete her question. "After that, there's only one place to go — Yin Bo, my natal family's home village. Hopefully someone there will be able to help us. Superintendent Wu knows the name of my home village, because I've told it to him every month for years now, but it will take the authorities a while to track down that information. We'll be out of the country by then," I finish, trying to sound confident.

I pull Ta-ming onto my lap and hold him tight.

Remembering Z.G.'s and my drive to Green Dragon, I'm fearful of what we might see once we turn off the main highway. But we encounter no dead or dying people either on the road or in the fields as we bounce along the dirt road. We see no children abandoned in pits. Yes, it's November and the climate is warmer this far south, but Kwangtung province is also farther from the capital. It doesn't seem to have been as badly affected by the strategies of the Great Leap Forward. What's the old saying? "The mountains are high and the emperor is far away," meaning that the farther you are from the capital and the emperor's policies, the easier it is to live your own life.

The driver drops us off just outside Wah Hong, since the village was built centuries ago and was not designed for automobiles. We hurry to the cousin's house. He's surprised to see us, but he welcomes us, offering tea and giving thanks.

"If not for the money your sister sends," he says, "we would have gone hungry."

"Soon you may not be so grateful," I tell him. As I explain our situation, his eyes become hooded. "We need clothes for Z.G., whatever food you can spare, and water. As soon as we leave, you must take the money May has sent to the village and bury it. Don't lie to the police when they come. Tell them you saw us and you chased us off."

"Where shall we tell them you went?"

"Macau."

This is not where we are going, but it will be safer for the Louie relatives if they don't know the truth. But the main thing is they'll send the police in the wrong direction.

We're in Wah Hong for less than an hour. Z.G. trades his elegant Mao suit for a set of dirty peasant clothes. Remembering my escape from China many years ago and how the bandits who boarded our ship recognized a well-off girl from the rest of us by her shoes, I get Z.G. to trade his Shanghai street shoes for a pair of sandals. I give the cousin five twenty-dollar bills. He falls to his knees and puts his forehead on my feet in gratitude. Then we walk out of Wah Hong. I hold Ta-ming's hand, Joy has the baby in her sling, and Z.G. carries several water flasks and a basket filled with rice balls. He still looks out of place — like a goat without fur.

So, on to my family's home village, Yin Bo, a place that has lived in my memory. I left when I was three, so I don't know how to get there. We know we shouldn't walk together, but we're afraid to separate. When we see someone coming toward us — a peddler or a farmer taking produce to market — some of us split off from the group, go into a field to pretend they are working, or walk ahead or lag behind, while one of us asks the way to Yin Bo. It sounds like it will be about a ten-mile walk along dirt roads or on the raised pathways that separate rice paddies. Not for one second does Dun leave my mind. I'm scared and worried for him, but I keep putting one foot in front of the other.

After two hours, we see a car approach. The desire to run is fierce. I slow down, Joy speeds up, and Z.G. and Ta-ming — who don't speak Cantonese — step into the fields. The car stops next to Joy. After leaning down and listening to the driver, she points to her left. The car comes to me and stops.

"We're looking for troublemakers," the driver says. "Have you seen them?"

"There are many people on the road," I answer. "How can I tell which ones are troublemakers?"

"The man was well dressed, like a three-pen cadre."

"Three-pen cadre? I've never heard of one of those. But if you say one man looks like our great Chairman, only thinner, then yes, I saw him and the others. They went that way." I point to my right — giving a completely different direction than Joy did — and hope that my shaking hand and my nervous sweat aren't too noticeable.

It's early evening when we enter Yin Bo. To me, it looks like any other small village — low houses made from gray brick, openings where glass windows should be, and pigs, ducks, and chickens wandering the alleyways. Maybe three hundred people live here, maybe fewer. A young mother with a baby on her hip comes out of her shack to stare at us. Soon others — a few children, a teenage girl, two farmers with piles of hay strapped to their backs — stop to ogle us.

"Excuse me," I say. "Can you help us? We need some food and a place to stay. My name is Zhen Long — Pearl Dragon. I was born here. My natal family name is Chin. You are Chins too. I am part of your family. We're all related." But these people are too young to remember me. "Is there a grandmother or grandfather I could talk to?"

They stare at me slack-jawed. No one wants to risk doing anything wrong.

"You are Chins. I am a Chin," I repeat. "My father was born here. I was born here. This is my daughter and my granddaughter. I may have uncles or aunts still living here. They would be my father's brothers and their wives. I need to see them." When no one moves, I

518

point to the teenage girl. "Go get the headman. Do it now!"

Then we stand there, waiting, as the girl runs down an alley on her bare feet. A few minutes later, she returns with not one man but several men — all of them older, all of them crowding and pushing each other to get to the front of the pack. This is my father's home village, so it doesn't surprise me that the men — again, all of them Chins — resemble him. They have his slightly bowlegged gait, weak jaw, and slope to their shoulders.

As they near, one of the men hurries forward. He's older, probably the headman. He extends his arms and calls, "Pearl?"

I shake my head, trying to dislodge memories that have no place right now.

"Pearl, Pearl."

The man stops a couple of feet in front of me. He's shorter than I am. Tears stream down his face. He's countryside old — his skin wrinkled and brown from the sun — but there's no question it's my father.

Pearl

Fate Continues,
Fortune Abounds

"Baba?" I say, stunned. The man before me can't possibly be my father. I know he can't. But he is. "I thought you were dead."

"Pearl."

When I was a girl, my father never once hugged me, but now he puts his arms around me and holds me tight. Not in ten thousand years could I have imagined this reunion, not now, not ever. I have so many things I want to say and so many questions I want to ask, but I have the others with me and we're in a desperate flight. Reluctantly, I pull away from him.

"Baba, I want you to meet some people. This is your granddaughter, Joy. The baby is your great-granddaughter. And you must remember Z.G."

My father looks from face to face. His tears don't stop. Now others around us weep too. Family reunification isn't about processing forms and getting permits. It's about this. Four generations together after too many lost years.

"Where is May?" Baba asks.

His question hurts. May was always his favorite.

"May and I made it to Los Angeles —"

"*Haolaiwu*," he says, nodding. That's what he planned for us. Then comprehension comes over his features. "But why are you here?"

"It's a long story and we don't have much time. What's important is that May is waiting for us in Hong Kong. We're trying to get to her. Can you help us?"

"Maybe," he says. "Come with me."

We follow him down an alley. The gawkers trail behind us. I should be more worried about that. When the police come, I don't want these people to tell them everything. But then this is my ancestral home. Would they rat out one of their own?

We enter my father's house. Several villagers crowd in as well. The longer we're here, the more show up to listen to and stare at their cousins. I've always hated the poverty of the countryside, but I don't see that now. The house is small, but it has actual windows. The furniture is nice. Jars, cans, and bags of food fill the cupboards. I haven't been here since I was three, but little memories pop into my mind. I remember the basket that hung from the ceiling. I fell on that step and skinned my knee. I liked to sit on the footstool next to the carved chair where my grandmother rested her feet.

Someone pours tea. Joy mixes a bottle of formula for the baby. My father hands Ta-ming an orange. An orange! What an incredible sight after all these months

521

of privations. My father squats on his haunches and starts talking. He may live in a village now, but he was once a Shanghai businessman.

"They say about a hundred people cross the border illegally every day," he begins. "But if you talk to a guard or a policeman, he'll tell you they catch many more than that every day too. Even more die in the process of trying to leave." He pauses to let that sink in. "How much money do you have?"

For the first time, I suspect my father's motives. Can he be trusted?

"If you have money," he continues, "you could take the train and bribe the guards."

"I tried that," Joy says. "It didn't work."

"I imagine things are different down here," Baba responds. "Gangs organize escapes by train, but you need to pay —"

"Oh, Ba, don't tell me you're involved with a gang again."

He pretends not to hear my comment. "You could hire a sampan or fishing boat to take you down the Pearl River to Macau or Hong Kong," he suggests, "but that traffic is also controlled by gangs."

"The Pearl River," Joy echoes. "Surely that has to be a good omen."

My daughter, so anxious to get out, isn't thinking clearly.

"We'd have the same problems here as we would have had in Shanghai," I remind her. "Do you know the schedules of the patrol boats?" I ask my father.

He ignores my question to offer another idea. "You could stow away on a ship, but that doesn't sound practical with so many of you. Some people prefer to float down the river on an inner tube or a piece of driftwood —"

"You seem to know a lot about it," Z.G. cuts in. He is forever a Rabbit — cautious and reserved.

My father juts his chin diffidently. He used to do that when he didn't want to discuss something unsavory with my mother.

"But how are you going to float down the river with a baby and a little boy?" my father continues after a pause. "And it's the dry season and the river is low. And you still might be caught by the patrol boats."

My shoulders sag. We've come so far. What will happen when we're caught?

"There is another way," my father says. "Our village is part of a twenty-village commune. Our villages have ties to Hong Kong and Macau that are centuries old. Those ties have not been broken just because the Communists have taken over." He sounds like the man at the family association in Hong Kong, which gives me renewed hope. "Goods still need to pass over the border. People from our commune cross into Hong Kong's New Territories every day to sell our products and then buy and bring back other provisions."

"Your products?" Joy asks, dubious since the Dandelion Number Eight People's Commune didn't make anything to sell.

"We process and make ingredients used for Chinese herbal medicine," my father answers.

"Chinese herbal medicine?" Joy echoes doubtfully.

"Didn't your mother give you traditional medicine when you were a little girl?" Baba asks. Then he turns to me. "Your mother would have been disappointed to hear you didn't raise your daughter properly."

My face heats with resentment and exasperation. This man abandoned us. His gambling led directly to May's and my arranged marriages, to May, my mother, and me having to flee Shanghai, to my mother's death and my rape, to May and me having to leave our home country . . .

"Of course, Mama gave me herbs and tonics," Joy jumps in, defending me and protecting him from my anger. "I hated them."

"So how do you think those ingredients got to *Haolaiwu*?" Baba asks.

He's right. Even after China closed, people in Chinatown bought ginseng, powdered deer antler, or some other terrible-tasting ingredient to cure a cough, indigestion, or trouble in the marriage bed.

"We grow and prepare ingredients for traditional medicines," he goes on. "We sell our goods at the wholesale market in Hong Kong. We also sell pigs, chickens, ducks . . . Our commune has several trucks, and we cross the border at the Lo Wu Bridge almost daily. Peking wants and needs foreign exchange with Hong Kong. We're some of the people who provide that."

"What are you saying? That we can just drive to Hong Kong?" Z.G. asks, sounding even more skeptical than Joy.

"More or less," Baba answers. "The border is about eighty Western miles from here. I think we can get you over the border and into the New Territories. Once there, you ought to be able to take a bus the last twenty miles into Hong Kong proper."

"Why didn't you tell us that in the first place?" Joy demands indignantly.

My father gives me a look. *Have you not taught my granddaughter any manners?*

But Z.G. agrees with Joy. "That's right. Why didn't you tell us? I mean, if it's so easy, then why haven't *you* left China?"

Baba stares at me as he answers Z.G.'s last question. "I deserted my family, leaving them to an uncertain fate. I was a no-good man." (He won't get an argument from me.) "I've stayed here because this is my ancestral home. The fallen leaves return to their roots. I have a house. I stay out of trouble. I do my work —"

"Baba, the police are after us," I interrupt. "They'll come here — if not tonight then in the morning."

"Then we'd better hide you," he says, "because it's too late to leave today."

He packs some food, hands us quilts, and walks us far out into a field. "You'll stay here tonight. Try to keep the baby up as long as possible. She'll need to be asleep for the crossing. I'll get you in the morning."

"Baba, can't you stay? Don't you want to talk?"

"Maybe stories and memories are destined to be incomplete," he answers. "Besides, it will be safer if you remain here. If the police come, we'll shout and make noise to alert you. If that happens, go south and hope

525

for the best. In the meantime, our other family members and I have to get things ready."

With that, he heads back to the village. We spread out the quilts. It's chilly but not unbearable. Joy paces back and forth with the baby, bouncing her, trying to keep her awake. I put my arms around Ta-ming. "Try to sleep a little," I say. "Close your eyes."

I stare at the stars. My father is alive, but can he be trusted?

I wake with a terrified start just before dawn. I stay still for a few minutes, waiting for my heart to stop pounding. I'm afraid of what will happen today, and of course I'm in terror for my husband. It takes all my strength to quash those emotions because I need to be strong today.

Z.G. is already up, standing a short distance from the quilts, staring south. I get up and walk over to him.

"Z.G.?"

"This is as far as I can go," he says quietly.

This is not a moment to get riled up, but I'm outraged. "You aren't going any father? Are you kidding me? Dun took your place to keep the blood part of the family together and now you want to go home? Besides, you can't go back. They'll blame you for Joy's painting and for helping us escape."

"I know, but I've been thinking about what your father said last night. Maybe leaving China isn't the best thing. This is my home."

When I say, "You and I have never really talked about May," he turns his back to me. I pull him around to face me. "You cannot stand there and tell me you don't love her. I know you do." He doesn't try to deny it. "May is a few miles from here. Whichever direction you go has an uncertain future, but one of those ways has May."

"What if she doesn't want me? I was as bad as your father —"

"Don't be stupid!" Again, that came out a little louder and harsher than I intended. I address his second point first. "You're not like my father. You didn't desert your family. You went to war, believing in a cause. And you didn't know May was pregnant, right?" When he nods, I say, "And of course she wants you. She's always wanted you, just as you've always wanted her. Finally, when we started all this, I could understand why you didn't want to come, but I'll say this again. You *can't* go back. You *have* to leave."

With that, I return to wake up the others.

As the sun rises, we see two trucks on a roadway in the distance. When they stop, we crouch low so we can't be seen. Then I hear my father's voice calling, "It's us. It's time." He's brought with him a man — Hop-li, a cousin. We're given food to eat. My father hands Joy some liquid to pour into Sam's bottle to help her sleep.

"You don't look right," Hop-li says to Z.G. "You look funny."

And he does, with his too short pants, his white ankles showing above his sandals, his soft, pale hands, his wire-rimmed glasses.

"Here, let me fix you." Hop-li picks up some dirt and rubs it into the parts of Z.G.'s skin that show — his face, neck, hands, ankles, and feet. Hop-li stands back to survey his work — an artist working on an artist. He shakes his head, steps forward again, takes off Z.G.'s glasses, and tosses them into the field. Then he rubs dirt around Z.G.'s eyes. Yesterday I thought Z.G. looked like a bald goat. Now he looks a like a blind and bald goat.

"Much better!" Hop-li exclaims.

"But I can't see," Z.G. complains.

"But you look a lot more like my brother," Hop-li says.

"In our commune, only men drive trucks," my father explains. "Your two cousins go everywhere together. The younger cousin —"

"Comes with me on every run, and the border guards are used to him. They think he's jittery because his eyesight is so terrible. Now his nervousness can be a disguise for you."

The cousin gives Z.G. an identity card. When I see it, I understand why the cousin was so particular in getting Z.G. ready. It's not a particularly good physical match, but then I remember Sam's papers to get into America. He didn't look much like the boy in that photo either. The American inspectors didn't catch the discrepancy until many years later, when the photo was used as part of the proof of Sam's illegal paper-son status.

"What about us?" I ask.

"You'll ride in the back of the truck. We'll hide you when we get close to the border."

"Will it work?"

My father blinks. "Maybe. I hope so."

We cross the field to the trucks. Both have open beds with wood slats on the sides. The bed of one is filled with pigs wrapped in straw matting and separate baskets of piglets. The other is piled with barrels, jars, and bulging burlap sacks. We climb into the back of the second truck. My father and Hop-li drive. I worry about Ta-ming's stomach, but he seems all right, staring out through the slats as the countryside rolls by. Soon, we turn onto a paved road. The sun stays to our left as we head south. I wish Dun were with us, and I pray that he's all right. Fear and sorrow have me in a merciless grip. I take Joy's hand and we hang on to each other.

The closer we get to the border, the more traffic there is — wheelbarrows; pushcarts; donkey-, mule-, and water buffalo-pulled wagons; bicycles piled high with merchandise; trucks of every size; and people with baskets of produce strapped to their backs, slung over their shoulders on poles, or balanced on their heads. Our two trucks turn off the main road, head down an alley, and stop.

My father comes to the back, and we all jump down to the ground. The men pull one of the barrels off the back of the truck. My dad pries open the top. It's filled with dried sea horses. He scoops out the top layer to reveal a hidden compartment, and then he leans down to Ta-ming. "You need to get in the barrel and you need to stay very quiet."

Ta-ming looks up at me and begins to shake. He doesn't have his violin for comfort as he did when he had to hide in the trunk of Z.G.'s car. But that's not our only problem. Samantha is to be put in a basket with some piglets and driven across the border in the pig truck.

Joy shakes her head. "I'm not putting *my* baby in a basket with a bunch of baby pigs."

"You'll have to if you want her to get across," my father says, as obdurate as my daughter.

"Then we'll stay," Joy snaps back.

I put a hand on her arm. "As mothers, we sometimes have to do things that are really hard, really against our natures," I tell her.

"I won't put my baby in there," Joy repeats.

"The guards at the checkpoint don't like to inspect live animals, because they're smelly and dirty. And, if the baby starts to cry, they'll be less likely to hear her if she's with the pigs," my father says, trying to be helpful, but these are about the worst things he could have said.

Once before I heard Joy and Z.G. talk in a way I didn't understand. I turn to him now, needing his help.

"Joy, do you remember a few days ago when we were in the studio and we talked about the differences between love for a country, the love you feel for a lover, and all-encompassing love?" he asks.

Joy nods, but she's so damn stubborn I don't think she's really listening to him.

530

"But what about the love you feel for yourself and for your child?" he asks. "Don't you owe it to her to see her to a happy future?"

We watch Joy's face as she considers this. She's just where I was yesterday in the taxi. I didn't want to leave Dun, but I had to.

"Can I at least be in the truck with her?" she asks at last.

"You're willing to get in a basket?" The cousin looks at her like she's crazy.

"We don't have much time," Joy responds briskly. "We *must* get out."

Joy puts her sleeping baby in a basket with the piglets. Little snouts poke through the open sides.

Ta-ming has gone completely white. I can't think of anything to say or do that will make him feel better. Then I remember my mother. I take the pouch with the three sesame seeds, three beans, and three coins from around my neck and put it around Ta-ming's.

"This will protect you," I say. "You'll only be in there for a short time. I'll talk to you the whole way, but you must remain very quiet."

This child has been through so much, yet he obediently climbs into the barrel and hugs his legs. The false top is put on, the sea horses layered on top, and the barrel sealed.

Joy crawls inside a larger pig basket and is loaded into the middle of the truck. The basket with Samantha and the piglets is placed next to her, and then other pig baskets are pushed up against their sides and piled on top. I climb up on the truck with Ta-ming's barrel. I step into a burlap sack, hundreds of small snakes dried into neat coils are thrown on top of me, and then the bag is tied shut. I hear three doors slam and the engines start. The truck with Joy, Samantha, and Z.G. leaves first, and then the truck I'm in lurches forward.

I'm in total darkness, covered with dried snakes, petrified. I talk to Ta-ming, hoping he can hear me. I can't see anything and can only intuit what's happening from what I feel and hear. The truck begins to stop, wait, roll forward a few feet, and then stop again. I hear water. That must be the Sham Chun River, the border between mainland China and Hong Kong's New Territories, which means we're already on the Lo Wu Bridge. My father was right. This is a relatively easy crossing; the line moves fairly quickly.

I hear a man, presumably a guard, say, "Please produce your travel documents for inspection." I'm scared, but I smile. The truck with Joy and the baby was ahead of us. Whatever happens now, my daughter and granddaughter are out. Z.G. too.

"I haven't seen you in a while, Comrade Chin," the guard says to my father.

"We've been busy in the commune," my father replies.

"What are you bringing across the border today?"

My chest constricts, my stomach pushes up against my lungs, my heart beats so hard I can hear it.

"The usual. We're on our way to the wholesale medicine market."

"Ah, yes. All right then. I'll see you on your way back later today."

The truck's gears grind and we roll across the bridge. The truck makes a few turns to the left and then a right. Finally, we stop. The truck door opens. In a minute, my bag is untied. I stand and brush the dried snakes from my body. I pop open the top of Ta-ming's barrel and pull him out. He's ghost white and trembling. I hug him. "We made it," I tell him.

I help Ta-ming off the truck. My legs are wobbly from fear and from being scrunched in the burlap sack. Up ahead, the cousin and Z.G. are still moving the pig baskets. I hurry to them to help. In minutes, Joy and the baby — a little scratched up but still sound asleep — are on the roadway with us. We're so emotionally and physically exhausted that we don't cheer or hug each other. Still, I feel relief as three years of worry and stress begin to melt from my body. We're all in a bit of a daze, and it will take a long time for everything to sink in, but we're *out*. We might — and here's a thought that would have been unthinkable even a few hours ago — get to May's hotel in time for lunch.

"Here," my father says. He presses a satchel into my hand. "This is for you and May. These are photographs and some things I wrote about your mother, what happened . . . everything."

"I wish we had more time," I say.

"I wish we did too," my father says. "Maybe one day we can all be together. Maybe one day you can bring May here and we can meet. Do you think the two of you might like that?"

I nod. I don't have words for what I feel.

Then, to the cousin, he says, "We need to hurry. The earlier we get to market, the better prices we'll get." He gives me a last look before climbing back in his truck. "Continue on that road to the left. Pretty soon you'll see a bus stop. The bus will take you into Kowloon. Once there, you can take the ferry to the Hong Kong side of the bay."

When we reach downtown Hong Kong, the busyness of the international port, the women dressed in vibrant hues, the white buildings against the emerald green slopes, and even the openness of the sky make everything seem brighter, lighter, freer. We walk up the hill and then along Hollywood Road past little antiques stands, where even now old beautiful-girl posters of May and me flap in the breeze, waiting for tourists to buy them and take them home. The proprietor at the hotel doesn't recognize me, but she gives us May's room number anyway. We walk up several flights of stairs, down a dingy corridor, and knock on the door. No one answers.

I knock again and call, "May, it's me, Pearl."

Almost as one, our little group steps back as the door opens. But it's not my sister. It's Dun.

Ta-ming is the first to react, running forward, squealing "Baba!" — the first time he has said this — and being lifted into Dun's arms. And then we're all crowding forward, pushing Dun back into the room, hugging him, patting him, still not believing he's here. I think I can have no emotion left in me, yet my feelings are so very big, their borders can't be seen. I put my arms around him and hold tight, never wanting to let go of him again. My eyes brim with tears of joy.

"How?" I'm finally able to ask.

"I had all the papers I needed. I proved who I was. I said I was to go to Hong Kong for family reunification. You want to know what they told me at the border? I was one less person to feed."

"What about Tao?" Joy asks.

Dun smiles wickedly. "He was angry, but there was nothing he could do." He turns to Z.G. "It's a good thing you got out." Then, to Ta-ming, who is eye to eye with Dun in his arms, he says, "I brought you something. Look." And there on the table next to the telephone is Ta-ming's violin. "I brought everything with me, not that we need it now. But I have something you might like, Joy." He goes to a corner and picks up a cardboard tube. "It's your painting. They said there was no room for your bourgeois thoughts in China."

Joy takes the tube from his hands and shakes her head in . . . disbelief? Wonder? Gratitude?

"Where is May?" I ask.

"She's at the American Embassy. We'll all need papers, won't we? She thought she'd get started on that. She's pretty amazing, that sister of yours."

We go back outside to wait for May. Maybe we should have taken showers, because we all look ragged, filthy, like the poorest refugees. She won't be looking for us dressed as we are, but none of us want to risk missing the reunion. We sit on the hotel steps, chatting, happy. Z.G. can't see very far, but I can tell he's anxious.

I'm the first to spot May. She's walking up the hill, her head down, watching where she steps in her improbably high stilettos. She wears a dress with a full skirt, cinched at the waist with a skinny belt, and a short jacket with three-quarter-length sleeves in matching fabric. A funny round hat sits on top of her head. Her pink-gloved hands carry gaily painted shopping bags.

I stand. The others look up at me and then down the street. They let me go forward first. May glances up and sees me. My sister. I thought I'd never see her again. We hurry toward each other and embrace. There's so much I want to say, but somehow all I can do is extend my arm toward Joy and the baby as they approach. Is this a reunion with a favorite aunt or a favorite mother? As Joy shows Sam to my sister, I know I don't have to worry about that kind of thing anymore. My daughter will return to Los Angeles knowing she has two mothers who love her.

And then there is Z.G. Joy meets my eyes. Silent communication exists between sisters, but it's even stronger between mothers and daughters. Joy pulls away and I touch May's elbow.

"We've brought someone else," I say.

My sister follows my gaze. She sees Dun — a man in an ill-fitting Western-style suit, with his hands balanced protectively on the shoulders of a thin but sweet-faced little boy implausibly holding a violin case. Next to them stands a tall but slim man in grubby clothes, with pants too short, looking a bit like a mole blinded by the light. May's knees start to buckle, but I hold tight to

536

her elbow to steady her. I walk her the short distance up the hill, hand her to Z.G., and step back. Oh, this is going to be interesting.

When I left for China three years ago, I thought of something my sister once said to me: everything always returns to the beginning. I was returning home to my roots, to the place where I'd been so ruined as a woman, but where I once again discovered the person I was meant to be — a Dragon of great strength and forgiveness. I found my daughter and through sheer force of will — through the fierceness of the Dragon that my mother always warned me about — brought her out of China. I found Joy — and *joy* with Dun and Ta-ming. Now I'll return to what I believe is my true home: America. Miracles are everywhere, and as I watch my sister — forever beautiful, forever my little sister — staring into the eyes of the one man she ever loved, I know that indeed things do return to the beginning. The world opens again, and I see a life of happiness without fear. I gaze at my family — complicated though it may be — and know that fate smiles on us.

Acknowledgments

In many ways this novel couldn't have been written if not for Amy Tan and her wonderful husband, Lou DeMattei, who invited me to go with them to Huangcun Village in Anwei province, where we stayed in a seventeenth-century villa called Zhong Xian Di. They had been invited to the villa by Nancy Berliner, the curator of Chinese art at the Peabody Essex Museum in Salem, Massachusetts, who brought Yin Yu Tang, another villa from Huangcun, brick by brick to the museum. Ms Berliner answered numerous questions about life in Huangcun and the villa both today and during the Great Leap Forward by email and in person. Tina Eng, Amy's sister, also came to Huangcun. Her stories about the Great Leap Forward, what it was like to live in the countryside, her loneliness for her mother, as well as her insightful explanation of *hsin yan* — heart eye — helped to inform *Dreams of Joy*. Cecilia Ding, who works for the Village China project, was a wonderful translator, font of information, and traveling companion. Although many of the tragedies that happened in the novel didn't occur in Huangcun, I wish to thank the many people there who told us their stories, showed us how they live day to day, and gave us wonderful meals, many of which are present in these pages. I've changed much of Huangcun's geography to create Green Dragon Village, but visitors will readily recognize the ancestral temple, the stone bridges, the villa, and the beauty of the landscape.

In 1960, about 10 million dependents of Overseas Chinese and returned Overseas Chinese lived in China. During the three years of the famine, tens of thousands of Chinese attempted to leave the country. Many were caught and jailed, or died. Then, in 1962, the Chinese government allowed 250,000 to leave China and enter Hong Kong. Some estimates suggest that another 700,000 people had made their way to Guangzhou in hopes of escape. There are no reliable figures for how many succeeded. I want to thank Xinran, whom I met in England, for information on feminine hygiene in China, ghost villages, and how people escape China even to this day; Jeffrey Wasserstrom for information on Shanghai, and also for introducing me to people who had either lived through the Great Leap Forward or escaped China; Judy Fong Bates, who shared with me family stories of sending money and letters to China when it was closed. Others — in China and the United States — told me tales of their experiences during the Great Leap Forward, how they communicated with relatives when the PRC was closed, and all the ways that they or their parents left China in those days. Although they prefer to remain nameless, I want them to know how grateful I am to them for sharing their stories with me.

I am indebted to Pan Ling, Hanchao Lu, and Simon Winchester for their writings on Shanghai. Special shout-outs go to Spencer Dodington, an architect living in Shanghai who restores art deco buildings, and Eric Zhang, who knows much about Hongkew and off-the-beaten-track sights, for each taking me around the city. For the history of Chinese propaganda posters, I want to express my appreciation for the works of Melissa Chiu, Reed Darmon, Duo Duo, Stefan Landsberger, Ellen Johnston Liang, Anchee Min, Michael Wolf, and Zhen Shentian, but the most important source for me in terms of art was Maria Galikowski's *Art and Politics in China*. I give thanks to Ye Xiaoqing for her scholarship on the *Dianshizhai Pictorial* and Shanghai urban life; Derek Bodde, Edward John Hardy, George Ernest Morrison, Reverend H. V. Noyes, and Richard Joseph Smith for their written observations on the reverence for lettered paper; Theodora Lau for her encyclopedic knowledge of the Chinese zodiac; Patricia Buckley Ebrey, whose collection *Chinese Civilization and Society* gave me insights into the correct handling of love, marriage, and family problems in the early years of the People's Republic of China; Liz Rawlings, who invited me to tea with Consul General Bea Camp at the U.S. Consulate in Shanghai; and Mike Hearn, curator in the Department of Asian Art at the Metropolitan Museum of Art, for his fabulous private tour (again with Amy Tan) of the collection. Careful readers will notice that Madame Garnett had one *t* in her name in *Shanghai Girls* and two *t*'s in her name in this novel. I want to thank Trish Stuebing, Eleanora Garnett's daughter-in-law, who caught the mistake and has since written to me many wonderful stories of this Russian countess, dancer, dress designer, and all-round impressive woman.

It's not all that surprising that so little has been written about the Great Leap Forward. Those in the countryside who suffered the worst effects of the famine either died or remained isolated in their villages. There are a few scholars, however, who have done considerable research on the topic. I'd like to highlight Jasper Becker (*Hungry Ghosts*), Frederick C. Teiwes (*China's Road to Disaster*), Ralph A. Thaxton, Jr. (*Catastrophe and Contention in Rural China*), and Frank Dikötter (*Mao's Great Famine*, which was published just as I was finishing *Dreams of Joy*). Several people have written memoirs, histories, or biographies that include the years of the Great Leap Forward, or what it was like to live in China when it was "closed" or had just opened. I acknowledge in particular the writings of Peter Brigg, Nien Cheng, He Liyi (with Claire Anne Chik), Li Mo (with a special thank-you for our correspondence), Sidney Rittenberg (and Amanda Bennett), Peter J. Seybolt, and Ningkun Wu (in collaboration with Yikai Li). Chou En-lai's *Report on Adjusting Major Targets of the 1959 National Economic Plan and Further Developing the Campaign for Increasing Production and Practicing Economy* gave me a partial view of the government's position on what was happening in those days. I was greatly helped with the details of daily life in Shanghai by a fan, Helen Ward, who answered numerous questions about her experiences returning to Shanghai to live in August 1951 with her parents. Many details in

541

this book — what happened upon entering the PRC, what it took to make toast with butter, and what kinds of cosmetics were available in shops — are here because of her great memory.

Under the heading of you never know what you're going to find, I was lucky to stumble on *China Leaps Forward, 1958,* an amazing documentary produced by the CIA and distributed by the National Archives with footage shot on communes, at fairs, and on streets in China fifty-three years ago. At the UCLA research library, I found a series called *Communist China,* part of the Communist China Problem Research Series, published by the Union Research Institute in Hong Kong. The yearly volumes contain typewritten essays on China's relations with so-called imperialist countries, agriculture, steel, the arts, "natural calamities on the mainland," and issues concerning returned Overseas Chinese — all of which were invaluable to me. (At UCLA, I also found *Chinese Stories from the Fifties, Chinese Women Liberated, Chinese Women in the Great Leap Forward,* and *Women of China.* These books and pamphlets revealed precious details and popular stories about women's lives in China during this period.) On the Internet, I came across Joseph Rupp's website on his bound-feet project. In 1985, he went into the Chinese countryside to interview and photograph bound-footed women. These stories, particularly those of the women who were required to unbind their feet after Mao came to power, are heart-wrenching and helped to inform what happened to Yong.

Bob Loomis, my editor at Random House, is kind, wise, supportive, and funny too. I want to thank everyone else at Random House as well, in particular Gina Centrello and Susan Kamil for their thoughtful questions and suggestions. Once again, my agent, Sandy Dijkstra, and the wonderful women in her office have labored tirelessly on my behalf. Larry Sells, Vivian Craig, and Meiling Moore have helped me in all kinds of surprising and interesting ways. Millie Saltsman and I have shared some interesting moments this year. I thank her for her wise words, many of which found their way into these pages. Sasha Stone looks after my website with aplomb and good cheer, while Pattie Williams takes the best photographs.

It hasn't escaped my notice that my books are often inhabited by people who don't get along with each other and who fail each other in numerous ways. This strikes me as rather odd when my own family life is so joyous. I could not write the books I do without my family's encouragement. My mother, Carolyn See, is a constant inspiration. My sister, Clara Sturak, offers a critical eye with love and tenderness. My sons, Christopher and Alexander, are always sweet. I now have a beautiful and brilliant daughter-in-law, Elizabeth, who has made me the happiest mother-in-law on earth. Finally, my husband, Richard Kendall, keeps me calm and balanced, while reminding me never to give up or waver from my vision. You are all the *best*, and I love you all deeply.

A Note on the Author

Lisa See is the *New York Times* bestselling author of *Shanghai Girls, Peony in Love, Snow Flower and the Secret Fan* (now a major motion picture), *Flower Net* (an Edgar Award nominee), *The Interior* and *Dragon Bones*, as well as the critically acclaimed memoir *On Gold Mountain*. She lives in Los Angeles.

www.lisasee.com